Kristin looked at the young officer and smiled, then held him in a long, penetrating gaze. Mr. Bright, almost as if acting without control, moved his lips to hers in a kiss. Though he was young and, she guessed, inexperienced, his kiss was firm and possessive. It was more of a kiss than those she had shared with the young men of society, but nevertheless it was the kiss of a gentleman. It went only so far . . . then it stopped.

She knew that she was going to seduce the shy officer. It would serve the high and mighty Captain Andrew Roberts right. It would be sweet revenge for his actions. That was the only reason she was going to do it, she told herself. But she knew it was a lie. For already she could feel her blood flowing hot in her veins, and her breath came in short, ragged gasps. She was doing this because she wanted it. She wanted this young man!

Kristin leaned into him. "Have you ever made love to a girl?"

"N . . ." Mr. Bright started to say, but he stumbled over the word, coughed, then tried again. "No," he finally managed.

"Would you like to?" She rubbed his fingers across her lips, then took just the tips of them inside her mouth and sucked them.

"Are you . . . are you what they say you are?" he stammered.

"I'll be anything you want," Kristin said seductively, putting her arms around his neck and pulling him to her for another kiss. . . .

Other Pinnacle Books by Paula Fairman:

In Savage Splendour

Forbidden Destiny

Storm of Desire

The Fury and the Passion

PORTS of PASSION

Paula Fairman

PINNACLE BOOKS   LOS ANGELES

PORTS OF PASSION

Copyright © 1980 by Script Representatives, Inc.

An original Pinnacle Books edition, published for the first time anywhere.

First printing, February 1980

ISBN: 0-523-40697-5

Cover illustration by Bill Maughan

Printed in the United States of America

PINNACLE BOOKS, INC.
2029 Century Park East
Los Angeles, California 90067

Ports of Passion

CHALMERS FAMILY TREE

John David Chalmers
born: 1810
died: 1868
m.
Virginia Towers
born: 1812
died: 1870

Charles Edward Chalmers
born: 1835
died: 1890
m.
Margaret Coy
born: 1840

Lee Martin Chalmers
born: 1839
died: 1861
m.
Constance Ann Hughes
born: 1837

Miles David Chalmers
born: 1869

James Amon Chalmers
born: 1860
died: 1881
m.
Cynthia Holt
born: 1862
died: 1881

Kristin Lee Chalmers
born: 1881

Chapter One

The most dominating building on the Boston waterfront skyline of 1901 was the Chalmers Building. It was designed by William Le Baron Jenney, the architectural genius who gave the world its first skyscraper when he built the ten-story Home Life Building in Chicago, in 1884. The Chalmers Building wasn't as tall—it was only six stories—but it did cover an entire block, and Bostonians showed it with pride to visitors to their fair city.

The top floor of the building was for the exclusive use of Constance Chalmers, Chairwoman of the Board of Directors of Chalmers Shipping Lines. She had her executive offices there, and she also maintained her living quarters there, seldom returning to Ocean House, the fifty-room mansion that was built by her father-in-law years before, and was itself as prominent a Boston landmark as the Chalmers Building.

1

Constance ruled the Chalmers shipping empire with the authority and wisdom of a queen. In fact, Victoria of England once commented after a particularly trying session with her ministers: "Would that my cabinet were as responsive to me, as Constance Chalmers's Board of Directors are to her. I should feel truly a ruler."

Constance was a widow, and had been for forty years. Her only son, James Amon, and his wife, Cynthia, were lost at sea in a yachting accident nearly twenty years before, and as a result, Constance was left with the responsibility of her granddaughter, Kristin.

Kristin, now twenty, lived with her grandmother, and Constance was the only family Kristin had ever known. It was a warm, and loving relationship, and Kristin didn't miss what she'd never had. She was as content with Constance as Constance was with her.

In Kristin's bedroom, there was a fine telescope in a window that overlooked the bay. The telescope was mounted on a brass swivel that Kristin polished daily, because the telescope, a gift from her grandmother some years before, was one of Kristin's proudest possessions. It was very powerful, and through it she could see the faces of the men on the decks of the great ships that slipped in and out of the Chalmers piers, without any of the men knowing they were being watched.

Had anyone been able to observe the observer, they would have seen a strikingly beautiful girl whose naturally blonde hair turned to gold in the sunlight, and whose eyes were as blue as the brightest summer afternoon. She was slender of build, but generously enough endowed with curves to cause many a man to harbor lascivious thoughts when looking at her innocent beauty.

Kristin knew, without having to be told, that what she was doing was akin to invasion of privacy, but she couldn't give it up. She didn't even look away during the summer of her thirteenth year, when, quite by accident,

2

she saw through her telescope an event that helped her to understand the strange and disquieting feelings that were already beginning to manifest themselves in her rapidly changing body.

She had been peering intently through the telescope, then quite new, when she saw one of the many women who walked along the docks approach a moored ship and call out to a sailor. She had asked her grandmother about those women once, wondering if they were part of the sailors' families, but her grandmother had dismissed the question with no satisfactory answer. Now, perhaps, she would find out, for she saw the sailor who had the anchor deck watch, and who was thus alone on the ship, invite the woman aboard. At his invitation, she disappeared into the deckhouse with him. Because it was in the heat of the summer, the overhead hatch was raised and propped open by the sailor to catch the breeze. Through her telescope and from her elevated angle, Kristin was able to look down through the deckhouse hatch, right into the room.

The woman pulled off her hat, then shook her head so that her hair fell free. She laughed, though from this distance Kristen heard not a sound. The woman's fingers plucked at the lacings of her bodice, until a moment later it was removed, and she stood before the sailor with bare breasts that were creamy white, high-pitched, and tipped by dark nipples.

Kristen was shocked that the woman would disrobe before the sailor, but was strangely excited too, as she realized that the mysteries of life were being played out for her on her own private stage.

Kristin self-consciously felt her own breasts, comparing the small mounds of flesh that were just now beginning to bloom with the well-developed orbs of the girl on the ship.

The man removed his shirt also; then he and the woman moved together for an embrace. Kristin was surprised to see the woman's fingernails raking across

3

the man's back, leaving in their wake scratches in his flesh. But the action, instead of angering the man, seemed to drive him closer to her.

The sailor drew the woman's skirt and petticoats up to her waist and Kristin was shocked to see nothing beneath them except a dark tangle of hair, and a pink, glistening cleft. That was not a revelation to Kristin, for her growing, changing body had already made her more like a woman and less like a little girl. But when she saw the sailor drop his pants, she gasped, for in viewing his anatomy she was seeing a nude man for the first time. And since the man was a fully aroused adult, it was an imposing sight.

The two naked bodies met on the bed, bestowing kisses on each other, yet thrashing about savagely so that the tenderness was intermixed with an unexpected and strange fury. Thus, even with the boat's curtain slightly open, Kristin realized that there were things left hidden from view, and for every question answered, two more were posed. Was this fire and ice a part of all lovemaking, or was it just the action of these two? Were such things pleasurable or painful? These were questions Kristin hoped would be answered by other such observations, but never again did she have the opportunity to see anything like the tryst she witnessed that afternoon, seven summers before.

There were times when Kristin would recall that afternoon, and her blood would run hot, and her body would come bewilderingly alive. Secretly, she wished she could happen upon another scene and, even more secretly, she wondered what it would have been like, had *she* been that woman. Then, even as her body was reacting to those erotic thoughts, her mind would thrust them aside angrily, and she would be flooded with a sense of profound guilt. What she had done was wrong, and it was even more so to dwell on it as she did. No decent woman would have dared watch such a scene,

4

let alone recall it with such obvious pleasure. She knew that she must keep such lustful musings in check.

Besides, she told herself, there were other pleasures to be enjoyed with the telescope. She could watch, with more than detached interest, the problems the tug captains had in docking the seagoing ships. Some were definitely more skilled than others, and she enjoyed watching those who could make the ship slip in as easily as walking up to a rail.

The sea captains of the great ships had little control over their own vessels during docking, for they were brought into their berths by chugging, wheezing tugboats. This was true of all the seagoing vessels, whether they were propelled by steam or sail. Though Chalmers had converted almost all of their Atlantic shipping to steamers, the vessels that plied the Pacific were still under sail. That was because there were few coaling stations along the rugged west coast of South America and virtually none beyond Hawaii. This lack of fuel made the Pacific Ocean exclusive property for windjammers for many, many years after the Atlantic was given over entirely to steam.

Kristin liked the sailing ships better than steam anyway. They were long and narrow, graceful of line and, when under sail, the most beautiful of all man's creations.

She also liked the captains of these ships. They were an independent lot, dashing and romantic, to be sure, but aloof from the rest of the world. When they stood on the quarterdeck as their ships were under tow, their faces were magnificent to behold. It was as if they had turned their souls over to another for safekeeping, and they watched fearfully and distrustingly the action of the captain of the tug. They were sure he intended to sink their ship, or run it aground, or bring some other foul circumstance upon it. Then, when their ship was safely docked, and their fate was restored to their own

5

hands, the relief on their faces was so obvious that Kristin sometimes laughed. Afterward, she would quickly look around to assure herself that her laugh had, indeed, fallen on an empty room.

Kristin did not confine herself to the telescope. She took an active interest in the operation of the shipping company, and since her grandmother encouraged her interest, Kristin already knew her way around the docks and warehouses.

Kristin would have enjoyed the same freedom on board the ships, too, but they were the exclusive domain of their captains, and whereas some welcomed her aboard, there were others who were less cordial. She learned early which captains welcomed her company and which ones didn't, and though she could accept a captain's wish to keep his ship sacrosanct and didn't hold a grudge against him, she was naturally more friendly with those who gave her free run of their vessels.

As Kristin stood there, sweeping the telescope along the docks, she heard the toot of a tugboat, and so swung the instrument toward the bay to see what ship was arriving. At first the arriving ship was blurred because of the difference in focal length, so Kristin turned the lens until the vessel came into sharp focus.

The ship was the *Morning Star,* a three-masted barkentine. It had a beautiful clipper bow, with a long jib boom, a graceful waist, and a rather arrogant stern, as if she were used to showing her backside to steamers and other sailing ships less swift. In this day of steel sailing ships, the *Morning Star* was made of wood, painted black, and shining brightly under the afternoon sun. Though figureheads were rapidly being considered to be a thing of the past, the *Morning Star,* Kristin noticed, boasted a fine carving of a nude woman, chiseled by some unknown but skillful artisan, flowing in line with the rake of the ship's hull. The carved woman held her head up, her arms back, and thrust her breasts

6

forward proudly. Kristin knew that some would consider the figurehead obscene, others would see her as beautiful, but no one would see her without comment.

There was something about the *Morning Star* that triggered a memory, and after a moment, Kristin recalled when she first heard the name. It had been a little over three months ago, and she was in her grandmother's office, answering some correspondence for her, when her cousin, Miles Chalmers, and his mother, Margaret, came into the office.

Miles was thirty-two years old. He was actually Kristin's second cousin, since his mother had been married to Charles Edward Hold, the brother of Constance's husband, Lee. But as far as Kristin was concerned, even a second cousin was too close, for there was nothing likable about Miles. He was a complainer, a compulsive gambler, and openly jealous of the fact that Constance Chalmers, and not he, held the reins of power in Chalmers Shipping.

Margaret, Kristin knew, was just as bad. In fact, she was probably to blame for Miles's attitude, for it was her intention to see control of the company passed to her son, rather than to Kristin, and she had spent a lifetime grooming Miles for that eventuality.

"Aunt Constance, I have great news," Miles said, bursting into the office with his mother, not bothering to knock, feeling that his relationship to her gave him entrée anytime he wanted.

"Wait until you hear this, Constance," Margaret put in, beaming proudly. "I'm telling you, we are very lucky to have someone with Miles's business sense on the scene. You've done an admirable job to be sure, Constance, but every day I realize more and more the importance of having men around to make the major business decisions. I don't know how you've handled it all these years. Certainly no other woman could do it."

Constance, who was making entries in a ledger, sighed and put the pencil down. She let Margaret's comments slide by for what they obviously were, and turned to Miles, who stood before her desk, smiling broadly.

Perhaps it was the smile, Kristin remembered thinking. Maybe that's why she didn't like him. It never seemed genuine, and it, like everything else about him, seemed studied, as if all activity of any kind had only one purpose, and that was to gain some personal advantage for himself. Besides, she thought, the smile just made his already big mouth look bigger, and his small, water-blue eyes look smaller.

"What is your great news?" Constance asked.

"I've found a ship to replace the *Gretchen*. As you know, that fool captain ran her on the rocks, and it has left us short in our Pacific fleet."

"That fool captain, as you call him, was forced onto the rocks by a storm. Not only was he found blameless by a board of inquiry, but he also managed to save his entire crew, and he was cited for heroism," Constance said.

"Well, be that as it may, the *Gretchen* was lost," Miles said, unperturbed by his aunt's caustic reply. "And we are in the market for a replacement ship, are we not?"

"Yes, we are," Constance agreed.

"Well, I've found a captain who has an excellent ship to sell. One that is perfect for our needs, and we have him right where we want him."

"Oh? And where is that, Miles?"

"Desperate for money, and nowhere to turn," Miles said triumphantly.

"Who is this captain, and what is his ship?"

"His name is Andrew Roberts," Miles said. "His ship is the *Morning Star,* a barkentine of one hundred and fifty feet tonnage length. It's perfect for us."

"How much is Captain Roberts asking for his ship?"

"Asking? What difference does it make what he is asking?" Miles replied, dismissing the question as not worthy of an answer. "I'm telling you, Aunt Constance, he will take just what we give him. He must sell to us, or lose his ship by confiscation. He has no choice."

"How much is he asking?" Constance asked again.

"I . . . I think twenty-five hundred dollars," Miles replied. "But as I said, that doesn't matter."

"Twenty-five hundred dollars sounds like a fair price for a ship such as you describe. We'll pay it."

"But . . . but, Aunt Constance, that isn't necessary."

"Why don't you listen to Miles, Constance?" Margaret asked. "After all, he's just trying to save us money."

"How much will he save us, Margaret?" Constance asked. "One thousand dollars? Fifteen hundred? Even if he saves us two thousand dollars, it isn't worth cheating a man, is it?"

"Cheating? This isn't cheating, this is shrewd business," Miles replied, blustering over the accusation.

"And I say it is cheating," Constance said. "Twenty-five hundred dollars is the going price for such a ship. The captain has every right to ask that for the *Morning Star*. If we don't give it to him, one of the other companies will."

"No, they won't, for I have entered into an agreement with them. They will abstain from the bidding, and we will reciprocate in kind on some future deal."

"And you don't call that cheating?" Constance said. "Just offer the captain twenty-five hundred dollars, and forget about the agreement."

"But I can't, Aunt Constance," Miles said. "I've already told the others we will go along with them. It's a matter of honor."

"Honor!" Constance said. She laughed.

"I . . . I shall do as you wish," Miles said, his face flushed in anger. He turned sharply and left the room, but his mother stood her ground for just a moment. Finally she spoke, in a voice dripping with venom.

"Constance, you have hated me for over forty years.

9

But it is unfair that you transfer that hatred to my son. He has done you no harm and wishes only to do the best for this company."

"You are wrong, Margaret," Constance said easily. "I haven't hated you. I have merely tolerated you."

"Charles didn't have one inch of backbone," Margaret said, "or our positions would be reversed today. But Miles isn't like his father. Miles is ambitious and smart. And if you think he and I are going to sit back and let this company fall into the hands of some snippet of a girl," she pointed to Kristin, "then you've got another think coming."

"Margaret, the way I see it this company is in my hands now, and I intend for it to stay there for quite a while yet. Now, if you'll excuse me, I do have work to do."

"Oh, yes," Margaret said sarcastically. "I mustn't forget that you are the chairwoman of the board. Well, I mustn't keep you from your busy schedule. Good day, Constance."

"Good day, Margaret."

"Good day, Aunt Margaret," Kristin said.

Margaret grunted an answer, or she may have just grunted, but she left the room with no further comment.

"Think you can handle them after I'm gone?" Constance asked.

"Grandmother, you're not going to be gone for a long time yet, I hope," Kristin said, walking over to put her arms around the older woman's neck. It seemed inconceivable that her grandmother would ever go. She hadn't changed one iota in appearance for as long as Kristin could remember. At sixty-eight Constance was tall and striking . . . maybe that's where Kristin got her tall build . . . and she had silver hair, which Kristin thought was beautiful, and vibrant blue eyes, which could look right through a person. In a world of changes, Kristin was glad that her grandmother was unchanging.

That had been over three months ago, and now the *Morning Star* was arriving at the Chalmers's port facility in Boston for the first time, under the command of her captain, Andrew Roberts.

As the *Morning Star* approached the inner buoy, Kristin brought her telescope to bear on the restless man walking the quarterdeck. Captain Roberts moved with grace and smoothness, somewhat belying his great size, for he was easily six feet four inches tall, and broader in the shoulders than any man Kristin knew. His eyes were creased, as if permanently held that way against the sea glare. From this distance Kristin couldn't determine the color of his eyes, though she wished she could, for there was something about him that moved her strangely. She felt a reaction to him, a sudden, unbidden eroticism that hit her with fully as much impact as had that forbidden scene she watched so long ago. Her knees grew weak, and she rose away from the telescope, gasping in surprise. What was this? How could the mere sight of a man affect her in such a way?

Then reason took over, for Kristin was nothing if not a logical person. It was a simple enough answer. She had been thinking earlier of the incident between the sailor and the woman. Those thoughts were of themself unnerving. With such images in mind, the sight of a handsome, and heretofore unknown man, would quite naturally cause confusion of thought.

But she must make a more positive effort to control herself, she decided. For such thoughts were most unseemly and could cause her some embarrassment if she didn't keep them in check.

Now that the logic was clear in her mind, Kristin decided it would be wise to take another look at Captain Roberts, just to prove she was right. But just in case she wasn't, she took a deep breath and braced herself before she looked.

* * *

Chapter Two

Captain Andrew Roberts stood on the quarterdeck and watched the tug pulling his ship into shore. The tug was an ugly, toad-looking affair, squat and fat, with its beam widened even more by the paddle wheels that beat at the water on either side. Smoke and soot billowed from the stack, and from back where he was, Roberts could see the ash beginning to settle on the teak decks of the *Morning Star*. He hated it when his ship had to be towed, for the smoke and the smell seemed to stay with it for days, and the sailors sometimes thought he'd gone a little daft, keeping them at cleaning parties long after the obvious dirt was gone.

Perhaps it was in his imagination, but if so, the men who sailed on his ship would have to get used to the fact that Andrew Roberts had no love for steam or anything about it, and he took special pains to free his ship of any of its foul contamination.

His ship. Roberts laughed a short bitter laugh, responding to a secret joke. A joke that was on him, for he had taken a chance in buying wheat cheaply in Galveston, with the intention of delivering it for a great profit in Honolulu. But the wheat had gone bad, and he had to put in to San Francisco. There were bills to pay in San Francisco, including a final payment for the wheat, and the only chance he had of avoiding a sheriff's plaster on his mainmast was to sell the ship.

Roberts had been surprised when he received an offer from Miles Chalmers that matched his asking price. He was certain that he would be cheated, and felt a degree of loyalty toward Chalmers now, because he wasn't. And with a clause in the contract that gave him an option to buy the ship back in one year, Roberts felt as though he was emerging from his ordeal in much better shape than he had a right to.

It wasn't his fault that the wheat went bad. The wooden plug that served as the stopwater between the keel and the garboard strake had popped out, and water had run in. Not enough to put the ship in danger . . . but enough to make the wheat turn sour. The cargo, which should have made a rather handsome profit, turned into stinking garbage one thousand miles out to sea. There was nothing Roberts could do but jettison his cargo and make for San Francisco.

In San Francisco, Roberts sold his ship to Chalmers Shipping, with the provision that he be kept on as captain and be allowed to buy it back in one year; then he loaded fifteen hundred bales of cured leather and started round the Horn for Boston.

Roberts stopped his pacing and leaned against the railing, looking down at the water that slipped by the sleek, wooden hull as the *Morning Star* followed the tug. He heard a sound on deck, and looked around to see Josiah Crabbs tossing a pan of scraps overboard. The sea gulls that had been following the ship in on long, graceful, seldom-moving wings, suddenly folded their wings in and dived like arrows toward the scraps, catching most of the pieces before they hit the water.

Crabbs was the cook, a man who gave his age as sixty but was thought by everyone to be at least seventy. Crabbs had a magnificent white beard and a full head of white hair and, by his own calculations, had spent less than one month per year ashore for the last forty years. "And so drunk then, as to scarcely be able to discern day from dark," he would tell, laughing.

Crabbs was the only hand Roberts knew from before. He had paid his crew off when he reached San Francisco and, with little chance of sailing with the *Morning Star* again, his crew had, to a man, signed with other ships. It had been a skeleton crew provided by Chalmers, who helped bring the ship on to Boston, and there, Roberts would sign on a new crew of his own.

"So this be Boston, eh?" Crabbs said, wiping his hands on his apron, which, from the condition of that fouled garment, did nothing to clean them. He shielded his eyes against the glare as he examined the skyline.

"This is Boston," Roberts said. "Have you ever been here?"

"Not sober," Crabbs answered. He spit overboard. "Cap'n afore we sail outta here, I think you oughta check our water tanks."

"I'll do that, Crabbs," Roberts promised.

14

The tug rolled in the swells, and the paddle wheels lost purchase for a moment. When they regained the water, the tug shot forward, with the result that the jerk was transferred along the line to the *Morning Star,* causing it to pause, then lurch forward. The lurch caught Crabbs unaware, and he grabbed the railing to keep from falling.

"That slab-sided, stinking, smoking son of a bitch!" Crabbs swore angrily, shaking his fist at the tug. "Put those loggerheads under sail on a real ship, and they wouldn't know whether to scratch their ass or go blind!"

Roberts laughed at his cook, then looked up to see how far they had to go. Fortunately, they had just passed the inner buoy, and even now the tug was swinging around to berth the ship.

Just as Roberts looked up, a flash of light caught his attention, and he squinted toward the building from which the flash had come. It was a huge building, with the words CHALMERS SHIPPING LINES, INC., painted in huge white-on-black letters across the facade of the building. The painted banner was between the fifth and sixth floors, and the flash of light had come from a window on the sixth floor, just above the letter *H* in the word SHIPPING. Roberts looked at the window for just a moment, wondering what caused the flash; but the crew came on deck at that moment, and he turned away from the building to look at them.

The crew was carrying their seabags, packed with all their worldly possessions. Roberts knew that wouldn't be much; maybe a couple of sea outfits, a set of woolen underwear, and a good coat for the Cape Horn weather, a rain slicker, some leather boots, a pair of shore shoes, and a shore shirt. Hell, he thought. He didn't own much more himself, especially now that this ship didn't belong to him.

Not much to show for someone who was already over thirty and had spent half his life at sea. Ah, he thought. But there is experience. What price is experience? What price would he put on the unique experience of having his nose broken by the mate of the *Governor Phelps,* because the mate thought no sailor should have the profile of a stage actor, not even one who is only fifteen years old?

Roberts smiled and tried to remember the mate's name, but he couldn't. He could remember the *Governor Phelps,* though. She was the first ship he had sailed on. He had worked his way a thousand miles cross-country from Nebraska after his mother died, just to fulfill a boyish ambition. The *Governor Phelps* was a three-masted schooner carrying lumber from Oregon, across the Pacific to Hawaii. He learned to splice rope and a dozen other things while sailing before the mast. He learned to develop a feel for the ship, so that at any given moment, he knew how the vessel was behaving from the keel to the truck, and from the jib boom to the sternpost. But, most of all, he learned the psychology of the sailor and what it took to earn his loyalty.

Those lessons learned in the forecastle had never deserted Roberts, and the basic philosophy of his command was built around that experience. He had been a second mate for a brief time on a China clipper, then, after acquiring his master's papers, he took command at the age of twenty-three.

Command set well with Andrew Roberts, and he had the size to allow it to ride easily on his shoulders. At six feet four, and two hundred thirty-five pounds, he was nearly as strong as two average men. He had never been a roughhouser, even in his younger years, sailing before the mast. But he very seldom had to prove himself. Most of the time a word or a glance was enough to ward off any would-be antagonist. On those rare occasions where he did need to assert himself, he did so convincingly.

Captain Roberts had likes and dislikes, the same as any man. He disliked suits, and men who wore them, labor unions and, of course, steamships. He liked steering the ship at night under a canopy of stars, beautiful women, and, surprisingly to those who knew him only casually, good books and music.

The tug gave three shrill toots on his whistle, then dropped the hawser and pulled away sharply, leaving the *Morning Star* to drift gently toward the dock, where three men stood ready to catch the securing line and make her fast.

"Stand by the bowline," Roberts called.

"Bowline ready, sir," came the answering call.

"Stand by abeam."

"Abeam ready sir!"

"Stand by stern line."

"Stern line ready, sir!"

"Away all lines!"

The sailors whirled the lines over their heads for a few turns, like cowboys chasing steers, then threw them toward the dock. The bowline and the abeam line were caught by men on the pier, but the stern line whistled into the water. No matter, one line would have been enough to draw the ship snug, and though he received a little good-natured razzing, the sailor on the stern line simply pulled it back in and tossed it out a second time.

"Cap'n, port inspectors are ready to board, sir," one of the sailors reported.

"Run out the gangplank," Roberts ordered, starting for his cabin for the papers the inspectors would need. Every year, it seemed, the amount of paperwork accompanying each voyage grew and grew, until one day, he was sure, the tonnage of paperwork would exceed the tonnage of cargo on any given trip. He had all the necessary papers laid out on his table by the time the inspectors boarded. There were bills of lading, port clearance certificates, port fee receipts, tax receipts, ship ownership statement (amended to show Chalmers, where his name had been), his personal master's papers, the ship's log, brought up to date and signed, crew pay-books, and nationality statements on each of the crew.

"Well, Cap'n, I see you have everything all ready for me," one of the inspectors said.

"Aye, I've been here before," Roberts replied. "Though I scarce see why it takes the two of you to certify a ship no larger than the *Morning Star*."

"Oh, only one of us is from the Port Authority," the man who was looking at the papers said. "That's me. Abner Johnson's my name. This other fella is Jack Lemmings. He's with the seaman's union."

"He's with the what?" Roberts asked sharply.

"I'm with the seaman's union, Captain," Lemmings said, holding his hand out to shake with Roberts. "The law of the state of Massachusetts gives me the right to be here."

Roberts wanted to refuse to shake his hand, but to do so would be a serious breach of his own code of etiquette, so he accepted the handshake, making it as perfunctory as possible. He noticed as he held the man's hand that it was smooth and uncalloused. If that hand had ever pulled a rope, it had been a long time ago.

"Captain, is anyone on your crew a union member?" Lemmings asked. "If so, we have the right to speak in private about the conditions on board your vessel."

"Lord, I hope not," Roberts said.

"Ah, I see. And so you are against the rights of the common seaman?"

"Not at all," Roberts said. "You can ask any man jack that has ever sailed with me. I treat all my men fair and square. Aye, and pull a watch with the best of them. I was eight years before the mast myself," he added.

"Were you still before the mast, captain, I feel you would be more generous toward our noble cause," Lemmings said. "For I'm certain you are aware of the oppression many of our brothers of the sea suffer."

"Then let those as may suffer oppression organize,"

18

Roberts said. "But the law still permits the captain to refuse to ship with organized men. And since the law is on *my* side in this matter, sir, I will not have a union man on my crew."

Lemmings smiled the smile of one who had been through all this before with many other captains. "You are quite right, sir, the law is on your side now. But the time is rapidly coming when the union will grow to the point that a captain who thinks as you do will find himself unable to muster a crew. What will you do then, Captain? Reactivate the impressment gangs?"

"I will cross that bridge, Mr. Lemmings, when the time comes," Roberts said. He looked at the port inspector. "Is all in order, Mr. Johnson?"

"It certainly appears to be, Captain," Johnson replied. "I congratulate you on your books. They are well kept."

"It's part of the job," Roberts said. "Now, if you gentlemen will excuse me, I must meet with Mr. Chalmers shortly, and I wish to change clothes."

"Yes, of course," Johnson said. He stamped all the papers with the seal of the Boston Port Authority, then smiled a bureaucratic smile and departed, taking Lemmings with him.

Miles Chalmers was walking toward the *Morning Star* when he saw Johnson and Lemmings leaving it.

"What's that man doing here?" Miles asked Johnson, pointing at Lemmings. "I told you I don't want any union organizing going on on any of my ships."

"By law he has a right to see if there are any union complaints on newly arrived vessels," Johnson explained patiently.

"And agitate the crew, just to make sure there are," Miles said. "You keep him off my ships."

"He can't keep me off," Lemmings said. "I can come on with a police officer, if need be."

"Then keep the hell out of my sight," Miles ordered.

19

Lemmings smiled. "That I shall do, gladly," he answered.

Miles cursed the union under his breath as the two men went on their way. If he had the power that his aunt had, there would never be a union problem. He would crack down on them, and crack down hard. The problem was Constance Chalmers was just too damn soft. Not only on the union men, but on everyone else. Chalmers Shipping Company stood on the threshold of greatness . . . but only if someone took it over who could lead it with a strong hand. Someone like him.

And that was the real reason he wanted control of the company. The fact that he was badly in debt from some gambling losses and needed money that he couldn't get to was just one added reason, an annoyance that had sped up his schedule. Of course, the men to whom he was indebted were a rough lot, uncouth and unable to understand the way things were. Just because he was a Chalmers, and technically a millionaire, he couldn't necessarily get his hands on vast sums of money right away. Oh, he had personal accounts to be sure and a rather substantial income. Unfortunately, his gambling losses had been very large, and credit had been extended him because of his association with a business like Chalmers. When the hoodlums with whom he was gambling learned that his personal income wasn't enough to cover the extent of credit, they took him to see Louis Prefontaine, the czar of the underworld, who demanded that he take money from the company.

Miles had laughed rather weakly and explained that such things weren't done. Mr. Prefontaine had not enjoyed the joke, and after roughing him up slightly ("Just a taste of what might happen, you understand," he told him) he asked him again to get it.

Miles grew frightened and finally begged off, promising to give them double his debt if they would just give him six months.

"Six months? What's going to happen in six months?"

"I'll be in control of the company by then," Miles said.

"Yeah? Well, you'd better, Mr. Chalmers. Because if you don't have fifty thousand dollars by then, you are going to regret it."

"Fifty? But no, I only owe you a little over twelve. Twice that amount comes to less than twenty-five thousand dollars."

"Let's call it interest," Prefontaine said. "Fifty thousand dollars, six months from now, or all the money in the world will do you no good. Because you'll be dead."

"I'll get the money," Miles promised. "I have a plan."

"It better be a good one."

"It is," Miles said.

Was it? he wondered. Perhaps so. But it was a plan born of desperation, and in any such plan, a lot of things could go wrong. That's why he intended to take care of the first, and largest obstacle right now, right after his meeting with Captain Roberts.

In fact, it was because he had something else to attend to that he decided to meet Captain Roberts on board his ship rather than wait for the captain to show up at his office as they had planned.

Chapter Three

There was no one left on deck when Miles stepped aboard the *Morning Star,* but he felt no compunction about poking around. After all, it was his ship. Of course, some captains were rather fussy about people on their boats, and they grew very proprietary about it, until Miles reminded them that they might be the captain, but *he* was the owner. For the most part that was all that was needed. Though there had been a few captains who quit in protest, and good riddance to them, as far as Miles was concerned.

Miles strolled aft to the captain's cabin, and without knocking, pushed the door open and stepped in. Roberts stood there, stark naked, reaching toward a high shelf for a shirt.

"Don't mind me, mate, I just live here," Roberts said in an annoyed tone of voice.

Miles just stared at the captain in astonishment. The

22

captain's body was all muscle, hair, and skin. He had a barrel chest and a flat stomach, and he was endowed with a badge of manhood that was overpowering.

"Are you planning on buying me?" Roberts asked.

"I beg your pardon?"

"The way you are looking me over, I feel as if I am going on the auction block," Roberts said. He stepped into his trousers, then pulled the shirt on, tucking the tail into his waistband. "What do you want?" Roberts asked, still looking at Miles. "I've already cleared my entry and paid my port fees."

"Oh . . . uh . . . no, it isn't anything like that," Miles stammered, recovering from the embarrassment of having walked in on the captain as he was changing clothes. "Captain Roberts, I am Miles Chalmers."

"Miles Chalmers?" The irritation on Roberts's face fell away under a genuine smile, and he extended his hand warmly. "Well hell, man, why didn't you say so? You didn't have to come down here. I was coming to your office."

"I have another appointment that I must keep," Miles said. "I thought it would expedite things if I came to you."

"Whatever you say, Mr. Chalmers. I want to tell you again how much I appreciate the way you handled our business. You know, there are many companies that would have realized my degree of desperation and tried to heave taut until I came around. You didn't do that."

"There are some in our company who would have done that, had they been allowed to," Miles said. "But I don't believe in that sort of thing. I like to keep an honest relationship between the ship masters, and me."

" 'Tis a fine way of doing things," Roberts agreed.

"Oh, here is your hatch money, Captain Roberts."

"Hatch money? You mean I'm to get a bonus?"

Miles smiled broadly. "Of course. All our captains get bonuses if they bring the cargo in on time, and with no damage."

Roberts took the envelope. "I must say, this is something I didn't enjoy when I owned my own vessel. Though since the vessel was mine, all profit was mine."

"When you could get a cargo, captain. With us, you need never go without a cargo."

"Careful now, I'll get the feeling you're trying to talk me into not buying back my own ship," Roberts said, laughing.

"No, no, that's in the contract and I'll honor it. As I told you, captain, I'm an honorable man, and I like to do business with honorable men. Besides, if you wish, after you buy the ship back there may even be arrangements whereby we can throw cargo your way."

"That would be very decent of you, Mr. Chalmers. But that is a year from now. In the meantime I am a captain in your employ, and so you shall have services and my loyalty."

"Ah, and therein is the point of our visit, Captain," Miles said. "Your loyalty."

"Surely, sir, you do not question it?" Captain Roberts asked.

"No, of course not. But I want to explore the limits of it."

Roberts squinted at Miles, then walked over to his table and opened a cigarette box. He pulled one out and lit it before he answered.

"Mr. Chalmers, I'm not certain about where you are heading right now, and I'm not certain I want to be," he said with studied slowness. "I shall be loyal to Chalmers Shipping in all ways legal. But because my papers would be on the line for any nefarious activity, I will not risk them. If that is disloyalty, then so be it."

Miles laughed easily. "My dear fellow, such a comment from you only reinforces my belief that you are the right man for me. Heavens, sir, I would not have you do anything illegal. No, sir. When I said I wanted to explore the limits of your loyalty, I was talking about something else. An internal affair."

24

"Then what do you mean?" Roberts asked, still guarded.

"As you know, Chalmers Shipping Lines is a family-owned enterprise. There are some other shares out, parceled as rewards for long service and so forth, but controlling interest is within the family. The head of the Board of Directors is my aunt, Constance Chalmers. Without going into the details, I will tell you that there will shortly be a new board election, and I hope that I shall become the new Chairman of the Board."

"Well, I wish you all the luck then," Roberts said.

"I will need more than your luck, Captain. I will need your help."

"How can I help?" Roberts asked. "I certainly won't have a vote."

"No, you won't. But if I have your loyalty, as well as that of the other sea captains, then I shall be able to use that in a most persuasive way."

"I see," Roberts said. He ground his cigarette out. "Mr. Chalmers, I don't believe it would be appropriate for me to show partiality toward one Chalmers over another, at this point. To me you are all the same. You are all Chalmers Shipping Lines, Incorporated."

"But we are not all the same," Miles said. "To begin with, you received full price on your ship, Captain, because *I* authorized it. And, I might add, I took a great deal of abuse from my aunt in arranging the deal."

"I did receive full price for my ship, and I am grateful for that," Roberts said.

"Are you a labor union man, Captain? Would you favor sailing your ship by consent of the sailors? Commanding by committee?"

"No sane master would, sir," Roberts said.

"Precisely my point. If my aunt has her way, all of Chalmers will be unionized, and captains will no longer command, they will request."

"And your aunt seriously hopes to stay in business with such a policy?"

25

"I'll be honest with you, Captain. I fear my aunt has neither the stamina nor the mental alertness required to run this company. She is, after all, sixty-eight years old, and Chalmers Shipping Lines is one of the largest shipping companies in the world. She has done well by it for forty years, all things considered. But she is no longer equal to the task. She is my aunt, and I love her dearly, so I cannot be ruthless in my dealings with her. Therefore, I must assume control gradually, painlessly, and ease her out from under the burden, so that her final years can be spent in the luxury and comfort she has so richly earned."

"I can understand the delicacy of your position, Mr. Chalmers," Roberts said.

"And I can count on your support?"

"Aye, for what it is worth."

"Good, good. Then I shall consider your word your bond."

"It is," Roberts said.

Miles pulled a watch from his pocket and looked at it. "Dear me, I am very nearly late for my appointment. Captain, you may recruit your own crew and pay whatever wages you wish. As you know, when you take a consignment from us, you are also given a mutually agreed upon sum of money. From that money you will provision your ship as you see fit, pay your men, and pay yourself. In that way it is not unlike the arrangement you've already had, as the owner of your vessel."

"Indeed it is not, sir," Roberts said.

"Some of our captains fare even better, finding ways to economize on the ship's provisions," Miles suggested.

"I will not be miserly in that department, sir. A well-fed crew is a happy crew, and a happy crew means an efficient ship."

"I couldn't agree more," Miles put in quickly. "I merely pointed it out to show the degree of latitude we allow our masters. Well, good day to you, sir. I must be off."

"I will walk with you to the gangplank," Roberts said.

The two men walked across the deck, then down the gangplank to the pier, alongside which lay the ship. They shook hands, then Miles walked away quickly, hurrying to his next appointment.

A young woman, attractive in an overmade way, waited until Miles was gone; then she sauntered quickly out to the gangplank. "Ahoy aboard," she called out.

Roberts, who had started back up the plank, stopped just before he regained the deck and looked back. He smiled.

"Well, what's the matter, could you find no one to play with?" he teased.

The girl smiled, and Roberts saw that she was in fact very pretty. He was surprised to see her in this occupation, for it had been his experience that most of the girls of the dock aged quickly and wore their dissipation like a sign, proclaiming their profession.

"The others weren't invited," the girl said.

"Oh? And why not?"

The girl raised one arm to the rigging. It was a seemingly innocent move, but one of design, for in so doing, her breasts thrust against the blouse she wore, and her hip jutted out. It was a provocative pose, and the girl knew it, and that was why she did it. She smiled a small, proud smile. "They can't afford me, Captain. I'm not a sailor's doxy. I'm a captain's lady."

"Any captain's?"

"Any captain whose purse can accommodate me," she said. "And I'm not cheap."

"You've a high opinion of yourself, madam," Roberts said.

"It's justified, Captain. Truly it is," the girl said. She moved one leg just slightly, and it caused the skirt to flatten against her abdomen; Roberts could see where her pelvic bone was and, though it may have been his imagination, the small rise of her pubic mound. It was an enticing pose, and even though he knew that she had done it for that reason and he was disgusted with himself for allowing it to affect him, it did, and he caught his breath.

"Come into my cabin," he invited.

Kristin was shaking. It wasn't a violent shaking, like a chill or anything. But she was shaking severely enough that she couldn't hold her hands still, even when she clasped them together and tried to hold them tightly.

She walked away from the telescope and sat down on her bed, feeling hot and out of breath, weak in the knees, and she had a strange fluttering in her stomach that somehow managed to extend down into her loins. And, underlying it all, she felt shame.

Kristin had watched it all. She had been unable to take her telescope off the new captain from the moment his ship had arrived. She managed to stop for a while, when the reflection off her telescope nearly gave her away; then she saw her cousin Miles walking toward the ship, and so she looked through the scope again. She told herself that she wasn't watching the captain, she was just curious as to why her cousin had visited the ship. Then, as her cousin left, she saw Captain Roberts approached by the woman, and Kristin knew what was going to happen.

"Please, don't let me see anything," she prayed silently, while at the same time searching every facet of the captain's cabin, looking for a vantage point similar to the one she had found on the deckhouse on that other ship, so long ago. That she didn't find it left her with conflicting emotions. She was glad she didn't find an opening because she wanted to so badly that she knew if she had, she would have shamelessly watched everything that went on. If she had watched, she couldn't have borne the guilt of it, she was positive of that. And thus, though disappointed, she was thankful that the burden was not placed on her.

It was bad enough just knowing what they were doing. Was he fire and ice? she wondered. Was he gentle and violent, or was he cold and mechanical? Without going any further, she felt that she knew the answer. Making love with Captain Roberts would be a savage experience, she felt; yet somehow she knew that his savagery would be couched in such tender caresses that it would leave her crying with the sweetness of it all.

Kristin felt a rapidly spreading dampness between her legs, and a flush of heat diffused through her body. She closed her eyes and clenched her fists, then angrily pounded on the bed, letting a little cry of frustration escape from her lips.

"Kristin, dear, are you all right?" Constance called from the hall just outside her door.

The call surprised Kristin and jarred her from her erotic musings. "Yes, Grandmother, I'm fine," she answered.

"I thought I heard you cry out."

"I was having difficulty with a buckle on my shoe," Kristin said. "But I have it now." She walked over to the door, opened it, and smiled at her grandmother, to reassure her that nothing was wrong.

"Dear, I'm going to spend a few days at Ocean House. Would you like to come along?"

"Oh, yes, I'd *love* to," Kristin said. "Just let me pack a few things."

"Very well. I'll send Mason up directly to take your bag. The flowers are coming up and the trees are budding now; I think it will be lovely over there."

Kristin kissed her grandmother on the cheek. "Thank you for thinking of it," she said. "I'll hurry and pack, I promise."

This was just what she needed, Kristin decided, as she happily selected the clothes she would take. A few days in Ocean House, with the opportunity to stroll about the grounds and breathe the salt sea air, free of

29

the fetid odors of the docks, would clear her mind of the disturbing thoughts that had occupied it of late.

With the stern window shutters open to catch the breeze, the late afternoon sun splashed into Roberts's cabin in streams of light, laying golden bars on the floor. Roberts lay there, comfortably, with his arm stretched over his head. His bed was large, primarily because it was a captain's prerogative, and he, as a big man, needed a large bed. Thus it was that the girl who came to his cabin was also comfortable between his sheets.

"Hmm, what time is it?" the girl in bed asked. Her name was Marcene, and she was redheaded. At this moment, her deep red hair spilled out over the pillow, fan shaped.

Roberts smiled as he looked at her. She was as beautiful now as she had appeared to be on the docks. Roberts knew from experience that a man's strong need often did more to enhance a woman's beauty than all her art with makeup and creams.

"It's about eight bells," he said.

"What time would that be in shore language?"

"Four in the afternoon," Roberts said. "Say, I'm famished. Do you know someplace where we could get a good meal?"

The girl looked at him in surprise. "You don't want to go to a restaurant with me," she said.

"Why not?"

"Because, I'm a . . . a . . . " Marcene couldn't say the word.

"You are a beautiful young woman," Roberts said. "And I like to be in the company of beautiful young women. Now, do you know such a place or don't you?"

"Well yes, I do," Marcene said. "But it isn't near here. All the places close to the docks know me, and they know my profession. I'm not welcome in them."

"Then we shall go where you are welcome," Roberts said.

"Oh, I'd like that," the girl said, her eyes shining in excitement. "I'd like that very much. My hair," she said, putting her hand to her head. "Oh it must be a mess. Do you have a mirror?"

"Aye," Roberts laughed. "It's a small one, and not like you're used to. But it'll do for your needs, I suppose."

Marcene got out of bed and padded, naked, over to a small mirror that hung on a bulkhead above a wash-basin. She had a total lack of self-consciousness over her nudity, and she looked over at Roberts and smiled. A patch of sunlight from the mirror fell upon her face and made her smile dazzling. "May I use your hair-brush?"

"It's there, by the basin," Roberts said, pointing.

He watched as the girl brushed her long, copper-colored hair, and he enjoyed the sight of her supple body, with the skin rippling like silk in a breeze, and her breasts bobbing with each stroke of the brush. He enjoyed the picture thus displayed before him so much that he felt the stirrings of desire being reawakened, and he called her name softly.

"Yes?" Marcene said, looking toward him. Then she recognized the look in Roberts's eyes, and the even more obvious sign of his renewed interest, and she put the brush down. "I thought you were hungry," she said, again smiling at him with that dazzling smile.

"The food can wait," Roberts said. "I have an appetite for something else."

"I can see that," Marcene said.

"How much for a second time?"

"Uh, uh," the girl said, shaking her head no. "For this, there will be no charge."

Roberts pulled aside the sheet of the bed and Marcene crossed over to it again. "I want to thank you for making me feel so welcome in Boston," he said.

"I'll bet you have a woman to welcome you in every port."

"I've been welcomed to a few," Roberts admitted.

"And, speaking as an expert, Captain, which port city gives you the finest welcome?"

"The one I'm in at the time," Roberts answered. He pulled her to him, feeling the entire length of her nude body against his.

The girl, as she had promised, justified her high opinion of her worth, and she responded eagerly to Roberts's prodding. Within moments he was over her again; their legs intertwined and their bodies joined as they shared each other a second time.

Chapter Four

A bird's song awakened Kristin, and for a moment
she wondered how a songbird had managed to find its
way to the Boston waterfront. Then she realized that
she was in her bedroom at Ocean House, smiled happily, and stretched gloriously, enjoying the sensuous
feel of silk sheets and pillowcases against her skin.

A bright, though not harsh, morning sun streamed
in through the casement windows, and she got out of
bed and walked toward the golden light on the far side
of her room. She pushed the window open to better
enjoy the song of the bird, and looked out across the
great expanse of lawn, freshly green with the young
spring, toward the hedgerows, three hundred yards
away. There was a sculptured fishpond halfway toward
the hedgerows, and around the pond were bright yellow jonquils, purple asters, and tiny white roses.

Kristin started to close the window, when she saw Mason coming toward the house carrying a bouquet of freshly cut flowers. Mason was well over seventy and had been a servant with the Chalmers family for fifty years.

"Not a servant, child," her grandmother had corrected her once, years ago, when Kristin was a child. "A domestic."

"What's the difference?" Kristin wanted to know.

"There is a great deal of difference. One can take pride in being a domestic. It is a title for a profession that has respect and dignity. To call one a servant, on the other hand, smacks of servitude, or indenturing, even slavery. No, we much prefer to be called domestics."

Kristin laughed.

"What's so funny?" Constance asked.

"You are, Grandmother. You said *we* much prefer to be called domestics. You aren't a domestic."

"Oh, but I was, dear," Constance said.

"You were?" Kristin asked, her eyes growing large in wonder. "Where?"

"Why, right here. I was a domestic in this very house. For your great-grandfather."

"But you are a Chalmers. How could you be a domestic for Great-Grandfather?" Kristin wanted to know.

Constance chuckled softly, and patted her lap. "Come, sit on Grandmother's lap, and I'll tell you a story."

Kristin responded eagerly, for she loved her grandmother's stories more than anything in the world. She realized she was lucky to be living with her grandmother, for all the other seven-year-old girls she knew got to see their grandmothers only when they visited. Of course, the other seven-year-old girls she knew had a mother and a father, while she had neither. But that didn't matter. She wouldn't trade her grandmother for a hundred mothers and fathers.

"Before I married your grandfather, my name wasn't Chalmers, you know," Constance said.

"It wasn't? Why not?"

"Because I wasn't married yet."

"But I'm not married, and my name is Chalmers."

Constance laughed. "You were born a Chalmers, girl. I was born a Hughes."

"Where were you born, Grandmother?"

"In London, England," Constance said. "My mother and father were domestics too. In England, we say that someone who is a domestic is 'in the service.' It's a very honorable profession, and people who are in the service pass the profession on to their children, and then to *their* children. But there was a panic in London in 1855, and there weren't as many jobs for domestics as there once were."

"What's a panic?"

"It just means that there isn't as much money," Constance said. "In my case, it meant that if I wanted to remain in the service, I would have to leave England. So, I came to America."

As Constance told the story, she rocked Kristin, and Kristin closed her eyes and listened to the tale. The story was told with such expressiveness, and was made so vivid, that Kristin could practically live it as her grandmother told it. In her imaginative mind, she almost became the young, twenty-two-year-old woman stepping off the boat in a new country.

The pier had been as crowded as the busiest London street, and Constance clutched her suitcase securely, afraid that someone would grab it and run away. All she owned in the world was in that bag: two additional dresses, a well-used, but fine, warm coat that Lady Haversham had given her, not needed now in the summer, an envelope containing four shillings and sixpence, and a letter of introduction from Lord Haversham to John David Chalmers.

"Here, lads," a man was calling to the arriving immigrants. "Here, lads, I'm the man that can find you work. Here, lads, come to see me and I'll treat you fair. Here, lads."

Constance walked over to the man, who had already gathered up several of the arriving men and was trying to collar more.

"Excuse me, sir," she said.

"Sorry, missy," the man answered. "I'm recruitin' for a railroad. You don't look near on to strong enough to swing a pick or a hammer."

The others laughed and Constance blushed.

"No, sir, and indeed I shouldn't attempt to undertake such a task. I was wondering if you could kindly direct me to the home of Mr. John David Chalmers?"

"What do I look like, missy, a road sign? Now be on with you."

"Do you know where I could inquire of his location?" Constance asked.

"I said be on with you," the man said again, this time more gruffly than before. "I get paid by the number of men I sign up, 'n you're costin' me money with your gab."

"I'm terribly sorry," Constance said. "I've no wish to be a bother." She left contritely and the man went back to his recruiting.

Constance was at a loss as to what to do, when she saw among the ship's cargo being unloaded, several crates that were consigned to Chalmers Shipping Lines. She let out a small shout of joy and hurried over to the crates to read the address. The address was 15 State Street.

Armed with an address, Constance was able to enquire about the direction. A few minutes later, tired from carrying the suitcase the entire way, but happy at seeing a sign that proclaimed the building before her to be Chalmer's Shipping Lines, she walked through the front door.

"Miss, we book our passengers through an agent," a man behind a counter said when he looked up and saw Constance carrying luggage.

"I've no need for additional passage," Constance replied. "I've been off the boat but an hour now."

"Then what can I do for you?"

"You could direct me to Mr. John David Chalmers. I saw that this building bore the same name, and hoped that they would be one and the same."

The man smiled. "You were correct in your chance, lady. But what business would you have with Mr. Chalmers?"

"That is for Mr. Chalmers, sir," Constance said.

"Well, but you see, as an employee of Mr. Chalmers, I have to look out for him. I can't let just anyone come in and talk to him anytime they want to."

"I . . . I wish to speak to him of my employment," Constance said.

"Well, then, there you are, you see? I can take care of that for him, and we won't have to bother him at all. Mr. Chalmers ain't hirin' nobody right now."

"I would prefer to hear that from Mr. Chalmers himself," Constance said.

"Miss, I done tole you . . ."

"I think the lady has a right to see John David, don't you, Paul?" a new, well-modulated voice said.

Constance turned toward the voice and saw that someone had come in behind her and was standing close enough to overhear the conversation.

"Mr. Coy, sir, how are you today?" the clerk asked.

The man addressed as Coy was well dressed and obviously a gentleman, and Constance was grateful for his intrusion.

"Where is Mr. Chalmers?" Coy asked.

"He's gone home, sir. He's expectin' a new servant girl and he wants to meet her himself. You know how he is about such things."

"Indeed I do," Coy said. He looked at Constance.

"I shall be driving out to Ocean House. Would you like to come along?"

"Ocean House?"

"That's where Mr. Chalmers lives," Coy explained.

"Oh, yes, then I should like to go."

"I expect he'll be surprised to learn that you showed up here, when he went home to meet you, don't you?" Coy said, perceiving at once that Constance was the girl he was waiting for.

"I expect so, sir, yes," she answered.

"Well, why didn't you tell me you was the servant girl in the first place?" the clerk asked. "We could have saved all this trouble."

"It was not your place to know, sir," Constance said. "And besides, I prefer to be referred to as a domestic."

Coy laughed and reached for Constance's suitcase, but Constance stopped him.

"I only meant to carry it for you, girl," Coy explained.

"It wouldn't be fitting, sir, as you are a fine gentleman and I am but a domestic. The clerk can carry it." She walked out of the office, accompanied by Coy's laughter, and followed by a surprised clerk struggling under the load of her case.

An elegant liveried rig was parked in front of the office, and a young woman just a few years younger than Constance sat on one of the rear facing seats.

"Margaret, this is the new servant girl the Chalmers were expecting," Coy said, introducing his daughter. "Oh, I'm sorry, you prefer to be called a domestic. I didn't get your name, by the way."

"Constance Hughes," Constance said. "My parents are in the employ of Lord and Lady Haversham, and they . . ."

"Really, Father, there is little need to introduce me to a common . . . 'domestic' . . . ," Margaret said, letting the word *domestic* slide distastefully from her mouth.

"Margaret, where are your manners?" Coy asked.

"Manners are to be used among people of equal stations," Margaret said.

"Missy, may I remind you that in this country we are all of the same station," Coy said. "And you should thank your lucky stars for that, for we have nothing left but our fine Boston name, and that is scarce little to trade on."

"Father!" Margaret said. "Must you tell everyone our business? When Lee and I are married, I shall have all the money we need. That is, if you don't ruin everything with your loose talk."

"Move over," Coy said gruffly.

"Move over?"

"Constance is riding with you. We are taking her out to Ocean House."

Margaret moved over in protest, and Constance climbed into the seat, spreading her skirt to take more of the seat than necessary, because she knew that it would cramp Margaret, who intended to stay as far away as possible.

"So you see, Kristin," Constance said, still holding the child in her lap. "I was a domestic myself, and I know what it's like to have to earn a living by the sweat of one's brow. And I know about things like dignity and respect and just good manners. So I hope you are never cruel or take unfair advantage of your position over anyone."

"I won't, Grandmother, I promise," Kristin said, surprising Constance, who thought the little girl had fallen asleep.

"Good morning, Mason," Kristin called from her bedroom window.

"Good morning, Miss Kristin," Mason replied. "Your grandmother is taking breakfast on the sun porch."

"Good, good, I'll be right down," Kristin said, closing the window and hurrying to get dressed.

When she stepped onto the sun porch a few moments later, she saw her grandmother reading the paper and sipping coffee.

"Have you already eaten?" Kristin asked, an edge of disappointment in her voice over the thought that she may have missed sharing her breakfast.

"No, dear," Constance said, smiling at her and holding her cheek out for a good-morning kiss. "I've been waiting for you." She folded the paper and laid it to one side.

"Grandmother, have you ever met Captain Roberts?" Kristin asked, as she spread marmalade on her toast a moment later.

"Met him? I don't even know who he is."

"Yes, you do. He is the captain of the *Morning Star.*"

"Oh, yes, that is the ship we bought a few months ago, isn't it? No, I haven't met the captain. Why do you ask?"

"No particular reason. It arrived yesterday, and I happened to see it from my window. Cousin Miles had a nice long chat with the captain, I noticed."

"No doubt convincing the captain that it was he who insisted on giving full price for the *Morning Star,*" Constance chuckled.

"Grandmother, why are Cousin Miles and Aunt Margaret so mean?" Kristin asked.

"They aren't mean, dear. They are merely ambitious."

"Ambitious and greedy," Kristin said. "I think it's awful the way they are always talking about what's going to happen 'after you've gone,' as if you were on your deathbed. Well, for my part, I wish you could boss the company for the next hundred years. I've no ambitions at your expense."

"You can't blame Miles, child. He's had this

40

drummed into his head from the time he was a baby."

"Why does Aunt Margaret dislike you so, Grandmother? Is it because you married Granddad when she wanted to?"

"If you ask her, I think that is what she would tell you," Constance said. "But in truth, after your grandfather told her he didn't wish to marry her, she turned her sights on your Uncle Charles without missing a step. You see, she didn't really want Lee or Charles. She just wanted a Chalmers."

"Was Granddad a handsome man?"

"Oh, yes," Constance said. She looked up, as if seeing something in the distant shadows of time. "He was a very handsome man."

"I'll bet he was a big man, over six feet tall," Kristin said. "With huge, huge shoulders."

Constance laughed. "No, nothing at all like that. He was quite bookish, rather thin, and no more than five feet eight or nine inches tall. He was very ordinary in appearance, but he was a wonderful, wonderful man. Who did you describe, by the way, your dream man?"

"No . . . no, of course not!" Kristin said, flushing a deep crimson even as she realized that she had just described Captain Roberts.

" 'Tis no crime to have an idea of a dream man in mind," Constance said. "In fact, Kristin, you're twenty years old now, and it's about time one man started standing out over the others. Who would he be?"

"I don't have such a man in mind, Grandmother."

"Surely you do. You can tell me; haven't we always shared things? Who is it? Let me see, would it be Titus Logan?"

"Titus Logan? Grandmother, you aren't serious!" Kristin said, thinking of the awkward, gangly young man whose father was Chairman of the Board of Directors of the Seaman's Bank and Trust.

"No? Perhaps Edward Hamilton?"

"You mean the future president of the United States?" Kristin replied, laughing. "At least, that's what he says he's going to be."

"No?" Then perhaps men of noble aims are not your cup of tea," Constance said, carrying the teasing on. "I daresay you fancy one of the sailors, a strong, handsome . . ." Constance stopped when she saw Kirstin looking down at the table. Her cheeks, once more, were aflame. "Kirstin, you haven't met a sailor have you?"

"No, Grandmother."

"Thank God."

"Anyway, I thought you were always making a thing about everyone being equal."

"Touché," Constance said easily. "But in this case, I really should make an exception. Marry whomever you will, dear. Marry a banker, a soldier, a ditchdigger if you must. But never marry a sailor. They are the most undependable of all God's creatures."

"You need have no fear on that score, Grandmother," Kristin said. "From all I've been able to find out, sailors aren't the marrying kind."

"Then I'll amend my admonition," Constance said. "Don't have anything at all to do with a sailor, in marriage or otherwise."

"I have no such thoughts in mind," Kristin said.

"Good. In the meantime, to help you find your young man, suppose we have a party? Would you like that?"

"Yes, Grandmother," Kristin said. In truth, she would just as soon not have one, but she knew that her grandmother loved them so and was using this an an excuse. It was little enough effort on her part to pretend that she liked them as well, and it made her feel good to make her grandmother happy. She smiled broadly. "I would love a party."

Chapter Five

Captain Raymond Woodward, of the Boston Police Department, ran his fingers over his waxed mustache, satisfying himself that it was neat and proper, as befitting the commander of one of Boston's most populous precincts. Then, squaring his cap upon his head, he stepped out of the carriage and walked up the foot-polished concrete steps to the precinct station house to start a new day.

"Cap'n Woodward, Diamond Willie is here to see you," the desk sergeant said as Woodward stepped inside. There were half a dozen policemen in the room, and they stood respectfully, until Captain Woodward indicated with a slight wave of his hand that they could be at ease. There were also a handful of petty crooks and vagrants in the room, but they made no move as Captain Woodward walked by them.

"Diamond Willie, have you been keeping yourself

straight?" Woodward asked the rather nattily dressed young man who lounged against the wall just outside his office.

"Yes, sir," Diamond Willie replied. "I ain't been picked up for nothin' since that jewel heist on Tremont Street, six months ago."

"I didn't ask if you'd been picked up, I asked if you'd been keeping yourself straight."

Diamond Willie held up his right hand. "God's truth," he said.

"What do you want to see me about?"

"In your office."

"I don't take petty crooks into my office."

Diamond Willie smiled. "You don't want this out here."

Captain Woodward looked around quickly, then made an impatient motion with his hand. Diamond Willie stepped into the office, and Woodward followed him, then shut the door behind him. "What is it?" he asked gruffly. "You know better than to come here."

"Mr. Prefontaine wants to know if you want him to look into this business with the Reverend Wales for you." Diamond Willie said.

"What do you mean?"

"Simple," Diamond Willie said. "Mr. Prefontaine says that the reverend might cause trouble for all of us, and it would be a pleasure for him to look into it and see what he can do."

"You tell Prefontaine that Reverend Wales is a police problem, and we'll take care of it ourselves."

"Then does the . . . uh . . . arrangement you have with Mr. Prefontaine stay the same?"

"Of course it does. Why should it change?"

" 'Cause the reverend is stirring up all kinds of stink."

"I told you. I'll take care of the reverend. You just tell Prefontaine to take care of his own business."

Diamond Willie smiled and pulled an envelope from his inside jacket pocket. He slid the envelope on the corner of the desk, touched his hat lightly, then turned to leave. "I'll be seein' you," he said.

"You'd damn sure better be seeing me," Woodward said, sliding the envelope across the desk and dropping it into his middle drawer. "And stay out of trouble."

"Oh, I intend to, Captain. I intend to," Diamond Willie said. "After all, that's what this is all about, isn't it?"

Woodward watched the door shut; then he sat there for a moment, drumming his fingers on the desk. Sergeant O'Brien put his head in through the door right after Diamond Willie left. "Everythin' all right Cap'n?" O'Brien asked.

"Yeah," Woodward said. "O'Brien, bring me the morning paper."

"I was going to bring it to you, Cap'n. You should see what Reverend Wales said last night."

"Prefontaine wants to take care of Wales," Woodward said. "That's all we need now."

O'Brien handed Woodward the paper, and he opened it up to read the latest in the series of articles dealing with the crusading Angus Wales.

"The committee investigating Boston's police department has been literally turning the city inside out, as one turns an old stocking to examine its seamy side and see what has lodged in its dark recesses," the article began. "Dr. Angus Wales, the crusading cleric, and a leading member of the investigating committee, blasted the police department from his pulpit in the Back Bay Methodist Church last night. 'The police department,' Reverend Wales said, 'is a lying, perjured, rum-soaked, and libidineus lot.' Reverend Wales went on to say that he has gathered evidence to implicate no fewer than ten precinct captains, and claims that the average precinct captain, in addition to his salary, draws as much as $3,500 in paid fees from gamblers, liquor dealers, and bawdy-house operators, said fees to ensure immunity from prosecution."

Woodward folded the paper and laid it to one side, swearing under his breath. He pulled out the middle drawer and opened the envelope given him by Diamond Willie. Inside were six crisp twenty-dollar bills, this week's payoff. Despite himself, he smiled, for Reverend Wales was way off on his figures. Woodward made almost twice as much as Wales claimed.

But Wales needed to be cut down to size. He was tempted to let Prefontaine, who was the kingpin of all criminal activity in Woodward's precinct, have his way. Just the slightest indication of assent on his part, Woodward knew, and Prefontaine would have Wales killed.

And that, Woodward realized, would cause the governor to launch his own investigation, with the result of destroying everything Woodward and the others like him had built up so carefully over the last twenty years. After all, Woodward told himself, what was he really doing wrong? Where was the harm in a little gambling, or drinking, or even a whorehouse? No one got hurt by those so-called crimes, and if he could make a little money on the side, it was his due. Whereas the other criminal activity—the murders, muggings, strong-armed robberies, and so forth—Woodward and his men guarded against those assiduously. And without finding this way of raising a little extra money, they would be sorely paid for such dangerous work.

That was why he agreed to help Miles Chalmers.

Woodward got up from his chair and walked over to the window. From there he could see only the masts of the ships at dock, but the trucks of the greatest majority of the ships bore the flag of the Chalmers Line: a silver lion on a field of green. If he could get Miles Chalmers indebted to him, then the problem of Reverend Wales would go away. For Chalmers, with all his money and power, could exercise great influence over public opinion.

Woodward hadn't spoken of that to Chalmers as yet. That wasn't the sort of thing you sprung right away. Woodward knew that he had to play Chalmers, give him line and offer him bait until, like a great fish, he was hooked. And once Woodward had him hooked, he would land him properly.

Woodward chuckled. Until a few days ago, he had thought his carefully constructed empire was going to come crashing down upon him. Then Chalmers contacted him and asked if he would be interested in "earning one thousand dollars."

Woodward knew that that kind of money would be offered only for the most nefarious of schemes. He agreed to meet with Chalmers, not so much for the money, but to find out what Chalmers had in mind, to see if, in fact, it could be turned to his advantage.

The appointment was for four o'clock the previous afternoon, and the place where they agreed to meet was a warehouse belonging to Chalmers. Woodward, from his experience as a policeman, had learned long ago that it was best to have an edge before keeping an appointment with an unknown. Therefore Woodward went to the warehouse not at four, but at two, and he checked it out thoroughly. Then he took a trusted aide with him, hid him near the agreed-upon meeting place, and provided him with a tablet and pencil for the express purpose of taking notes.

After the meeting place was checked out, Woodward sought out Miles Chalmers, locating him at around two-thirty in the afternoon, and secretly following him until the time of the meeting, just to make certain that Chalmers didn't spring any unwelcome surprises on him.

When he saw Chalmers meet with the captain of the *Morning Star,* he sent Marcene to visit the captain, to find out what Chalmers and the captain talked about.

47

Marcene did not report back to him the night before, as she had promised. It didn't matter that much, because the meeting with Chalmers had given Woodward all the ammunition he needed.

"Captain Woodward," Chalmers had greeted, when Woodward walked into the meeting place, five minutes late.

"I'm sorry I'm late," Woodward said. "I had some police business to take care of." That was a lie, of course. There had been no police business at all, and contrary to being late, Woodward had been two hours early. But even this, he knew, helped to give him a slight edge.

"That's quite all right," Chalmers said nervously. "After all, where would our city be without our fine police force?"

"There are some who would say we would be better off," Woodward said.

"Troublemakers, Captain. Troublemakers and agitators. Believe me, among my crowd, we very much appreciate what you and all our boys in blue, are doing."

Woodward didn't answer. Instead he stared pointedly at Chalmers. The staring and the protracted silence made Chalmers even more nervous, and he began sweating. That was exactly what Woodward wanted, for that, too, would give him an edge. He knew that nervous men tended to talk too much, to give away things they had no intention of giving away, and to overlook the obvious.

Chalmers pulled a handkerchief from his jacket and began patting at the beads of perspiration on his face. "It's hot for this early in the spring," he said.

"I suppose it is," Woodward said. He added no more to his statement. He would say just enough to keep his ploy from being obvious, but little enough to keep Chalmers nervous.

Chalmers looked around before he spoke this time, and Woodward knew that he was coming right to the point. "Captain Woodward, since you agreed to meet me here, you are no doubt interested in my offer of one thousand dollars."

"Yes," Woodward said. "I am interested."

Chalmers cleared his throat. "Captain, in your line of work, dealing with dangerous people, I imagine you find it necessary to use physical force?"

"Yes."

"How much physical force?"

"As much as may be needed."

That wasn't the answer Chalmers wanted, so he cleared his throat and started again. "Have you ever . . . uh . . . found it necessary to . . . kill . . . anyone?"

"Yes."

"And you have no qualms about it?"

"It was part of my job."

"Could you kill a woman?"

"If I had to."

Chalmers began to sweat even more profusely, and he wiped his face again before he went on.

"You understand that what we say from here on, must be treated with the utmost discretion?" Chalmers said.

"Of course," Woodward said easily.

"I . . . uh . . . am coming to you, because I have been told that you are the type of man who understands loyalty. And I was told to mention the word *excalibur*."

The word hung in the air for fully thirty seconds, hovering over them as if emblazoned on a balloon. So, Woodward thought during the pregnant pause, you have done your homework, eh? Excalibur referred to Gerald Carson, past Chairman of the Board of the Atlantic Brokerage Company. Past Chairman of the Board, because he was found dead, last fall, floating face down in Boston Bay. The murder was being in-

investigated by Captain Woodward. Carson had been killed for a price, and the code word for the operation was *Excalibur*. Only two men knew that word; Scott Pendleton, the current Chairman of the Board of Atlantic Brokerage, and the killer himself. By saying that word, Chalmers was now telling Woodward that he knew that the killer of Gerald Carson was a murderer for hire. He was also saying that he knew that Woodward was that murderer.

"What do you want done, Mr. Chalmers?" Woodward asked.

"I want you to kill someone."

"I see. Mrs. Constance Chalmers, right?"

"No," Chalmers said. "I want you to kill my cousin, Kristin Chalmers."

"What? Why kill *her*?"

"I have my reasons, Captain. She should be no harder to kill than my aunt. And believe me, there would be less row raised over it. She is little more than a decoration at the social events of the season. No one would miss her. My aunt, on the other hand, is head of one of the most powerful organizations in the world. If anything happened to her, there would be a terrible cry of outrage, and I would lead it."

"But why would you want to kill the girl?" Woodward asked again. "What good can it do you?"

"Do I have to give you a reason? I'm paying to have it done."

"But the girl is, what, nineteen?"

"Twenty."

"Twenty years old," Woodward said. He ran his hand across his mustache.

"I'll raise the price to two thousand dollars, Captain, but I'll go no higher."

"It's not the money," Woodward said. "It's just that I find it difficult to kill a twenty-year-old girl for no reason."

"But I told you, Captain. I do have a reason," Chalmers said. "Besides, a human life is a human life. How can you draw a moral judgment between a twenty-year-old girl and a fifty-eight-year-old man?" Chalmers was referring to Carson.

"All right, I'll do it," Woodward said. "When do you wish it done?"

"Within the week."

"I'll take half the money now."

Chalmers smiled. "I rather thought you would." He opened his jacket and pulled out his wallet. "And, as you can see, I brought a thousand dollars, thinking also, that you would force me to raise the price." He handed the money to Woodward, and as the latter took it, he had the sudden realization that the edge in this meeting had, somehow, passed over to Chalmers.

Woodward said nothing to Chalmers about Reverend Wales. That would come later. For now, he would wait.

There was a knock at the door of Woodward's office, and his mind dismissed the rather uneasy meeting of the day before. "Yes?" he called out.

"A lady here to see you, Cap'n."

"Send her in."

Sergeant O'Brien stepped out of the way and held his arm out, inviting the visitor into Woodward's office. A woman came in, hatted, corseted, and bustled, as befitting the president of a ladies' tea club. She looked as if she might be representing just an organization, ready to request police assistance for an afternoon cotillion. She looked nothing at all like she did yesterday afternoon, when Woodward last saw her.

Woodward smiled. "Marcene, I've never known anyone who can change her appearance so much."

"It is a necessity," Marcene said. "If I couldn't become respectable, I would never be able to enjoy the fruits of my labor."

Woodward laughed. "I see what you mean." He stopped laughing. "Where were you last night?"

"You sound like a jealous husband," Marcene teased.

"I'm not a jealous husband. I'm a man who can throw you in jail for prostitution and you know it."

"Then why would you ask such a question?" Marcene replied. "You know where I was. I was with Captain Roberts."

"What's his name?" Woodward asked, holding a pencil to a tablet.

"Andrew Roberts," Marcene said, saying the name distinctly. "He used to own the *Morning Star,* but he had some bad luck and had to sell it to Chalmers."

"What did Chalmers want with him?"

"Just routine shipping matters," Marcene answered.

Woodward slapped Marcene sharply, but not brutally. It came quickly and unexpectedly, and Marcene put her hand up to her face in fear and surprise.

The expression on Woodward's face didn't change. "I asked what Chalmers wanted with him," he said again. "And don't tell me routine shipping matters. He doesn't go to meet every new ship."

"I . . . I'm not really sure," Marcene said, her voice colored now by fear of the police captain.

"You were supposed to find out."

"We talked, but he doesn't say a great deal. He's the strong, silent type." Despite the precariousness of her situation and the fear of the moment, a passing thought of her afternoon and night with the captain came to her as she mentioned the words strong and silent, and she smiled a small, satisfied smile.

"I can see that," Woodward said. "But tell me what he *did* say. Anything can be significant, even if you don't think it is."

"Loyalty," Marcene said.

"What?"

"I asked him once, you know, flippantly so as not to arouse suspicion, what Chalmers wanted of him, and he said Chalmers wanted loyalty."

Woodward smiled broadly. What was it Chalmers had said to him? That he was the type of man who understood loyalty? Yes, that would be what Chalmers wanted with the strong, silent sea captain. Maybe he could use that.

"Do you know what he meant?" Marcene asked.

"Yeah," Woodward said. "Loyalty. That's a word you wouldn't understand." He looked at Marcene, and his eyes grew deep, with tiny red dots far in the bottom. "Tell me," he asked. "Was he better than me?"

"Better than you could ever hope to be," Marcene answered, knowing she would suffer for her words, but wanting to show Woodward that she could understand loyalty as well as he.

Chapter Six

SHIP'S LOG, Barkentine *Morning Star*. At anchor in Boston Harbor, tied up to Chalmers's Pier Fifteen.

April 13, 1901

Begins calm. Middle the same.
Last of leather off-loaded. Received orders for new cargo. Molasses, consigned to Golden Gate Distillery in San Francisco.

Under direction of Josiah Crabbs, took on following provisions and staples: 2,000 pounds flour, 800 pounds bacon, 8 gallons vinegar, 400 pounds sugar, 350 pounds beans, 4 gallons pickles, 200 pounds dried beef, 200 pounds cheese, 100 pounds salt, 4 dozen boxes of matches, 300 pounds coffee,

100 pounds apples, 50 pounds rice, 20 pounds pepper, 20 pounds tea, 10 pounds of baking soda.

Water tanks aired.

Begin signing on crew today.

Julian Truax, a tall, handsome man, with penetrating brown eyes and dark hair, moved over to the table that was set up in the corner of the seaman's hiring hall, and read the hand-printed sign.

FOR SAN FRANCISCO
The Barkentine *Morning Star* under command of Andrew Roberts, will leave her dock at Chalmers's Pier 15 for the above port on Wednesday next, April 17th. Hands being signed on.
NO UNION MEN!

"I'd like a berth on your ship, Captain," Truax said.

"Able-bodied, or ordinary seaman?"

"Able-bodied it is, sir. Eight years on a windship."

"Do you have any papers?"

"Aye, Captain." Truax reached his hand down in his seabag and pulled out a dog-eared, much-read, well-traveled batch of papers. They were official discharges from previous vessels, and Roberts scanned them quickly, knowing exactly where to look for the information he wanted. He looked up in surprise. "Truax, all you have to do to get mate's papers is pay the fee. You could be an officer, man."

"Aye, Captain. But I've no wish to leave the forecastle," Truax said.

"You've had a few problems in the past," Roberts said.

"Aye, with brutish first mates whose brains are in their ass. I'm a good sailor, Captain, all the papers say that . . . despite the run-ins I've had."

Roberts cupped his chin in his hand and studied the papers for a moment. The reports were excellent as far as seamanship was concerned. But there were four occasions where the captain had entered a report of "sometimes has difficulty in accepting the authority of those appointed over him."

"I run a tight ship, Truax, and I'll expect discipline. But I've respect for my fellowman, having spent my own time before the mast."

Truax smiled. "Captain, I'm certain you'll be pleased with me."

Roberts sighed, and ran his hand through his hair. There was something about this sailor which disturbed him. It wasn't just the trouble he'd had with the mates. There were few sailors with more than one voyage who hadn't experienced some kind of trouble. But there was something else, a sort of contained insolence, which oozed out of this man, like tar on a hot deck. Still, Truax appeared to have skills and experience, and he'd already experienced a surprising amount of difficulty in signing able-bodied seamen.

He had mentioned that difficulty earlier in the day, and one of the clerks at the hiring hall informed him that there was a boycott among AB's, against those captains who wanted no union men.

"You'd have no trouble signing on men, Captain, if you'd change your mind," the clerk had said.

"I'll not change the sign," Roberts insisted. "If need be I'll sail to San Francisco with nothing but ordinary seamen on board, and I'll train them myself until they are as good as they come. I've a special requirement for this passage, and I'll be wanting men loyal to me and not to the union."

"You're the captain," the clerk had replied with a shrug of his shoulders.

"Truax," Roberts said, remembering his conversation with the clerk.

"Aye, Captain?"

"Have you not heard of the AB boycott?"

"Aye, I've heard."

"And you've no wish to join?"

"No, Captain," Truax said.

"Well, I'm glad to have you aboard. I've only signed one more AB, and he's over fifty. We may have to conduct a school."

Truax smiled. "I've played nursemaid before, Captain. I can do it again."

By four that afternoon, Roberts had signed all sixteen men of his crew. He did manage to sign one more AB, a large man called Pig Iron. That gave him a crew of sixteen, but with only three who had the skills to take the helm or work aloft. Considering what Roberts had agreed to do on this voyage when he accepted the passage orders from the distillery representative, the lack of AB's was going to be critical. Had he known this, he might not have agreed to the distillery's conditions. But he had agreed to them, and he was going to do it, with or without AB's.

Roberts closed his book, picked up his sign, and returned to his ship. He had an interview there at five with James Bright. Bright had applied to be his mate. Roberts wondered if Bright would have applied had he known what Roberts agreed to do.

Bright was pacing up and down Pier 15 alongside the ship when Roberts got there. He was twenty minutes early, and Roberts took that into favorable account, for he equated punctuality with dependability, and to his way of thinking, it spoke well for the young man.

Bright was young, probably no more than nineteen. He was rather smallish, with dark, slicked-down hair. He was clean-shaven, and he was wearing an officer's uniform that, until this moment, had never been exposed to salt air. That was obvious because of the brightly shining brass buttons.

"Did your folks buy your sailor suit for you?" Roberts asked.

Bright blushed, then smiled self-consciously. "Yes, sir. For graduation from the Academy Del Mar."

"Academy Del Mar?"

"It means School of the Sea, sir," Bright explained quickly.

"You don't say?"

Bright blushed again. "I'm sorry. Of course you would know what that means. It's just that I'm so used to apologizing for the dumb name all the time."

Roberts decided he liked Bright, and he laughed. "Don't apologize, kid. Hell, be glad you got the chance to go. Have you ever been to sea?"

"I've had two voyages as a midshipman, sir."

"Did you get a chance to handle a watch under way?"

"Aye, sir."

"Well, the job's yours, if you want it."

"Thank you, sir," Bright said, beaming proudly.

"Wait," Roberts said, holding his hand up. "I don't want to dampen your enthusiasm, but I think you ought to know that I've got only three AB's."

"Only three, sir?" Bright asked.

"Aye. And thirteen ordinary seamen. I'll give you two of the AB's in your watch, and I'll take one in mine."

"Captain, are you going to stand a watch?" Bright asked in surprise.

"Aye, that I am, Mr. Bright. Unless you wish to take your watch *and* mine."

"There'll not be another mate, then."

"No. A captain who goes along for the ride is unnecessary," Roberts said. "With the money that would have paid the other mate's salary, I can feed us a little better. Any objections?"

"No, sir."

"There's one more thing you should know about," Roberts said. "This voyage has a rather unique aspect to it. We are carrying molasses to San Francisco, consigned to the Golden Gate Distillery. They are going to start bottling a new rum, and, if we meet their conditions, they will call the new rum *Morning Star* after this ship, and pay me $5,000 in prize money."

"That's great!" Bright said. "What are the conditions?"

"We must be in San Francisco by July fifteenth."

"July fifteenth?" Bright did some rapid calculations. "Captain that's only ninety days or so."

"It is eighty-nine days, Mr. Bright," Roberts corrected. "The exact amount of time it took the *Flying Cloud* to race from New York to San Francisco. But since we are leaving from Boston, we would be establishing a new record. Golden Gate figures to sell a lot of rum by naming it after the ship that sets the new record. So you can see why it is important to make it by July fifteenth."

"But, Captain, that isn't possible," Bright protested.

"It is not only possible, it is going to happen. Mr. Bright, I intend to share that prize money with you and the crew. Three-eighths for myself, one-eighth for you, and four-eighths to be divided among the men. Your share would be $625 and the men would get $156.25 each."

"Six hundred and twenty five dollars? That's a small fortune!" Bright said. "And for the crew, why, that's more than double their regular wages. Captain, we certainly should have the incentive to try for the record."

"And I have even more incentive," Roberts said. "For if we make it, I shall have the money to buy my ship back. Now, what about it? Do you still want to ship with me?"

"Aye, aye, sir," Bright said, grinning broadly.

"Then get your gear aboard. The mate's cabin is aft, just across from mine."

Bright walked over toward a piling and only then did Roberts see his enormous seabag.

"My God, son, are you bringing all of Boston with you?"

"I . . . I thought I'd rather bring too much than take not enough," Bright said. He hesitated as if embarrassed by his riches. "But I can leave it behind if you wish me to."

"No, no, its your gear. Besides, you have a good point. You can always jettison excess baggage, though it's hard to find a slops commissary in the middle of the ocean. Bring it on."

Bright smiled, relieved that his captain agreed with him, and hefted the bag over his shoulder. It was nearly as big as he was, and halfway as heavy, and he staggered under the weight as he climbed up the gangplank of his first ship as a full-fledged officer.

Roberts watched Bright climb the gangplank, remembering at that moment his own first voyage as an officer. He'd come to sea at the age of fifteen, and he'd worked his way up. As soon as he realized what he wanted out of life, he realized also that it would take an education, so half of all his earned money was spent on books. Before he started his study of the sea, he studied other things, things he would have learned in school, had he stayed. He studied grammar and math. He read history, and then, quite as a bonus, discovered his love for literature, turning the orlop deck of a schooner into the grassy fields of England as he read *Ivanhoe,* and listening to the clash and clang of swords through the reading of *Macbeth.*

The older sailors took a liking to the studious young man, and they helped in his instruction. The seamanship he learned from books was augmented by the wisdom of the sailors, who passed on to him the very special kinds of knowledge that couldn't be found in books, but was discovered, refined, and passed down from sailor to sailor through all the centuries of windship sailing.

After eight years before the mast, studying every minute of his spare time, Roberts took the exams for an officer's appointment and got his first berth as a second mate on a China clipper, the *Flash of the Waves*.

Clippers were beautiful ships, long, thin, sharp pointed, and carrying as many as four or five masts, crowded with sail on every inch, slamming across the waves in the reckless quest for speed, speed, and more speed. And in that the ships excelled, though great sacrifices had to be made for that speed. The ships themselves had little cargo space, and their construction wasn't sturdy, so that they had been known to break up in only moderately heavy seas. Also, they carried so much sail that yardarms, and sometimes even masts, were snapped under the pressure.

But it wasn't only the equipment that snapped under pressure. Men buckled as well. The clipper captains were under orders from the owners to make even faster and faster passages, and they drove their crews relentlessly.

Captain Roberts knew about the pressure of the mad pursuit for speed from firsthand experience, and when the distillery representative first made him the offer this morning, Roberts had turned it down.

"But Captain," Hayden, the representative, had said, leaning back in his chair and crossing his hands across his rather large stomach. "You must admit that $2,500 is a great deal of money. Certainly you will at least try?"

"I will deliver your molasses for you," Roberts said. "And you will get it in plenty of time. But I've served with speed-merchant captains. I've seen what such relentless pressures can do."

"What was your best time?"

"Ninety-two days from New York to San Francisco," Roberts said. He looked through the window of Hayden's office, out toward the ships in the harbor, and in his mind's eye, he could see again the *Flash of the Waves,* now sunk in a storm near French Frigate Shoals. "We could have broken the record on that passage, had we made a clean run of the Cape," he said. "And if I had been in command, we would have.'

"Aha!" Hayden said. "So, the sporting blood does run in your veins, Captain. Then surely you will accept this challenge?"

"Surely I will not, sir," Roberts said. "I've no wish to subject my crew to such an arduous passage, just for the empty quest of speed."

"It is not an empty quest, Captain. I've already explained to you that the record would ensure the sale of many, many bottles of our product. That means a great deal of money to us. And the $2,500 should certainly mean something to you. Particularly since you recently lost your ship."

"So, you know about that, do you?'

"Yes, Captain. I also know that you will be permitted to repurchase this ship in one year, provided you have the money. This would ensure that you have the money."

Roberts cupped his chin in his hand. "Double the ante," he said.

"Captain, I would not have taken you for a greedy man," Hayden complained.

"Double the ante," Roberts said again. "So that I may provide a generous share for my crew, and I'll accept the challenge."

Hayden smiled. "Consider the ante doubled." He got up from his chair and walked over to a liquor cabinet near the window, took out a bottle, and poured two drinks. "And now, Captain, let us drink a toast to the venture. I think you'll like this. It, too, is one of ours."

Roberts held the glass up, captured a sunbeam in the amber liquid, then drank it down.

* * *

Now, as he stood on the deck of the *Morning Star,* he thought of the challenge and of the job that lay before them. He had learned a great deal during his voyage with the *Flash of the Waves,* and he hoped to be able to apply some of the lessons learned to the upcoming voyage. He knew ways to hang extra sail so that the *Morning Star* could have nearly the same ratio of sail to displacement as the clipper ships, but with the advantage of far greater strength.

It had long been Roberts's theory that a sturdier ship, with slightly less speed but the ability to sustain a better average because of fewer breakdowns, would have a good chance of breaking the existing record. In fact, he had discussed that very concept with Captain Helgen, the chief and only instructor of the Helgen School of Navigation, the small academy that offered a cram course in taking the exam for a master's papers. Roberts had gone to Helgen's school after leaving the *Flash of the Waves,* and there was certificated as a captain. Through Helgen, Roberts learned that the owner of the *Cauldwell Morrison* was looking for a new captain. Roberts got the command, and later bought the ship, changing its name to the *Morning Star.*

As Roberts recalled his personal history, he looked over toward the hatch of the deckhouse. There, ornately carved into the wood, was the name, *Cauldwell Morrison,* the only place where the name had not been changed. It was beautifully carved by some unknown sailor, who, long ago, must have whiled away the lonely hours of his midnight watch. The letters were cursive and flowed into each other with as much grace and style as the figurehead itself. When the *Cauldwell Morrison* was undergoing extensive repairs and modifications at the time of the name change, one of the shipyard workers started to sand the name out.

"No," Roberts had protested, seeing the worker just before he started.

"I was just going to take that name off, Cap'n,"

63

the worker explained. "She's the *Morning Star* now. And with the new rigging, planking, and fixtures, she's near to bein' a new ship."

"But, like me, this ship has a past. Keep the name there. If ever I get so high and mighty as a captain and owner that I can't remember what it's like in the forecastle, I'll look at the name carved there, and it'll remind me."

"Aye, Cap'n. It's your ship," the worker had said.

Now Roberts recalled his statement, and he walked over to rub his hand across the letters. He wondered if he had sold out his principles in agreeing to go for the record.

Josiah Crabbs came on deck at that moment, dusting his hands together, leaving a puff of white from the flour he had been parceling out into a bin in the galley. He saw Roberts rubbing the name and he smiled at him.

"Aye, laddie, and you've done her proud," Crabbs said. "Any man jack as has ever sailed with you will testify to that."

Roberts looked around quickly, embarrassed that Crabbs had been able to peer into his soul. He cleared his throat.

"Make damn sure you double sift that flour, Crabbs. I don't want weevils this voyage," Roberts said gruffly.

"Aye, sir," Crabbs replied, not understanding the reason for Roberts's reply, and a little hurt by his sharp retort. "I'll do that."

Roberts watched the old sailor shuffle back down into the hold. So, he thought, angry with himself. The pressure had already started.

Chapter Seven

A short ferry ride across the bay from old Boston lay the island of East Boston. There, along a road that ran by the sea, sat half a dozen homes, as grand and elegant as anything in Back Bay or on Beacon Hill. The most elegant of these elegant homes was Ocean House. It sat in the middle of twenty acres of rolling green lawn and garden, and one end of the lawn rose to a moderately high bluff, overlooking a sandy beach and the Atlantic Ocean. There was a beautiful view, with the ocean sparkling like faceted gems in the sun-dance days, or winking like diamonds on velvet in the silver-mooned nights.

On the second night after Constance and Kristin returned to Ocean House, Constance gave her party. As the late afternoon softened into evening, and the western sky turned from red to purple, the carriages began arriving. They were elegant vehicles, pulled by tassled, matched teams, and they moved grandly up the long, treelined drive. The liverymen drove them under a portico where uniformed attendants greeted the guests and escorted them into the house.

Music spilled from the house and rolled across the lawn to welcome the arriving guests. The music was not from the ordinary party band of five or six pieces, but came from an entire orchestra of woodwinds and brasses, strings, and a full section of percussion instruments. Despite the fullness of the band, the music was nearly drowned out by the chatter and the laughter and the clink of glasses, as the partygoers toasted each other and admired the gowns and the jewelry.

Inside the massive house in the main dining room, a table that could seat forty in formal dining, was now laden with hors d'oeuvres. There were several bars working, one in the parlor, one in the game room, and another in the main ballroom. But the most popular was the one set up in the garden, lighted with Japanese lanterns strung on wires from tree to tree, making bubbles of golden light in the velvet blue night.

Though it was a little too early for the official "season," Constance alibied the party by insisting that it was for Kristin. "It will help you get rid of the cobwebs of the business. You are just too young to work so hard," she told Kristin.

"But I don't mind, Grandmother. Really I don't. I find the work fascinating."

"It may be," Constance said. "But it isn't the best way to meet young men."

"Grandmother, are you serious? I thought you were teasing. Doesn't it seem a little like going to the market to find a husband?"

"So what if it does?" Constance asked. "At least I'm letting you meet several, so that you can make up your own mind. Be thankful that I'm not marrying you off to some titled gentleman in Europe, trading money for the right to be called duchess. That is all the rage now, you know."

"Why, Grandmother, don't you think the duke of Manchester would have given me a tumble if he had met me before Helena Zimmerman?" Kristin teased, referring to the Pittsburgh Steel heiress whose marriage to the duke of Manchester had made the society pages of the world.

"Maybe it's my English background," Constance said. "But I'm not as easily impressed with phony gentlemen as the Zimmermans were. No. You'd do better, girl, to find yourself a banker or a railroad owner or a steel millionaire right here in America."

Kristin smiled at her grandmother. "You're no different from the others," she said. "You just read a different geography book. But if it'll make you feel any happier, I shall look at all the men tonight, with an eye toward possible involvement."

"Not just involvement, dear, matrimony. And not all the men," Constance said. "Only the unmarried ones."

"But Grandmother, some of the most interesting ones are already married, and that leaves only involvement," Kristin joked, laughing at her grandmother.

Kristin was still laughing when she stepped out into the garden to mingle with her guests. That was when she saw her Aunt Margaret. The sight of her aunt caused her mirth to be short-lived. Nevertheless, she put a cool smile on her face and went over to speak to her.

"Hello, Aunt Margaret. I'm glad you came to the party."

Margaret held her cheek out for a kiss, and Kristin bussed her lightly.

"You didn't think I would miss this party, did you?" Margaret asked. "Heavens, child, I've attended every social event at Ocean House for over fifty years, including the ones in which your grandmother worked as a servant girl."

"Yes," Kristin said. "I know. Would you excuse me, Aunt Margaret? I must see to our guests."

Margaret watched Kristin walk away, so young, so beautiful, and with everything before her. She envied Kristin. She envied her and she resented her, for in truth Kristin shouldn't even be. There was a Kristin because Constance had married Lee. Her Lee and that servant girl. It was still hard to take, even after nearly half a century. It was here, on these very grounds, that Lee had double-crossed her. It was almost fifty years ago, with Lee dead now for more than forty. But she would never forget that terrible afternoon.

"I'm glad you asked me for a walk," Margaret had said on that afternoon so long ago. "It will give me an opportunity to tell you about our wedding."

Lee didn't answer. Instead, he bent down and plucked a dandelion spore, then blew the seeds into the air.

"Don't do that," Margaret said. "Such things can cause consumption."

Lee tossed the stem aside. "Margaret, I want to talk to you."

Margaret went on talking, as if she hadn't even heard Lee. "Did you know your mother said there would be over five hundred people at our wedding? Imagine that. Five hundred people! Why, it shall easily be the social event of the season, and maybe of the decade."

Lee let a sigh escape his lips. "Margaret, I want to talk to you," he said again.

"Talk? Talk to me about what?"

"I want to talk seriously about something. You never let me talk, Margaret."

"Heavens. The next thing I know you'll be off on something you read in one of your books," Margaret said. "If you're so all fired up to talk, go talk to Constance. She doesn't fool me, reading all those books. She just does it to impress you. Doesn't she know her place? She just makes me sick."

"Margaret, I won't have you talking about Connie that way."

"You won't have me . . . well, I never. It's about time you got something straight around here, Mr. Lee Martin Chalmers. It isn't proper for you to pay as much attention to a servant girl as you pay to Constance. I know you mean only to be courteous, but snippets like that girl don't understand common courtesy. The next thing you know, she'll get it in her mind that . . . well . . . never mind what she'll get in her mind. The point is, after we are married, I shall dismiss her. I'll give her excellent references and she will have no trouble finding employment elsewhere, but she'll not work here."

"Margaret, I don't want to get married," Lee said. "That's what I've been trying to tell you."

"What?" Margaret asked in a small voice. She wasn't sure she understood what he said. It couldn't have been what it sounded like.

"Just what I said. I don't want to get married."

"But . . . but . . . I don't understand," Margaret said. My God, she thought. It's true. He did say that. "We've been planning it for ages. The invitations are all sent out . . . your mother has made all the preparations, how could you change your mind so suddenly?"

"I haven't changed my mind," Lee said. "Margaret, the truth is, I never wanted to get married in the first place. It was all your idea. Yours and my mother's." Lee laughed. "She has it in her mind that marrying into the Coy blood will erase some of the stain of our past. The mighty Chalmers Shipping Lines. Legitimate now, but built on the blood and suffering of countless thousands of the poor Africans my father and uncle brought over here."

"Lee, Lee, don't be hasty," Margaret said. "Listen, I know that people get frightened just before a wedding. Everyone does. Why, I would myself, were it not for the fact that there is so much to do. Why don't you just take a walk and think about it for a while? I think you'll discover that the institution of marriage isn't as bad as you believe."

"Margaret, don't you understand? Is there no way I can make you listen to me? It isn't marriage that I'm afraid of. It's you."

"Me?"

"Yes. From the time I've known you, you've been rushing me pell-mell to the altar. If it wasn't you, it was my mother. I tried to say no, I tried to stop it, but the two of you were just too much for me. Now I've decided that it's too late to be subtle or polite. If I don't do something now, I will find myself married to you, and both of us will be miserable for the rest of our lives. I don't want that, and I don't want to marry you."

Margaret slapped Lee hard in the face.

"You bastard!" she yelled. "You have let me make a complete, absolute ass of myself. And now, just because you are getting cold feet, you want to back out. Well, I won't let you. I will sue you for breach of promise!"

"That's just it, Margaret. I've never promised anything!"

"Then you gave your assent through your silence," Margaret said.

"I haven't been silent, Margaret. You just haven't been listening."

Margaret started hitting Lee, slapping him in the face, hitting him on the shoulders, crying and screaming at him as she did so. Lee made no effort to defend himself, he just stood there letting the blows rain down on him. Finally, when Margaret fell to the ground, exhausted and crying, Lee looked down at her.

"Margaret, if you are honest with yourself, you will recognize that the tears you are shedding now are not tears of heartbreak. They are tears of anger. Be angry if you wish. But don't be foolish."

"Get away from me," Margaret said in a muffled voice. "I hate you. I hate you with all my heart!"

"I'm sorry," Lee said, turning and walking away.

Margaret lay there for a long time after Lee left. Finally she composed herself and stood up, then walked slowly toward the bluff that overlooked the rocky beach and the ocean. For one insane moment, she wished it were high enough to use for suicide. That would show Lee. Everyone would hear what happened, how he had jilted her at the last minute, and they would all hate him. He wouldn't have a friend left in the world.

As Margaret stood there, she saw a lone figure trudging by the sea. She shielded her eyes against the afternoon glare, the better to see, and saw that the solitary stroller was Charles Edward, Lee's brother. Charles Edward was four years older than Lee, and it was whispered in polite society that he was of "notorious dissipations and soiled reputation." In fact, Margaret suddenly remembered once he'd even flirted outrageously with her, knowing full well that she was his own brother's fiancée.

Margaret wiped her eyes, touched her hair, and straightened her dress, then started down the path toward the sea.

"Let's go down to the sea!" one of the young men shouted, and his shout jerked Margaret back to the present. Margaret looked over at the young man, a handsome ne'er-do-well from one of New England's wealthier families, and wished that he, or someone like him, could marry Kristin and take her away from here. But she could tell from Kristin's face that that wasn't likely to happen.

"I have no wish to get wet," Kristin said, wishing she could just watch from the sidelines, without getting involved.

71

"What? Have you no sporting blood?" the young man, whose name was Jack, challenged.

"Do come, Kristin," one of the girls pleaded. "It would be ever so much fun with you."

"And a beastly bore without you," Jack said. "Now do you want it known throughout Boston, Newport, and New York, that you, Kristin Chalmers, were responsible for ruining a party? My dear, you will become a social outcast."

The others laughed; then one young man pulled a flower and held it over his breast, falling backward and lying supine on the ground, as if displayed for burial.

"Have reverence, dear friends," he said solemnly. "Have reverence for the dearly departed."

"Shh!" Jack shushed loudly, placing his finger over his lips and admonishing the others. "We must have reverence for the dearly departed."

"Tell me, oh dearly departed," one of the girls asked, tittering with glee. "Who is the dearly departed who is dearly departed?" She laughed at her play on the words.

"My initials are K.S.S.," the man on the ground said in a rolling, sonorous voice.

"Who is K.S.S.?" Jack asked.

"Kristin's Social Standing," the man shouted, bursting into a peal of laughter. He hopped up and handed the flower to Kristin. "But have no fear, fair damsel, for I have risen from the grave to save you. Come, a mere dunk in the water, a baptism as it were, and your social standing will be reinstated forever."

"And honorably so, madam," Jack said. "For should your social standing ever be impugned after this, I shall leap to the forefront in valiant defense."

"And I, madam, as well."

The group started toward the water . . . by now four young men and three young women, with Kristin reluctantly among them.

Down on the beach the sound of the surf drowned out the revelry from the house. Even the loud guffaws of the men and the tinny shrieks of the women were carried away in the wind and smothered in the thunder of the waves that crashed on the shore.

"Oh, look," Jack exclaimed. "Look how big that wave is."

The wave Jack pointed to rolled toward the shore, moon-silvered and flashing white at the top but not yet breaking, as it gathered more and more momentum, and grew larger and larger.

"Come," Jack said, running into the water with all his clothes on. "Let it break on us."

"Jack, you nut, you're getting all wet," one of the girls said, laughing at his antics.

"Come on," Jack called, coming back and grabbing one of the girls and pulling her with him. Then all went, including Kristin, who was half dragged, and half persuaded.

Kristin felt the water climbing up her dress, heavy, sodden, pulling at her, and much colder than she would have expected.

"Here it comes . . . *now!*" Jack shouted, and the huge breaker snapped forward right on top of them, cresting as high as their heads, hitting them with all its fury, and knocking them off their feet.

Kristin went under the water, tasted the brine, and felt herself being dragged along the sand and shells until, wet and muddy, she was deposited on the beach with the others. She lay there, with the water rushing around her back to sea, feeling the sand giving way under her with the sucking, hydraulic action, so that by the time she got up there was a large depression in the sand.

She looked at the others, at their debauched countenances, their wet hair hanging in strings, their sopping, muddy clothes, and realized that she was one of them, seemingly no different. They were laughing, but Kristin felt a vague uneasiness, not just discomfort from the mud and sand, but a gnawing, almost guilty impropriety over what they were doing. She found it impossible to join in the laughter, and she started away from them, walking up the beach, leaving them, the house, and the party behind her.

As Kristin started walking away, she saw a fisherman stretching his net out in the sand, preparing it for the next morning. She wished she could avoid him, but there was no way short of turning back, and she wasn't going to do that. She wanted to keep walking forever, following the stretch of beach as far as it went, just keep on going until she ran out of Boston . . . out of Massachusetts, out of America . . . out of the world!

The fisherman looked up as she passed him. He was of an indeterminate age, perhaps as young as thirty-five, or as old as fifty-five. He had worked a lifetime and he showed it, by the creases in his face and the muscles in his arms and shoulders. He looked at her but said nothing. He didn't have to speak. His eyes were eloquent spokesmen for him. Look at you, his eyes seemed to say. You have money, position, and power, and yet you squander it in such foolish ways. I have a purpose in life. I catch fish so that people may eat. What is your purpose? What are people like you and your friends good for?

Of course, the fisherman said none of this. He didn't have to, for Kristin was saying it for him, putting the words in his silent mouth, to match the accusation in his screaming eyes. But Kristin, her own eyes stinging with tears of self-recrimination, looked away from him, silent in response, even in her own mind. For she had no answers to give.

Chapter Eight

Julian Truax stood just behind the curtain that hung as a covering over the anteroom door at the union house on Newhall Street. He peered through it at the gathering audience.

"We've got a good crowd tonight," he remarked to the man with him.

The man with him was John Lemmings, the union representative who had boarded the *Morning Star* when it docked. Lemmings stepped across the room and peered through the curtain at the gathering of seamen.

"Better than I thought we would have," he admitted. "Though I wonder if they are here to hear me speak, or merely to eat our sandwiches and drink our coffee?"

"What difference does it make why they are here?" Truax asked. "The point is, they are here." He smiled at Lemmings, then put his hand on the other man's shoulder. "Besides, once you start speaking, they'll listen to you."

"I hope so."

"They will, believe me. You've got that about you, John. When you talk, you can stir something up in a man."

"I wish I could introduce you," Lemmings said. "I think it is a brave thing you are doing."

"No, don't dare do it," Truax warned. "If word got back to Chalmers Shipping, or to Captain Roberts that I was a union man . . . especially if he knew I was one of the organizing officers, he'd set me off his ship before we ever got started and it would ruin everything. His is the only Chalmers ship with an all-new crew. If we are to bust Chalmers, we must do it on Roberts's ship."

"I suppose you're right." Lemmings looked at Truax, finding much to admire in the big, handsome man. If all seamen were like him, there would be no trouble in organizing. He was a skilled sailor, a well-read, self-educated man, with a certain revolutionary fervor about him. It was the same kind of revolutionary zeal, Lemmings knew, that was present in the founders of the nation. And why not? Didn't Truax share with the founding fathers the same dedication to the fundamental dignity of man? In fact, Lemmings thought proudly, he himself shared those same ideals and, in a sense, he knew that he and Truax, and a handful of the other, dedicated workers were founding fathers in their own right. Yes, he rather liked that theme. Founding fathers of a new order. He turned the phrase over in his mind, looking at it from every angle. That, he decided, would be the theme of his speech tonight.

"You ought to go out there now, John," Truax suggested, peering one more time through the curtain. "They are ready. Wait too much longer and they might get restless."

Lemmings cleared his throat and stood there for just

a moment, composing his thoughts then, pulling his dedication about him like a royal robe, he stepped through the curtain. Three men who were planted in the audience to start the "spontaneous" applause, saw Lemmings, and as instructed, they began clapping. The others joined in, some of them not knowing why they were applauding, or even that they were about to listen to a speech.

Lemmings held his hands out to quiet them, smiling in appreciation, speaking to a few of the men, calling by name those he knew. It wasn't exactly a standing ovation, but it was enthusiastic enough to sustain Lemming's spirits, and he felt buoyed, almost jubilant, as he began to speak.

"Seamen," he began. He paused for just a moment. "Notice, would you please, that the word is sea . . . *men*. You are not slaves, you are not beasts of burden, you are *men!*"

This time the applause was spontaneous, and Lemmings, feeling that he had a good crowd, went on, wishing that he was addressing the Congress of the United States, or the Supreme Court, knowing he had it within him this night to move either of those august bodies.

"Toward the close of the eighteenth century, our founding fathers set forth on this continent a new nation," Lemmings began. "They dedicated themselves to liberty and individual dignity. But while they were securing liberty for the Americans ashore, our brothers at sea were being treated like vermin, forced to labor under brutish officers, and provided with a diet that barely kept them alive. Midway through the nineteenth century, our nation fought a war to free the negro from the bondage of slavery. The world rejoiced when, at long last, that evil practice was abolished. But all the while, our brothers at sea were held in the chains of oppressive conditions. Their lot had not improved one bit over the lot of their fathers, and their grandfathers who had preceded them in maritime commerce.

Now, we are in the twentieth century. Modern science has given us such marvelous inventions as the telephone, the electric light, gasoline engines, and the typewriter. But we who labor at sea labor under the same conditions as did our fathers, and their fathers, and their fathers before them, and, yes, their fathers too, for one thousand years!"

Lemmings's voice reached an impassioned peak, and as he shouted the last few words, the men leaped to their feet with a mighty roar.

Lemmings paused to let the demonstration continue, and he drank a glass of water. He felt it now, this sense of power in persuading others with the spoken word. Finally he held his hands out to signal for quiet, and the audience regained their seats.

"Just as our founding fathers set forth a new nation," he said, "we are setting forth a new order. An order of basic worker's rights. An expression of common needs. A manifesto of human dignity!"

Again applause and cheers.

"We, you and I, are the founding fathers of this new order. We must go out to our brother sailors and organize them. We must convince them to join us, show them that our cause is just. And then, with a united front, we will bring down the despots of the sea! Now, tonight, I am authorized to tell you of a bold plan one of our members is putting into effect. I am not yet at liberty to tell you who it is, for his design is so risky that it could be very dangerous, and there may be spies among us. However, I will tell you that one of our number has signed a sea letter with a Chalmers ship, with a captain who has refused to let union men ship with him. It is our man's intention to organize that ship to the man, so that when it reaches its destination, it will be the first Chalmers ship to be one-hundred-percent union!"

There was more applause.

"I need not tell you of the risks here. The slightest miscalculation, and all our plans could go awry. And yet, this must be done, for if we can prove to our brothers that a Chalmers ship that has an antiunion captain can be organized . . . and organized one hundred percent, then we can prove the power of our movement. Our prayers will go with this brave fellow, and I ask now for a cheer for his courage!"

The men in the union hall jumped to their feet once more and cheered and applauded wildly. Lemmings, his eyes shining in excitement, left the front of the room and passed through the crowd, shaking hands with the men, accepting their words of praise, and pointing out the printed literature that was available to them.

"Take several broadsides," he told them. "Become a crusader for our cause. Urge the boycott of nonunion ships, even among nonunion men and brothers, and we will win our battle."

The men milled around for several minutes more, commenting on the speech, reading the broadsides, arguing the merits of various approaches, drinking coffee and eating sandwiches. Finally, when the coffee and sandwiches were gone, the arguments grew less spirited, the broadsides were folded and put away, and one by one the men departed until the hall was empty.

Truax had listened to the speech from the anteroom behind the speaker's platform, and now that all were gone, he came out into the large room. The floor was littered with paper wrappings from the sandwiches, and coffee cups were scattered about the room. The rows of chairs, which had been neatly aligned before the speech, were now pushed aside in disarray, some of them lying tipped over on the floor.

"Johnny, that was some speech," Truax said.

Lemmings, who was standing in the middle of the hall, turned around to look at Truax. Truax was surprised to see Lemmings's eyes brimming with tears.

"I've passed the torch on to you, my friend," he said. "Don't let it drop."

Truax grabbed Lemmings's hand, and the two men stood there, clasped in a handshake, a tableau of determination for their cause.

When Captain Woodward saw Kristin leave the others on the beach, he stepped back into the shadow of the seawall. He had come to Ocean House tonight hoping to have an opportunity to take care of Kristin. When he arrived, he saw that a party was in full swing, and he cursed his luck and started to go back. But, just as he turned to go, he saw Kristin and a small group of people break away from the main party and go down to the beach. He followed, keeping always in the distance, remaining in the shadows, until he reached the seawall. He could go no further without crossing open beach, so he remained hidden, watching them, waiting to see what was going to happen. He was an enterprising police officer, with many years of experience on stakeout. He knew that patience was a stalker's most valuable asset, and he was prepared to exercise patience tonight. Then his patience was rewarded, for he saw Kristin leave the others and walk down the lonely stretch of beach. There was a fisherman about fifty yards down from the others but, once she passed the fisherman, there was no one.

Captain Woodward followed Kristin's movements, keeping abreast of her, though still several yards away, and still hidden by the dark shadows of the seawall. On they went, fifty, one hundred, two hundred yards beyond the fisherman, and still she walked on, moving with a singleness of purpose that made her oblivious to time and distance. Finally, when they were so far away that the built-up area stopped and the seawall ended and there was nothing left but a smear of iridescent sand, dark, shining rocks, and the cold, rolling sea, Captain Woodward knew that he could make his move. It would be easy to kill her here. All he had to do was grab her and pull her into the surf. Then, he could simply hold her under the water until she drowned. There would hardly be need for a coroner's inquest . . . she had merely wandered into the surf and been dragged down by the riptide in the heavy, wet clothes.

Captain Woodward opened a bottle and poured ether onto a handkerchief. He had to turn away when the strong fumes hit him suddenly, but a quick breath of fresh air cleared away the dizziness. Then, looking around one last time to ensure that no one was watching, he sprinted across the beach, running silently in the sand. He slipped up behind Kristin before she even knew she was in danger and forced the handkerchief over her nose. She passed out with scarcely a struggle.

Chapter Nine

SHIP'S LOG, Barkentine *Morning Star*, at anchor in Boston Harbor, tied up to Chalmers's Pier 15.

April 14, 1901

Begins with freshening seaward breezes. Loading molasses today.

Replaced all sail with new. Double-braced masts and spars, added rigging for spinnakers and try-sails. Removed 1,000 pounds of ballast to make hull ride higher in the water. Will allow more speed, but increases the danger of capsizing. Installed new, gasoline-operated bilge pumps.

Diver contracted to examine hull for barnacles and other such sea growth as might impede progress.

"That hull's as smooth as a baby's butt, Captain," the diver said, after completing his inspection. He was putting dry clothes on in Roberts's cabin. "She'll slip through the water like a greased eel."

"I had her hauled out of the water in San Francisco, after I sprung the leak on the wheat," Roberts said. "We gave her a good cleaning then, and treated her hull with a concoction that is supposed to retard sea growth."

"Well, whatever the hell it was, it's doing its job," the diver said. "I've seen new vessels with rougher hulls."

Roberts smiled broadly. "That's good news to hear. I appreciate your inspection." The diver finished dressing, and Roberts handed him a Chalmers voucher for payment.

"Anytime you're in port, Captain," the diver said, taking the voucher. "But tell me. If you just had the bottom cleaned, why did you bother to check it again so soon? Most of the time no one bothers until they've got a regular sea garden growing down there."

"I was just interested, that's all," Roberts said, thinking it would be best not to speak of his intention to go for the record.

Roberts walked with the diver to the gangplank, then after bidding him good-bye, started back to the chart room. When he turned, he saw Josiah Crabbs standing near the galley door, wearing an apron and a cap, polishing a copper kettle, looking on in silence. Roberts nodded to his cook, then started back to his charts. He was studying currents and known, prevailing winds, trying to plot a course which would give him the maximum possible advantage. But he no more than rolled the charts out, when there was a knock on the door.

"Come in, Josiah," Roberts called, knowing who it would be without asking.

Josiah stepped inside. "Cap'n, I'd like a word, if you don't mind."

"You've got it," Roberts said.

"We've off-loaded ballast."

"The cargo will compensate for it."

"We took on all new canvas this mornin', too," Josiah said.

"Aye, we did."

"Cap'n, most of the canvas we had was in first green, 'n I doubt if any of it was out of second green. There wasn't no need to take on all new canvas."

Roberts smiled. "Well, you know how these big companies are, Josiah. They have money to burn. If this was my ship, the canvas we had would have been good enough. But the Chalmers Shipping Company wants all new sails."

"Uh-huh," Josiah said. "But the fella came to inspect the hull, too."

"That's natural enough, isn't it?" Roberts asked. "I mean, after all, we lost that load of wheat because of a leak. We don't want that to happen again, do we?"

"He wasn't looking for leaks, Cap'n. He was looking for sea growth."

"He might as well have, while he was down there."

"You've rigged for spinnakers and trysails. And now you're studyin' the charts, extra particular. Cap'n Roberts, you're gettin' this ship ready for a speed run."

Roberts cupped his chin in his hand and studied the white-haired, full-bearded man before him. He knew there would be no sense in lying, and he knew that Josiah was too smart not to notice the preparations. Finally he sighed. "Aye, Josiah. I'm going to try to beat the record of the *Flying Cloud*."

"You're going to try and beat . . . ?" Josiah started, then he stopped in midsentence, in disbelief. "Cap'n, if that record could ever be beat, someone would'a already done it. Hell, Cap'n, there was more than speed involved there, and you know it. He held fair winds, smooth seas, and he slipped around the Horn with dry decks, and all canvas flying, as easy as rowing a boat across a pond. I've served aboard them what took two months to beat through the straights, aye, and come up to fifty south with kindlin' wood for spars."

"Nevertheless, we are going to try and do it," Roberts said.

"Now, laddie," Josiah said. "You're the cap'n of this here vessel, 'n I've sailed with you now for better'n four years. You're a good man, Andy, and a hell of a good seaman. But by God this is crazy, 'n if anyone else had told me you was goin' to try this foolishness, I'd have turned my back on them for bein' a liar."

"You don't understand, Josiah," Roberts said. Roberts noticed that Josiah called him by his first name, and knew also that it was well-meaning. Josiah would never have become so familiar if there had been a chance of anyone else hearing them. That was not because Captain Roberts was standoffish; that was just a cardinal rule of the sea.

"No, sir, I don't understand," Josiah went on. "I've served on speed ships. I've seen the men drove to the edge of mutiny by a cap'n who had no choice, if he wanted to keep up the time. Now Cap'n, there's only one way you can take a shot at that record, 'n that's to drive your crew till they drop. Can you do that?"

"If I have to," Roberts said.

Josiah stood there for a moment, looking at Roberts with his face registering his disbelief at the statement. "I don't believe a fella can change that much," he finally said.

"I've no choice, Josiah," Roberts said. "If I can beat that record, the Golden Gate Distillery is going to give me a very, very large bonus."

"It would have to be large, to make you try something this foolish."

"It is large," Roberts said. "It's large enough to give every man a bonus that's more than double his wages, and still have enough left over for me to buy my ship back."

Josiah sighed. "Yeah," he said. "Yeah, it would have to be something like that." He walked over to a porthole that opened onto the sparkling bay and rubbed his hand lightly on the ledge. "Cap'n, nobody's heart was broke more'n mine when you lost your ship back in Frisco. And I can understand you wantin' to do this thing to try 'n buy her back. But believe me, you can't do it. You can't do it lad, and you'll only bust your ass tryin'. And your heart too, I'm thinkin'."

"I've got to try," Roberts said. "Don't you see that, Josiah? I have no choice."

"Well, I *do* have a choice," Josiah said. He untied the apron and began taking it off.

"What are you doing?" Roberts asked.

"Cap'n, I've loved you like a son these last four years. Aye, 'n been proud of you to boot. But if you are serious about this crazy scheme, you're goin' to have to turn against every principle you've ever stood for. The men are going to become just another part of the ship to you. You'll not give one damn about any of 'em, and you'll drive 'em until they can't be drove no more, and then you'll drive 'em some more. When that happens, the ship's compliment will split in two. The officers will be on one side, and the men on the other. I'd be havin' to side with the men, laddie, and I don't want to go agin' you. The only way I can prevent that is to leave the ship before it ever starts. You are goin' to have to get yourself another cook."

"Josiah, no," Roberts said, putting his hand out to stop the older man. "Please, don't go."

"The way I see it, I ain't got no choice," Josiah said.

"No," Roberts replied. "I have no choice. But you said you did. Please, exercise it by staying with me. I need you on this trip, old friend. There'll not be a man aboard that I know, if you aren't with me."

"I don't know, Cap'n," Josiah said, his face reflecting

his true anguish over the decision. "I want to stay with you. But you're honest to God headed for trouble."

"Maybe you can help me avoid it," Roberts suggested.

"The only way you can avoid it is to give up this crazy notion of settin' a new record."

"No," Roberts said. "I've got to try for that. But if I have you aboard, you know, as a liaison between the crew and me, maybe we can work things out."

Josiah stood there for a few seconds longer and then tied the apron around him again. "Oh, what the hell," he said. "I'm dumb for stayin', but then I never was very bright. If I had been, I wouldn't have gone to sea the first time."

"Thanks, Josiah. I appreciate this."

"I just hope neither of us winds up regrettin' it," Josiah replied.

About seven miles from the *Morning Star,* as the crow flies, stood Ocean House. Its lawn was littered with residue from the party of the night before, but the laughter and the music and the clink of glasses were gone. Napkins tumbled across the lawn swept before the offshore breeze, and one of the Chinese lanterns tapped lightly against a pole as it danced in the wind.

The house appeared to be totally deserted, though in fact it was not. Inside there were nearly a dozen people, gathered in the library, talking animatedly. Occasionally, one would remind the others to "keep it quiet" and then point upstairs to Constance Chalmers's room, indicating that they might wake her up with their chatter.

But Constance wasn't asleep. She was sitting in a chair in her bedroom, gazing morosely through the large French doors leading onto her private balcony, which overlooked the ocean. Constance had a lap robe around her, and at this particular moment she looked every one of her sixty-eight years. Her eyes were red-rimmed from crying, and she clutched a tightly wadded, tear-stained handkerchief in her hands.

"Oh, Kristin," she said softly. "Where are you? What has happened to you?"

It had been some time before anyone at the party missed Kristin. The group of young people who had dragged her with them down to the sea spent another thirty minutes cavorting in the surf. Finally thoroughly soaked, and literally caked with sand, they returned to the party, laughing gaily and admonishing the others for being unable to appreciate the pleasures of Neptune. When they were chastised for being childish, they defended themselves by saying that Kristin had joined their merry band, and because she had a reputation for levelheadedness, such criticism was unfounded.

"But where is she now?" the others wanted to know, not believing Kristin had been with them.

"Oh, she was having so much fun that she decided to take a walk along the beach," Jack said. "When she returns, though, you shall see that she is as thoroughly debauched as we. And then we shall hear if your tune is the same."

The party went on, buoyed along by music and drink and laughter until well after midnight. It wasn't until the level of merriment began to wind down that some-one made the observation that Kristin had not yet returned from her walk. Then the chilling realization hit them. She had been gone for over four hours! That was highly unlikely, unless some ill fortune befell her.

A search party was immediately organized and sent out, and they searched all through the night. When the sun rose from the flat, silver sea the next morning, it disclosed more than a dozen young men, still attired in formal, evening wear, vainly patrolling the beach for miles in both directions from Ocean House.

Is there some god of the sea? Constance wondered. Is

there some sea deity who extracts payment in kind? The sea has given the Chalmerses so much . . . must it always claim its dues in human lives as well? Thus far there had been a Chalmers sacrificed to the capricious god of the sea from every generation. Was this necessary to balance the scale? Was it now Kristin's time to tithe?

Constance made a mental note of the Chalmerses who had been lost at sea. The first to be taken was Lee Amon Chalmers, who, with his brother John David, started the shipping empire. Lee Amon was the captain who went to sea, and John David the broker who stayed home. The brothers amassed a quick fortune by transporting slaves. Ironically, Lee Amon had survived slave uprisings, mutinies, and pirates during those tumultuous days, only to be swept overboard during a hurricane long after the Chalmers brothers had given up the slave trade.

Lee Amon, being always at sea, had no family other than his brother. That brother, John David, never went to sea, but he didn't have to. He had ships, and captains to sail them, and two sons to leave his empire to. His two sons were Charles Edward, the eldest, and Lee Martin, the youngest, named after John's brother. Lee had been the husband of Constance.

As Constance thought of Lee, she remembered the afternoon of the wedding, and how tender and loving he had been. Strangely, it wasn't her wedding with Lee she thought of most often. It was the wedding of Charles Edward and Margaret Coy.

Constance had worked hard, as had the others of the household staff, to prepare Ocean House for the wedding. Margaret had wanted a garden wedding, and Virginia Chalmers, Charles and Lee's mother, had agreed that such a spot would be a beautiful setting. While the maids were preparing refreshments, gardeners manicured the lawn, shrubs, flowers, and trees, so that everything was perfect, and afterward, Constance stood on the balcony of the master bedroom to look down at the splendid spectacle.

There were hundreds of people at the wedding, and as they moved through the garden, their gaily colored clothes added a moving rainbow to the already colorful afternoon. There were music and refreshments, and all who came commented that never was a wedding more resplendent.

"Margaret should be truly happy now," a voice said.

Constance gasped, for she had not heard anyone come in, and she knew that she shouldn't be out here. Virginia Chalmers had given very explicit instructions. Any domestic not actively engaged in support of the wedding would stay out of sight.

"Oh, what are you doing up here?" Constance asked, surprised to see Lee. Lee was standing there in very casual clothes, as if he had no intention of attending the wedding. "Shouldn't you be down there?"

"All things considered, I think it's just as well I stay away from down there," Lee said. "It seems a bit awkward as it is. My being there would just remind everyone that this wedding is being played with a substitute cast."

"Poor Charles," Constance said. Then realizing what she had said, she gasped and put her hand to her mouth. "Oh, forgive me!" she said.

Lee laughed. "Forgive you? For saying exactly what I've been feeling ever since she turned her efforts toward him? Connie, there is nothing to forgive, believe me. You are right to pity my brother."

Lee walked out onto the balcony with Constance and leaned against the brick half-wall, which formed the protective rail. He looked at Constance and smiled. "But the truth is," he said, "I'm so glad that it isn't me down there, that I find it difficult to feel anything but joy at this moment."

"I'm glad you aren't marrying her, too," Constance said.

"Oh?" Lee's eyes sparkled in amusement. "And why, pray tell?"

"Because. I fear there would have been no more long conversations between us had you become the husband of Margaret Coy."

"You would miss those conversations?" Lee asked.

"You know I would," Constance said.

"Then you can understand that it was to protect those conversations that I told Margaret I had no wish to marry her," Lee said.

Constance felt her heart leap into her throat. What was he telling her? Was this a declaration of some deeper feeling for her? Oh, if only it were so! Constance had been in love with Lee for over three years, but it was a love that stayed locked in the secret, innermost recesses of her heart. For Lee was a Chalmers, and she was a chambermaid, and she knew that nothing could ever come of it but heartbreak.

"You shouldn't say things like that, Lee," Constance said. She often slipped into using his first name when they were alone. It was easier by the fact that he was two years younger in age, and sometimes, she felt, many years younger in life. His world seemed composed of books and ideals, and though he wasn't naive, he was withdrawn and met strangers with great reluctance.

It was Lee's discomfort in crowds and around strangers that led to the beginning of the "conversations" they were speaking about. When the Chalmerses would entertain, Lee would endure the meal, then, at the earliest opportunity, slip away from the others. Constance once caught him slipping away, and when he saw her, he smiled sheepishly and begged her not to give away his secret. They began talking then, and it became a regular occurrence at all social functions. It wasn't a very great step from meeting during the social functions to meeting at other times, and though there had never

91

been a declaration to the effect, or a physical expression of any kind, Constance knew that she had fallen in love with her employer's son.

"Come with me," Lee said. "I feel a strong need for another of our conversations."

"No, I . . . I'd better not," Constance said.

"Oh? But you've never refused me before. Why would you now?"

Lee was right. Constance had never refused him before, because the conversations had become so important to her. But always before, she had been able to hide behind a facade of it being no more than a friendly conversation. Now, with words nearly spoken, that carefully constructed facade might crumble, leaving her defenseless. If he wished, he could have her heart and wear it as a trophy. She knew that if she went with him, she would no longer be in control of the situation. She mustn't go with him, she told herself. She mustn't.

And yet despite the desperate shouts of her mind, the pleading of her heart won out, and Constance found herself following Lee through the hallway, then up the back stairs through the floor where the domestics lived, and on up into the attic. There, in the subdued light of the dormered windows, and in the shadows of discarded furniture, trunks, and old paintings, Lee and Constance had created their own little world.

Constance knew that Lee wasn't bringing her up here for conversation, and she knew that wasn't why she came. She felt light-headed, and warm, and her heart was beating so hard that she was certain Lee would be able to hear it.

Lee closed the attic door behind them and locked it; then he reached out and took Constance's hand. That was something he had never done before, but it seemed so natural that Constance would have been surprised had he not done it. Hand in hand they walked over to the large horsehair sofa that had once sat in the great parlor of Ocean House, until Virginia Chalmers saw one just like it in the governor's mansion.

Lee pulled Constance to him and they kissed. It was as if this too, had been planned, and Constance melted in his arms, letting all opposition to his intentions slide from her. She was no more able to hold onto her resistance than she was to grab quicksilver, and from that moment, events unfolded as if in a dream.

Constance found herself on the sofa. She knew she was nude, because she could feel the texture of the sofa against her bare skin. She didn't remember removing her clothes, but it didn't matter. She was not in the least self-conscious over her nudity. Time lost its meaning then. Lee was over her, kissing her, and caressing her, and they were making love, and she couldn't even remember when it started. It was as if they were always making love, had been forever, and would continue to do so for all eternity. When she was lifted to the heights of rapture, it went on and on without ending, and then it ended too soon.

Lee asked Constance to marry him that day, and he was so insistent that he broke down all her resistance. Constance knew that Virginia would be against it, but she also knew that John would be supportive. She asked Lee if he was willing to live with his mother's ostracism, and Lee replied that with her he could endure anything, whereas without her, there could be reward in nothing.

It was a quiet marriage, with only Lee's father and brother in attendance. Margaret begged illness and Virginia stayed home to tend to her daughter-in-law. No matter. The only one needed to make it the happiest day of Constance's life was Lee himself.

Virginia never forgave Lee, and even when Constance bore Virginia a grandson one year later, she didn't soften. Thus it was that when Lee left for England on business for the company, he was accompanied to the ship by Constance, their son James, and John, but Virginia did not send so much as a message of good-bye.

Constance cried that day, not only because she and Lee were parting for the first time in their marriage, but also because she knew the hurt Lee felt from his mother's treatment.

"Don't cry, darling," Lee told her. "If I had it to do over again, I would do it. I never knew what happiness was until this last year, and if I grieve over Mother's attitude, it is only because she had made her life so much poorer by not knowing you as I do, and I pity her for it."

Lee's ship never reached England. Not a man or a stick of it was ever seen again, and once more the sea had claimed a Chalmers.

"Aunt Constance," a voice called softly, and suddenly the curtain drawn across the years tumbled back into place, and Constance was again sitting in her chair, looking around quickly.

"Have they found Kristin?"

"No, Aunt Constance, I'm afraid not," Miles said. "We have searched everywhere, and we have knocked on every door of every house for miles around. I've even checked the hospitals and the churches. She is nowhere to be found."

"Oh," Constance said, giving a little cry and biting her fist.

"Aunt Constance, I know it is very difficult, but I'm afraid you are just going to have to accept it."

"Accept it? Accept what?" Constance asked.

"Accept the fact that Kristin is . . . dead," Miles said.

"No," Constance replied. She stood up and walked over to the French doors, then pushed them open and stepped out onto the balcony. The sea spread before her, mocking her with its beauty, intimidating her with its immensity. She turned to look at Miles, and tears

94

glistened in her eyes. "I lost my husband to the sea. And my son as well. I will not give up my granddaughter," Constance said softly. Then, turning back to the sea, she shouted into the fresh morning wind, shaking her fist angrily at the nameless demon who lived in those waters: "I will not give you Kristin! Do you hear me? I will not give you Kristin!"

Miles, standing behind her, made a small signal, and another man came forth. The man looked at the old woman yelling at the sea and his face registered shock. He looked at Miles, but Miles held his hand up, as if cautioning the man against saying anything. Finally, he spoke.

"Aunt Constance, please, you must get hold of yourself," Miles said.

Constance turned quickly, and fixed a sharp glance toward her nephew. "Don't you worry about me, young man. You just get busy and find my granddaughter."

"I'll do what I can," Miles said.

"And what is that?"

"I've called in the police. They've assigned their best man to the case."

"And who might that be?" Constance asked.

"Captain Raymond Woodward."

Chapter Ten

Miles and the man with him left Constance's room, and started back downstairs to join the others. The man with Miles was named Tony Norton, and he was Miles's lawyer.

"Do you see what I mean, Tony?" Miles asked. "She is so overwrought from this that I feel she is no longer in control of her faculties. I fear for the stability of the company, if it stays in her hands."

"Miles, I can scarcely ask a judge to declare a woman incompetent just because she has not lost hope that her granddaughter is alive."

"It's more than that and you know it," Miles said. "You saw the way she stood out there and shouted at the sea! Is that the act of a sane woman?"

"It is the act of a distraught woman," Tony said.

"But her mental instability began even before this happened," said Miles. "And as much as I grieve for my dear cousin, I must not lose sight of the fact that Chalmers Shipping is a major company, with responsibilities to thousands of people. It has taken the unfortunate drowning of one girl to bring matters to a head."

"How do you know she is dead?" Tony asked.

"Because I can accept it calmly," Miles replied. "Come on, Tony. It's quite obvious what happened, isn't it? She had too much to drink, and she wandered along the beach all alone. She probably went back into the surf, was knocked down by a wave, and pulled out to sea by the riptide. With those wet, heavy clothes, there would have been no chance for her to save herself. It is a very tragic thing, and I am, as I say, most grieved by it. But I have maintained my balance."

"It's a tragic thing," Tony said. "Kristin was such a lovely girl."

"Yes, she was. And I feel nothing but sorrow over it, and sympathy for my aunt. Believe me, Tony, I've no wish to do this to her, but I feel it must be done. You must get her declared incompetent."

"What you are asking for is an adjudication of non compos mentis," Tony said. "Judges are very reluctant to make that declaration, and against someone as powerful as your aunt, they would be even more so."

"Even if, by her action, she was jeopardizing the entire company?"

"If it could be proved that she is unable to administer her own affairs, then, a judge would act, for he would feel as much obligation toward the company as toward the individual. But it would be very difficult to make that case."

"What would it take?"

"Testimony from a family member, to begin with."

"There are only two members of the family remaining. My mother and me."

"Are there no blood relatives?"

"No. She had no brothers or sisters, her son died twenty years ago, and there was only Kristin."

"Then there would be no offsetting testimony from family members to counteract the statements of you and your mother?"

"None," Miles said.

"Well, that would be a point in our favor," Tony said. "When families divide, the judge almost always goes with the defendant. There would be need for a doctor's examination."

"I can obtain that," Miles said.

"And statements from business associates to show examples of incompetency in her transactions."

"I have one example that occurred a few months ago," Miles said. "It substantiates my claim that Aunt Constance has been slipping, even before the shock of losing Kristin. I can prove, through several sources, that she recently bought a ship and paid five times more money for it than was necessary."

"Five times more?" Tony asked, surprised by the statement. "Are you sure of that?"

"Yes."

"Why would she do such a thing?"

"I have no idea," Miles said. "I pleaded with her not to waste money so. In fact, my mother was with me then, and she, too, tried to talk Aunt Constance out of doing such a foolish thing. But Aunt Constance was bound and determined to do it, and there was little we could do to stop her. I must say that her action did upset other shipping companies, for it disturbed existing agreements pertaining to methods of bidding for ships."

"I see," Tony said. "But, taken alone, that is not enough to get a ruling at this point. I'm afraid you are going to have to have several more such examples if we are to have any hope for a favorable ruling on our petition. And we are going to have to have the testimony of some disinterested observers as well."

"But such a thing is possible?" Miles asked.

"Yes. Though . . ."

"Though what?"

"It would be much easier if we found Kristin."

"Why?"

"Because either way, whether she is dead or alive, a judge could view that as a resolution of the problem. As long as Kristin is missing, and there is hope that she is alive, a great deal of what might otherwise be classified as irrational behavior, could be discounted as normal anxiety under such conditions. That will make the adjudication very difficult to come by. What we need, Miles, is the girl's body."

"But what if it was swept away to sea?" Miles asked. "Good Lord, man, we may never find it!"

"In that case, it may take two years to win our case."

"Two years? She'll have run the company into bankruptcy by then."

"If we have proof of that, we can expect action more quickly," Tony said. He looked at Miles with narrowed eyes. "But of course, we shall not likely have proof of that, will we? I mean just between the two of us."

"What do you mean?"

"I think you know what I mean. My fee for this service, Miles, will be high."

"I imagine it will be," Miles said. "But I'm prepared to pay it, no matter how high it is."

"It shall be very, very high," Tony said conspiratorially, "for it shall be difficult to make a judge see what is not there."

When the two men reached the parlor, they saw a police officer there, questioning all the servants who had worked at the party the night before.

"Where is Captain Woodward?" Miles asked the officer. "I was told that he would be handling this case."

"Oh, he is, sir," the police officer replied. "He is out this very minute, interviewing people who live along the beach, asking them if they saw the young lady."

"Why is he wasting time with all that?" Miles asked. "It seems to me to be a simple matter. Surely her body is lying somewhere along the beach."

"Oh, God, sir, I hope not!" one of the maids said, putting her hand to her mouth in quick horror.

Miles realized what he had said, and he stammered as he tried to recover quickly. "Well, of course, I hope not too," he said. "What I meant was, we, uh, must face up to that possibility. And if my poor cousin is dead, it would be better to know it than to linger on in false hope."

"Quite right you are, sir," the policeman said. "And I'm sure Captain Woodward is doing all he can to alleviate all the sufferin' your family is goin' through."

"I, uh, shall be in the study, should you or Captain Woodward need me," Miles said. "Tony, you get right on what we were talking about."

"Very well, Miles," Tony replied, taking his cue to leave. "Perhaps we will have a rewarding end to all this after all."

"Oh, let us pray that we do, sir," said the maid who had spoken earlier. She, of course, had no idea that Tony was talking about the economic rewards he and Miles stood to gain, and Tony couldn't quite hide the smile as he left them.

Miles walked across the large foyer and into the library. It was a room of tremendous size, lined on three walls and in two partitions with books. Toward one end of the room, there was a bay-window area, looking out over a rose garden. There, in the bay-window area, a leather sofa and two leather chairs sat opposite each other. Nearby was a rosewood liquor cabinet, and Miles went straight to it to pour himself a stiff drink.

What in the hell did that fool Woodward do with Kristin's body? he wondered. He had paid him a thousand in advance to do a job. Well, he damn sure wasn't going to pay Woodward the second thousand until he had proof before his eyes, of Kristin's demise. Dammit! This was just complicating things more! Why the hell did he depend on Captain Woodward in the first place? Why didn't he do it himself?

Miles was on his second drink, when he heard a commotion in the entry foyer. There were several loud voices, and he got up quickly and walked to the door to see what was going on.

In the entry foyer, stood four of the young men who had been at the party the night before. Though it was by now afternoon of the following day, all four of the men were still dressed in the party wear of the previous evening, and their faces were shadowed with the stubble of a day's growth of beard. Two of the four men were holding, and holding rather roughly, a fifth man, an older one, dressed in work clothes. They were the clothes of a fisherman, and, in fact, Miles could smell the fish upon him, even from the door of the library.

The man was powerfully built, and it looked as if he could easily handle the four effete young gentlemen who held him prisoner. But one of them was holding a pistol, brandishing it about proudly, and it was that pistol which held the fisherman in check.

"We've caught the beggar, Miles!" the one with the pistol shouted.

"You've caught who?" Miles asked, stepping out into the foyer. "Who is this man?"

"Jack remembered him," the man with the gun explained. "Last night, when Kristin took a walk up the beach, this man was there, watching her."

"I saw her. I did not watch her," the man said.

"Then what were you doing on the beach?" a new voice suddenly asked, and Miles looked toward the door to see Captain Woodward.

"Where the hell have you been?" Miles asked, blurting it out angrily.

"I've been doing my job, sir," Captain Woodward

answered smoothly. "And now if you will allow me, I will continue to do so." He walked over to stand in front of the fisherman. "I know you, don't I?"

The fisherman looked away quickly, but Woodward put his hand on the fisherman's cheek, and turned it back so he could see his features. "Yes," Woodward said. "We've met before, haven't we, Mr. Stansilos."

"Yes," Stansilos said quietly. "We meet before, Captain Woodward."

"You may recall the incident, Mr. Chalmers," Captain Woodward said. "About one year ago, when someone cut the anchor lines on all the Chalmers' ships in the bay?"

"Yes," Miles said. "I remember that."

"This was the gentleman who did it. His name is Nick Stansilos and he claims to be a fisherman."

"I *am* fisherman," Stansilos said resolutely.

"Sometimes you are a fisherman, sometimes you are an anchor cutter," Woodward said.

"Why did he cut the anchors?" the youth with the gun wanted to know.

Woodward noticed for the first time that the young man was waving the gun around as casually as if it were a pipe, and with an exasperated sigh he reached over and grabbed it from the boy's hand, broke it down, and ejected the cartridges. They fell to the floor with a heavy clatter. "Put that thing away before someone gets hurt," he said gruffly, handing the pistol back. Then, to answer the question just put, he said: "Mr. Stansilos claimed that Chalmers cut his fishing net, and he was just paying them back in kind."

"They *did* cut my net," Stansilos said. "It cost me much money, so I did something to cost them money."

"Yes, I suppose you did," Miles said. "In fact, you cost us over a thousand dollars."

"You could more better pay the thousand dollars than a poor fisherman such as myself could pay the hundred dollars you cost me," Stansilos said.

102

"So you just paid them back, is that it?" Woodward asked.

"Yes."

"And last night, maybe you decided to pay them back a little more?"

"I don't understand what you say."

"Sure you do, Stansilos. Last night, were you really working your fishing net on the beach, or were you there like these people say? Were you just *watching* Kristin Chalmers?"

"I tell you before. I see girl, not watch her."

"Weren't you looking for a chance to get her alone?" Woodward said. "Maybe you thought you could hurt her, and pay back the Chalmerses even more?"

"No," Stansilos said. "That is not true."

"And I think it is you who is lying," Woodward said. "I think you saw her leave the others; then you followed her, and you killed her."

"I did not," Stansilos said. "I could not do such a thing."

"Can you prove that?"

Stansilos suddenly smiled. "Prove it? Yes, I can prove it."

"How?" a woman's clear voice asked.

"Aunt Constance," Miles said. "You shouldn't be down here listening to this sort of thing. It will only serve to upset you."

"Maria, help my aunt back to her room," he said, speaking to one of the maids who had come with the others to the foyer to observe the drama played out here.

"Nonsense, Miles, quit treating me as if I were an invalid," Constance dismissed with a wave of the hand. "Now, tell me, Mr. Stansilos. Can you prove that you did not do as the police captain says? Can you prove that you did not follow my granddaughter up the beach and kill her?"

"Yes, miss," Stansilos said. "Soon, short time after

103

young people leave the beach, my crew come to help me with net. They are my . . . how you say . . . alibi. Yes, they are my alibi that I did not follow girl up the beach."

"You are prepared to let me question your crew, I suppose?" Woodward said.

"Yes," Stansilos said. Stansilos looked at Constance Chalmers, and his eyes softened. "Mrs. Chalmers, when I cut the anchor, I was not mad at you. I was mad at the company who cut my nets. You are very nice woman. All people say this. Also, they say how sad that you lose your husband and your son to the sea. I would not want to make more sorrow for you. I did not hurt your granddaughter, this I swear to you."

"I believe you," Constance said. "Look somewhere else, captain. You are on the wrong track here."

"I guess my theory was correct in the first place," Miles said. "Kristin must have fallen into the surf and drowned. I'm sorry, Aunt Constance."

"No," Stansilos said.

Miles looked at Stansilos, surprised at the comment. "What do you mean no?"

"The girl did not drown."

"How can you be so sure of that?"

"Is easy," Stansilos said. "When I hear about missing girl, I remember I see her walking north on beach. So, I know if she drown last night, this morning her body will beach at Rocky Spit. I go to Rocky Spit, but there is no girl's body. No one has found girl's body at Rocky Spit, so the girl did not drown."

"Thank God!" Constance said.

"Aunt Constance, you mustn't get your hopes up over the homespun wisdom of some fisherman," Miles warned.

"It is currents, Mr. Chalmers. I am a fisherman in these waters for forty years. I know the currents. I know if someone drowns where the girl was, then that person's body will be taken by currents to Rocky Spit.

104

It is not homespun wisdom to know that a floating body cannot move against the current."

"I knew it," Constance said. "I knew Kristin was alive!" She clasped her hands, and her eyes sparkled in such excitement that the excitement became contagious, and several of the maids rushed to her and embraced her and began crying with joy.

Miles watched the scene in frustration, then looked at Captain Woodward. "Is there any need to keep him?" he asked.

"No," Woodward said. "You can go, Stansilos, but be around in case I want to ask you some more questions."

"Yes," Stansilos said. He put his hands on the chest of the two who were holding him and pushed them away, gently but firmly. Then, making an elaborate show of brushing his shirt sleeves where their hands had been, he bowed slightly to Constance Chalmers and left the house.

"Captain Woodward, may I see you in the library for a moment?" Miles said.

"Certainly, Mr. Chalmers," Woodward answered.

A moment later Miles closed the large, oaken doors behind them, then motioned for Woodward to go over to the leather sofa, across the room from the doors, so they could speak in privacy.

"Now," he hissed. "Suppose you just tell me where in the hell Kristin is?"

"No, Mr. Chalmers," Woodward said. "I don't think I'll do that."

"What? What are you talking about?"

"Have you ever heard of Reverend Wales, Mr. Chalmers?"

"Reverend Wales? I . . ." Miles got a confused look on his face. "Woodward, what the hell are you talking about? Who is this person Wales, and what difference does it make whether I've heard of him or not? That isn't the issue here."

"Oh, yes, but it is," Woodward said easily. "You see, until you silence Wales and his committee, Kristin Chalmers will remain alive, ready to be a witness against you for attempted murder."

"What? Alive?"

"Yes, Mr. Chalmers," Woodward said, smiling easily. "I have her now, and I will keep her for awhile. You get Wales to call off his investigation, and I'll provide you with a body. If you don't get him to call it off, I'll provide you with a witness. Now, which will it be?"

"How am I supposed to get him to call it off?" Miles asked in exasperation.

"Oh, that's not my worry, Mr. Chalmers. You are a man of power and influence. Use it."

Chapter Eleven

When Kristin awakened, she was aware of a vast, dark emptiness. She was frightened and confused, and wondered where she was and how she got there. Her head hurt, and she felt nauseous; when she tried to move, she discovered with alarm that she was tied down!

Kristin tried to call out then, to yell for help, but there was a gag over her mouth, and though she tried to scream, all she could manage was a desperate little sound which could do nothing to help her.

Finally she managed to beat down the panic that had nearly overtaken her, and she lay there quietly, trying to pull herself together, fighting to hold onto her sanity. She was truly worried about her sanity, for she knew one could be driven out of their wits with fear. And in the dark and quiet of this great emptiness, Kristin's mind was playing tricks on her. She spent some time trying to decide if she was still alive. Certainly I'm alive, she told herself. For if I were dead, I wouldn't be posing such questions.

But, she questioned, have I not accepted the fact that the soul survives the body after death? And what is the soul, if not the mind? It would be logical to assume that a mind which is intact would be a questioning mind, even after death.

And yet, if this is death, she reasoned, why am I bound? The soul cannot be restrained by ropes, only the body. And if my soul is with my body, then I am still alive.

And thus, by logic and reason, Kristin determined that she was alive. That having been settled, she tried to determine where she was and how she got there. She listened carefully, and after sorting out the sounds of her own breathing and the beating of her heart, she began to hear other sounds. A clanging bell in the distance, which she knew to be a buoy bell. There was a train. Once she heard a wagon, with the steel rims of its wheels humming on pavement. A horse blew. A door slammed. Then she heard the sound of hollow footsteps coming toward her, and from the time it took the steps to cross to her, she knew that she must be in a large room. Perhaps an empty warehouse.

"How is she?" a voice asked as the steps drew very near.

"I think she's still asleep," another voice answered. "She was really given a dose of that stuff. Another few hours and it'll be twenty-four hours she's been unconscious."

"Don't worry about it, he's handled that stuff before. Besides, she ain't dead yet, is she?"

"Well, no, but . . ."

"Then she ain't gonna die."

Kristin heard a match strike, and a moment later a man held a lantern over her, examining her in the spill

108

of yellow light. She opened her eyes and looked up at him.

"Well now, lookie here," the man said. "She's opened her eyes nice and purty for us. You're still alive, ain't you, missy?"

Kristin's eyes were wide in fear, and she tried to make out the face on the other side of the shining lantern. She could see only the rough growth of a beard and a rather large nose. She tried to talk but, as before, could make only a grunting sound.

"Say, Pierce, this here girl's a purty un, she is," the man with the lantern said.

"Yeah," the disembodied voice, which was Pierce spoke from the darkness. "I been admirin' her myself a bit."

"Are we gonna have to kill her?"

"I dunno. He didn't say."

"Itta be a shame to waste it," the man with the lantern said.

"See here, Jesse. What you got in mind?" Pierce asked.

Jesse put his hand on his crotch and rubbed himself unashamedly. When he pulled his hand away, there was a great bulge in his pants.

"I'm gonna have myself a little fun," Jesse said. "Are you gonna join me?"

"I don't know," Pierce said. "I'm a bit afeared to. What if the cap'n finds out?"

"You think the cap'n ain't plannin' on doin' this hisself? Onliest thing is, we're gonna beat him to it, that's all."

"Jesse, I . . ."

Jesse put the lantern on the floor, and as he stood looking down at her, his features were underlit so that they were glowing beneath and shadowed from above. It was a terrifying sight, made the more so by Kristin's realization of what was about to happen.

"Get her clothes offen her," Jesse ordered as he started removing his own.

"You mean you want me to get her nekkid?" Pierce asked.

"Yeah," Jesse replied. "Maybe it'll make your blood flow like a man and you'll be wantin' to take your turn at her."

Kristin closed her eyes to blot the horror out of her mind. She turned her head to one side as she felt Pierce's fumbling, rough hands tugging and pulling at her clothes. He was rough and impatient, and by the time he had her clothes removed, mostly by ripping them from her, her breasts were bruised and her nipples stinging from the abuse inadvertently inflicted.

"Lookie here, hold that lantern up, Pierce," Jesse ordered. "I ain't never seen me no blonde girl down here before, and I want to take a look."

Once more the yellow light spilled across Kristin, this time falling on her smooth, naked skin, giving it a shining, golden hue.

"It ain't blonde," Jesse said in disappointment.

"Yeah, sure it is," Pierce said. "Look, see? It's just that it ain't been out in the sun like her hair so it ain't had no chancet to lighten up."

As Pierce talked, he ran his hand across the triangle of hair which was the object of their observation, and Kristin shuddered as she felt his callused fingers there.

"Jesse," Pierce asked, his voice thick now with barely controlled lust. "Have you ever had anythin' as pretty as this girl?"

"Naw," Jesse said. "I ain't never had no one 'cept whores and the such. But the one's purty much like the other, I s'pose." Jesse started to climb up on the table where Kristin was tied.

"Wait a minute," Pierce said, holding his hand out to stop Jesse.

"Wait a minute? What for?"

"I ain't never had me no one pretty enough as to

110

make me want to do this to before. But I'd like to now."

"What are you talkin' about?"

"Watch," Pierce said.

Kristin watched in fear as Pierce bent down, then, to her surprise, she felt his mouth close over her breast. She closed her eyes and held them tightly shut, afraid that he was going to bite her. Maybe he intended to bite it off!

But he didn't bite. Instead, he sucked, gently, and then she felt his tongue flicking across her nipple. And then, the most shocking thing of all! The nipple grew instantly erect, and the sensations his tongue evoked raced through her body like an electric shock! Involuntarily, she trembled, and she tried to cry out for him to stop . . . not because it was hurting, but because it was unexpectedly and unacceptably pleasurable.

Pierce raised up and looked over at Jesse. "You wanna try that?" he asked.

"Naw," Jesse said. "I ain't some baby suckin' at the teat. I'm a man, 'n I got a man's needs. Now get outta the way. When I'm finished with her, you can suck around all you want."

Jesse climbed onto the table and then came down over Kristin. Kristin felt the bile of fear climbing in her throat, and she struggled in vain against the ropes. Above her, on the high ceiling, she could see the shadows that were cast upward by the lantern on the floor. They were huge, grotesque images, pulled and distorted so that they could have been reflections of hell's own demons.

"Pierce, untie that leg and pull it out," Jesse said, struggling with his task. "I can't do anythin' this way."

Kristin felt the rope being removed, and when her leg was free, she made a desperate try to kick at them, but Pierce laughed, and held it, then pulled it open.

"Now," Jesse said. "Now, that's more like it."

Kristin felt him poking around, heard him curse a

111

couple of times, and then . . . "Uhhnnnggg!" she cried out in pain, as Jesse, with a grunt of victory, accomplished his foul purpose.

The pain was excruciating as it shot down both legs and up her body. She felt as if a red-hot poker had been held to her, and she bit her lip and bore down against him, trying to expel that which had forced its way into her body.

Jesse grunted and strained, and a moment later let a hissing sigh escape from his lips, and she felt him collapse on her. He stopped thrusting at her then. She didn't know why, but she was glad he had.

"I'm finished with her," Jesse said, getting off the table. There was a dampness on his groin, which reflected in the light.

When Pierce followed Jesse, Kristin lay there, no longer feeling a sharp pain, but crying out inside for the ordeal to end. Once Pierce took her nipple in his mouth and again she felt the strangely pleasurable sensations. Also, Pierce was more gentle with her, and once or twice, unbidden and immediately suppressed as soon as she was aware of them, she felt tingling feelings, which weren't that unpleasant. That was more frightening to her than Jesse's painful thrustings, for it was an unwanted look into her own wanton nature.

Thankfully, Pierce finished with her in as short a time as did Jesse, and after he climbed off her, she was left alone, uncomfortable in the stickiness they left with her, but otherwise unhurt.

They left the room, taking the lantern with them, and once again Kristin was plunged into darkness. She knew little more than she did when the two men arrived. There was a third, a captain, possibly a ship's captain, but he wasn't there, only mentioned.

Why was she here? Then she remembered reading once about the very rich shieks who paid money to have women captured and brought to them for their harem. Could she be a victim of such a bizarre plot?

Then a cold, heart-stopping fear numbed her. One of the men had asked the other if they were going to have to kill her. At the moment she recalled that, she was so frightened that she had difficulty in breathing. Then she called on logic again. She forced breath back into her body and lay very quietly, fighting back the panic. Logic. Of what use would she be to a shiek, if she were dead? Of course they wouldn't kill her. But, wouldn't any decent woman rather be dead than be subjected to such a life? Decent, perhaps, Kristin thought. But a logical woman would cling to life, and she expected to do just that.

Captain Woodward leaned against the front of the building, waiting for the coach and four. It seemed a bit melodramatic to him, but experience had proven that the safest way to talk to anyone without fear of being overheard was to do so in a moving coach. There was no chance for a secret opening leading into another room, where prying ears could listen in on all your secrets.

The coach, a big, black, closed landau, approached, and Woodward checked quickly to make certain that it was safe to get in. If he saw anything out of the ordinary he would give a casual signal to the driver, and the driver would continue on. But the way was clear, so the driver stopped, and Woodward stepped into the coach and pulled the door shut behind him.

"Good evening, Captain Woodward," an enormously fat man said. He sat on a seat that was designed for three people, and his corpulent body flowed over it from one side to the other, filling it completely. He was wearing the most expensive suit, but still he was ugly in his obscene grotesqueness. His neck hung in rolls over his collar, and a layer of chins started nearly on his chest and worked their way up to a mound of flesh that was his face. The mouth seemed unusually small for so large a man, and Woodward sometimes wondered

113

how so small a mouth could ingest enough food to keep so large a body. But even now, the man was eating. "Won't you have one of these cream cakes?" he asked. "They are quite delicious."

"No, thank you," Woodward said. "What is it, Prefontaine? What do you want?"

Prefontaine laughed, and his laughter shook the coach. "I thought you might be interested in a proposition that came my way tonight."

"What kind of proposition?"

"To have you killed," Prefontaine said. He laughed again.

"Well, you'll excuse me, Prefontaine, but I don't find that funny."

"Oh, but you would, Captain, if you knew who wanted to have it done."

"Who?"

"None other than Mr. Miles Chalmers," Prefontaine said.

"What? Why, that lily-livered son of a bitch!" Woodward swore. "I ought to kick his teeth in."

"Well, after all," Prefontaine said, "the man does have cause to be upset with you. He paid you for something, and you didn't deliver."

"Yeah? Well, why would he come to you? What have you got to do with it?"

"Mr. Chalmers owes me fifty thousand dollars," Prefontaine said, licking the cream off his finger, then reaching into the sack to pull out another cake. "Are you certain you won't have one?"

"No," Woodward said. "How does he owe you that money?"

"It's a . . . uh . . . business arrangement we have," Prefontaine said. "But he does have a point, Captain. He tells me that he can't get his hands on the money until he can control the company. And he can't control the company until he has the proof that his cousin is

114

dead. Now, you were supposed to take care of that for him, and you didn't do it. Why didn't you?"

"I thought I might use her for a little leverage," Woodward said. "Prefontaine, somebody like Chalmers can kick up quite a bit of public support for whatever he'd like. He could grease a few palms, grant a few favors, and the next thing you know this investigation of Reverend Wales would be over with."

"It is over with now," Prefontaine said.

"Oh? What do you mean?"

"I mean I had the good reverend killed, no more than an hour ago."

"You fool!" Woodward spat. "Don't you know what you've done?"

"Yes. I've taken care of a troublemaker. Don't worry. I think the others will get my message loud and clear. I think the investigation will be terminated."

"If it isn't, Prefontaine, and if I go down, by God, you're going down with me."

Prefontaine smiled. "Then I think we should see that neither of us goes down, don't you?"

"And how do you intend to take care of that?" Woodward asked. "There will be other Reverend Waleses."

"And others to kill them," Prefontaine said easily. "Now, about Mr. Chalmers."

"Never mind. With Wales dead, I might as well go ahead and give Chalmers what he wants. That way you'll eventually get your money."

"No," Prefontaine said.

"No? What do you mean no?"

Prefontaine smiled. "I'm a very greedy man, Captain Woodward. Why should I be satisfied with fifty thousand dollars, when I could have more? Much, much more."

"How?"

"Your idea was a good one, Captain. Use the girl to

have leverage against Chalmers. But your ambition was too limited. If we can control him, we can control Chalmers Shipping."

Captain Woodward smiled. "Yes," he said. "Yes, I see what you mean. But the girl. I can't keep her here; it's much too hot."

"Then send her away," Prefontaine said.

"Where? How?"

"Oh, Captain, I leave *that* up to you. You are a resourceful man. I'm certain you will come up with a way to get her safely out of the city for awhile."

"Yeah," Woodward said. "Yeah, I think I do know a way."

Chapter Twelve

SHIP'S LOG, Barkentine *Morning Star* at anchor in Boston Harbor, tied up to Chalmers's Pier Fifteen.

April 16, 1901

Squalls in morning. Clear by noon.

Cargo all loaded. Manifest in order. Hatches battened down, ready in all respects to get underway.

Crew aboard today.

Andrew Roberts stepped into the crew's mess, and Julian Truax, who was seated at the head of the table, looked up and saw him.

"Gentlemen, our captain," Truax said.

"Please, continue eating," Roberts said quickly, when everyone stopped and looked toward him expectantly. "I thought I'd join you for coffee, if you don't mind."

"We don't mind a bit, Captain. Do we, gents?" Truax said. "Cookie, a cup of coffee for our captain, if you please."

"I've been serving him coffee for four years without having to be told," Josiah replied gruffly, already starting toward Roberts with the captain's personally monogrammed cup in his hand. "And don't call me cookie."

"I'm sorry, mate, I meant nothing by it," Truax said, apologizing easily. He looked up at Roberts. "Captain, speakin' on behalf of the crew, I'd like to tell you that we greatly appreciated tonight's supper. We know that fresh roast beef is not in the ship's stores, and we know that this meal came out of your pocket. It was a fine meal to send a man off to sea."

"Aye," the others assented, and there followed a few comments of how much so-and-so ate, or how full another's stomach was now.

"I'm glad you enjoyed it," Roberts said, smiling at the men's comments. "And, I'm glad you understand that such fare is not the routine. But, as the steward mentioned, we have served together for four years now, and I think he can do more with dried beef and salt pork than any man afloat. You'll find your meals pleasant enough, I wager."

"Cap'n, when'll we be gettin' under way?" one of the men asked.

"We'll weigh anchor at six bells o' the midwatch. The tug *Dauphine* will take us in tow, and we'll be under wind power by eight bells."

"Cap'n, is it true we'll be standin' heel-to-toe watches this voyage?"

"Aye," Roberts said. "That isn't unusual for a vessel of this size. Your wages are time and a half other windjammers for that very reason. It was in the sea letter you signed."

"But four on and four off . . . that's likely to get hard on a man," one of the sailors complained.

"I'll not be asking any of you to pull more than his share," Roberts said. "And I'll be pulling my watch, same as the rest of you."

"Might we do this, Captain?" Truax asked in his smooth, confident voice. "Might we take eight on and eight off?"

"Eight hours is a long watch," Roberts said.

"Aye, and eight hours off is long enough for a body to get some sleep," Truax said. There were several others who agreed with him.

"Very well," Roberts said. "If that is preferred, I'll have no objections." He laughed. "Listen to me. Damn me if I don't sound like a captain arbitrating with the union."

The sailors laughed at his statement.

"Now, lads, I'll like to get to know all of you. Josiah, fetch young Mr. Bright, would you? I think he should be here during the introductions."

"Aye, sir," Josiah said.

Josiah returned with Mr. Bright a moment later, just as Roberts was finishing with his own introduction.

"And that brings me here," Roberts was finishing. "Eighteen years at sea, from the forecastle to the master's cabin, but I'm the same man I always was. I want anyone of you to feel he can approach me . . . but I don't want any of you to make the mistake of considering me an easy berth. I'll be fair with you, but if you can't come up to my standards, I'll be hard. And my standards are high, mates. They are very high."

Roberts punctuated his remarks with a slurping swallow of his coffee, and looked at the faces of the men to see how his comments had registered. Most seemed to take it at its face value, but one, Julian Truax, just sat there staring back at Roberts with his face fixed in the seemingly permanent, insolent smile. What is there about him? Roberts wondered. He knew that some

119

men had as a natural expression a frown, or sneer, or a look of surprise. Perhaps that was the case with Truax. Perhaps the expression on his face was natural, and there was nothing Truax could do about it. At any rate, Roberts hoped to withhold judgment until Truax had given him something more than a mere facial expression to worry about.

"Mr. Bright," Roberts said, looking at his young first mate. "Would you care to fill us in on your background, sir?"

"As you can tell by looking at me, I've not much background to fill in," Mr. Bright said. The others laughed politely. "I've had only my midshipman cruises and my schooling for navigation and other skills in seamanship. My real experience I hope to get from you men. But, because I know that only three of you are ABs, perhaps I can pay for my experience by helping the rest of you acquire those skills necessary to get AB papers."

"Speaking for the crew, Mr. Bright, we'll be glad to work with you in any way," Truax said.

"Truax, why is it that you continually speak for the crew?" Roberts asked.

"I beg your pardon, sir?"

Roberts set his coffee cup on the table, then stood up and folded his arms across his chest and leaned against the after bulkhead. "Two times tonight, you have prefaced your statement with the words, 'speaking for the crew.' Have you been selected as a crew spokesman?"

"Why, uh, no sir," Truax said. "I was just using a figure of speech, sir."

"I don't like that as a figure of speech," Roberts said. "You see, using such figures of speech causes you to assume certain prerogatives that aren't yours to assume."

"I'm sorry, sir; I meant nothing by it."

"Gentlemen," Roberts went on, explaining his outburst. "You may recall when you signed your sea letter with me, that I specifically prohibited union men from shipping with us. There is a reason for that. I am not against the rights of the seaman. In fact, I am quite liberal in my dealings with the men, as anyone who has ever served with me will testify."

"That's a fact, lads," Josiah put in quickly.

"If a ship is a cruel ship, then perhaps I could see a need for a union, for then a union would be the lesser of two evils. But any man who belongs to a union on my ship, has traded his rights as an individual for the questionable advantages of collective bargaining. Your union representative would have as much power to govern your life as I would. And a union representative can be just as dictatorial as the sternest captain afloat. You don't need anyone to speak for you, gentlemen. The door to my cabin is always open to any sailor with a legitimate complaint. Or, a helpful suggestion. We can have a good ship, lads, if we'll work as crewmates and not as adversaries."

"I'll remember that, Captain," Truax said.

"Good. Now, perhaps we can continue with the introductions."

Truax was next, and he informed the men that he had been at sea for twelve years. The list of ships he had served on was impressive and, by the time he finished, it was obvious that he was no ordinary sailor. He did not inform the men that he had only to pay the fee to be given mate's papers.

Gershom was also an able-bodied seaman. He was "somewhere over fifty" he said, and had worked everything from garbage scows to clipper ships. He "thought he had a family" in San Francisco, but he wasn't sure. At any rate, he hadn't seen any of them in well over twenty years.

Pig Iron Moore was the remaining AB. Pig Iron was six feet nine inches tall and weighed 285. He had worked on windships and steam, and it was said that he once broke a bear's back when he agreed to get into the ring with it at a circus in Turkey.

Josiah didn't say much. His age and appearance spoke for him. The ordinary seamen went through their introductions; Bradford, Sanders, McQueen, Duke, Evers, Hunt, and on down the line until one name ran into another, like one history ran into another. There were only thirteen ordinary seamen, plus the three ABs, and Roberts would have seven of the ordinaries in his watch. Those, he would learn first, and within a short time he would know the others as well. That was one advantage about a long voyage on a small vessel. No one could remain a stranger.

McQueen was a black man, the only one on the ship, and he was nearly as large as Pig Iron. From his experience and his demeanor, Roberts felt that McQueen probably was as skilled as most ABs. He may have been denied his papers by reason of color. Roberts had seen that happen before. He made a mental point to see to it that McQueen had his papers by the time this voyage was completed.

"Captain," Truax asked, after the introductions were completed. "We'd like to . . ." he started; then he stopped and smiled easily. "That is, *I'd* like to know," he corrected, "whether the story I read in the paper is true."

"What story is that?" Roberts asked.

"Why, this story, Captain," Truax said, sliding a folded paper across the mess table.

Roberts picked it up and looked at the story that, by the way the paper was folded, had the most prominent position.

CHALMERS SHIP, *MORNING STAR,* TO TRY SPEED RECORD

Mr. Robert Hayden, of the Golden Gate Distillery of San Francisco, announced in a news conference today, that the three-masted Barkentine *Morning Star,* under command of Captain Andrew Roberts, will depart from her Boston Pier on the 17th, instant, for San Francisco. Her cargo will be molasses, and Captain Roberts hopes to make the passage in 89 days, thus establishing a new world's speed record.

The *Morning Star* has a clipper hull, and the Barkentine rig has been modified to carry more sail than such a vessel usually can spread. Mr. Hayden is confident that the record can, and will be, broken. "The molasses carried by the *Morning Star* will be used in the manufacture of rum, said rum to be named *Morning Star,* after the ship," Hayden said. "We believe that bottles of *Morning Star* rum will be much in demand, after the successful passage of Captain Roberts's vessel," Hayden concluded.

Roberts tossed the paper back on the table. "Yes," he said. "That is true. Though I hoped to be able to tell you the news myself."

"Captain, I've worked aboard windships that were commanded by speed-hungry masters. The work gets a bit hard."

"Work under sail is always hard," Josiah reminded him. "If you can't take it, you should sign aboard a steamship, where you can lay around on the deck all day suckin' on oranges."

The others laughed at Josiah's outburst.

"I won't lie to you, Truax. The work is much harder when you're trying for a speed record. But the rewards are higher too."

"Yeah? What kind of rewards?" one of the men asked.

"Prize money," Roberts said. "Gentlemen, if we can set that record, there'll be a pretty penny to split up.

You'll each get a bonus that is more than twice your regular pay."

"Well now, I don't know about the rest of you, but that sounds pretty good to me," McQueen said.

"Yeah, I could go with a bonus like that myself," Sanders said. And within a short time all agreed, including Truax, that the prospect of so much money made the effort of trying to establish a new record worthwhile.

"And we'll all go in the record books," Bright pitched in.

"Well, gentlemen, I suggest we break down the watches. Truax, McQueen, you'll be in my watch. Mr. Bright, you will have Gershom and Pig Iron and any six others you wish to choose. Those men who are not in Mr. Bright's watch will be in mine, and we shall commence watch at midnight. As soon as you are tolled, I suggest you try and get some rest."

"Aye, sir," Bright said.

Josiah Crabbs, who as the steward had no watch, picked up the newspaper from the table and began looking through it.

"Anything interesting?" Roberts asked, casually, before he returned to his cabin.

"Yeah," Crabbs said. "Boston's a real interestin' town. We got us a good murder here, some preacher fella."

"A preacher? Someone murdered a preacher?"

"Yeah. His name is Wales. Seems he's been preachin' all fire 'n brimstone about cleanin' up the crime in the city. Anyhow, he must'a said the wrong thing about somebody, 'cause they found him dead this morning."

"That'll teach you to watch what you say around here," Roberts said. "What else?"

"Nothin' much else," Crabbs said. "Some society lady got herself drowned the other night. Seems like she was at a party, and went swimmin' with all her clothes on."

124

"If she didn't have any more sense than to do that, it looks like someone around her would have at least had sense enough to pull her out," Roberts said.

"You wanna see this when I'm through with it, Cap'n?" Josiah asked.

"No, I guess not. I've got a little work to do yet; I think I'll just get right on it, then try and grab a few winks of sleep. Midwatches get awfully long."

"Aye, sir," Josiah said. "I'll fix an early breakfast for you."

"Thanks," Roberts replied. He left the crew mess, climbed the short ladder to the deck, and walked quickly to his cabin.

How many days had she been here? She had no idea. She was no longer certain where she was, or even who she was. Jesse and Pierce had come again in the night or in the day; the darkened interior of the warehouse made it difficult to distinguish one from the other, and they had used her, time and time again. Between the sexual assaults, there was only the endless waiting, and the quiet and the dark. The longer Kristin stayed there, the farther removed she became from reality. She tried to put together a sequence of events, a scenario of what happened, but she couldn't do it. She found that thoughts, almost as soon as they were constructed in her mind, broke up and drifted away. The harder she concentrated on something, the less distinct it became, until soon she gave up concentration altogether and just drifted with the flow of time.

Kristin heard a woman's voice, and she was puzzled by it. She had neither heard, nor seen anyone except Jesse and Pierce for so long that she wasn't at all sure but that Jesse and Pierce might be the only other people in the world. Certainly they seemed to be the only other people in her world. But now, as she heard them approach, the sound of their advancing footsteps was altered by one additional person. Then she heard them speaking and the voice of the additional person was a woman's.

"Oh, my God," the woman gasped, as she approached Kristin. "What have you done to her?"

"Why, we've had a little fun with her, that's all," Jesse said.

"Fun? Look at her! You've treated her no better than an animal!"

"Now, Marcene. You're a whore," Jesse said. "You ought to know that a man can't keep a purty woman like this'n tied up, without havin' hisself a little fun."

"Get her untied," Marcene ordered angrily. "Get her untied and get her cleaned up. You disgust me! Why have you treated her like this?"

"I tole you," Jesse said. "We was just havin' a little fun."

"Well, you'd better get her cleaned up and fast. If the captain gets here and sees her like this, there's going to be hell to pay."

"She's right, Jesse," Pierce said, his voice laced with fear. "I told you we oughtn't to have done all this."

"Don't give me all that, you son of a bitch. You was enjoyin' it as much as I was."

"We don't have time for all that now," Marcene said. "You, Jesse. Go get some water. And you, Pierce, get her dress."

"Her dress ain't naught but rags now," Pierce said.

"Then get her something to wear," Marcene said.

The two men hurried off on Marcene's orders, and Marcene helped Kristin to sit up. It was the first time Kristin had been able to sit up since she was captured, and for a moment she was so dizzy she didn't think she could do it. She started weaving around.

"Here," Marcene said, offering Kristin a helping hand. "Take it easy."

"Who are you?" Kristin asked.

"My name is Marcene," she said. Marcene saw a

126

scratch on Kristin's breast, and she tried to examine it in the dim light. "I hope that doesn't become infected," she said.

"Marcene, help me to escape," Kristin said, putting her hand on the other's shoulder. "Help me to escape this terrible place."

"I . . . I can't," Marcene said.

"Please," Kristin begged. "You must help me escape."

"I tell you, I can't," Marcene said. "You don't know what they would do to me if they caught me."

Marcene bent down to light the lantern and now she held it up to get an even better look at the bruises, wounds, and scratches on Kristin's body. That was when Kristin saw Marcene's face clearly for the first time.

"You're the girl on the ship," Kristin said.

"What? What are you talking about?"

"I saw you," Kristin said. "I saw you go aboard the *Morning Star*."

"How did you see me?"

"I . . . I don't know," Kristin said. "I don't remember." She put her hand to her head. "Please," she said again. "Help me."

Something in Kristin's pitiful plea touched Marcene, and in a sudden, bold decision, she made up her mind.

"All right," Marcene said. "I'll help you escape. But afterward, you must help me, do you understand?"

"Help you? Yes, yes, of course," Kristin said. "I'll do anything for you. What do you want?"

"I want to get out of Boston," Marcene said. "You can help me. You own all those ships. Put me on one going to San Francisco. I have a sister in San Francisco. I'll help you escape here and you help me escape Boston. Will you do that?"

"Yes," Kristin said. "Yes, I'll get you to San Francisco."

"Wait here," Marcene said. She turned and walked

across the warehouse floor, beyond the golden circle of light projected by the lantern, and into the cloak of darkness on the far side of the room.

Kristin waited for her for what seemed an eternity. Finally, when she wasn't sure she had even spoken to another woman in the first place, Marcene returned. She was carrying an overcoat.

"Put this on," Marcene said, handing the coat to her. "Come on, I have a buggy outside. We have to hurry."

Kristin got off the table, but she was so weak that she nearly fell. Marcene put her arm around Kristin's shoulders, and half carried, half supported her as they started across the room of blackness.

"Hurry," Marcene begged. "Oh, please, hurry."

Finally they reached the other side, and Marcene pushed the door open. A blast of fresh night air hit Kristin, and never in her life had anything smelled or felt so good.

"Marcene, Marcene, what a disappointment you are," a man's voice suddenly said from the darkness.

"Captain, no, I . . ." Marcene started, but her pitiful plea was cut off by the loud popping of gunshots.

Kristin felt Marcene's body sag as she heard the gunshots, and she saw the brilliant orange flashes of light with each shot. She realized, without having to be told, that Marcene had been killed, and she thought the man with the gun was trying to kill them both. Kristin screamed and turned to run, but she was still too weak, and there was such darkness in the room that she couldn't see where she was going, so that after a few steps she fell.

"Stop her!" a man's voice yelled. Kristin heard other footsteps running toward her, and she saw that they were carrying battery torches, playing the long, white beams through the darkness, searching her out.

Kristin stayed on the floor. She could feel that it was concrete, and she crawled through the darkness as the flashlight beams crisscrossed above her.

"Where'd she go, Jesse?"

"Beats the hell outta me. But she can't get outta here," Jesse answered.

Kristin lay still for a long time, listening to them swearing in frustration, watching the lightbeams play around the big room. Then, she saw one of the beams disclose a door. If she could just get there!

Slowly and quietly, Kristin crawled toward the spot where she believed the door to be. Once a beam fell on it again, and she corrected the direction of her crawling, until finally, unable to restrain herself, she stood up and ran the final few steps until she reached the door. She tried to open it, but it was stuck. She let out a cry and jerked on the handle, pushing against it with all her strength.

"Jesse, listen, she's at the side door!" Pierce called.

The flashlight beams converged on her, and Kristin screamed and pounded in frustration at the stubborn door, but it wouldn't budge. Finally, realizing that the door wouldn't open, she tried to run away, but the flashlight beams held her trapped, and she had gone no more than a few steps when she was grabbed.

"I've got 'er!" Jesse yelled.

"Hold on to her until I can get some of this down her," Pierce said, arriving at about the same time. He held a bottle in his hand and he put it up to Kristin's lips. "Drink this," he said.

Kristin jerked her head aside and closed her lips.

"Drink it, little lady," Pierce ordered. "Or I'll pour it down you. Either way, you are gonna drink it, so you might as well make it easy on yourself."

"What . . . what is it?" Kristin asked.

"It's just somethin' to make you sleep, girl, that's all," Pierce said.

Suddenly all the fight seemed to leave Kristin. She was terrified, and hurting, and tired, and confused. She had a small fear that what they were offering her was poison, but at this point, even that seemed better than whatever else. She surrendered totally and drank the liquid down, willingly, almost eagerly.

"That's a good girl," Pierce said, holding the bottle turned up until she had drunk all of it. "Now, come on back to your table like a good girl. You're gonna take a little nap."

Whatever it was, it worked fast, because even as Pierce spoke, his words seemed to come from farther and farther away, until it was as if he were speaking to her from across a great distance. And that was funny, because he was right there, holding onto her.

Chapter Thirteen

Kristin sat on the edge of the table and stared out of herself at the three men. That was exactly what she felt like she was doing . . . staring out of herself, as if the real person had somehow become much, much smaller, and then had retreated inside the body that had been hers. The body itself seemed cumbersome and non-responsive as it sat there, and only the tiny Kristin inside was alive.

And yet, strangely, it seemed as if Kristin were also outside her body, looking on from another place, watching as the three men discussed the woman who was sitting on the table.

"Can she hear us?"

"Of course she can hear us."

"Then why is she just sitting there? Why doesn't she say something? Why doesn't she act like she hears us?"

"It's the effects of the laudanum."

"What does it do to her?"

"It makes her drunk, but it leaves the mind open to suggestion."

"What do you mean?"

"It's a little like hypnosis."

"You mean magician stuff? I don't believe that."

"Watch."

From inside herself, Kristin saw the man lean over and stare into her eyes. She laughed. Or, she thought she did. Actually, there was no sound. But whether there was audible laughter or not didn't matter. She laughed inside, because she knew he was looking for her, peering through the eyes to see if he could see her. "You can't find me," she shouted. "I'm hiding in here!" And though she thought she yelled the words as loud as she could, not one sound came out.

"All right, she's ready now," the man said. He looked at her. "What is your name?"

It sounded as if he were speaking from the bottom of a well. The words echoed, and reechoed, and she tried hard to concentrate on them.

"What is your name?" the man asked again.

My name, Kristin thought. He wants to know my name. But even as she was considering the words, she knew she couldn't answer him. She couldn't answer him, because she didn't know her name.

The man raised up and smiled at the others. He looked back at Kristin. "Your name is Rose," he said.

"My name is Rose," Kristin heard herself say.

"You are a prostitute, Rose. Do you know what a prostitute does?"

"Yes," Kristin said.

"What does a prostitute do?"

"A prostitute lays with men," Kristin said.

"That's right. Have you lain with men?"

"Yes."

"Who have you lain with?"

"A . . . a sailor," Kristin said, now seeing herself as the prostitute she had watched through her telescope so long ago.

"Damn, I thought we was gettin' a virgin," Jesse said.

"Hush," the third voice, the voice of the man Kristin didn't know, said. "Be fortunate that what you did didn't interfere with any of my plans. If it had, you would have paid, and paid dearly for your lustful pleasure. Besides, the girl is now hallucinating. She will construct any history I wish."

"Have you lain with others?" he asked Kristin.

"Yes. With many, many others. And once I was a harem girl for a rich shiek."

"Good, good. Now, Rose, you know it is against the law to be a prostitute and you are going to have to be punished. You understand, don't you?"

"Yes," Kristin said. "I am going to be punished."

"That's right. But you won't be punished in Boston. You will be punished in San Francisco."

"I have a sister in San Francisco," Kristin said, now confusing herself with Marcene. "I must get to San Francisco."

"And you shall," the voice said. "I will help you. But you must do exactly as I say. Will you promise me that?"

"I will do as you say," Kristin said.

The knock on the door awakened Captain Roberts, and he rolled over, thinking that midnight had arrived awfully early. "I'll be right there," he said. "Has the watch been called?"

"Cap'n, it's me, Mr. Bright. It's not time for your watch yet, sir."

"Then what the blue blazes are you waking me up for, Mr. Bright?"

"Sir, I didn't know what else to do," Bright said. "I couldn't take on this responsibility on my own."

"Just a minute," Roberts growled. He thrust his hand

around in the darkness until he located his trousers; then he pulled them on and padded across his cabin and opened the door. Mr. Bright was standing in the dim glow of the corridor gimbal light. He was still wearing his shore-fresh uniform. Behind him was a man in a police officer's uniform, and behind him, a girl. From the amount and type of makeup the girl was wearing and from the style of her dress, Roberts knew at a glance that the girl was a whore.

"Dammit, Mr. Bright," Roberts swore as soon as he had taken it all in. "You mean you woke me up just because the police caught a whore on our vessel? Just throw her off."

"No, sir," Bright said. "He didn't catch her on the ship. He wants to put her on the ship."

"Put her on . . . what do you mean?"

"I want you to take this girl to California, Captain," the police officer said.

"Officer, look, whoever you are . . ."

"Woodward. Captain Raymond Woodward."

"Captain Woodward, this isn't a passenger vessel. This is a freight vessel, and in case you didn't read the papers today, this is the vessel that is going to try for the speed record. I can't take her. There's no way."

"Captain, may we speak in private for a moment?" Captain Woodward asked.

Roberts sighed. "It'll do you little enough good," he said. "But I'll talk to you. Mr. Bright, take the young . . . lady . . . ," he said, setting the word apart from the others, "into the crew's mess and give her a cup of coffee. She looks as if she could use it."

"Aye, Captain."

"All right, Captain Woodward, what is it?" Roberts asked after Bright and the girl had gone.

"Mr. Chalmers did speak to you of loyalty, did he not?"

"Aye. What's that got to do with it?"

"It is to his best interest that this girl be taken to

San Francisco as soon as possible. And as quietly as possible."

"I don't understand. There are trains leaving Boston for San Francisco every day, and they are much faster than we are."

"And much more public," Captain Woodward said. "The trains must stop in every major city between here and San Francisco. If the wrong person talked to this girl at any one of those stops, it could cause Mr. Chalmers a great deal of difficulty."

"How?"

"Use your imagination. The girl is quite pretty, or didn't you notice?"

"I noticed she was a whore."

"Exactly. She is a whore who has decided to add to her income by blackmail. She was bleeding Mr. Chalmers dry. Finally, he had no recourse but to complain to the police. Unfortunately, if we arrested the girl and allowed her to tell her story here, it would ruin Miles Chalmers. Then I found out she is wanted by the San Francisco police for a multitude of crimes, so we arranged extradition papers. Here they are," he said, handing an envelope to Roberts. "And here she is. Take her to San Francisco. When you get there, there will be a police officer waiting on the docks for you. And, Mr. Chalmers's problem is solved."

"Dammit!" Roberts said, slamming his fist into his hand. "Doesn't Chalmers realize what he is asking me to do?"

"As a matter of fact he does," Captain Woodward said. "That's why he has authorized me to give you this." Captain Woodward opened his vest pocket and pulled out a neatly packaged stack of currency. "Here is one thousand dollars," he said, fanning through the bills.

"A thousand dollars?"

"Yes. It isn't a fortune, I know. But it may compensate for your extra trouble in taking the girl."

135

Roberts considered the money. Even if he didn't break the record, a thousand was ample reward for the trip. And that money would be there whether he broke the record or not. It was good insurance.

"All right," he finally agreed. "I'll do it."

"Mr. Chalmers will be very grateful," Captain Woodward said, smiling broadly. "Of course, you can understand if he doesn't wish to show his gratitude in person."

"This is gratitude enough," Roberts said, taking the money from the police captain. "Mr. Bright," he called.

"Aye, sir."

"Bring the girl aft."

A moment later Mr. Bright and the girl reappeared. Roberts looked at her again, and noticed that she looked strangely confused.

"Is the girl all right?" Roberts asked.

"Yes. Why do you ask?"

"She appears dazed."

"It's shock from the arrest," Woodward said. "That happens often. Being under arrest is an experience anyone would find disturbing, especially a young woman. She will be all right when she gets over that."

"Has the girl spoken to you, Mr. Bright?" Roberts asked.

"No, sir," Mr. Bright answered.

"What is your name, girl?" Roberts asked.

"Tell him your name, Rose," Woodward said.

"My name is Rose."

"Tell him what you do, Rose."

"I am a prostitute," the girl said.

"There, you see? There is nothing wrong with her," Woodward said.

Roberts rubbed his chin and looked at the girl. Despite the police captain's assurances, he wasn't so sure. The girl spoke, but it was almost as if she didn't know what she was saying. Still, he was no doctor, nor did he have much experience around women in situations of stress. In fact, he had very little experience around women at all, he realized, having spent most of his time at sea.

"Mr. Bright, she'll have your cabin. You'll bunk in the chart house."

"Aye, sir."

"Has the girl any more clothes?" Roberts asked.

"No," Woodward said.

"Mr. Bright, you're about the same size, and you've too much dunnage. Would you be so kind as to provide some clothes for her?"

"Aye, Captain, I'll be glad to."

"I'd post a guard outside her door if I were you, Captain," Woodward suggested. "At least while you are in port. She is likely to recover from this stuporous state at any moment, and if she does, she may try to escape."

"Aye, that's a good idea."

Woodward started to leave, then he turned and looked back at Roberts. "I feel I should also warn you that she is a woman with a marvelously inventive mind. She once escaped an officer by convincing him that she was the daughter of the mayor." Woodward laughed and Roberts joined him. "You can well imagine that officer's embarrassment when he learned how he had been taken. Her pattern, I understand, is to try and pass herself off as someone grand: the governor's daughter, the daughter of a millionaire, and the like."

"I am not likely to fall for any such fabrication," Roberts said. "But I appreciate the word of warning."

Roberts accompanied Woodward to the gangplank. "Well, you'll be off in the morning then, Captain Roberts. I hope you have a pleasant voyage, and good luck in your attempt at the record."

"Thank you," Roberts said. "And I hope you catch the preacher-killer."

"You what?" Woodward asked with a start.

"The preacher-killer. Wasn't there a preacher murdered in Boston last night?"

"Oh, oh, yes, there was," Woodward answered. "Yes, that caused quite a few ripples, believe me."

"Well, good luck with it," Roberts said.

"Yes, yes. Thank you, Captain Roberts. I'll tell Mr. Chalmers that he has nothing to worry about."

Roberts stood at the rail until the police captain was clear of the pier; then he pulled out his timepiece and looked at it. It was only thirty more minutes until his watch would be called. That wasn't enough time to go back to bed, so he went into the mess to pour himself a cup of coffee. He sat on a stool that was secured to the starboard bulkhead, and from his position he could see the door to the mate's cabin. There would be no need to post a guard as long as he could see it. Besides, few of the men were aware that the girl had even come aboard, and he thought it would be best if it was kept quiet until they were already put to sea.

Roberts took a sip of his coffee and stared at the door, as if he could see through it to the other side. There was something haunting about that girl. Perhaps it was just as Woodward said. Perhaps it was the state of shock the girl found herself in. Whatever it was, there was something in her which disturbed him . . . which agitated a part of him. One thing he would have to admit. Even behind the whore's clothes and the makeup, she was a girl of great beauty. And, despite the vulgarity of her profession, there appeared to be a degree of helplessness about her that appealed to his male instinct for protectiveness. He could really see how such a girl could convince the unsuspecting person of her innocence. He would have to be ever on his guard with her.

Inside the cabin, Kristin stretched out on the bunk. It was the first bed she had seen in over four nights, though her confused brain didn't realize that. She knew only that she was sleepy, so sleepy, and the bed was so comfortable. She crawled into it and closed her eyes.

There was something about the man she just met. She had seen him somewhere before. Oh, yes, she remembered now. She had gone to bed with him, and she had watched herself through the telescope.

The convoluted logic of that statement didn't seem disturbing to Kristin. For the girl who was, above all, a creature of logic was not logical at all now. Her mind was befuddled with tincture of opium, and all perceptions, visual or cognitive, reached her through the distorted lens of drug intoxication. She was like a feather dropped before the winds, with no control at all over her ultimate destiny. And, like a feather, she drifted down, down, down, until she was in a deep, deep, dreamless sleep.

Chapter Fourteen

Dust motes hung in the air, illuminated by the afternoon sun. Spears of gold slashed through the venetian
blinds of the Chalmers Shipping Company boardroom
and lay in bars of light and shadow across the long,
polished mahogany table.

Constance Chalmers, as Chairwoman of the Board
of Directors, sat at the head of the table. To her right
and occupying the position of vice-president sat Miles.
Margaret sat next to Miles, and on her right was Jason
Morris, Director of Steamship Operations. Next came
Richard Cooke, Director of Warehousing, Melvin
Speldman, Overseas Operations, Amanda Coy, widow
of Margaret's brother, Stephan, and holder of a small
amount of shares of the company, then William Roache,
Director of Windship Operations. There was an empty
chair between William Roache and Margaret, and that
chair was for Kristin.

Constance had summoned the board for the meeting and was already there when the others arrived. They took their seats quietly and waited for her to speak. She looked up at them, challenging them with a cool, steely glance. As she stared at each of them, they looked away, unable to meet her glance. All, that is, except Margaret. Margaret returned her stare with one equally as defiant. After all, she seemed to say, she had accepted Constance's challenge for forty years, and she wasn't going to back down now.

"This board meeting will come to order," Constance said, though in fact there was little need to make the statement as there was absolute silence among everyone waiting to see what would happen.

"As you no doubt know, the whereabouts of my granddaughter is still unknown."

There was a quiet but general expression of sympathy from the others, and Constance held her hand up. "I have hope and faith in the Lord that Kristin is all right and will be found and returned to me," she said. "I'm certain that you all share my hope, if not my faith."

"Of course we do," one of the men said.

"What you may, or may not know," Constance went on, "is that my nephew is attempting to have me declared legally insane for harboring such faith."

"Constance, what a thing to say!" Margaret said quickly. "You know that isn't true!"

"Isn't it?" Constance replied. "Tell your mother, Miles."

"That isn't true, Aunt Constance," Miles said easily. "I have no wish to have you declared insane. Why, under the circumstances, you are bearing up very well. It would be a very cruel thing to bring on more problems by attempting such a thing."

"Then would you mind telling me what is the purpose of the adjudication you are seeking?"

"I would be glad to tell you and the board," Miles

said. "Though I must say that any such talk is premature. I haven't filed a petition yet, and I may not."

"Oh, you may not? And what, pray tell, would be the deciding factor?" Constance wanted to know.

Miles smiled. His aunt couldn't be playing more into his hands if he had written her role. "It's quite simple, Aunt Constance. The deciding factor is the fate of Chalmers Shipping. As long as I am convinced that the best interests of the company are being seen to, I will be perfectly satisfied with things as they are. But should I see that your distraught state is causing an impairment of judgment with regard to company matters, then I may indeed file an adjudication of non compos mentis. But, Aunt Constance, that certainly would not mean you are insane. Only that your judgment has been temporarily impaired by your grief."

"How prettily you say the words, Miles," Constance said. "But saying them is one thing and getting them put into effect is another. I have no intention of being declared incompetent, and I have no intention of relinquishing my position as chairwoman of the board."

"Aunt Constance, I am certain you would not surrender your position voluntarily," Miles said. "If I thought you would, there would be no need for an adjudication. But if such a time comes that I feel your continued occupancy in that chair is detrimental to the company, I shall do all in my power to have you removed and I shall do so with the board's blessing."

"The board's blessing?" Constance said. "May I remind you that I vote fifty-one percent of the stock? You, your mother, and Amanda are board members by charter, but the others are members at my sufferance. What good would the backing of the board do you? And what makes you think you would have it, anyway?"

"The decision of the board, regardless of its impotence with regard to establishing company policy, would nevertheless, carry a great deal of weight with the court. And I would have their backing, Aunt Constance, because I don't intend to do anything unless the situation becomes in extremis."

"Do as you wish, Miles," Constance said. "I will not be budged from my rightful place."

"Your rightful place!" Margaret shouted, pounding on the table so hard that the others jumped. Her sudden reaction shocked the board, who had thought they were witnessing a dialogue between Miles and Constance.

"Mother, it's all right," Miles said, comfortingly. He put his hand on his mother's arm, but Margaret jerked her arm away angrily. She stood up and walked a few paces away from the table, then spun around and pointed an accusing finger at Constance.

"You have no more right to occupy that chair than the throne of England. That should have been my husband's chair. And by rights, after he died, my chair, and then my son's chair. My son is a Chalmers, Constance Hughes. A *Chalmers*! He has a right to that position by blood. You are there only because you married my Lee, and then, after my poor Lee was gone, *you became John David's whore!*"

"Margaret, you are out of order!" Constance said.

"The truth hurts, doesn't it?" Margaret said. "The secret that was no secret is finally out in the open. Do you think no one knew? Do you think Virginia didn't come to my house, crying because of what was going on? Oh, she knew, all right. And so did everyone else. You slut! You sneaked around, sleeping with John David, telling him lies about his son, until Charles's own father lost faith in him and transferred controlling interest of the company to you. So don't you sit there on your high-and-mighty chair and tell us that it is your rightful place!"

Margaret finished her tirade in a flood of tears, and Miles stood up quickly and helped her back to her chair. There was an embarrassed pause for several seconds, and finally Constance cleared her throat. "Let us get immediately to business," she said. She picked up

143

a sheet of paper that was in front of her. "I have here a recommendation filed by Miles Chalmers that Chalmers Shipping establish a Department of Internal Security, and hire Captain Raymond Woodward, presently of the Boston police force, as Director of Security. Said position would entitle Captain Woodward to a seat on the board. Is there any discussion on the matter?"

Miles cleared his throat. "The recent tragedy that befell Kristin points out the need for such a move, I think."

"But isn't Captain Woodward under some sort of investigation?" Roache wanted to know.

"No," Miles said. "Other than the fact that he is a member of the Boston police force, and at the moment the entire force is under suspicion."

"Maybe we would be better off getting someone from somewhere else," Morris said.

"Captain Woodward has worked closely with us for many years," Miles said. "He could move into the new position with little difficulty."

"I agree with Miles," Constance said.

There was some surprise at that, and the others looked at Constance with faces that registered their surprise.

"I think we should have our own security force, and I think Captain Woodward's first job should be to find Kristin."

"And I agree, Aunt Constance," Miles said. "That certainly should be his first job."

"I . . . I will not override the board on this," Constance said. "I will abide by majority decision. It has been proposed that we hire Captain Raymond Woodward of the Boston police force as the head of our own security force and offer Mr. Woodward a seat on our board. All in favor, signify by saying aye."

The vote was unanimous.

"So be it," Constance said. "Is there further business?"

144

It was obvious to everyone that Constance was barely able to hold back the tears since Margaret's outburst. Margaret, silent now, made no effort to try, and she sat in her seat, dabbing at her eyes with her handkerchief. There was in the boardroom a sense of uneasiness, as if the outburst might recur, this time involving them all. No one wished to precipitate such an event nor remain in the room under such a tense atmosphere.

"We stand adjourned," Constance said.

There was a scraping of chairs and a quick exodus to the door. Constance sat there, bracing herself for another attack, either from Margaret or Miles, but mercifully they left without further comment.

Constance was alone, and now that it was no longer necessary for her to keep her defenses up, she cried.

Word was carried to Raymond Woodward, via special messenger, of the outcome of the board meeting. It wasn't at all a surprise to him, and he had already submitted his shield and letter of resignation to the Boston Police Department. The idea of demanding to be appointed Director of Internal Security was Prefontaine's idea, and Woodward had to admit that it was a good one. This would put him in position to hijack entire shiploads of valuable cargo without the slightest risk. It was a foolproof scheme that stood to make millions.

When the messenger gave Woodward the letter, he distributed cigars, then hurried across town to assume his new job and to meet with Miles Chalmers.

"I hope this will keep you satisfied, Mr. Woodward," Miles said with barely controlled anger.

"Oh, it will, Mr. Chalmers, it will," Woodward said, looking around the office that would be his. It was several times larger than his captain's office at the precinct and, even as he stood at the window, he could see the workman putting his name on the door window in gold gilt lettering.

"It certainly should. Your salary will be ten times

greater than your police salary. And your first job should be easy enough. Aunt Constance has directed that you locate Kristin."

"I'll do that for you, Mr. Chalmers," Woodward said. He saw a cigar box on the large, new desk that was to be his and he walked over and opened it. It was full, and he looked up and smiled. "Now that's what I call the right touch. It was very nice of you to make certain that my cigar box was filled." He removed a cigar and prepared it for lighting. "I have to hand it to you. You people certainly know how to live over here." He struck a match and held the flame to the end of the cigar.

"I assure you, I, personally, had nothing to do with filling your cigar box," Miles said. "But back to Kristin. Where is she?"

Woodward took several puffs before he answered, wreathing his head in blue smoke. Then he laughed. "She's trying to set a record," he said.

"Trying to set a record?"

"She's on the *Morning Star* bound for San Francisco."

"My God, man, are you insane? What do you mean by such a thing? She'll tell the ship captain everything! We'll all go to jail!" Miles said.

Woodward smiled around the cigar that he held in his mouth loosely, confidently. "Mr. Chalmers, you shouldn't get so upset over things like that," he said. "After all, as your security officer, I'm around to take care of you. She can sing to the captain all she wants. I've arranged it so that he won't believe a word she says. And before they get to San Francisco I will telegraph ahead to have her picked up before she can reach anyone who might believe or recognize her."

"You are sure you have everything covered so that nothing can go wrong?"

"Absolutely sure," Woodward said. "The only remaining question is: What shall we do with her once she arrives in San Francisco?"

"What do you mean?"

"Well, I can have her brought back on the next ship out, or . . ." Woodward pulled the cigar from his mouth and examined the end of it before he finished the sentence so that the word *or* hung ominously. "Or," he said again, "I could have her killed. It is up to you, Mr. Chalmers. Which would you have?"

"I would have her dead, Mr. Woodward. Dead, as we agreed."

"Then it is dead she shall be, Mr. Chalmers," Woodward said, flicking the ash of his cigar into Miles's jacket pocket.

Chapter Fifteen

"We're running full and by at your command, Mr. Bright."

"Thank you, Gershom. Truax, have you measured our speed?"

"Aye, sir. Eighteen knots and holding."

"Eighteen knots? Good, that'll warm the captain's heart. Keep her close to the wind, Gershom. Truax, have we more canvas to spread?"

"Mr. Bright, we're flying everything now but the cook's drawers."

Like a cork surfacing from the depths of a pool, Kristin floated slowly back to consciousness. She lay there for a moment, not knowing where she was nor how she got there. She could hear the conversation taking place between the men, but it made little sense to her. Then she realized that she was on a ship and, since she could perceive a definite pitching and rolling, she knew that the ship was at sea!

Kristin was on a small bunk and she tried to sit up quickly, but the quick move made her head spin with dizziness, and she fell back on the bunk. She had to fight to stay conscious, for the dizziness was so severe that she very nearly passed out again.

When Kristin regained control of her reeling senses, she looked around at her surroundings. She was, as she had already discovered, lying on a small bunk, which, as is customary on ships, was attached solidly to the wall. Above the bunk was a round porthole, and it was open to allow a salt sea breeze to cool the room. It was night, but a huge, brightly shining moon hung clearly visible through the porthole, and it laid a wide carpet of silver across the sea into the interior of Kristin's small cabin. There was a gimbal-mounted lantern on the wall just above Kristin's head and a waterproof box just below the lantern, bearing the legend MATCHES.

Kristin raised up to check the box and when she found that it did indeed contain matches, she removed one and lit the lantern. The cabin was illuminated at once by the bright orange glow, and she could then take better measure of her surroundings.

Kristin remembered being tied before and noticed with relief that the ropes had been removed. She unconsciously rubbed her wrists. How did she get free of that awful place? Or was she free? Certainly she was on board a ship, and the ship was at sea. The question was, what was this ship, and for what purpose was she brought aboard?

Suddenly Kristin remembered Marcene, and she gasped and put her hand to her mouth. Marcene had been shot trying to help her escape! That meant that whoever shot Marcene was responsible for her being here! She was still in danger!

At that moment there was a knock on her door, and

149

Kristin jumped back in fear, staring at it with trepidation.

"Rose?" a voice called from outside the door. "Rose, are you awake?"

Rose? Who was Rose? Kristin wondered.

There was another knock. "Rose? Rose, I see your light. Are you awake yet?"

"Who . . . who is it?" Kristin called hesitantly. "What do you want?"

"My name's Josiah Crabbs, Rose. I'm the ship's cook. You've slept around the clock, girl. I figured you might be hungry. Would you like your supper now?"

Supper? Kristin suddenly realized that she was ravenously hungry and couldn't recall the last time she had eaten.

"Yes, oh, yes," she said. "Please, bring me something to eat."

"She can eat in the crew's mess same as everyone else, Josiah," a new voice called out. "And from now on there will be no special invitations issued to her."

"Aye, Cap'n," Josiah answered. "Rose, I'm sorry, girl, but you're gonna have to come to the mess to eat."

"I'll be right there," Kristin said. She opened the door just a crack and peered through cautiously. There was an older man standing just outside her door and he was wearing a full white beard and long white hair. He had a benign, almost pleasant smile on his face, and she felt instinctively that she had nothing to fear from him. She pulled the door the rest of the way open and just stood there.

"Well, come on, lass," Josiah said. "You heard the cap'n. You have to come to the mess to eat."

"I don't know where it is," Kristin admitted.

"Sure you do, Rose. It's where you had your coffee when you first stepped on board. Come along, it's just forward a way. Watch your step, now."

Had she drunk coffee when she came aboard? She

150

couldn't recall that, but she also couldn't recall coming aboard.

The door that led into the small cabin Kristin was using was actually a hatch, with a very high sill, designed to prevent water from coming into the cabin when the ship was awash. Kristin had to step over the sill and bend her head at the same time in order to exit. She stepped out of the room and saw then that she was in a small hall or passageway. Across the passageway was another cabin much larger than hers. She could measure its size because the door was open and she looked inside. There she saw a large bed rather than a bunk and a table, or desk, that dropped down from the wall. There was a man sitting at the desk, but since he didn't look around, Kristin was unable to see his face. The end of the passageway opened through another hatch onto the deck, and when Kristin stepped across it, she felt the soft breeze of open air for the first time since her capture. She stopped, luxuriating in the sensation, enjoying the freedom of the moment.

Once on deck, Kristin was able to get a better look at the ship. There were running lights on the quarter-deck, mantled in green and red so that they splashed squares of color against the deck, mizzenmast, and deckhouse. The ship was heeled over under a fair breeze, and a billowing white sail blossomed from every stick and line. A young man who didn't appear to be even as old as Kristin, was walking the quarterdeck. He looked at Kristin and Josiah.

"Come along, Rose," Josiah called back, noticing that Kristin had stopped.

Kristin quit the deck reluctantly, but she was even more hungry for food than she was for fresh air, so she followed Josiah willingly through another hatch that led below deck. There she saw a long, rough-hewn wood table surrounded by benches.

"You just sit there, missy, and I'll give you a bowl of soup the likes of which you've never tasted before."

"Thanks," Kristin said, taking the seat offered her.

Josiah put a steaming bowl before her, then looked at her with a proud smile. "Smells good, don't it?"

"Yes," Kristin said. It did smell good, but Kristin believed that her state of hunger had reached the point that she would have eaten anything.

"Would you like a little coffee, Rose?"

"Yes, thank you," Kristin said, shoving a spoonful of the hearty soup into her mouth.

Josiah put a coffee mug before her, and it too was a welcome sight with an appetizing aroma.

"You said your name was Mr. Crabbs?"

"Josiah, lass. You can call me Josiah. Mister is what you call officers, 'n we only got two of them aboard. There's the cap'n, he's the one you seen in his cabin, 'n young Mr. Bright. He's the one you seen on the quarterdeck. This here is his first voyage, but I reckon he'll make out all right. I've broke in a lot of 'em, 'n I can generally tell from the first hour how they're gonna be. How 'bout you, Rose? This here your first voyage?"

"Why are you calling me Rose?" Kristin asked.

"Why? Well, 'cause that's the name you give us, miss, when you come aboard."

"I've never told anyone my name was Rose."

"Why, you surely did, lass. You said it to me when I give you coffee the first time we met."

"Are you telling me we've met before?" Kristin asked.

"That we did. 'Twas in the middle of the night, last night. You come in here with young Mr. Bright and drunk a cup of coffee while the cap'n 'n the police figured out what to do with you."

"The police?" Kristin said. "You mean there were police on board and I was brought in here to hide from them?"

Josiah laughed. "Lord, girl, you ain't makin' no sense at all. I think you musta slept too hard today. That

152

sometimes happens, you know. A person can go to sleep like you done, sleep near on to twenty-four hours, 'n when they wake up they are struck dumb. It's like as if they ain't woke up good yet."

Kristin pinched the bridge of her nose for a moment, trying to gather her senses. Had she really been on board this ship for twenty-four hours? Had she drunk coffee at this very table? Finally she looked up at Josiah. "I'm awake now," she said. "But I don't remember coming on board this vessel. Josiah, am I still a prisoner?"

"Yes," a new voice said. "You have been remanded to my custody."

Kristin looked around quickly and saw that the captain had come into the mess. He was standing just inside the door, leaning against the bulkhead with his arms folded across his chest.

"Then, am I to be killed?" Kristin asked in a quiet resigned voice. "And thrown into the sea?"

"Killed?" Josiah said, barking out the word in surprise. "My God, girl, why would you ask such a thing?"

"That is what I was told after the kidnapping," Kristin said. "I was held, tied head and foot in a dark warehouse. I heard the men say that the captain would have me killed. I take it, sir, that you are the captain."

"Cap'n, is this girl makin' any sense to you?" Josiah asked.

Captain Roberts smiled. "I think I understand," he said. "I was told that she had an inventive mind. I believe we are merely witnessing an example of her creativeness." Roberts stepped over to the coffee pot and poured himself a cup of coffee, then sat at the table across from Kristin. It was at that moment that Kristin recognized him as the captain she had watched through the telescope when the *Morning Star* had arrived.

"You," she said. "I know you. You are Captain Andrew Roberts."

"And you are Rose Page," Roberts said, slurping his coffee through lips extended to cool the hot liquid.

"No, I'm not," Kristin said. "There has obviously been some sort of mistake. Captain, look, if the girl you are supposed to kill is Rose Page, then you have the wrong person. My name is Kristin Chalmers. I'm not Rose Page."

"What are you talkin' about?" Josiah asked. "You told us yourself that your name was Rose Page when you come aboard. And we ain't gonna kill you or nobody."

"I tell you, I don't remember coming aboard!" Kristin said. "I assure you, Captain, I am *not* Rose Page. I am Kristin Chalmers. My grandmother, Constance Chalmers, owns the shipping line. In fact, she owns this very ship. I would appreciate it if you would take me back immediately. In fact, sir, I make that more than a request. I *order* you to put about at once."

"Miss Page, there is only one person who gives orders on this ship, and you are looking at him," Roberts said.

"But . . . but . . . you don't understand! Please, I'll see to it that you are adequately rewarded. My grandmother would be most generous!"

"Cap'n, my God, do you suppose the girl is tellin' the truth?" Josiah asked.

Captain Roberts laughed. "Rose, my girl, I must give you credit for that little invention. It is even better than the time you convinced an arresting officer that you were the mayor's daughter."

"The mayor's daughter? Arresting officer? What are you talking about? Why would I want to tell anyone I was the mayor's daughter? And why would I be arrested?"

"You were arrested for prostitution before and you thought that passing yourself off as the mayor's daughter would get you out of trouble. As it turned out, you were right. It did work that time. But it won't work this time, Miss Page. I know all about you. Captain

154

Woodward warned me of your lies and tricks when he brought you aboard."

"Then I was brought aboard by force!" Kristin said.

"You were brought aboard under arrest, Miss Page. But you came aboard under your own power, at which time you told me your name and admitted the charges that had been made against you."

"But . . . but I couldn't have," Kristin said. "My name isn't Rose, and I would never confess to . . . to *prostitution*!"

"You did, madam. And I have the extradition papers that authorize me to transport you to San Francisco to turn you over to the police there. You can try your inventiveness on them. They have several prostitution charges awaiting you there too, I understand."

"San Francisco? But that is impossible. I've never been in San Francisco in my life! Has the world suddenly gone mad? What is happening here?"

"Please, Miss Page, spare me the dramatics. You are a whore. Now, as a rule, I have nothing against honest whoring. But you have become a blackmailer as well, and I feel it an exercise of good citizenship to assist the police in transporting you to San Francisco to face the charges against you."

"I . . . I think you are serious," Kristin said. "I think that you really do believe I am who you say I am."

"Yes, Miss Page. I am serious."

"Thank God, then at least you are not in league with those killers! Oh, Captain, what a relief this is."

"You speak of relief as if I had granted you some concession, madam. I assure you, nothing has changed. You are going to San Francisco, as scheduled."

"But . . . but surely since you have no evil motive for taking me there, you would be satisfied by turning me over to another police department. Any police department. There I can prove my identity and be returned to my grandmother."

"I am turning you over to the San Francisco Police

155

Department as per my instructions," Roberts said.

"No!" Kristin said. "No, take me back, sir! Take me back at once!"

"I'm taking you nowhere but San Francisco."

"No!" Kristin screamed. She jumped up from the table and scrambled up the short ladder to the deck. "Mr. Bright, Mr. Bright, please, help me! I'm being kidnapped!"

Captain Roberts grabbed her before she was halfway to the startled Mr. Bright, and he dragged her roughly across the deck, through the passageway hatch, and then into the small cabin she had occupied. As soon as they were in the room he pushed her forcefully toward the bunk, where she fell across it, unable to maintain her balance.

"Now, you listen to me, Miss Page, and you listen well," Roberts said angrily. "If you ever do anything like that again, I will keep you confined to this cabin for the entire voyage. Is that clear to you? And if the cabin should prove insufficient to alter your behavior, I shall confine you to the brig."

"Please, Captain, I beg of you. All you have to do is put back into Boston or into any port, and I can prove my identity."

"I am not putting into Boston or anyplace else until we make San Francisco," Roberts said. "So you had better resign yourself to that fact."

"But you don't understand. I'm . . ."

"No, you don't understand," Roberts interrupted. He pointed his finger at Kristin. "The truth is, at this very moment it wouldn't make any difference to me whether you were telling the truth or not. I will not break this passage. Do you hear me? *I will not break this passage!*"

Roberts left, slamming the door behind him, and Kristin collapsed in tears on her bunk. It was obvious that she was in the clutches of a madman, and there was nothing she could do about it.

Chapter Sixteen

Because Kristin had slept around the clock, she lay in her bed long after Roberts left, unable to go back to sleep. After several restless hours, she sat up on the bunk and looked through the porthole at the water, which winked back blackly under the waxing moon. She heard four bells and knew from the number of hours she had tossed that it must mean two in the morning. Finally she decided that if she wasn't locked in her room, she would go up on deck. She got out of the bunk and crossed over to try the door. It wasn't locked, so she pushed it open, stepped across the sill, and found herself in the long, narrow, and dimly lit passageway just outside the captain's door.

Kristin paused by the door. It was shut now, and she listened closely. She could hear a gentle snoring coming from within, and she breathed easier, knowing that the captain was asleep. She moved quietly down the passageway, then stepped out onto the deck.

As before, Kristin was struck with the delicious sensation of freedom, of air blowing unrestricted across her skin. She stood there for a moment, then crossed over to the port rail. The ship was heeled slightly to port, and as she leaned against the rail she could feel the spray in her face and taste the salt of the water.

"Beware the line at your feet, miss, that you don't trip over," someone said.

Kristin looked around and saw Mr. Bright standing on the quarterdeck just above her.

"You are Mr. Bright, aren't you?" she said.

"Yes, ma'am," Bright said. He touched his hat in deference to her. "Are you sure it's all right for you to be on deck?"

"I have not been restricted to my quarters," Kristin said rather haughtily, "unless the captain has given you such orders. But in any case, I will not return willingly. You may be assured of that."

"No, ma'am," Bright said quickly. "I've received no such orders."

"Then I shall remain above," Kristin said. "I've enjoyed so little fresh air that I find this much too dear to pass up."

"I've no objections, miss," Bright said. "As long as you stay out of the way."

"I've been aboard vessels before, Mr. Bright. I'll not be in the way."

Kristin wandered around the deck then, sometimes looking out to sea, sometimes looking up at the sail which ballooned out under the steady breeze. She noticed that the sailors all seemed to be watching the sail with a great deal of interest, and if one of the sheets showed the slightest sign of spilling wind, there would be an immediate adjustment to a stay so that the canvas would once more puff full.

After several minutes on deck Kristin felt the need

for a cup of coffee, so she stepped into the messroom to get one. As she sat there, all alone, looking back through the open hatch at young Mr. Bright and the sailors of his watch, she suddenly realized how really pleasant this could be under other circumstances. From the time she was a very small girl watching the great windships slip in and out of Boston Harbor, Kristin had entertained fantasies of such a voyage. She knew that her grandmother would never have approved of such a thing, but the circumstances of this voyage were beyond the reaches of her grandmother's approval or disapproval.

Finally, realizing that this was no fantasy but a real-life situation, Kristin returned her thoughts to her present condition. She finished her cup of coffee, then with a sigh of resignation returned to the deck. She saw Mr. Bright calling to one of his men.

"What is our speed, Truax?" Bright called.

"Nineteen knots, sir!"

"Nineteen knots?" Kristin said. She walked back to the quarterdeck and looked up at young Mr. Bright. "Mr. Bright, did that sailor say we were making nineteen knots?"

"Aye, he did."

"But, why so fast? Six knots is the average."

"Haven't you heard, Miss Page? We're out to set a new record. Captain Roberts intends to reach San Francisco in eighty-nine days!"

"Impossible," Kristin said. She put her hand to her mouth. "So *that's* why he won't break the passage!"

Suddenly Kristin's fear fell away to be replaced by anger. This captain was a fool. Somehow he had been tricked into aiding the foul villains in her kidnapping, and now she discovered that his quest for the new record was the real reason he would not put ashore and verify her identity. Well, she would certainly take care of that!

Kristin left the deck again and stepped into the

159

passageway leading to the captain's cabin. She banged angrily on the door.

"Captain, I would have a word with you!" she shouted.

"What is it?" the captain's muffled voice replied. "Is there trouble?"

"You have no idea the trouble there will be if you don't open this door at once!"

Kristin heard a muffled swear word, and a few seconds later the door to the captain's cabin was opened.

"What do you want?" Roberts asked angrily, tucking his shirt into his trousers.

"I know now why you won't break this passage," Kristin said. "You are bound on some fool's mission to reach San Francisco in eighty-nine days."

"It is not a fool's mission," Roberts said. "I intend to do it."

"At my expense, sir?"

Roberts ran his hand through his hair and sighed. "Look, Miss Page . . ."

"I told you my name was Chalmers. Kristin Chalmers."

"I have a funny habit," Roberts said. "I tend to address people by the first name they give me. You told me your name was Rose Page, and that's how I shall know you."

"I am not Rose Page! I am Kristin Chalmers, and I can prove it if you would just put ashore. Put ashore anywhere, sir, and we can settle this by a simple telegram. Please, I beg you!"

"I will not put ashore."

"Is it because you are committed to trying to break the record?"

"That is partly the reason," Roberts admitted.

"But what could be so important about an empty record?"

"It's more important than you can ever know,"

Roberts said. "If I break that record, I'll be paid enough money to buy my ship back."

"Is that all? Captain, I have already told you, my grandmother would be most generous with her reward. If you take me back now, I'll see to it that the *Cauldwell Morrison* is returned to you."

Roberts got a shocked look on his face. "The what? What did you call this ship?"

"The *Cauldwell Morrison.* That's the name that was on the original papers of the . . . Oh, wait, that's right, the name was changed to the *Morning Star,* wasn't it?"

"How did you know that?" Roberts wanted to know.

"I told you. When we bought your ship I had the registry brought up to date for my grandmother. The original papers listed the name of this ship as the *Cauldwell Morrison.* Because of that, I've filed it under that name, with a cross-reference under the name *Morning Star.* It is natural for me to think of it by the original name."

"Stop it!" Roberts said. "I . . . I've got to think for a moment."

"You mean you believe me?" Kristin asked excitedly.

"No. I mean . . . I don't know," Roberts said. "Please, come inside."

"Oh, thank God," Kristin said. "Captain Roberts, if you had any idea what all I've been through. I . . ." she started to cry, but even as she cried she was smiling. "I'm sorry I'm crying," she said. "It's just that I'm so happy that you finally believe me and that this nightmare is about to end."

"I'm not certain that I do believe you," Roberts said.

"But you'll at least listen to me now."

"Yes."

Roberts pulled a chair out from beneath his desk. He offered it to Kristin, then he sat on the edge of his bed. "Now tell me your story."

"There are a lot of blank spots in my story," Kristin

161

began. "Because I don't know myself what happened. I don't even know how I got on this vessel. The last thing I remember is walking along the beach at Ocean House. There was a party, and a few of us went down to the surf. I . . . I grew tired of the frivolity . . . in truth, somewhat shamed by it . . . so I walked along the shoreline alone. I was trying to gather my thoughts when I was grabbed from behind. I remember struggling briefly, then . . . nothing . . . until I awoke sometime later. I discovered at that time that I was being held a prisoner. I was tied to a table of some sort in what I believe was a large warehouse."

"Who captured you?" Roberts asked.

"I don't know the answer to that, sir. But in the warehouse there were two men. Their names were Jesse and Pierce, for I heard them address each other. Do you know them?"

"No," Roberts said.

"They were foul creatures. Very foul." Suddenly Kristin's voice left her. It was as if she had been functioning on pure courage and determination, and now that the immediate danger seemed to be passed she was able to let down her defenses a tiny amount. She began crying.

"Go on," Roberts said.

"They . . . they abused me," she said quietly.

"Abused? You mean . . . see here, you mean they *raped* you?"

"Yes," Kristin said. She wiped the tears with the back of her hand, but Captain Roberts stood up and pulled open a small drawer from the desk. He removed a clean handkerchief from the drawer and handed it to her, and she accepted it gratefully. Finally after a moment to compose herself she went on. "I'm sorry," she said. "It's just that I had managed to put it out of my mind until this moment. I couldn't let myself think about it, you see? For if I had dwelled on it, I wouldn't have been able to go on."

"That's quite understandable," Roberts said, now beginning to show some solicitation for the girl and her plight.

"I don't know how long I was kept in the warehouse," Kristin said. "I only know that they came to me, again and again. Then, there was a woman. She tried to help me, but they discovered us and she was killed. Her name was Marcene."

"Marcene? Did you say Marcene? What did she look like?" Roberts asked.

Kristin remembered at that moment seeing Marcene with Captain Roberts. "It was the same girl," she said. "The one who visited you."

"How did you know she visited me?"

Kristin wondered if she should tell Captain Roberts that she had seen it through her telescope but decided not to. If the captain knew she had been spying on him, it would sour the newly found friendliness. "She . . . she mentioned it to me," Kristin said. "Or maybe someone else said something about it. I don't know."

"It doesn't matter," Roberts said. He looked at her with an embarrassed expression on his face. "Forgive me, madam. I should feel shame over being exposed as someone who receives visits from prostitutes, but my shock of learning about the poor girl's fate is such that concern over my pride seems unjustified."

"And that is as it should be," Kristin said.

"Please continue with your story."

"I ran, after poor Marcene was shot. But I was caught and forced to drink from a cup. I was told that the draft would make me senseless. As you and others have stated, I walked aboard this vessel under my own power and identified myself as Rose Page. I remember none of that. I remember nothing else until I awoke a short time ago and was taken by Josiah Crabbs into the crew's mess for a meal."

Roberts got up and paced back and forth for a moment. He stopped and looked at Kristin with a pained expression on his face. "Lord, girl, if what you tell me is true, then I've been as guilty as the others in your unlawful detention."

"It wasn't your fault, Captain," Kristin said. "You were the victim of a cruel hoax."

"But the man passed himself off as a police officer," Roberts said. "He had a badge and identification papers, and the extradition papers appeared authentic. Believe me, I've looked upon enough legal papers in my day to be able to judge the difference between documents that are forged and those that are genuine. These had all the appearances of the genuine article. Kristin, please forgive me. I was only doing what I thought was right."

"Then, then you do believe me, and you will take me back home?"

Roberts put his hand gently on her shoulder. "Aye, lass. I'll take you back."

The relief so overjoyed Kristin that she leaned into him and began crying into his large chest. He put his strongly muscled arms around her and pulled her to him, cradling her as he would a small wounded bird. He held her as she cried in racking sobs and because he didn't know what to do or say, he said nothing. Finally after several moments Kristin stopped crying. They stayed that way, in each other's arms for awhile longer, and then Roberts felt his cheeks beginning to flame in guilt and shame. For, holding her against him, with his arm around her slender, soft body and feeling the hard mounds of her breasts against his chest, he had begun to get aroused. He cleared his throat and dropped his arms and walked away, turning slightly to hide the unexpected and unwanted bulge that had risen in his pants.

"I'll go on deck and bring us about," he said.

As Roberts turned away from Kristin, she turned away from him, for she had noticed his condition, had, in fact, felt the bulge grow against her, and for an

164

instant she felt fear as she thought of what she had been subjected to by Jesse and Pierce. But the fear was quickly replaced by a sense of bemused awareness that she had embarrassed the captain. And though she was loath to admit it, she was not without a certain degree of pride that she could arouse him. That pride, she knew, bespoke some reciprocity of feeling on her part. There was no further proof needed of the difference between Roberts and the two men who had used her than the fact that the captain could be embarrassed by the situation, certain evidence of his concern for her feelings.

That was when Kristin saw the bathtub. It was a large wooden tub, and it sat on the far side of the cabin. She gave a small squeal of delight. "Captain Roberts, you have a *bathtub*?"

"Aye," Roberts said. "It's one of my vain affections, I'll admit. But I like a bath now and then. Would you like to use it?"

"Oh, would I? But at this hour of the night, I would hate to ask someone to fill it for me."

Roberts smiled, walked over to the tub and turned a handle. Water began pouring into the tub through a spigot.

"I have a special tank that supplies this tub with water," he said. "It's warmed by the sun during the day and will hold the heat through the night, when weather permits. I can also heat it with a fire when necessary. There's just enough water for two baths per week, provided you don't allow it to go over that mark there," he said, pointing to a painted mark halfway up the side of the tub. "Here's soap," he added, removing a piece from a shelf. "And the towels are in there. I'll stay out long enough for you to enjoy your privacy."

"Oh, Captain Roberts. Oh, I can never thank you enough."

"Please, Kristin. Don't thank me. Just forgive me, if you can."

But Kristin was already drawing the water and looking at it with eager anticipation in her eyes. She was nearly oblivious to Captain Roberts now. He smiled and left the cabin and the beautiful young girl who was inside. What an amazing turn of events had befallen him on this voyage!

Chapter Seventeen

Kristin watched as the water poured into the tub. It didn't spew forth a satisfying cloud of steam, but she tested the temperature of the water several times as the tub was filling, and if not hot, the water was at least warm. Besides, it had been so long now since she had a bath . . . in fact, she had no idea how long it really was because she had lost all track of time. She would have taken a bath in cold seawater had that been the only thing available.

When the water was completely drawn, Kristin hurried out of her clothes and stepped into the tub. She dipped the soap into the water, then moved it across her body, feeling the luxurious sensation of soap bubbles sliding across her skin and frothing in the water. At this moment, she doubted if a marble tub with golden spigots could have given her a more enjoyable bath. And the strong, lye smell of the soap was as pleasing to her as the most elegantly scented cleansing bar in her bathroom at home.

As Kristin bathed, she thought of Captain Roberts. He was as handsome in person as he had been through the telescope.

"They are green," she said aloud and then laughed at herself. For she remembered that she had been unable to ascertain the color of his eyes through the telescope, and now realized that even while fighting with him she had subconsciously noticed their hue. They were green with flecks of gold like the sun dancing on the surface of the sea.

But she had noticed more than his eyes. When his arms were around her, she had felt their strength, and they had been as thrilling to her as she had imagined they would be. She was attracted to him, there was no denying that.

Kristin held her leg up and stretched it out over the edge of the tub. She looked at it critically. It was smooth and unmarked and showed no sign of the harsh treatment she had just undergone.

Kristin thought of what had happened in the warehouse. Was there any way she could appraise her reaction to the abuse she had undergone? Not really, she decided. For, in truth, she had been so frightened for her life that the loss of her virginity had become a secondary thing. How unimportant such things as sexual innocence become when one is faced with a life or death situation. Should she feel unclean because she had been used by her two attackers? Well, to a degree she did. But the feeling was one of a fouled body rather than soiled spirit.

Kristin thought of her experience with Jesse and Pierce. She had already determined that a sexual experience should be like fire and ice, and there should be a proper balance between the two. She knew that not only from watching the girl and the sailor so long ago but because her own body yearned for just such an experience. All sugar and no spice could make sex as insipid and uninspiring as an afternoon tea. But brute force with no sweetness made sex painful and revolting. That she had already discovered from experience.

How would Captain Roberts be, she wondered? She thought about that for a moment. In truth, she had already experienced fire and ice with him. As her captor, he had held her fate in his hands. He had been cruel to her, even mocked her, and that was certainly a savage experience. But he had softened to her cries, and was finally convinced by her pleas, and that was truly sweet. Then he held her tenderly, comforting her sweetly with arms that were strong as steel encased in velvet. Then when she leaned against him, she felt the pure animal response of his maleness rising unchecked to bulge against her, and that bold, savage thrust was dampened by sweet concern and embarrassment. Yes, the fire and ice ingredients were all there, she decided. Sex with Captain Roberts would truly be a sweet-savage experience. He would be capable of bringing her to the highest peaks of ecstasy.

Suddenly Kristin blushed. How objectively she had pursued that line of reasoning. The logic that had always done her in such good stead had been used for erotic musings, and she had felt no guilt! She was surprised by that. She had entertained erotic thoughts many times before, but always these thoughts were chased away by profound feelings of guilt. Now this wasn't the case. What had changed?

But even as Kristin asked herself that question, she knew its answer. She was no longer a virgin. Her innocence had been taken from her . . . not by her own will but by brute force. Thus the "jewel of womanhood" that the magazine articles insisted should always be protected was no longer hers to protect. She was freed of that burden, and with that freedom came the ability to divest herself of the yoke of unreasonable guilt. She had come face to face with reality in its most brutal aspect and emerged from that experience with an ability to recognize life for what it was and to establish priorities as they should be.

When Roberts left the girl in his cabin and stepped out onto the deck, Bright saw him immediately and came to report to him.

"Captain, what are you doing up, sir? You should be sleeping."

"Hello, Bright, how's it going?"

"Fine, sir, just fine. We've a close following wind, and we're logging nineteen knots." Bright smiled proudly. "I'd hoped to be able to surprise you with our position when the watch changed."

"You're a good lad," Roberts said. "And I'm sure I would have been most pleasantly surprised. Unfortunately, I think we're going to have to . . ." Roberts paused in midsentence because his eyes had just fallen on the deckhouse hatch. There carved in cursive letters was the name *Cauldwell Morrison*. He examined it for a moment.

There was silence during that time, and nothing was heard save the running of the sea and the creaks of the ropes and the muted thunder of sails answering the wind. Finally Bright, confused by the long pause, spoke up.

"Yes, sir?"

"What?" Roberts asked, still looking at the name carved above the hatch.

"You said you thought we were going to have to do something . . . but you never said what," Bright said.

"Oh, uh, well, belay that. Mr. Bright, was the girl on deck tonight?"

"Yes, sir. Captain, I've received no orders to the contrary; I hope I wasn't remiss in keeping her below."

"No, I, uh, didn't specify," Roberts said. "How long was she on deck?"

"Quite awhile, sir. She wandered around the deck,

she leaned against the rail, and she looked at the sea. She went into the mess once. I saw her drinking coffee."

"Damn!" Roberts swore.

"Captain, is anything wrong?"

"Yes, Mr. Bright. But not to worry, I think I discovered it in time. Continue steady as she goes."

"Aye, aye, sir."

So, Roberts thought. She knew the ship was called the *Cauldwell Morrison* because she filed the papers on it, did she? Or could she have seen the name carved above the hatch? And there was something about that story she had told him too. What was it? She was walking along the surf when she was captured? That sounded suspiciously like the story Josiah had mentioned from the newspaper. He stepped down into the galley and began looking around. He wanted to wake Josiah up and ask him where the paper was, but he knew that Josiah would probably wake on his own if he stayed long enough in the galley. Finally his theory was proved as Josiah stepped inside.

"I thought I heard someone in here. Can I get somethin' for you, Cap'n?"

"Aye," Roberts said. "You can get that newspaper for me."

"Newspaper? What newspaper?"

"You know the one, dammit. The one that had the story about the rich, young society girl who drowned?"

"It's on the condiment shelf," Josiah said. "I'll get it for you."

Roberts poured himself a cup of coffee while he waited for the cook to get the paper. A moment later Crabbs found it and handed the by now dog-eared paper over to the captain.

"Is this what you wanted to see, Cap'n?" Josiah asked. "It's got food stains on it. Hope it can be read."

"Oh, I'm sure it can be read all right," Roberts said. He took the paper and sat down at the table with his coffee to read. The more he read, the angrier he became.

Finally when he had read the last paragraph, he wadded the paper up, stepped over to an open porthole, and tossed it angrily into the sea.

"Cap'n, what is it? What's wrong?"

"She's played me for a fool, Josiah."

"Sir?"

"That girl in there. She nearly had me believing her story, even though I was warned about her. Fortunately I discovered just in time how she tricked me."

"I don't understand," Josiah said.

Roberts stood up and looked at the confused cook. "I'll explain it all later," he said. "You go on back to bed."

Josiah Crabbs had spent enough years at sea with enough captains to know that they didn't always behave in ways that could be understood by the average seaman. And he knew better than to try and figure them out, so as the captain suggested he returned to his bunk.

Kristin stepped out of the tub. Her skin was pink and glowing, not only from the bath but from the flushed reaction to her erotic contemplations. She was just reaching for a towel, with her arm extended, her breast fleshed full, and the nipple upturned, when the hatch from the passageway opened, and Captain Roberts stepped into the room.

"What . . . what are you doing here? I thought you were going to allow me some privacy! Can't you knock?" Kristin was so angered and surprised by the sudden, unannounced entry that, for the moment, she made no effort to cover her nudity.

"I am the captain of this ship," Roberts said.

"And I, sir, am the owner," Kristin snapped back. She realized then that Roberts was staring at her openly and unashamedly, and she took the towel and wrapped it around her, restoring a degree of modesty to the scene.

"No," Roberts said. "You aren't. Although I must give you credit for having me believing it for awhile."

"What are you saying?" Kristin asked, realizing now that something had happened to change Roberts's mind. "Are you saying that you don't believe me now?"

"I was warned of your inventiveness," Roberts said. "And I should have been prepared for your quick mind."

"But . . . but you said you believed me," Kristin said.

"And I did. Until I saw how you were able to manufacture your lies."

"Manufacture lies?"

"The part about the *Cauldwell Morrison* was the best," Roberts said. "I believed you when you said that it was the name on the registry. I guess it's just that the ship is referred to as the *Morning Star* so much that when I hear anyone else use its original name I'm shocked. What I had forgotten, momentarily, was that the name *Cauldwell Morrison* is carved right above the deckhouse hatch for all to see. It would be a simple thing for you to see it, then put together the story of having filed the registry papers."

"But . . . the kidnapping. You believed me when I told you that."

Roberts smiled, not a pleasant smile but one that masks anger. "Oh, yes. Until I read all about Miss Kristin Chalmers in the newspaper."

"In the paper? What paper?" Kristin asked. "Is there something about me in the paper?"

"No, Miss Page. There is nothing about you in the paper. There is, however, a story about Kristin Chalmers. It details quite nicely everything you would need to know to compose your little story. It tells of the party, it tells of the girl going down to the surf, and it names all the names so you could drop them in your tale to make it seem all the more plausible."

"But, I'm not lying! I'm not, I swear to you!"

"You should have read further, Miss Page," Roberts said angrily. "For if you had, you would have discovered that Kristin Chalmers is dead."

"What? No, that's not true."

"But it *is* true, Miss Page. Kristin Chalmers drowned in the surf."

Suddenly Kristin saw the grief Constance must be going through, and her own plight seemed insignificant compared to the suffering she knew her grandmother was experiencing. Her heart went out to the poor old lady, and she began to weep uncontrollably. She raised both hands to her face and, when she did so, the towel fell to the deck, exposing her nakedness once again.

"So, Miss Page, your game is up," Roberts said cruelly.

Kristin didn't answer him. In fact, she didn't even hear him, so far immersed was she in her own sorrow.

"Cover yourself, woman. Or is the power of your sex your last weapon against me?" Roberts asked.

Kristin still didn't hear him, and she made no response to his statement.

"I said cover yourself!" Roberts said angrily. He stepped over to her, reaching her in three, brief strides. He picked up the towel and made a futile attempt to put it around Kristin, but as she made no effort to help him, it fell again.

"My God, woman, have you no shame? Must you torment me so?" Roberts said, his voice now showing the strain of the situation. What was there about this woman that affected him so? He had seen other harlots just as beautiful. He was not a man who denied himself the pleasures of a willing woman, so it was not as if he had no experience upon which to base his resistance. And yet, the sight of this girl, slender and vulnerable, was fanning a fire in his loins that threatened to erupt into an inferno. Her skin was smooth and blemish free. Her breasts were small and perfect, and the gently flowing fullness of her hips maddened his senses to an insatiable desire.

Roberts let a small groan escape from his lips. He didn't know if it was a cry of anger with himself for surrendering to the lust that was consuming him or a cry of acknowledgment over his own helplessness to resist her. He crushed her naked body against his, and when Kristin dropped her hands in surprise, she gasped as he pulled her face to his for a kiss.

There had been no kissing during the brutal rape by her two captors and, indeed had there been, she may have been even more repulsed by that than she was by the other degradations that were performed on her.

Kristin had been kissed before. There had been the innocent brushing of lips in the shadows of the garden, and quick, dry pecks under the security of party mistletoe. But never had she been kissed like this.

The kiss took Kristin's breath away and all thought and reason left her at that moment. It was a kiss of hunger and urgency, and it set her head spinning. She felt his tongue brushing across her lips and she was surprised by it, for she had no idea that the tongue played any part in kissing. Certainly it had never played a part in any of her kisses. The tongue was gentle and rough, tentative and demanding, enticing and frightening, all at the same time, and, as if of its own volition, her mouth opened to allow his tongue entry.

For the moment, the sensations so overwhelmed Kristin that she lost sight of who and where she was, and she let herself go limp against him. Roberts put his hands on her body. One big hand covered a breast, then gently caressing it before moving farther down. His hand burned a searing path down her body and across her stomach, drawn in tightly now in fear and surprise. When he stopped, his hand was between her legs at the center of all her feeling.

Kristin's knees turned to water, and she began to fall, then as if in the same motion, she fell and was caught

175

up and carried by him over to the large bed. There she was unceremoniously dumped, and she lay there, floating in the partial stupor that was brought on by extreme sexual arousal. She watched through disbelieving eyes as Captain Roberts removed his clothes. Then with her blood turning to hot tea and a sweet aching in her loins, she managed to muster one, pathetic plea for him to stop.

"No," she said though her body was trembling with fire under his touch.

Roberts moved down over her, taking her small hands in his huge palms and pinning them to the bed. With a large, hard-muscled leg, he spread her thighs and though she tried to resist him, he was too strong and her own passions too rampant to make any resistance effective. She felt him thrust deeply into her.

Kristin gasped loudly. There was no pain as there had been during the brutal rape by the two ruffians. There was no numbness as there had been later. There was only exquisite pleasure, silken sensations unlike anything she had ever experienced and far more wonderful than anything she had ever dreamed. She raked his bare back with her fingernails, and even as she did so, she got a mental image of the scene she had witnessed so long ago. In her mind and in her present sexual inebriation, she wasn't sure but that she *was* that girl, and this was then, and then was now, and all her dreams, and musings, and desires had come together in this one, intense instant in the continuum of eternity.

Kristin gave as well as took and became as much the aggressor as the victim. She took his lips and tongue eagerly and gave herself up to him to receive him deeply into her, fighting not against him but with him in the headlong rush toward something mysterious and wonderful, waiting for her in all its potentiality.

Then it started, a tiny sensation that began deep inside her, buried in the innermost chamber of her soul. It began moving out then, spreading forth in a series of concentric circles like waves emanating from a pebble cast in a pool. The waves began moving with more and more urgency, drawing her up tighter and tighter like the mainspring of a clock until finally, in a burst of agony that turned to ecstasy, her body attained the release and satisfaction it had sought. There were a million pins pricking her skin, and involuntary cries of pleasure came from deep in her throat. She felt as if she lost consciousness for just an instant, and brilliantly colored lights passed before her eyes as her body jerked in orgasmic, convulsive shudders.

There were two more after that: one nearly as strong, then another not quite as strong but intensely satisfying in its own right. Then, when she felt Roberts reach his own goal, it was as if she was struck by lightning when a new, unexpected orgasm burst over her, sweeping away all that had gone before it and bringing her to a peak of fulfillment so intense that every part of her being, from the tips of her toes to the scalp of her head, tingled with the kinetic energy of it. She hung precariously balanced upon the precipice for several seconds, and during those rapturous moments her body became so sensitized that she experienced not only her own, sweet pleasure but could feel, through Roberts, the muscle-jerking release of pent-up energy that was his release. The waves of pleasure that swept over him moved into her own body so that his climax and hers became one massive burst.

As Kristin coasted down from the peak, she fell, not like a stone, but floated like a leaf, meeting new eddies of pleasure, rising back up a bit before slipping farther down. Finally, after all the peaks and valleys had been explored, and there was nothing left but the warm, well-banked coals of a blazing fire, Roberts got up from her and sat on the edge of the bed, looking morosely at the floor.

"Please, madam," he said in an odd, choked voice. "Return to your own cabin now."

Chapter Eighteen

Constance opened the big double doors with the key that hung from a silver chain around her neck, stepped into the Big Room, then closed the doors behind her. Heavy, dark-green drapes hung across the row of windows that opened toward the sea, and only a thin crack of light spilled in around the edges so that the Big Room was dark.

The Big Room. It was always pronounced as if the letters were capitalized, and it had been John David Chalmers's private room. He did most of his work from there and most of his relaxing as well since the Big Room was, in addition to an office, a small library. And though John David kept his clothes and personal things in the master bedroom, it was a well-known fact that he slept in the Big Room. In fact, the Big Room was practically his entire world after his stroke because he was too vain to be seen using a cane.

The Big Room was closed after John David died by order of Constance Chalmers, who, to the surprise of everyone, became the new mistress of the house. Now only she had the key to its doors and only she could enter. She kept the room just as John David left it. There were three books on the table and they had been there since the day John David died. A walking cane stood in the corner, and a smoking jacket was draped loosely across the back of a chair. There was even a half-smoked cigar in the ashtray and a shaving brush with the soaped bristles, long since crystalized, by a small basin on a shelf beneath a mirror. On the floor, in the exact position in which it fell, was a copy of the *Boston Daily Evening Transcript,* dated May 11, 1868. John David had been reading it at the very moment he died.

No one knew that such things were still in the Big Room or that Constance regarded them as sacred to her own, personal shrine. Had they seen, they wouldn't have understood, and had they asked, Constance wouldn't have explained.

Constance pulled the drapes open. She knew just how far to open them, to allow the sun to fall upon the painting of John David. The painting was made in 1863 when John David was fifty-three years old. It showed a man with a full head of silver hair, eyes that had a magic light caught perfectly by the artist in hues of dark blue and purple, and a rugged, square jaw. The painting was made two years after Lee had been lost at sea and after the courts had declared him legally dead. That was thirty-eight years ago, but as Constance looked at the man in the painting, she could very nearly hear him speak.

"Let the boy be, Connie. He's just getting his sea legs about him," John David said from the chair where he was sitting for the painter.

"But I fear he will distract the painter, and the likeness will be flawed," Constance said, picking up young

Jimmy, who had been running wildly through the room.

John David laughed. "A flaw might be an improvement. Besides, I hired Monsieur Thibideaux because he is very experienced in these things. I'm certain he has encountered children at his sittings before, have you not?"

"Oui, monsieur," the artist replied, dabbing color on the canvas even as he spoke.

"So there, you see? There is nothing to worry about."

Constance walked around to stand behind the painter, and she looked at his work critically, and then at John David. "What a handsome man you are," she said, then blushed almost as soon as she said it.

John David threw back his head and laughed heartily. "And what an honest breath of fresh air you are, Connie girl. But come, there is nothing to be ashamed of in complimenting your own father-in-law now, is there?"

"No, of course not," Constance said.

"Monsieur Thibideaux, haven't you dabbed enough for today? I grow tired from sitting so long."

"Oui, monsieur, if you wish, we are *fini* for the day."

"I wish," John David said, standing up and stretching, "that you would go now, paint your naked women, and enjoy yourself."

"Papa Chalmers!" Constance gasped, but she couldn't suppress the laugh that bubbled from her.

The artist carefully covered the easel, then closed his box of paints and left. John David walked down the stairs with him, and when he returned to the Big Room a moment later, he saw Constance staring down at Jimmy, who was asleep on the sofa.

"He hasn't a care in the world," John David said, closing the door softly behind him.

Constance looked up at him and smiled. "Isn't he a beautiful baby, Papa Chalmers?"

"Of course he is. But he is my grandson, and I am prejudiced." John David walked over to stand beside

Constance, and he looked down at the sleeping child. "He looks just like Lee did when Lee was that age."

"Oh, I wish Lee could see his son grow up," Constance said, and John David put his arm around her to comfort her.

When Lee was alive, Constance needed no one else. She and Lee were a bastion against Lee's mother and against Margaret. They were complete in themselves, and Constance's world was a happy one. But since Lee's death, Constance found that she had lost much more than a husband and a lover. She had lost the only comforting voice there was in the vast sea of conspiratorial silence. Thus the gesture of comfort offered by John David seemed all the more sweet because of her isolation, and Constance involuntarily turned toward him and began crying.

Constance wasn't aware of when the platonic patting turned to passionate petting. It was all so gradual, so natural, that the progression couldn't be measured. They were holding each other in mutual comfort one moment and grabbing each other in sexual need the next. She had been without a husband for two years, and she had lost Lee when she was in the early bloom of womanhood. John David had been denied his wife's bed for many more years. He was a virile man whose normal appetites had been frustrated. With mutual needs and genuine affection for each other, the wonder wasn't that it happened but that it took as long as it did to happen.

Constance and John David became lovers after that. He became her solace; she, his fulfillment, and they passed the next five years in private, self-contained happiness.

Then Margaret discovered them. Margaret wasn't supposed to be there. She and Charles had left early in the morning by train to take Virginia to New York. They were going to spend two days in New York and then six weeks in Newport before returning. The house servants, too, were gone. Some were on private vacation, but most had gone ahead to Newport to open up the house there. Constance remained behind by mutual agreement, and John David, pleading work, agreed to meet the others in Newport in one week.

Thus the stage seemed set for a week of leisurely togetherness without the necessity of surreptitious meetings in the middle of the night or stolen moments in the afternoon. On the first night they slept together, but ironically they had not made love. They were lying together, talking, when Margaret opened the door to the Big Room and caught them.

"Margaret, what are you doing here?" John David asked, pulling the cover up to his chin in shock over seeing her.

"I came back from New York," Margaret said. "I had hoped to persuade Constance to join us in Newport. I can see, however, that she has a good reason for staying behind."

Margaret's voice dripped venom as she spoke, and Constance felt her stomach dropping as if she were in a great fall. She felt no fear for herself, only sorrow for the nasty situation she had created for John David.

"Why the sudden concern as to whether I come or not?" Constance asked.

"You are part of the family, Constance, dear," Margaret said in forced sweetness. "It is only natural that we try and accept you. Though some of us, I see, are more willing to accept you than others." The statement was pointed and made directly to John David. "Poor Virginia. This will break her heart."

"And of course, you will have to tell her," John David said.

"She is my mother-in-law," Margaret said. "More like a mother, than a mother-in-law. I feel it is my duty to tell her that she has taken a viper to her bosom."

"You care nothing for her feelings, Margaret," Constance said. "You just hope to further discredit me in her eyes when, if truth were known, I doubt that anything I could ever do would make her think any less of me than she does now."

"Then let us just say that I will give her ample justification for her feelings toward you," Margaret said.

"What do you want, Margaret?" John David sighed.

"I want peace and harmony in this family," Margaret said.

"And what else?"

"Why, Papa Chalmers, are you trying to buy my silence?"

"What else do you want?" John David asked.

"I want Charles to be named president of Chalmers Shipping."

"I don't think Charles can handle it," John David said.

"He can handle it. I will help him. Besides, who else is there? Charles is your only heir."

"Not true," John David said. "As Lee's widow, Connie becomes as much an heir to the company as Charles."

"What?" Margaret asked, nearly choking on the word. "You can't be serious!"

"I am very serious," John David said. "When I die, I shall leave fifty-one percent of the stock to one of my children, and forty-nine percent to the other. As Lee has preceded me in death, his share will go to Constance."

"Why fifty-one and forty-nine?" Margaret asked. "Why not fifty-fifty?"

"Someone needs the power to make decisions, or nothing will ever get done."

"But . . . but who will get the fifty-one percent?"

"The person I think is best qualified to run the company," John David said.

"But surely, you don't think that would be Constance?"

"I have not yet made that decision," John David said.

Margaret stared in disbelief for a while; then she got an evil smile on her face. "If you've no wish for Virginia to find out about this pretty little scene, then I suggest you make that decision now, and I demand that you make it in favor of Charles."

John David got out of bed. He had been sleeping nude, and he walked openly, defiantly, over to the chair where his clothes were, and started stepping into them. Margaret gasped when she saw that he was naked, and she turned away from him, blushing. Despite the trauma of the situation, Constance couldn't help but laugh at the scene.

"Margaret," John David said easily. "I don't give a damn whether Virginia knows or not. You go right ahead and tell her if you want to."

"Perhaps you don't care about yourself, but what kind of position do you think it will put your precious Constance in if I tell Virginia what I found this morning?" Margaret asked, still facing away from him.

"I think it will put her in a pretty good position," John David said, smiling at Constance. "Because, if you do tell Virginia, I will assign fifty-one percent of the stock to Constance immediately, just to protect her interests in this family. Now you go right ahead, Margaret, and do whatever you feel you have to do."

Margaret gasped and turned back to face John David. Her face went from a flushed pink of embarrassment to the deep crimson of rage. Tears sprang into her eyes, then rolled down her cheeks. She looked at Constance, and Constance knew that if it were possible to wish a person dead, Margaret could have killed her that very instant.

"I hate you, Constance," Margaret finally said. "And I will hate you until the day I die."

Margaret spun on her heel and left the room. Constance heard the slam of the door to the bedroom she

184

was sharing with Charles, and its hollow boom rever-berated through the big, empty house.

"I'm so sorry," Constance said.

"So am I," John David replied. "But we can't unring a bell, Connie girl. What has happened, has happened."

John David started back toward the bed, but after a few steps he stopped, and got a queer, pained expression on his face.

"John! John, what is it?" Constance asked.

"I . . . I don't know," John David said, just before he collapsed.

John David Chalmers had suffered a stroke, though in 1868 the illness was called apoplexy. He had a spon-taneous recovery of about seventy-five percent of his motor functions, but he seemed to lose his will to live. He retreated into semireclusion, seeing only immediate members of his family, and confining himself to the Big Room, twenty-four hours per day.

The running of the company, by necessity, was passed on to someone else, and that someone else was Charles.

But Charles's handling of the company was a total disaster. Within four months he had cost hundreds of thousands of dollars in unwise decisions, and there was danger of a total collapse of the company. Charles realized his inabliity to cope with corporate complexity as well as anyone, and it was his suggestion that control be turned over to Constance.

"You know what that means, don't you, boy? If Connie is running this company, she gets fifty-one per-cent of it, after I die."

"I understand, Father," Charles said. "But the way I see it forty-nine percent of a going concern is worth more to me than fifty-one percent of a bankrupt com-pany. I'm a fool about a lot of things, but I'm no fool when it comes to recognizing my own shortcomings. The truth is, I can't handle it."

185

"What about Margaret? Will she understand?" John David wanted to know.

"No," Charles said. "She won't understand at all. She is a very ambitious woman."

"Don't you think this is going to make things even harder for Connie than they are now?" John David asked.

"I'm sure it will," Charles said. "But Constance can handle it. She can save this company, and she can handle anything my wife or my mother throws at her." Charles grinned, the same slow, dissipated grin that had become his trademark. "But of course, I'm sure you already know that. I'm sure there is nothing I can tell you about Constance."

"What is *that* supposed to mean?" John David asked shortly.

"Anything you want it to mean, or nothing at all," Charles answered easily. "Believe me, Father, I'm not here to pass judgments. If judgments are to be passed, I would be the first to suffer."

"I guess I'm a little self-conscious," John David answered. He sighed. "But I am glad that you understand what I must do."

"I not only understand, Father, I encourage it," Charles said.

Margaret and Virginia were outraged at the turn at events, but they were unable to do anything about it. John David died, six months after the stroke, and less than two months after taking control away from Charles and giving it to Constance. As he stated he would do, he left fifty-one percent to Constance, and forty-nine percent to Charles. Virginia was left a sizable amount of personal cash, and was guaranteed to be maintained in the manner to which she had become accustomed for as long as the shipping company was able to provide such a standard of living for her. Charles immediately gave six percent of his stock to Margaret's brother, Vernon Coy. Vernon was at the time vice-president of warehousing, and was handling not only his own job, but helping Charles do his as well. The gift of six percent was Charles's method of paying Vernon Coy back for his services. Even though Vernon was Margaret's brother, Margaret protested the transaction vigorously. However, Charles, who seemed to have no gumption, at least had a surefire way of handling his overbearing wife. He simply ignored her.

From that day to this, the distribution of the stock had remained substantially the same. There had been some dissemination of shares, equally apportioned from Constance's holdings and from Charles's holdings, but voting rights had been retained. Today, Constance actually owned only forty-one percent of the company, and Margaret and Miles owned thirty-six percent. The remaining shares had been parceled out as retirement bonuses, though without the right to vote the shares. Constance still voted fifty-one percent, Miles, with his mother's proxy, voted forty-three percent, and Amanda Coy voted six percent.

It was because of that delicate balance that a judgment of noncompetence against Constance would have a permanent effect. For the charter read that the chairman of the board would vote as much of the stock in public as is necessary to give the seat fifty-one percent. If Miles were appointed chairman of the board, even temporarily by the court, he could then elect himself to that position permanently, and legally, merely by exercising the charter. Miles knew that, Constance knew that, Tony Norton, Miles's attorney knew that, and every member of the board knew it. The result would have an immediate and lasting effect on the lives of thousands who were dependent upon Chalmers Shipping in one way or another for their livelihood. For that reason, the conflict between Constance and Miles was thoroughly observed by all as if it were taking place on a stage.

A loud knock on the door disrupted Constance's reflections, and she looked toward it with a start. Never, in all the years since John David had died, had she been disturbed in the Big Room. Even Virginia, for the two remaining years of her life, had stayed away from the Big Room.

"Yes, who is it?" she called.

"Aunt Constance, it's me, Miles. May I come in?"

"Miles, you know I don't like to be disturbed in here."

"But it's about Kristin, Aunt Constance," Miles said.

"Kristin? Yes, yes, of course. Come in, please."

The door opened and Miles came in, followed by Tony Norton and two other men. Miles was carrying a brown paper bag.

"What is it, Miles? Have they found her?"

"No, Aunt Constance," Miles said. He put his arm on her shoulder to comfort her. "You're going to have to be brave, Aunt Constance. It is beginning to look as if I'm right. I'm certain now that she is dead."

"Oh!" Constance gasped, putting her hand to her breast. "What is it?"

Miles opened the sack and pulled out a badly torn dress. "This is her dress. It was found in a warehouse, down on the docks," Miles said. "It has already been identified as hers by several who were at the party. Do you recognize it?"

"Yes," Constance said in a quiet, resigned voice. "It is hers."

"As you can see," Miles went on. "It is badly torn. And here," he turned the material back in his hand, "you can see blood, no doubt."

"Please, please, take it away," Constance said, pushing at it and turning her head aside. "I don't want to see it."

"But, Aunt Constance, you must be reasonable. You must accept the evidence that is available. You can't merely close your mind to it and cease functioning."

Constance knew that Miles was baiting her. She

knew that every word he said was studied to further his case, but she was too grief-stricken to say anything. She could only sob quietly.

"Aunt Constance, really, you should pick up in here," Miles said, looking around the room. "And air it out too. It's terribly stuffy." Miles started toward the newspaper that lay crumpled on the floor.

"No!" Constance suddenly screamed, galvanized by his movement into quick action. "No, leave it alone! Leave everything in this room alone, do you understand? Don't touch a thing! Get out! Get out of here, all of you!"

"Aunt Constance, please, try to control yourself," Miles said easily. "I'm afraid you'll take total leave of your senses if you continue to act in such an irrational manner."

Constance knew exactly what Miles was doing. What's more, she realized that he had, somehow, discovered the secret of the Big Room and knew that she had made it into some sort of a shrine. And he calculated his actions to derive the greatest benefit from her grief. She knew exactly what Miles was doing, and a certain, detached part of her mind was able to look down on the scene and observe the mechanics in perfect detail. But despite all that, she was unable to control herself. Her grief, anger, and fear worked in concert to bring her to the edge of hysteria, and she could only observe with the rational part of herself the action of her irrational being. Seeing and understanding but being unable to do anything about it made it all the worse.

"Leave me alone!" she screamed. "Quit hanging over me and over my granddaughter like some sort of vulture! Get out of here! Get out, get out, get out!"

"Dr. Peters, perhaps you'll leave a draft for Aunt Constance to take to calm her down some," Miles suggested to one of the two men with him.

"He's a doctor?" Constance asked. "You brought a

189

doctor to observe me, and then you baited me? What kind of fiend are you, Miles?"

"I am but a loving nephew, Aunt Constance, concerned with your mental well-being. I forgive you your outburst. I know you don't mean it."

"I mean it!" Constance shouted. "I mean every word of it!" In her anger, and without thinking, she took a book from the table. It was the first time the book had been moved in nearly forty years, but in her rage she didn't stop to think about that. She just grabbed it and threw. Then when she saw what she had done, she screamed again.

Miles led the other three men out of the room and shut the door behind him. He looked at the two doctors with an expression of anguish and concern on his face.

"Gentlemen, as you can see, my aunt's mental condition is deteriorating daily. I'm sorry you had to witness such an unpleasant scene, but I knew that you would want to base your opinions on actual observation."

"You are quite right, Mr. Chalmers," one of the doctors said. "And even without making a clinical examination of your aunt, I am willing to make a declaration of incompetence."

"And you, Doctor?" Miles asked the other.

"I tend to agree with my colleague," the other doctor said. "However, I would prefer a clinical examination, just to further verify what I feel that I already know."

"And that is as it should be, doctor," Norton said in his eloquent, lawyer's voice. "For in the final analysis, this shall be a legal decision, and the judge will certainly want as much information as may be made available to him in rendering the verdict."

Both doctors nodded their heads in solemn agreement, then started down the hall. Behind the doors in the Big Room, they could hear Constance crying, and Tony Norton and Miles Chalmers looked at each other, exchanging a victorious smile.

Chapter Nineteen

SHIP'S LOG, Barkentine *Morning Star,* April 20, 1901.

Three days out of Boston, position 60 degrees west, 36 degrees, 45 minutes north.

Begins fine, with strong, favorable winds. Gasoline bilge pump broken.

Winds hold through middle. 311 miles this day, noon to noon. Have maintained average of 13.6 knots. Must maintain 8.8 average to effect record passage.

Miss Page, who insists that she is the missing heiress, Kristin Chalmers, of the Boston Shipping Chalmers, is calm and cooperative at this time.

Captain Roberts lay the pen down and looked at the entry he had just made. What if the girl was telling the truth? Would this entry be sufficient evidence that he actually believed the girl to be Rose Page? Or would he be held guilty for aiding and abetting kidnapping by keeping the girl aboard the ship by force?

Roberts closed the book angrily, snapping it closed so that the *pop* filled the cabin. What the hell was he doing, anyway? If there was absolutely any chance that the girl was telling the truth, he would put into the nearest port and check it out. He was only two days out of Norfolk, Virginia, right now. Two days out, one or two days in port, then two days back. Six days added onto his passage . . . and the chances were probably one in a thousand that the girl was telling the truth.

No, he would not put into port, and he would not worry about the entries in the log. After all, he had the legal papers on her. And the documentation and evidence of a police officer certainly should carry more weight than the fabrications of a felon. Especially since he was warned about this very thing.

Of course, the girl nearly fooled him once. She had him believing her fantastic tale. Until he realized how she managed to put her story together. Then after they had sex in his cabin, her strange reaction to it merely fortified his opinion that she was just who the police officer claimed she was.

Roberts felt a quick flush of heat and desire as he recalled that incident, but he brushed his hand through his hair as if brushing the thought out of his mind. He got up from his desk and stepped out into the passageway. When he looked through the hatch, he saw the girl leaning over the port rail, looking down at the sea. She was wearing some of Mr. Bright's clothes, but there was no mistaking her for a sailor. Her position at the rail, and the cut of the clothes, greatly accented the shape of her hips and the smooth, feminine line of her thighs and legs. Even the shirt clung to her womanly curves.

Watching her, Roberts felt the return of the flush of desire he had experienced a moment earlier.

It had been nearly two days since the incident in his cabin. He had sent her back to her own cabin because afterward he had suffered greatly from anger and guilt. Anger with himself for not being able to keep his lusts in check, and guilt for forcing himself on the girl.

But the girl puzzled him. She did not seem to harbor any feelings of anger over what had happened. She did not seem to feel used or abused. In fact, she was friendly toward him, almost coquettish. And that reaction reinforced Roberts's belief that she was a prostitute. For after all, any innocent girl so despoiled would scarcely even look at her attacker, let alone converse with him on a friendly basis.

That proved to Roberts that the girl was not only experienced in sexual matters, but, in fact, was adept at using them for her own purposes. And that reasoning led Roberts to believe, somehow, that he was not the attacker but the victim. She had used her sexual charms on him, trying thereby to persuade him to violate his principles and his commission.

As Roberts stood looking at the girl, she seemed to sense his gaze on the nape of her neck and she turned to return his gaze. She smiled prettily.

"It's a beautiful day, Captain. Are you going to take some air?"

Roberts made some noncommittal answer, then turned quickly and disappeared back into the passageway.

Kristin was hurt and puzzled by the captain's odd behavior. Why would he act so? Surely she had displayed by her action that she held no grudge against him for taking advantage of her. She knew that proper behavior dictated that she should be revolted by the sight of him, after what he did. Proper behavior was formulated by society. In the case of her upbringing, Boston society. But Boston society was nine hundred miles behind them. That was another world, another time, even another girl.

"Rose, girl, toss me that belaying pin, would you?" one of the sailors called, and Rose reached for it, then flipped it toward the man who was working with the running rigging.

Perhaps I am Rose, she thought. Perhaps Kristin is dead, and Rose has been reborn.

The more Kristin considered that idea, the more it appealed to her. Oh, she knew that she was the girl who had been Kristin. She had the same flesh, blood, and appearance. But she was not the same girl. Her world had been so drastically changed that the creature who existed now was an entirely new person, born in ordeal and nurtured by the will to survive.

Perhaps she had a premonition of this on that night when she left the others frolicking in the surf and wandered along the beach, vaguely uneasy with the lack of purpose in her life. She remembered the fisherman and the look in his eyes. Despite her situation, she smiled, a small, bitter smile. If she could look that fisherman in the eyes now, she wouldn't blink. She had learned the bitter lesson of survival and had paid her dues, the same as he.

And there, standing at the rail, Kristin came to a new realization. The captain would never be convinced of her true identity, and that meant that this ship wasn't turning around. She was going to San Francisco, and there was nothing she could do about it. Therefore, she had best accommodate herself to the situation.

Kristin sighed, and turned from the rail. She looked toward the passageway again, but Roberts had not come back. She wondered again why the captain was acting so strangely toward her. Could it be that the whispers and the magazine stories were right? Were men such creatures that they wanted only to despoil a girl, and once having accomplished their foul purpose, dismiss her from their minds entirely?

Kristin didn't know the answer to that question. She did know, however, that having sex with Captain Roberts had been more wonderful than her wildest imaginings. But if this was the price a girl paid for it, if she had to be subjected to a man's total rejection afterward, then it was not worth it, for all the thrill of it.

Kristin left the deck and stepped into the galley to pour herself a cup of coffee.

"Who's there?" Josiah called from the pantry.

"It's me," Kristin said. She paused for a moment, then added resignedly, "Rose."

Julian Truax had been waiting for the girl to leave so he could slip down through the forward hatch and get into the bilge unobserved. After she stepped into the galley, Truax looked around, noted the position of every man on the watch, then quickly and quietly raised the hatch and dropped down into the forward hold.

It was dark in the hold, and Truax could hear the groans and creaks of the barrels of molasses as they rode in the pitching ship. He could also hear the trickle of water and he smiled. That meant that his plan had worked.

Truax picked his way through the barrels until he reached the forward seacock. He had loosened the seacock a couple of hours earlier . . . just a few turns to allow a small amount of water to enter. Now he tightened it back, then dried it with a rag, so that when examined the seacock would show nothing. He sounded the bilge and found six inches of water. Good. That wasn't enough water to damage the cargo or endanger the ship. But that much water could slow the speed of the ship, and the captain would want it out. With the gasoline bilge pump out, that meant using the back-breaking hand pumps.

Truax knew that working heel-and-toe watches and manning bilge pumps, while also working constantly to take advantage of the lightest breath of air, would soon wear on the men. They would become tired and irritable and begin to complain. Then they would be ready to listen to some of his ideas. His ideas about organizing.

Truax felt a degree of guilt about what he was doing. After all, plugging up a fuel line so the bilge pump wouldn't work, and opening a seacock to allow water in, was sabotage. But he told himself that he was doing it for a greater good, and the end justified the means.

Truax turned away from the seacock and picked his way back to the hatch cover. He raised it slightly, looked around, and, when he saw that the coast was clear, came back on deck. This wasn't his watch, so he hadn't been missed. But someone might question his being on deck, so he pretended to check lines, until he was near the helm. Gershom was steering, and Mr. Bright was trying to tie a knot.

"Here, sir, would you like me to do that?" Truax offered easily.

"Aye," Bright said. He laughed, a young, boyish laugh. I guess I was much better in navigation than I was in knot tying, while I was in school."

" 'Tis a sailor's job anyway, sir, not an officer's."

"But we're a small crew, Truax, and committed to a common goal. It's best if we work together."

"Aye. As long as the goal is for everyone, and not just the vested few."

Bright looked at Truax with a puzzled expression on his face. "I don't know what you mean by that," he said.

"I mean nothing, sir," Truax said. "Though sometimes I look at the vessels I'm serving on, and I realize the amount of money each passage makes for the ship owner, and how little it makes for these of us who sail her, and I wonder about the fairness of such things."

"Truax, are you an anarchist?" Bright asked.

Truax laughed. "Heavens, no, sir," he said. "But I am a man who thinks. And a man who thinks is not always satisfied with his lot, now is he? After all, sir, isn't that how the world gets ahead? A person isn't satisfied with where he is, so he moves on. That's progress."

"You are a strange one, Truax," Bright said. "I've studied your papers. I know you could be an officer if you wanted. You could probably have your own ship if you wanted. And yet, you're naught but an able-bodied. Why is that?"

"Here you go, sir," Truax said, finishing the knot. He smiled at the young mate's question. "Well, now, why is that, indeed? Perhaps it's because I have a sense of responsibility to my fellowman. Perhaps it's because I know what's right and I feel it's right for me to stay in the forecastle."

"But surely you have some ambition," Bright said.

"Indeed I do, sir," Truax said. "I have a grand and glorious ambition. So grand and so glorious that it is too big for one person, and so I don't have it for myself but for all my fellow sailors. It is my ambition to see dignity and justice for all seamen, regardless of their station."

"You are a man who talks in riddles, sir," Bright said.

"If by that you mean I am a man who asks questions, then I agree with you," Truax said.

"I can understand asking questions," Bright replied, "for I've a few of my own."

"Oh? You are a young man, already an officer, with nothing before you but ships to command. What sort of questions would you have?"

"Well, for one thing, the girl," Bright said.

"The girl?" Truax replied, surprised by the sudden change of subject.

"Yes. Who is she?"

"Why, her name is Rose Page, I've heard."

"That's not who she claims to be," Bright said.

"Who does she claim she is?"

197

"She says she is Kristin Chalmers," Bright said.

"Kristin Chalmers? The granddaughter of the woman who owns Chalmers Shipping?"

"Aye. You've heard of her?" Bright asked.

"Of course I've heard of her. She represents that class of people I've been talking about," Truax said. "She wears fine dresses, and drinks the best wine, and lives in the most elegant mansion because she profits off the misery of the common seaman. It should be the duty of every man jack at sea to know of the likes of her. But what would she be doing on the *Morning Star*? She would go to San Francisco by private railroad car, her kind would."

"That is what one would think, I am certain," Bright said. "But the girl claims to have been kidnapped and brought aboard by force."

"Didn't she come aboard under her own power, but under arrest? Josiah says she walked aboard and he gave her coffee."

"She did," Bright said. "And she told us her name was Rose Page. It was only later, after sleeping for twenty-four hours, that she changed her story. At that time she claimed that she had been given a potion to render her senseless."

"The captain doesn't believe her story though?"

"No," Bright said.

"Do you?"

"I don't know," Bright admitted. "There's something about her . . . a sort of residual quality that someone like Kristin Chalmers would have."

"Do you know someone like Kristin Chalmers?"

Bright smiled. "Not exactly. Although my family probably represents all that you dislike about our society. My father is a factory owner, and quite wealthy in his own right. Nothing to compare with the wealth of the Chalmerses, certainly, but his money has given me entrée into the level of society that is occupied by people like Kristin Chalmers. And that is why I have a nagging doubt in the back of my mind. That mysterious quality that I'm talking about, a sort of acceptance of one's position as a right, can never be acquired. It must be inborn. This girl has that."

"I'm told she's a prostitute," Truax said.

"I . . . I have to admit, Truax, that I've never known a prostitute," Bright said. "So I've no way to make the comparison. Have you?"

Truax laughed.

"Oh, forgive me," Bright said, blushing brightly. "I had no right to ask you such a personal question."

"Bless you, lad, you have every right. You're an officer, and I'm but an AB. But to answer your question, yes, I've known many prostitutes. There's scarcely a sailor afloat, rated or no, who has not. And I dare say that before you set foot in Boston again, you'll be able to make the same statement."

"Are they all like her?" Bright wanted to know. His eyes took on an eager shine, as if to say that if all were like this girl, he would willingly sample their wares.

"No," Truax said. "Though there may be many like her when they start. The life soon tells on them, though, and by the time the poor sailor gets to see them, they are old before their time. Slatterns, the lot of them, either so drawn and haggard that their tits are like ropes, or so fat and brutish that their breasts are like melons. I imagine there are pretty ones like this girl, but they'd be for the very, very rich." He laughed. "I guess it proves there is very little difference between the rich and the poor. The rich just have prettier whores, that's all."

"Mr. Bright, the wind's comin' aroun' sir," Gershom said.

"Aye, we'd better trim the yards then," Bright said.

Truax offered his help, and he and the men of Bright's watch began adjusting the sail.

Chapter Twenty

"Mr. Bright, did you sound the bilges?" Captain Roberts wanted to know.

"Aye, sir," Bright's muffled voice came back. Bright had already gone into the small cabin and climbed into his bunk, when Roberts left the deck to shout the question through the door.

"What was the reading?"

"Less than two inches, Captain."

"When did you sound?"

"When my watch began." The door to the cabin opened and Bright stood just on the other side. He was wearing bright red pajamas, and Roberts nearly laughed aloud. He had never seen a sailor in pajamas, officer or seaman. "Is there something wrong, Captain?"

The question brought the problem back to Roberts's mind. "Aye," he growled. "I just sounded nine inches of water."

"Nine inches? Captain, we must have a leak!"

"That's what I'm afraid of," Roberts said. "And that damned gasoline pump is out. Say, you don't know anything about gasoline engines, do you?"

"No, sir," Bright replied.

"Well, no matter. I guess we can handle it with the manual pumps. But I'll have to keep two men on the pumps for the whole watch. And you'll have to do the same."

"Aye, Captain. Do you need me for anything now?"

"No. You'd better rest while you can. It looks like things are taking a downturn now."

Roberts returned to the quarterdeck. Truax had the helm.

"Truax, didn't I see you up here during Mr. Bright's watch?"

"Aye, sir," Truax said.

"What were you doing?"

"I couldn't rest, sir. I took a turn about the deck, helped young Mr. Bright with trimming the yards when the wind came around. Jawboned awhile."

"Who sounded the bilge for Bright?"

"Pig Iron. He's experienced, Captain. He knew what he was doing."

"Damn it. I know the bottom is sound. I had it hauled out in San Francisco and checked by a diver in Boston. Where's the water coming from?"

"I don't know, sir," Truax said.

"Well, there's no sense crying over spilled milk. McQueen!" Roberts shouted.

"Aye, sir," the big black answered.

"Pick the smallest man. The two of you will man the pumps for two hours. After that, I'll relieve you with another team."

"Aye, Cap'n," McQueen answered.

Kristin heard the pump start, and she stepped out of her cabin and looked toward the mainmast where the manual pump was located. McQueen, his huge, muscular back shining blackly under the sun, worked at the pump effortlessly, while a small, older man named Hunt struggled with the other side. Kristin came up on deck.

"Miss Page, I'm going to have to ask you to stay clear of the pumpmen," Roberts said.

"You needn't worry, Captain," Kristin said. "I'll not be in the way." She walked to the rail and saw the water coming through the pump outlet. It was flowing in a steady stream. "Have we a leak, Captain?"

"Obviously," Roberts said.

"I would have thought you learned your lesson when you ruined your load of wheat. You should have had the leak repaired."

"I did have it repaired," Roberts started, then he stopped. He stared at her for a moment, as if surprised by her statement. Then he smiled at her, a knowing smile, telling her that he wasn't being fooled this time.

"You thought to catch me on that one, did you? No doubt you were going to tell me that you heard all about it when your grandmother bought the ship."

"No, Captain, I'm not going to try to tell you anything," Kristin said.

"Good," Roberts replied. "For that story is well known by the crew by now, and you could have heard it anywhere."

"You're quite right, Captain. I could have."

At that precise moment there was a *pop* as loud as a gunshot, and all eyes looked up to see the main topsail fluttering out like a flag, with part of the mast with it.

"Captain, we've got to get that down, or it'll set up a vibration that'll snap our mainmast," Truax said.

"Thank you, Truax, I'm aware of that," Roberts replied grimly. He started toward the mainmast on a run, and within a few seconds had already scrambled aloft. Kristin shielded her eyes with her hand and watched.

From down below he looked terribly small, and she knew that if he lost his footing or his hold, he would come crashing to the deck, and probably be killed.

"Som'bitch," one of the sailors said. "I ain't never seed no cap'n go aloft like that. He's quite a man."

For some, unexplainable reason, Kristin felt a warm glow of pride over the sailor's comment. She didn't know why. She certainly had no proprietory rights over Captain Roberts. He had been most specific in discouraging that. But she couldn't prevent the feeling, nonetheless.

"Miss Page, could you hold the helm, please?" Truax asked.

"What?" Kristin asked in surprise.

"The captain will need another hand to furl that sail. That'll be me. But the wheel has to be held, or the gaff could swing across and brush us off like a couple of flies."

"Well, yes, I'll do it," Kristin said. "Just show me what to do."

"Nothing much, miss. Just keep her by the compass, sou'-sou'east," Truax said, pointing to the instrument.

Kristin stepped behind the wheel and took it in her hand. She could feel the drag of the water on the rudder and the pull of the wind in the sails. It was somewhat frightening but very thrilling, and when Truax left her with the wheel, it was an exhilarating experience.

Truax started up the mast, but he had no more than started when a rather heavy swell hit the ship. Kristin was unprepared for the sudden pressure the rudder exerted on the wheel, and it jerked out of her hands and began spinning. The ship started to fall away from its course, and the gaff, the upper spar which supported the aft-mounted mainsail, swung around, knocking Captain Roberts off the mast.

Kristin screamed when she saw him fall, and even the pump, which had continued unabated, now stopped, as everyone looked aloft.

Roberts felt the swell and sensed the ship was falling away. Instinctively, he knew that the gaff would have to swing about, and he tried to prepare himself for it. But all this took place in the space of a split second, and he was unable to avoid being brushed off.

Roberts first reaction was anger rather than fear. Anger that he would be the victim of such a land-lubber's trick. For surely no one who had spent as many years at sea and as much time aloft as he could be brushed from a mast by a free gaff. As he tumbled down, he saw the ship below him. He could see the entire deck from jibboom to stern rail, and it seemed frozen in his mind like a painting on canvas. Odd, but he could see every plank, and every knothole, and every rope and every pin, perceiving them as clearly as if he were leisurely studying his vessel from this vantage point. He thought of Mr. Bright, and wondered if Bright would break the passage or return to port after he was dead.

And he thought of the girl. Why now, he wondered? He had spent his entire life going from port to port, and whore to whore, never meeting any woman whose face stayed with him more than an hour after he left her. But now it was different. This girl was with him in body and in spirit, all the time. Not just because she was on the ship with him, because he saw her even when she wasn't there. She had taken over his very soul . . . though until this moment he had never been able to admit it, even to himself.

And now it was too late, because he was about to die.

A rope passed into Roberts's vision, and he made a desperate grab for it. He missed it with his hand but caught it with his leg. He whipped his leg around the rope, feeling it burn as he slid through it, then finally feeling it catch as it formed a loop around his ankle.

The rope was part of the dangling stay from the broken topsail mast, and since it wasn't secured at the bottom, it swung free. Roberts hung from it like a human pendulum, and he was unable to stop himself as he swung in a long, sweeping arc, carried by the momentum of his fall into the gaff, which was now swinging back toward him. They came together in a crack that could be heard on deck, and Roberts was immediately knocked cold.

Kristin's scream had lasted just under a second, beginning when she saw Roberts fall and ending in a choking sob when she saw him get fouled in the rope and knocked out by the swinging gaff. Roberts hung by one ankle, his arms stretching toward the deck, swinging slightly now, like an animal in a snare.

"Oh, my God!" Kristin gasped. "Oh, I killed him!"

"No, you didn't, miss," McQueen said. The big black man was to the wheel in an instant, and he grabbed it and held the ship steady on course.

"I have it, Truax," he shouted up. "You get the cap'n."

"Lash the gaff," Truax shouted down.

By now the below watch was on deck, and Bright and Gershom hurried to lash the gaff to keep it from swinging back. Pig Iron climbed the mast with Truax.

"You, Pig Iron," Truax said. "I'm going to tie this line around the captain, then pass it over the spreader. You lower him to the deck."

Kristin watched with her heart in her mouth as the men worked. Truax worked his way out toward the captain, inching out on the sheet itself since there was no solid support at this point, holding to the top of the canvas and fighting the billowing effect as it answered the wind.

"I wouldn't do that for me own mother," one of the men said.

"A good puff 'n he's a goner," another replied.

There was absolute silence after that, as if even the spoken word could raise enough wind to alter the shape of the sail. Finally, after painstakingly inching his way out, Truax reached Roberts, and, holding onto the sail with one hand, he passed his slipknot loop over Roberts and freed his ankle.

"Hold onto it, Pig Iron. I'm going to cut the stay now."

"I got 'im," Pig Iron said.

Truax pulled a knife from his belt and started cutting at the stay which had grabbed Roberts's ankle. The rope was new and tough, and it took several seconds before he was able to cut through it. Finally, a loose piece of rope dropped to the deck, and when it first started to fall, Kristin, not knowing what it was, gasped.

"Easy, Rose. It's naught but the stay," Josiah said, and Kristin noticed that he was standing right beside her.

"Gershom, take the helm," McQueen called. "I'll get the cap'n when Pig Iron lets 'im down."

Gershom moved over to the wheel, and McQueen went out on deck, standing below the gently lowering body of Captain Roberts, holding his arms up, waiting to catch him.

"Easy, lads, easy with 'im now," Josiah said, stepping over to stand by McQueen.

McQueen took Roberts in his hand, and, holding him like a baby, carried him into his cabin. Kristin anxiously followed alongside.

"Put him in his bed," she said.

"You know anythin' about doctorin', Rose?" Josiah asked anxiously.

"No, I'm afraid not."

"I thought whores was kinda like nurses," Josiah said.

Josiah made the statement in all innocence, and Kristin was much too worried about the fate of Captain Roberts to take offense.

"I don't need any doctoring," Roberts said, coming around about then. He grimaced in pain. "Just let me lie here for a few minutes, I'll be all right."

"You sure, Captain? That was a pretty nasty blow you took. I think we should put into port," Mr. Bright suggested.

"No!" Roberts shouted, and the effort caused him to wince in a new spasm of pain. "No," he said again, softly. "We'll not break this passage."

"You go on about your business," Kristin said. "I'll watch over him."

Mr. Bright took one more look at the captain, then signaled to the others that they should leave. "Call me if anything happens," he told Kristin.

"Now just what the hell do you think is going to happen?" Roberts asked dryly. His eyes were tightly shut as he spoke, as if opening them would cause more pain.

"I, uh, well, uh, had better get back on deck," Bright said. The others had left at his signal, and now he too departed, leaving only Kristin and Captain Roberts.

"Why do you have to be so rough on everyone?" Kristin asked. "Are you afraid someone might get too close to you?"

"I thought about you," Roberts said.

"What?"

"Up there, when I started falling. My last thoughts were of you."

"They were?" Kristin asked, puzzled by the remark. "Why was that?"

But Captain Roberts couldn't answer her because he had passed out again.

Chapter Twenty-one

SHIP'S LOG, Barkentine *Morning Star*, April 21, 1901

Four days out of Boston, position 58 degrees West, 33 degrees, 30 minutes North.

Entry made by James Bright, First Officer.

Captain Andrew Roberts is laid up in his quarters with a bad bump on head, having suffered a blow from a swinging gaff. The blow has rendered him senseless at times, though there are times when he is quite lucid. He is being cared for by Miss Rose Page.

Winds have held, but due to loss of main topsail,

the speed has been greatly reduced. 166 miles this day, noon to noon. That averages to 6.9 knots.

Sounded bilges after pumping all water out. Level remaining constant ½ inch. The leak must have sealed itself.

James Bright signed the log with a flourish, noting with some satisfaction that this was the first logbook he had ever signed. It was unfortunate that the captain had to be injured in order to give the opportunity, but the circumstances did not detract from his pride of the moment.

There was a knock on the door of his cabin.

"Yes," he called out.

"Mr. Bright, it is I, Rose Page," Kristin called.

"Come in, please," Bright invited.

Kristin opened the door and stepped into the cabin. She was surprised at how small the first officer's cabin was. Smaller even than hers, and hers was not as large as the closet in her bedroom at home.

"What can I do for you, Miss Page?"

"The captain needs medical attention," Kristin said. "I'm afraid he has a skull fracture."

"I'm sorry, Miss Page. We have no ship's surgeon, I'm afraid. Our ship is much too small for that."

"I know you have no surgeon," Kristin said. "That's why I'm coming to you. You are the acting captain now. You must put in to a port, Mr. Bright. You must."

"Put in? Break the passage?" Bright replied. "No, no, I can't do that."

"You can't do it? But you must! Unless you want the captain to die!"

"Die? Surely he won't die. I mean, if he were going to die, wouldn't the blow have killed him immediately?"

"Not necessarily," Kristin said. "I don't know anything about medicine, Mr. Bright, but common sense tells me that if he continues to lose consciousness, then something is severely wrong."

"I . . . I don't know," Bright stammered. "The captain was quite specific, Miss Page. He gave me explicit instructions not to break the passage of this ship. I dare not do so. To violate those instructions could be grounds for having my papers revoked."

"And obeying them could mean that you are killing the captain," Kristin said. "How would that look to a board of inquiry? It could well appear that you took advantage of this accident to further your own maritime career."

"No, of course not!" Bright said. "Who could possibly think such a thing?"

"Anyone might, if they saw that you could have saved the captain's life by putting in for medical assistance and didn't do so. Believe me, Mr. Bright, he could die if he is not treated."

"I . . . I don't know what to do," Bright said.

For a moment, Kristin felt genuinely sorry for the young man. This was his first voyage, and he had suddenly been thrust into command. Now he had his first command decision to make, and it was a tough one. Should he follow the instructions of his captain, and continue the passage, or should he make his own decision and put into port to seek medical assistance?

"Mr. Bright," Kristin said softly. "You can't be held in contempt of orders if you do what you think best, under these circumstances. Captain Roberts may not have even been in his right mind when he ordered you to continue on. You know yourself he has been insensible at times since the injury."

"Yes," Bright said. "Yes, you're right. I'll put into port," he looked at the map. "I'm putting into Bermuda," he said. "That's the nearest landfall."

"Fine, fine," Kristin said. "Anyplace where there might be a doctor is fine with me. But hurry, Mr. Bright. Change course at once."

"All right," Bright said.

"Thank you. Thank you very much."

Bright and Kristin left Bright's cabin, but just before they started up the ladderway to the deck, Bright turned to look at her. "Miss Page, if I am making an error," he said, pointing at her. "If I am making an error . . ."

"Yes?" Kristin said, looking at him coolly and evenly.

Mr. Bright returned her gaze for a moment, then smiled self-consciously. "If I am making an error, I'll live with it," he said. "It probably won't be my last one."

"Mr. Bright, you've the makings of a good commander about you," Kristin said.

Kristin followed Bright onto the deck, then, as Bright gave the new heading to the helmsman, she returned to the captain's cabin.

Roberts had been nauseous and dizzy, and for the last twenty-four hours he had had long periods of unconsciousness. She had been very concerned over him, but his pulse had stayed strong and constant, and she was certain that that was a good sign. But when he was conscious, he couldn't remember what had happened, and he asked her once or twice what he was doing here, and she was sure that was a bad sign.

Roberts appeared to be resting comfortably when she returned, and she sat in the chair she had placed by his bunk and looked at him. His breathing was steady and unlabored, and that was reassuring.

There was a knock at the door.

"Yes? Who is it?"

"It's Julian Truax, miss. I thought I might have a look at the captain, if you don't mind."

"No, of course I don't mind," Kristin said. "I'm terribly worried. He keeps passing out."

Truax lifted an eyelid and stared at the captain's pupils. "The pupils are of equal size," he said. "That is

211

a good sign. Has he passed any clear fluid from his nose or ears?"

"No," Kristin said.

"Has there been any bleeding from the nose or ears?"

"No."

"Any twitching of the face muscles?"

"No," Kristin answered again. She looked at Truax in surprise. "Mr. Truax, have you had medical training?"

"Of a sort," Truax said. "I was assistant to a ship's surgeon. I know some of the signs to look for, but I don't know what to do if I find them."

"Well, what do you think about the captain? Is his injury serious?"

"Maybe not too bad," Truax said. "But I think Mr. Bright is right to put in to Bermuda. It would be best for a real doctor to have a look at him."

"I'm glad you agree," Kristin said. "Oh, and if no one has thanked you for him, let me say that it was a brave and fine thing you did to save his life."

"You like the captain, don't you?" Truax said.

"Yes," Kristin said. "Yes, I do." And even as she answered his question, she wondered if it could be said that she more than liked him. Could it be said that she loved him?

"Do you think your grandmother would approve of your taking up with a common sailor?" Julian asked.

"He is not just a common sailor," Kristin said. She looked at Truax with a strange expression on her face. "Why would you ask such a question, anyway? What makes you think I even have a grandmother?"

"You are still a young girl, miss," Truax answered easily. "I would say that the chances are very good that you have a grandmother."

"Well, I . . . I do. Still, in view of what everyone around here regards as my profession, that seems a strange question for you to pose."

"Perhaps so," Truax said, not offering any explanation. "I'd keep him warm, miss," he said, changing the subject. "I've got to go now. Call me if you think I can be of any help."

"I will," Kristin said. "And thank you."

Kristin stared at the door, even after the sailor left. There was something about him that disturbed her, and it nagged away at the back of her mind. There was something frightening about him, though he didn't seem ominous. What was it then? What was it that caused a thread of fear to weave its way through her?

"Is it time for my watch?" Roberts asked.

Kristin turned around and saw Captain Roberts trying to sit up.

"No," she said. "You must stay in bed."

"Stay in bed? What for?"

"Because you've had a nasty bump on the head."

"You aren't telling me anything that I don't already know, girl. I can feel it," Roberts said. He put his hand to the back of his head and touched it gingerly. "Ooooh," he said. "God, that hurts."

"Then you understand why you must lie down," Kristin said, gently putting her hands on his shoulders and pushing back.

"Of all the fool things to happen to me," Roberts said. "To get brushed off by a gaff."\

"Then you remember? You know what happened?"

"Of course," Roberts said.

"That's a good sign," Kristin said.

Roberts looked at her with a funny expression on his face. "Look here, have I been awake and not been able to remember what happened?"

"Yes."

"Uhmm, that's bad," he said. "I can see why you were worried. But, things are better now. I remember everything."

"Everything?"

"Yes. I remember climbing the mast to cut the top-sail loose. And I know you had the helm when the gaff swung across."

Kristin looked down in embarrassment and guilt.

"Rose, don't fret any about that," Roberts said easily and surprisingly gently, considering the way his behavior had been at times. "You couldn't help that. Why, with the broken stayline and the heavy swell, there aren't many who could have held her. It wasn't your fault, girl, and I don't want you worrying over it."

"You don't know how good that makes me feel," Kristin said.

"I'm hungry," Roberts said. "I think I'll go get something to eat." He sat up quickly, but when he did so, a wave of dizziness and nausea overcame him, and he nearly fell back down.

"No, wait," Kristin said. "You stay there, I'll bring you something."

"I'll not be waited on like an invalid, girl." Roberts tried to stand up but he couldn't.

"Then go ahead," Kristin said archly. "And after you've had a bite to eat, you may want to take a few quick runs around the deck."

"You've made your point," Roberts said. "If it wouldn't trouble you any, I would appreciate it if you would have Josiah fix something for me."

"I'll bring you something. You just wait here," Kristin said.

Kristin started for the door, and Roberts lay back on the bunk. "I did think about you," he said.

"What?" She turned to look at him and saw that he was eyeing her with a small, self-conscious grin.

"Up there. When I fell. They say a man's life flashes before his eyes. Mine didn't. But I did think about you."

"I'll get you something to eat," Kristin said, feeling a quick thrill over Captain Roberts's words. Maybe he hadn't rejected her after all. "We can talk about it when I return, if you'd like."

Kristin left the cabin and started toward the galley.

"Miss Page," Bright called.

Kristin stopped, then walked over to the young officer.

"How is he?"

"He is conscious," she said. "He seems to be doing well for the moment."

"He does? Then do you still think we should put in to Bermuda?"

"Absolutely," Kristin said. "Just because he is feeling better is no sign that he doesn't need medical attention."

"But if he's conscious, don't you think he should be allowed to make that decision?" Bright asked.

Kristin thought of Bright's question. In truth, she was about convinced that the injury was not as serious as she first feared. But she knew that if they didn't put into Bermuda, they wouldn't put in anywhere. And she would have lost her last opportunity to prove her identity. So for that reason more than any other, she was insistent that they land there.

"You know what he would say, Mr. Bright," Kristin finally said. "But just because he is lucid now doesn't mean he is entirely rational. I would say that the decision is still yours to make."

Bright folded both arms across his chest and leaned against the rail. Kristin wanted to laugh, for she had seen Roberts assume this same posture many times, and she wondered if Bright knew he was imitating his commander. "You are right," Bright finally said. "The decision is still mine to make. And I say we will go into Bermuda."

"Good," Kristin said. "Oh, but Mr. Bright, I wouldn't mention it to him yet if I were you. It would upset him, I'm sure, and that wouldn't be good for him in his present condition."

"You're right," Bright said. "Very well, I shall say nothing."

Kristin smiled, then left the young officer and continued on her mission. When she reached the galley, she saw Truax and Josiah drinking coffee.

"How's the cap'n?" Josiah asked.

"He's awake, and he's hungry," Kristin said.

"Hungry? That's good, ain't it?" Josiah said, smiling broadly. "Well, I'll fix him up good. I'll make him a big stew of . . ."

"A clear broth would be better," Truax interrupted.

"A clear broth?" Josiah said. "That ain't even like eatin'."

"Nevertheless, I agree with Mr. Truax," Kristin said. "A clear broth is what would do him the most good."

"All right, I reckon I can come up with that," Josiah said. Josiah got up and started picking through his condiments to prepare the broth. Kristin sat at the table, then looked over at Truax. She remembered again that there was something about him that was frightening, but still she was unable to put her finger on it.

"Tell me, Miss Page," Truax said. "Now that you've seen the plight of the common sailor . . . what do you think?"

"I don't understand your question."

"Well, it's just that all the fancy-dress parties and dinners, the fine homes and carriages, the luxuries that the ship owners enjoy are paid for by the blood and sweat of men like the ones you see on board this ship. Now that you have seen this side of it, do you think the sailor is treated fairly?"

"Why do you say now that I have seen this side of it?" Kristin asked, raising one eyebrow, "as if you assumed that I had seen the other side?"

"I assumed that you had."

"Why?"

"Miss Page, you are no ordinary woman," Truax said. "You are very beautiful and very cultured. I am certain that in your lifetime, you have attended the functions of the wealthy. I thought you might be able to draw a comparison."

"Oh," Kristin said. "Uh, yes, I guess I have attended a few of the functions of society."

Now Kristin knew why there was something about Truax that frightened her. She realized, from the tone of the conversation, that he may know who she was. But why should she be afraid? If he knew who she was, then couldn't he help her convince Captain Roberts? But, she also realized, he may know who she is because he is in league with those who kidnapped her in the first place. Was he alone on the ship, or were others with him? Was he her salvation or her most dangerous enemy? She had no idea of whether to trust him or not. Some instinct told her it was better for her, at the moment, to continue to play the game with Truax and to protect her true identity.

"It's nearly time for the watch change," Truax said. "I'd best get ready." He drained the last of his coffee, then left the galley. Josiah, who had the broth on the stove now, sat down across the table from Kristin. He picked up an empty can and spit into it before he spoke.

"I'm not sure I like that fella," he said.

"Why not?" Kristin asked.

"They's just somethin' about him that don't quite ring true, is all. He's a slick talker."

"He did save Captain Roberts's life," Kristin reminded him.

"Aye, he did do that," Josiah said. He looked at Kristin with narrowed eyes. "I don't mind tellin' you, miss, they's somethin' about you that don't ring true, neither."

"What is that?" Kristin asked.

"I don' know. I can't quite call it up to mind. But they's somethin' about you, 'n that's a fact."

Kristin smiled at Josiah. "What if I told you I was a witch, come to hex this ship?"

She had said it jokingly, hoping to elicit a laugh, or at least a smile from Josiah. But his eyes stayed narrowed and his face wrinkled, and he never cracked a smile.

"I might be believin' that," he said seriously.

Chapter Twenty-two

By the time the broth was done, the watch had changed, and when Kristin left the galley with the bowl of soup, she saw that the sun was setting in a magnificent display of color. Because of the altered course, the ship was headed nearly due west, and the bowsprit stretched out toward the setting sun, now a great orange disk, balanced like a ball on the horizon.

Just before the sun and stretching all the way to the *Morning Star* was a wide band of red, laid out before them as if someone had spread a carpet of roses in a magnificent welcome. The ship seemed poised on the road of roses, traveling down it as if it was a great highway. The few clouds that dotted the western sky had purpled, and even the billowing white sails of the ship were rimmed crimson by the sun.

"It's a lovely sight, isn't it, miss?" Julian Truax said, stepping up beside her.

"Yes," Kristin said, so taken with the beauty of the moment that she forgot to be uneasy around this strange man. "Until I came aboard this vessel, I had never seen the sunset at sea."

"It must be one of God's favorite sights," Truax said. "For he made the world seven-eighths ocean."

The surprising depth of feeling in Truax's voice somewhat embarrassed Kristin, and she coughed self-consciously. "I must get this broth to the captain," she said, excusing herself.

"Yes, ma'am. Good evening now," Truax said, touching his eyebrow in a small salute. The gesture was just short of mocking, and Kristin didn't know whether to be angered or amused. She decided to let it pass without a reaction and continued on her errand.

When she returned to the cabin, Captain Roberts was lying on his bunk again with his arms folded across his eyes. She thought he was asleep again or perhaps passed out.

"Captain Roberts?" she called, cautiously. "Captain Roberts, are you all right?"

"Aye, lass," Roberts's muffled voice came back. "I was just resting my eyes for a bit. This bump has left me with a headache."

"And it's no wonder," Kristin said. "You took a very bad hit, Captain. Here, I've brought something for your supper."

"Ah, good," Roberts said. He sat up. "What is it?"

"A nice broth," Kristin said.

"A broth?" Roberts complained. "Surely you don't call that supper."

"Can you truly eat more, Captain?"

Roberts looked at the bowl of broth for a moment, then grinned, a sheepish, almost boyish grin. "No," he finally said. "I don't suppose I can."

"Then try, at least, to get this broth into your stomach," Kristin said. She set the bowl on the dropdown table, and Roberts moved to the head of his bed to reach it. He dipped the spoon into the liquid and started it toward his mouth, but halfway there his hand started shaking and he had to put the spoon back in the bowl.

"Are you all right?" Kristin asked.

"Aye," Roberts said. "Just a bit woozy for a moment, that's all."

"Let me," Kristin offered. She took the spoon and held it to Roberts's mouth.

"Look at me," Roberts said. "Getting fed like a baby."

"Hush," Kristin said, wiping gently at his mouth with a napkin.

As Kristin fed him, Roberts began to gain strength with each spoonful. When the last bit had been consumed and Kristin was about to put the bowl away, Roberts wrapped his hand around her wrist. His grip was surprisingly strong.

"Don't leave, just yet," he said.

Kristin looked at his hand around her wrist, then smiled at him. "Why, Captain, how strong your grip is. Could it be that you have deceived me? Could you have fed yourself?"

"Perhaps so," Roberts admitted. "But I was enjoying it so that I saw little reason to change the situation."

"I won't leave you, just yet," Kristin said. "But I must put the bowl away lest a swell drop it on the bed." She removed her wrist from his grip and set the bowl across the table, bracing it with a crossbeam to keep it from sliding around. She looked at Roberts and smiled, remembering what he had told her earlier. "You said you thought of me."

"Aye," Roberts said. "As I was falling."

"What kind of thought."

"I think you know," Roberts said. "It was about us . . . about what we did."

It was funny, but though Kristin had only pleasant thoughts about what had happened between the two of

221

them, the fact that Roberts had mentioned it . . . brought it out into the open that way, suddenly caused her embarrassment. Her face flamed pink, and she looked down, quickly, with demure eyes. "I . . . I've thought of it too, Captain."

"Andrew," Roberts said.

"I beg your pardon?"

"Call me Andrew, please."

"Only if you call me . . ." Kristin started, then stopped. She was going to suggest that he call her Kristin, but she knew it would just cause trouble between them, so she stopped in midsentence and said, "Rose."

"Rose it is," Andrew said.

"You're not married, Andrew?" Kristin asked.

"No. Marriage is not for the seafaring man. I'm afraid I'm not cut out for it."

The reply stung Kristin slightly. Of course, any talk of marriage at this point was absurd anyway, and she had just asked the question as a conversational gambit. Still, she felt as if she had somehow been rejected.

"Of course, I'm certain that you would understand that yourself," Andrew went on. You're obviously not the marrying kind either."

"Why would you say that?"

"Well, now. What man would . . ." Andrew started, then stopped and cleared his throat nervously.

"What man would marry the likes of me?" Kristin finished for him, arching her eyebrows.

"What I meant to say was, what man could catch your fancy? I mean you knowing so many and all."

"Captain Roberts . . ."

"Andrew," Andrew corrected again.

"Andrew, maybe I had better explain something to you," Kristin said.

Andrew held up his hand. "No," he said. "Don't explain anything to me. Explanations are not needed."

"But it's not like you think," Kristin said. In her effort to make him understand, she sat on the bed next to

222

him, hoping that by her nearness, her intensity could be measured and Andrew would perceive the truth.

"It doesn't matter," Andrew said. He put his arms around her and drew her to him for a kiss. It was a kiss of passion, of soul and of feeling, and its suddenness caught Kristin unaware. Without an opportunity to muster her defenses against it, she found herself responding fully. Her mouth opened as she felt the strength of his kiss growing. She leaned against him as if she had turned to molten metal, melting to his searing kiss.

"I do not want it to be rape this time," Andrew said, finally breaking off the kiss. "I want it only if you want it as well."

"Yes, Andrew," Kristin said, her breath coming now in sharp gasps. "Yes, my darling, I want it. Oh, how I want it!"

Andrew smiled at her, though by now the light had completely faded with the setting of the sun, and she sensed, more than saw, his grin. He began removing his clothes.

"I'll lock the door if you don't mind," Kristin said, "I don't want anyone coming in on us."

"No one would dare come into my cabin without my permission," Andrew said. "But if it makes you feel better, be my guest," he invited. "I'll even close the port if you wish, so that no one will hear us and . . ." Roberts stopped in midsentence. "What is the *North Star* doing there?"

"What?"

"The *North Star*," Andrew said. "It's . . . my God! We're badly off course! We are sailing west!"

Andrew rebuttoned his shirt quickly and started for the door, but Kristin intercepted him. "Andrew, no, wait!" she called.

"Wait! I can't wait, girl! Don't you realize what this means? I have no idea how long we've been off course! Think of the time we've lost!"

"We're not off course!" Kristin said.

"What do you mean?" Andrew asked, stopping to look at her in bewilderment. "We're supposed to be sailing south-sou'west."

"We are heading for Bermuda," Kristin said.

Andrew, who was halfway to the door, came a few paces back toward her. "What?" he asked in a small, surprised voice.

"I talked Mr. Bright into altering course," Kristin explained.

"You did *what?*" Andrew shouted.

"We had to, don't you see? You were badly hurt, Andrew. You could have died! We had to get you to a doctor!"

"And, no doubt, allow you to escape?" Andrew asked in biting tones.

"No," Kristin said.

"No?" Andrew said. "You mean you had no intention of leaving the ship?"

"Well, yes," Kristin stammered. "But I wasn't going to try to escape, actually. I was just going to establish my true identity."

"Your true identity? And who are you now, miss? The niece of the president of the United States? Or perhaps the Princess Royal of England?"

"I am just who I have always said I am," Kristin said. "I am Kristin Chalmers, and I can prove it in Bermuda!"

"No," Andrew said, angrily. "You can't prove it in Bermuda because we aren't going there."

"But you must," Kristin said. "You must!" She reached for him, but he pushed her away angrily and roughly. So roughly that she nearly lost her balance and had to reach out for the table to keep from falling.

"Get your hands off me," he said angrily. He opened the door and stepped out through the passageway and onto the deck. "Mr. Bright!" he bellowed. "Mr. Bright, here at once!"

"Aye, aye, sir?" the young mate answered.

"What were your orders, Mr. Bright, with regard to course?"

"South-sou'west, sir," Bright said.

"And what is our course now, Mr. Bright?"

"Nearly due west, sir," Bright admitted quietly.

"And may I ask, sir, how came we by such a course?"

"At my orders, sir."

"Your orders, Mr. Bright? *Your* orders?" Andrew yelled. "And by what right did you give such orders?"

"By discretionary right," Bright said. "I was temporarily in command."

"No, Mr. Bright. You were never in command. You were merely officer of the deck underway. And I am relieving you of even that responsibility as of now."

"Yes, sir," the young officer said, his face flushing a deep, deep scarlet.

"You can't do that!" Kristin yelled.

"Josiah!" Andrew shouted.

"Aye, Cap'n?"

"Kindly see to this woman," he yelled.

"Rose, come along with me now," Josiah pleaded gently.

"I am not Rose. Do you understand me? My name is not Rose. I am Kristin Chalmers! *Kristin Chalmers!*"

"Helm!"

"Aye, Cap'n."

"Come to course south-sou'west!"

"Aye, Cap'n."

"Don't turn your back on me!" Kristin shouted, in anger and frustration, as Andrew stepped up to the quarterdeck. "I'll have you stripped of your command for this!"

"Rig the skysails," Andrew ordered, paying no attention to Kristin's shouting.

"Aye, Cap'n," Gershon said.

"Listen to me!"

"Josiah, I told you to see to that woman. Now you get that whore below deck at once!"

"How *dare* you!"

"Come along, miss, please," Josiah said. He reached for her.

"No," Kristin said, jerking away from Josiah's reach.

"Cap'n, I . . . I can't handle her," Josiah said.

Andrew laughed, a wild, wicked, angry laugh. "What's the matter, Josiah? Have you grown too old for a spirited woman? Very well, then I shall give it to someone a bit younger. Mr. Bright?"

"Aye, sir?"

"Take this woman belowdecks."

Mr. Bright looked at Andrew. He was still smarting from having been relieved, and then he looked at the hellcat of a woman standing there on the middeck with her hands on her hips and her eyes blazing fire. She was more than he wanted.

"Captain, I . . ." Bright started, his voice pleading already to be relieved of this odious task.

"Well, then, is there no one but me who can handle her?" Andrew shouted.

"Come along, Mr. Bright," Kristin finally said. "I will go with you."

"Careful with him, Rose," Andrew shouted. "He's a bit young yet." He laughed again, the same, wild, wicked, angry laugh as before. Oddly, the sailors were very quiet. They realized even if the captain didn't that his anger was brought on by hurt feelings. And the hurt feelings betrayed his genuine attraction for her. They knew that if they joined in his mockery, or even laughed at his cruel jests, they could be opening Pandora's box, and might be forced to close it later. Thus they thought it best to remain silent.

Kristin went into her cabin, followed closely by Mr. Bright. As soon as she was in her cabin, she crossed to the porthole and stared out at the reflection of the moon on the water. She, like Andrew, was hurt and angry, and she wanted to cry. She needed desperately to cry, to let it all out of her, but the tears wouldn't come. She made a fist and pounded on the wall beside the port, but try as she may the tears wouldn't come.

She needed some relief, some catharsis for her soul, or the anger and hurt and frustration would fester inside until it burst wide open, filling her body with poisons. If only there was some way she could get even with him, she reasoned. Some way to punish him for what he had done and was doing.

"Are you going to be all right now, ma'am?" she heard Bright's voice behind her.

At the sound of Mr. Bright's voice, Kristin knew what she must do. She turned to look at him. A moment before, she had been unable to bring forth tears of anger. But now, with feminine wiles, she was able to fill her eyes with tears of despair.

"Please," Mr. Bright said. "Please don't cry. I don't like to see a lady cry."

"I can't help it," Kristin said. She moved over to him and put her head on his shoulder. She began crying, and Mr. Bright instinctively put his arms around her. That was just what Kristin wanted, and she took advantage of it. She leaned against him, pressing her body against his, knowing full well that he would be able to feel the soft, heavy warmth of her breasts, and the insistent pressure of her flat stomach and thighs against his body. And within a short time she was rewarded by the sudden appearance of a bulge in his pants.

Mr. Bright drew away abruptly. "I'm sorry, Miss Page. Please forgive me. I had no right to take advantage of you like that!"

Kristin looked up at him and smiled, then held him in a long, penetrating gaze. Mr. Bright, almost as if acting without control over his own motor functions, moved his lips to hers in a kiss.

Though he was young, and, she guessed, inexperienced, his kiss was firm and possessive. It was more of

227

a kiss than those she had shared with the young men of society who attended the endless whirl of social functions, but it nevertheless was the kiss of a gentleman. It went only so far, and then it stopped.

"I . . . I'm sorry," he said, pulling away from her again.

"Don't keep apologizing, Mr. Bright," Kristin said. She knew now that she was going to seduce the young officer. It would serve the high and mighty Captain Andrew Roberts right, she felt. It would be sweet revenge for his actions. That was the only reason she was going to do it, she told herself. But even as she told herself this, she knew it was a lie. For already she could feel her blood flowing hot in her veins, and her breath came in short, ragged gasps. She was doing this because she wanted it! She wanted this young man!

Kristin looked at Mr. Bright's handsome, young features. They were probably just a few months apart in age, but, oddly, she felt many years older than he.

"Do you have a girl friend, Mr. Bright?" she asked.

"No, ma'am," Bright answered, swallowing hard.

"Have you ever had a girl?"

"A girl friend?"

"No," Kristin answered. She leaned into him. "You know what I mean. Have you ever made love to a girl?"

"N . . ." Mr. Bright started to say, but he stumbled over the word, coughed, then tried again. "No," he finally managed.

"Would you like to?" She rubbed his fingers across her lips, then took just the tips of them inside her mouth and sucked them.

"Are you . . . are you what they say you are?" Mr. Bright asked. "Are you a . . ." he swallowed hard. "Are you a whore?"

"I'll be anything you want," Kristin said seductively, putting her arms around Mr. Bright's neck and pulling him to her for another kiss.

From that moment, Mr. Bright became disassociated from reality. All thought and feeling were blotted out, with the exception of the white heat of the kiss and the spreading fire of his sexual arousal.

Somehow, he found himself in bed with her, feeling her wonderfully smooth skin, her soft curves and delightfully firm breasts. Her passionate, skillful love making beckoned him to the ultimate explosion. It wasn't until several moments later that Mr. Bright realized that it was all over, and that he had just been introduced to sex with a degree of intensity which so overwhelmed him that all other senses had been redirected to cope with it.

"Mr. Bright, if you are quite finished now, I could use your services above. We've a storm building," Andrew Roberts said coldly, his words falling like ice on a deck.

"Captain, my God!" Mr. Bright said, rolling quickly to one side and grabbing a blanket in a vain attempt to shield himself.

"Andrew, no!" Kristin said, gasping and covering her mouth in shame.

Andrew reached into his pocket and pulled out a coin. He tossed it into the cabin, and it hit on the floor with a metallic clang, then rolled up under the bunk.

"That should pay for his fun, Miss Page," Andrew said in a low, seething tone. "After all, it is tradition for a sailor's first experience to be financed by his shipmates."

"Captain, it wasn't like that," Mr. Bright said, trying desperately to get dressed. "You don't understand. Tell him, Miss Page."

"Please," Kristin said, now finding the tears which were so tightly locked up before. "Please, both of you. Just leave me. I beg of you, leave me alone."

Chapter Twenty-three

"Mr. Bright, we're into heavy seas," Andrew said when young Bright sheepishly reported to him on deck a few moments later. "We'll be needing your help to take in sail."

"Aye, aye, sir," Bright said. "Have the hands been turned to?"

"That they have, Mr. Bright," Andrew replied. "Had you not been otherwise occupied, perhaps you too would have heard the call."

"I'm sorry, sir," Bright said, his face flushing a brilliant red, though, thankfully, it was shielded by the dark of the night.

As Andrew had stated, a quick-building storm had hit them, and the *Morning Star* was plowing through heavy seas. As her bowsprit dipped and poked through a large swell, the wave broke over the bow and threw its spray the entire length of the deck.

"Reef the topsails," Andrew ordered, and the order was repeated by Mr. Bright. A handful of sailors, led by Julian Truax, scrambled up the foremast, as it was the only mast that was square-rigged, and thus required hands aloft to furl sail. "See that there is a proper furl, Truax," Andrew shouted into the wind.

"Aye, aye, Captain," Truax shouted back, his voice sounding thin in the wind that now buffeted them.

The wind was blowing with gale force now, and the ship was crashing violently through the waves. Andrew steadied himself at the rail and watched the men work. They furled the topsail with enough authority to satisfy him, but the wind continued to build until suddenly the great mainsail on the foremast ripped open from top to bottom.

"Pig Iron! Grab some men and lay up to furl that sheet before it blows to tatters," Andrew ordered.

"Aye, Cap'n," Pig Iron replied. "Sanders, Duke, with me!" he shouted.

The men climbed the mast and began working on the torn sail, but no sooner had they finished with it than the mizzen topsail tore loose and began flapping in the breeze, threatening to pull away and take with it the top part of the mizzenmast, which was now vibrating like a wand.

"Damn!" Andrew swore. "Gershom, take the helm, I've got to get up there."

"You're in no condition to go, Cap'n," Mr. Bright said. He started for the mizzenmast. "I'll go up."

Mr. Bright was in the rigging as soon as he shouted and within seconds was nearly to the errant sail. But now the howling wind was of near-hurricane velocity, and the mountainous waves were battering against the hull of the ship with the impact of a cannon ball. The *Morning Star* would be lifted by one swell, hang quivering over the trough between the waves, then slam back down into the sea, only to be caught up by another, even larger wave. That would have the effect of knocking the ship to the side, slapping at it as if it were a helpless victim in the claws of a tiger enjoying a macaber sport.

Mr. Bright made the mistake of trying to step from the braces to the weather spreader, but just as he did so, a violent roll of the ship jerked the spreader away and his foot came down on empty air. He had already committed the transfer of body weight from one foot to the other, so he lost his footing. He made a desperate grasp for the gaff, missed it and fell, pitching headfirst toward the deck more than seventy feet below.

Andrew was watching, and he gasped and felt his stomach rise to his throat as he saw Mr. Bright pitch forward. Mr. Bright didn't make a sound . . . or if he did, it was drowned out by the fury of the storm. He made a final, futile grab for the mainsail as he fell, but, as with the gaff, he missed, and a split second later he crashed onto the deck with a sickening thump, then lay very still.

Gershom was less than six feet from where Mr. Bright hit when he fell, and, in fact, was lucky that Mr. Bright didn't fall on him. He leaned down to examine the young sailor for a moment, then stood up and looked at Andrew, his eyes reflecting the shock of what he had seen.

"How . . . is . . . Mr. . . . Bright?" came the faint yell from atop the foremast. Truax was standing on the topsail yard, holding his hand cupped around his mouth.

"He . . . is . . . dead!" Gershom yelled back.

"Gershom, get him under canvas," Andrew ordered, feeling sick at heart over the young man's death.

"Aye, Cap'n," Gershom replied.

The rain began shortly after that, coming in large, heavy drops, blowing in sheets across the deck, mixed with the salty sea spray. Finally the ship was rigged out with storm sails, special sails, smaller, stronger canvas, triangular in shape and mounted close to the deck.

But even with the ship so rigged, the danger was great and there was no time for anyone to be thinking of the dead first officer, whose body now lay wrapped in a canvas shroud lashed with rope to the mainmast. All hands had to attend to their duty to prevent the storm from dismasting the ship or causing even more severe damage.

Below deck, in her small cabin, Kristin knew nothing of the accident that had befallen Mr. Bright. She had lain in her bed, crying until the bitter tears were expended. She was exhausted, and only then, after giving vent to all her own bitter feelings, did she begin to notice the condition of the ship. The curtains that hung over the porthole and a towel that hung from a hook near the small washbasin swayed back and forth with each groaning roll of the ship, sticking out at crazy angles, as if they were flying from a line in a strong wind.

"What's going on?" she asked, sitting up in bed.

Though she asked the question aloud, she could scarcely hear the sound of her own voice. Outside she heard only the crashing of the sea against the hull and the howling, screeching wail of the wind. The wood and the ropes creaked and popped under the twisting, rolling action of the ship, and she heard voices on deck, high-pitched and strained, screaming as loudly as they could, but sounding puny and insignificant in the storm.

Kristin got up, was nearly thrown down again by the pitch of the ship, and finally managed to work her way over to the door. She stepped out into the passageway, held onto the side, and finally exited onto the middeck. Needles of flying water stung her skin, and she could see the men working their way cautiously, with fear-strained faces, along the deck, tying off ropes and securing loose gear.

"What's going on?" she asked a sailor near her.

"We've got us a hell of a storm here, miss," the sailor said. "You'd best get below."

Even as the sailor spoke, the deck heaved up and then fell to starboard, then dipped sharply to port. The roll to port was much longer and deeper than the roll to starboard had been, and it seemed to hang over for several agonizing seconds. For a moment Kristin had the terrifying sensation that it wasn't going to recover, that it was going to keep going until the ship was capsized. Then, slowly, laboriously, the *Morning Star* returned to the upright position, then through the upright and back to starboard again.

Kristin had never been in such a storm, and for a brief instant she thought of the mother and father she had never known. They had been lost at sea when she was a baby. Was it like this? Did they know the same gut-wrenching terror?

Kristin knew that the sailor was right. She had no business on deck, but she didn't want to return to her cabin. She had the notion that if she was going to die, she wanted to die with the others and not be trapped in her small cabin. Then she thought of the crew's mess. If she could just make it there, she would be content to ride out the storm out of the way.

Kristin started toward the crew's mess, but just as she started, the deck seemed to fall away and she was thrown against the doorframe, cracking her head. She felt a hot, nauseating pain and saw streaks of brightly colored lighting. She held onto the sides of the door, steadying herself for a moment until the nausea and dizziness passed. Then she scrambled wildly across the deck, holding onto whatever she could find, trying to work her way forward to the hatch that led into the mess. Once she had to hang on for life as the ship rolled hard to port again. The angle of the ship was such that had she let go, she would have slid from the deck right down into the boiling, angry sea.

Kristin dragged herself up to the crew's mess, hand over hand, while the *Morning Star* dipped and climbed on monstrous swells, rolling back and forth as it pitched through the sea. The galley was a shambles. The benches were securely mounted around the table, so they and the table, also bolted to the deck, were still in place. But nothing else was. All the cabinet doors had swung open, emptying their myriad contents onto the floor. There was broken crockery and piles of sugar, flour, coffee, and beans. With each roll of the ship, the crockery slid from side to side, tinkling, cracking, and breaking into smaller and then still smaller pieces.

Josiah was in the crew's mess, paying no attention whatever to the clutter. He was sitting at the table, with his legs wrapped securely around the bench leg and his hands gripping the edge of the table. His face was gray and his mouth was set. He looked at Kristin with white-rimmed eyes, and she knew without looking in a mirror that her eyes probably looked the same.

"What are you doing in here?" he asked.

"I . . . I didn't want to stay in my cabin. Alone," she added.

"Can't say as I blame you much," Josiah said. Another severe roll of the ship sent Kristin sliding across the floor, and she had to reach out and grab the edge of the table to keep from falling.

"Here," the cook said. "Sit here the way I am. It's the only way to keep your place."

"Are . . . are we going to sink?" Kristin asked in a fear-tinged voice.

"No, girl, we aren't going to sink. The *Morning Star*'s come through worse blows than this, I reckon. Though it's a shame about poor Mr. Bright."

"Mr. Bright? What about Mr. Bright?"

"You mean you don't know, girl?" Josiah asked.

"Has the captain done some further meanness to him?" Kristin asked angrily.

"No, girl, the captain's done nothing," Josiah said. He looked at Kristin, and she could see all the gentleness and sorrow and suffering and pain of all the sailors of the world mirrored in his eyes. "The boy's dead, miss."

"Dead?" Kristin said, putting her hand to her mouth.

"He fell from the mizzenmast," Josiah said.

"Oh, my God," she said. "I just . . . he just . . ."

"I know," Josiah said, gently. "The captain sent me to fetch the boy when the storm came up. I saw what was goin' on, but I didn't want to interrupt. The cap'n wasn't so polite."

"You . . . you saw?" Kristin asked, shocked by the revelation.

"Aye."

Kristin's face flamed. "What evil you must think of me," she said.

"Why should I think evil of you?" Josiah asked. "The boy was a virgin, miss. Had it not been for you, he would have gone to his watery grave that way. You did him a service no other could have done. 'Twas a good deed you done the boy. More than that, 'twas a noble deed you done."

Kristin didn't answer Josiah. She couldn't, for there was no answer to give. Now, by her own actions, she seemed to have forever sealed her fate. There would be no one who could believe she was anything but a whore. And she had brought it on herself through her own lustful and hedonistic activities.

Kristin rode out the storm in the crew's mess. Occasionally, she dozed fitfully through the long night, but she was so lost in her own emotions, self-pity, sorrow for Mr. Bright, frustration, and fear, that she couldn't be sure when she was asleep and when she was awake. Occasionally Josiah would say something to her and she would respond, but for the most part the night was spent in silence.

"The captain's quite a man," Josiah said.

"I beg your pardon?" Kristin replied, startled by the statement coming at the end of a long period of silence.

236

Josiah was standing at the door of the mess, looking out onto the deck. Strangely, Kristin had not seen him stand, and she didn't know how he got over there. "I said the captain's quite a man," Josiah said again. "He took a blow in the head that would kill most men, but he stayed out there the whole night working harder than any of them."

Kristin was aware of the rich aroma of coffee and now noticed that the rolling of the ship had nearly stopped. From behind Josiah, she could see the gray light of dawn. She had been asleep and didn't even know it!

"Is the . . . is the storm over?" she asked.

"Aye, lass, I think it's run its course," Josiah said. "The men'll be wantin' their breakfast soon. And you? Would you be wantin' somethin' to eat?"

"No," Kristin said. "Nothing, thanks."

"I've coffee brewed."

"No," Kristin said. "Not even that." She stood up, somewhat shakily on legs that were cramped and sore from their position around the bench legs. "I think I'll just go to my cabin if you don't mind."

"Bless you, lass, I don't mind at all," Josiah said. He started picking up the broken crockery, and Kristin noticed that sometime during the night he had swept it into a pile.

Kristin stepped out onto the deck and looked around. It was a shambles. Men were lying exhausted on every space available, paying little attention to the wet boards. There were broken fixtures and dangling stays but, she noticed, the storm sails had already been replaced with the regular sails, and the *Morning Star* was flying all the canvas she could carry, making maximum speed. Captain Roberts didn't intend to let anything like a small storm prevent him from making a record passage, she noticed.

The sea was a dirty green, jagged-looking and frothy, but not boiling wildly as it had been during the night.

The sky was gray, with low-lying, scudding clouds that appeared to be held off by the very masts themselves. Indeed, the tops of the masts were obscured by the clouds.

Kristin glanced toward the helm and saw that the ship was being steered by Captain Roberts himself. Roberts was looking at her and she stared pointedly at him. Their gaze held for a moment, challenging and angry. Then Kristin broke off the gaze, fearful that she might allow Andrew to peer through the shield and into her soul.

Kristin had started toward the after-passageway and her cabin, when she saw the tarpaulin roll by the mainmast. She stopped and breathed in a sharp intake of breath. That was obviously Mr. Bright. She turned toward Captain Roberts.

"Are you just going to leave him there?" she shouted angrily. "Are you going to do nothing?"

"He is dead, Miss Page," Andrew said. "Just what the hell would you have me do?"

"Bury him, Captain."

"Aye, Miss Page. That I will do," Andrew said. "But I'd rather not just dump the lad's body in the sea if you don't mind. I'd rather have a Christian service for him."

"That's what I mean, and you know it," Kristin said. Andrew was mocking her. How *dare* he mock her about such a thing?

"Service at four bells, Miss Page," Andrew said. "I hope you can attend."

"I will attend, Captain," Kristin said. "My only regret it that it is Mr. Bright's service I shall be attending . . . and not yours."

If Kristin had entertained hopes of a response of equal fervor from Andrew, she was disappointed. He merely gave an order to tighten a stay, as if he hadn't even heard her outburst. She swallowed her anger and frustration and walked quickly across the deck and into the passageway that led to her own cabin.

Chapter Twenty-four

When Kristin returned to her cabin, she saw herself in the mirror.

"Oh," she said softly. She put her hands to her hair. "Oh, I look awful!"

And indeed she did, for the poor, wretched figure staring back at her from the mirror looked nothing at all like the beautiful young shipping heiress who was so well known to Boston society. Her hair hung in a shapeless tangle, her face was wan, and instead of the most fashionable dress, she was wearing a man's shirt and pants, soggy now from the storm.

It was little wonder she could find no one to believe her claim to be Kristin Chalmers, for when confronted with her own image, Kristin found it difficult to believe it herself. For a moment, she wondered wildly if she really was Kristin Chalmers. Or was she who everyone said she was . . . Rose Page, a prostitute?

No, of course I'm not Rose Page, she thought. But still, the nagging doubt persisted. After all, she had undergone a great deal of stress. What if she had merely heard of Kristin Chalmers, and in an attempt to escape reality she had convinced herself she was Kristin? After all, she introduced herself as Rose, and though she had insisted to everyone that she had no memories of coming aboard, that wasn't quite true. Occasionally, an image would pop into her mind, and she could see it with crystal clarity. She distinctly remembered standing in the dimly lighted passageway with Mr. Bright and the police officer and watching Andrew open the door to answer Mr. Bright's knock. She remembered nothing of the conversation and nothing of the police officer. But she did remember standing there, seeing Andrew's face when the door opened. And if that happened could the other be true? Could she be a prostitute suffering under the delusion that she was Kristin?

Kristin remembered watching the prostitute and the sailor through her telescope so long ago. Or . . . did she really watch them? Maybe she was the prostitute, and she just imagined that she had watched them. Maybe she was hallucinating the whole idea of being Kristin Chalmers. After all, her attitude toward sex was certainly that of a prostitute. She had enjoyed sex with Andrew Roberts more than she could admit. And she had been willing to have sex with him again, until he had become angry with her for talking Mr. Bright into changing course.

And what about Mr. Bright? she asked herself. She had not just enjoyed him, she had *seduced* him. That should certainly be proof that she was not Kristin Chalmers, for Kristin Chalmers would never have done such a thing. Kristin Chalmers was a proper, well-bred lady, with never a lascivious thought.

Oh? Kristin challenged. Then what about the telescope? And what about the aching longings she used to get . . . hungering for something before she even knew what she was hungering for? No, the truth is Kristin Chalmers had always been a woman with a passionate nature. From the time her blossoming body had been physiologically ready for such a thing, erotic thoughts had offered temptations in her mind. She had made a few, futile attempts to dominate the sexual side of her nature, and until the rape by the two villains in the warehouse she had been successful in maintaining her virginity, at least, if not in controlling her lustful feelings.

Thus it was that through logic, the tool of her mind that had always served her so well, Kristin was able to reestablish her identity. At least in her own mind. And, she told herself, for the duration of this voyage she would have to be content with that.

There was a light knock on the door.

"Yes?" Kristin called. "Who is it?"

"Captain Roberts," the voice from the other side answered.

At first Kristin turned her back to the door, angry that he would disturb her. What was he doing here? What did he want?

"May I come in?" Andrew called.

Kristin sighed, then walked over to the door and jerked it open. "You are the captain of this vessel," she said coolly. "I am sure you have entrée anywhere you wish. Why should my cabin be any exception?"

"Why, indeed?" Andrew answered. He stepped into the cabin then, carrying a seabag. He dropped the seabag on the floor. "I thought you might want to go through Mr. Bright's things."

"Go through his things? No, why?" Kristin asked. She shrank from the bag.

"Don't get the wrong idea," Andrew said. "I know you aren't the grieving lover. But you can wear his clothes, and I though you might want to find another outfit. The one you are wearing will be hard pressed to last the entire passage."

"Yes," Kristin agreed, common sense prevailing over her hurt and indignation. She stepped back to the seabag. "Yes, perhaps you are right."

When Kristin returned to Mr. Bright's seabag, it brought her in very close proximity to Andrew. She could feel his closeness, almost as if he exuded a wave of heat, and the heat infused her body, spreading through her, bringing a flush to her skin. She tried to ignore it, and to ignore him, as she looked through the bag.

"Look at that," Andrew said softly, as she went through Mr. Bright's clothes. "I guess he had visions of being the Beau Brummel of the sea. Poor guy, to get killed before he even got started."

The genuine sincerity in Andrew's voice startled Kristin, and she looked up at him with questioning eyes.

"You . . . you really do feel bad about the boy's death," she said.

"Of course I do," Andrew replied. "I liked the lad."

"You gave an awfully poor impression of it," Kristin said.

"I'm afraid you had certain advantages over me in showing your appreciation of him," Andrew said coldly.

Kristin's eyes welled with tears and she turned away from him.

"Madam, you need shed no tears of remorse on my account."

"Not remorse, shame," Kristin said.

"Shame? Shame, from a lady of your occupation?"

"I am *not* . . ." Kristin started to say, then she sighed, and shrugged her shoulders. "Forget it. I see no point in going into it again." She turned to walk away from him.

"No." Andrew said, reaching out to grab Kristin by the shoulders. "You're not walking away from me."

"Unhand me, sir," Kristin said angrily, try to push his hand off her shoulders. "What are you doing?"

Though his grip wasn't so tight as to be painful, it was much too strong for her to break, so after a few attempts she gave up in frustration.

"That's better," Andrew said when Kristin stopped struggling. "Now, you are going to stay here until we get something straight, once and for all."

"We have nothing to get straight," Kristin said angrily.

"Yes, madam, we do," Andrew insisted. "And I intend to take care of it before I leave this cabin."

"What is it you want, Captain?"

"You know what I want, madam. I want to raise San Francisco in eighty-nine days or less."

"It can't be done."

"It has already been done, madam. I merely intend to do it again."

"Captain, why don't you face up to the fact that the odds are already against you?" Kristin asked. "You were injured, we sailed for many hours off course, your first officer was killed, and the storm has probably cost us dearly. Your goal is no longer possible."

"My goal is possible, madam," Andrew said. "But I cannot fight the sea, the elements, the calendar, and you."

"Me?"

"Yes, you. From the time you've come aboard this vessel, you've been nothing but trouble. If you were a new piece of gear, I would have you thrown overboard. And I swear if my patience is too sorely tried, I may yet do so."

"I did not ask to come aboard, sir," Kristin said hotly. "And I have made it very clear that I don't wish to stay aboard. Why don't you put me ashore, and our mutual interests will be served?"

"I am *not* putting you ashore," Andrew said. "Until it be in the hands of a police officer in San Francisco. That, madam, is what I want us to get straight. You will not be able to convince me that you are anyone

243

other than Rose Page, a woman of the streets. It will do you no good to continue to try. Your very actions, madam, from the time we embarked, have only served to convince me that I am right."

"That is unfair, sir!" Kristin said, tears stinging her eyes. "You know that it was you and not I who initiated what took place between us!"

"Well, if you will forgive me, Miss Page, your resistance to the idea was very weak. In fact, it may be said that it was nonexistent."

"I was moved by genuine feelings of affection," Kristin cried. "And it is unfair of you to fault me for giving vent to my honest feelings."

"And the boy?" Andrew asked coldly. "Was that the result of honest feelings as well?"

"You are an incredibly cruel man, sir," Kristin said in a tiny, injured voice.

"I'm sorry," Andrew apologized. "I have no wish to be cruel, only realistic. I do not paint castles in the air, nor imagine feelings of affection when none are there."

"You can honestly say that you felt nothing in return?" Kristin asked.

"I felt nothing for you," Andrew said. He took his hands from her shoulders.

Kristin turned away and walked over to her bed. She lay down on it, and held her arm folded across her eyes. "Leave me," she said quietly.

Andrew crossed the tiny cabin in three steps, then stood over the bed looking down at her. "Why must you, of all people, ask for more from a man?" he asked in exasperation. "Surely you do not expect a declaration of love from all the men you are with!"

Kristin didn't answer. Then suddenly she felt Andrew on the bed with her and his arms moving around her. He pulled her to him and pressed his lips against hers, hard, so hard that she felt as if they would be bruised.

"Don't you understand?" Andrew asked, breaking off

the kiss. "You are not the kind of woman one falls in love with, only the kind one can make love to!"

"I will not be made love to," Kristin said, twisting away angrily.

"Aye, by God, you will be made love to," Andrew said determinedly. He grabbed her again, and with strong, sure hands, stripped away the wet clothes she wore. Then, holding her trapped on the bed, he removed his own clothes. He was naked in an instant, and his smooth, hard-muscled body was still wet from the storm and the deck spray. Kristin stared at him, at the wildness in his eyes. Shocked and hurt by his cruel action, she shuddered and fought against him, hitting him ineffectively on the chest with her small fists. And yet, even as she did so, she found herself trembling in ill-suppressed excitement at his nearness.

"No," she said, feeling herself losing the battle. "I do not want it like this. Can't you see? Don't you understand?"

"I understand perfectly," Andrew said. "I'm going to show you just how well I *do* understand."

Andrew moved over her and thrust into her. He offered her no love, no apology, gave her nothing but the driving flesh that was the badge of his manhood, and as he did so Kristin stopped fighting and wrapped her arms tightly around him. She cried with the joy of it, and felt her anger and resolve crumbling in an ever increasing flood of passion, until finally a searing flash consumed her, and she was swept away in an ecstasy more tempestuous even than the raging storm that had beat its fury upon the ship during the night.

"Do you still say you feel nothing in return?" Kristin asked a moment later.

Andrew sat up and looked down at her. His face was drawn into a mask of guilt and confusion.

"Who are you?" he finally asked.

"I told you who I am. I am Kristin Chalmers."

Andrew stood up, grabbed his clothes, and stepped back into them very quickly. All the time he was dressing he was staring at Kristin, but he said nothing. It was not until he was dressed that he finally spoke.

"No," he said. "I don't believe you."

Kristin sighed in defeat and raised up in the bed, looking at him with eyes that were clouded over with sadness and resignation. She was totally nude and, for the moment, completely uninhibited by her nudity. Unconsciously, she fell into a pose that would have pleased the great French impressionist painter, Renoir. Her knee was raised and her arm rested upon it so that her breast upon that side continued in a beautiful, unbroken line from her shoulder out to the small, upturned nipple. The other breast blended into the form and shadow of the rest of her body highlighted by the slanting bar of light that came in through the open porthole. There was an unconscious diagonal tension in the pose that directed the eyes of the viewer right to her face, despite her nudity.

The beauty of the scene thus presented Andrew was not lost upon him, and he looked away to keep himself from losing his composure. For at this moment he feared he might say anything the girl wanted him to say.

"I . . . I've work to do on deck," he said, starting for the door. He told himself that he wouldn't look back, but just before he stepped outside he found that he was unable to hold onto his resolve and he glanced one final time toward the bed.

It was as if Kristin had anticipated that, for she was staring directly at him, and around her lips, and in her eyes, there played just the suggestion of a smile. The resigned sadness did not leave her features, but the small smile shone through. It was an enigmatic smile, and Andrew wondered at its meaning.

Andrew regained the quarterdeck, and walked to the afterrail to stare at the wake. The water, so soon after a storm, had a thick, oily appearance, and the ship's wake was clearly visible all the way to the horizon behind the ship. Andrew had a theory about such a long ship's wake. It was a direct and visible link with his past. Somewhere, he felt, on the other end of that wake, everything that had ever happened to him was still happening. If he had a sailing ship swift enough, perhaps one thousand times faster than the swiftest clipper, he could follow the wake backward and reach the other end of it before the shifting sea carried it away. When he got there, he would see himself as if on a stage, as a young seaman, as a first officer, and as the owner of his own ship. And maybe by observing himself from such a vantage point, he would be able to find the answers to all the questions that haunted him.

But even that, he felt, would not enable him to answer the question of the girl. For despite what he told her . . . he did feel something for her. He didn't know what it was, but it was something he had felt for no other woman he had been with.

He wondered if it was love. No, of course not, he answered himself. One does not fall in love with a whore. He had known more than a dozen whores in ports from Singapore to New Orleans. All had been skilled and many had been exquisitely beautiful, but none had evoked the strange and disquieting feelings this girl had caused. Maybe what he was feeling was love. But then, having never experienced it before, he had no real idea what it was.

How could he love her? Didn't he see her with Mr. Bright? Yes, he answered himself. And that was when he realized that he did love her, for seeing her with the young first officer had hurt him more deeply than he would ever let anyone know. More deeply even than he wanted to admit to himself.

He wondered what love was, anyway.

He wasn't sure he could answer that question. But he did know that the girl dominated his senses as no other woman had. He knew also that in the second that he thought would be his last on earth she had filled his mind. He knew that when she came on deck, he wanted to look at her, and when she was below, he wished she would return.

Then why would he not admit it? Why could he not go to the girl and tell her that he was in love with her and offer to take her to the nearest port to give her a chance to prove her claim?

But he knew why. If they returned to port and the girl was who she claimed she was, she would return immediately to Boston and he would never see her again. On the other hand, if she was not who she claimed to be, then she was a prostitute. That seemed the most likely, and oddly that prospect frightened Andrew even more. For Andrew knew that he would not allow himself to be in love with a prostitute. No, it would be best for the girl to keep her mystery for the moment.

"Captain Roberts, sir?" a voice behind him said.

Roberts was somewhat startled that he had been so deeply engrossed in thought that he hadn't heard the sailor approach. He turned to see Truax.

"Yes, Truax, what is it?"

"Captain Roberts, we would like to ask a favor of you, sir."

"We? Are you speaking for the crew again, Truax?"

"Aye, sir, on this matter, I have been their appointed spokesman."

Roberts sighed. "Very well, Truax. What is it?"

"Captain, I'd like to ask you . . . that is to say, the crew would like to ask you, having selected me as their spokesman on this . . . if you would put in to Norfolk and send the boy's body back to Boston by train."

"What?" Roberts asked, surprised by the statement. "Are you serious?"

"Yes, sir, we're very serious," Truax said.

"But why on earth would you ask such a thing?"

"We just figured that the boy's family, being as this was his first time at sea, would prefer to have the body back," Truax said.

"Being buried at sea is part of being a deepwater sailor," Andrew said. "The boy knew that, and I'm sure his family knew it. The fact is, I don't know but that the family would prefer having Mr. Bright buried at sea. I know I would prefer that to be my own final resting place, and I'm certain the boy would too."

"I think that's a decision the lad's parents should be allowed to make, Captain," Truax said.

"Truax, you are asking me to add at least three and maybe more days onto our passage, just to give them a chance to do something that they may not want to do in the first place?"

"Captain, what difference do the three days make?" Truax asked. "Surely, you don't still plan to go for that record?"

"I most certainly do plan to go for the record," Andrew said.

"But after everything that has happened? We have a jinxed ship!"

"Nothing has happened, Truax, which couldn't have happened on any passage. And I am surprised that you, of all people, would speak of something like a jinxed ship. You are a fairly well-educated man, Truax. In many ways, more educated than I am. You know there is no such thing as a jinxed ship."

"Sure, I know it, Captain. But do all the men?"

"What do you mean?"

"Nothing in particular," Truax said. "It's just that, well, you know what a superstitious lot sailors are. I'm afraid that if the men get the idea that the *Morning Star* is jinxed, we are going to have a difficult passage without even thinking of the record."

"And you feel that taking Mr. Bright's body back to Norfolk will set their fears to rest, huh?"

"Aye, Captain, I do."

"Well, I'm sorry, Truax, but I'm not going to do it. The boy is going to get a burial at sea as prescribed. You pass the word to the crew that services will be at four bells."

"Aye, Captain," Truax said. "I'll tell them. I don't think they'll like it."

"I didn't ask for their opinion," Andrew said, turning back toward the sea, by way of dismissal.

At three minutes before ten o'clock, Andrew Roberts, wearing his uniform coat and hat, stepped out of his cabin and walked over to the starboard middeck, where a burial plank had been prepared for James Bright. His body was securely sewn in a shroud made of tent canvas, and it lay ready for the service.

Kristin was there, and so were Josiah Crabbs and the big, black sailor, McQueen. But not one other member of the crew was present.

"Where is everyone?" Andrew asked. "It's nearly time."

"They ain't comin', Cap'n," McQueen said.

"What do you mean they aren't coming?" Andrew asked.

"It's that fella Truax," McQueen said. "He's talked 'em all into staying below decks as a demonstration."

"A demonstration? A demonstration about what, for Christ's sake?" Andrew wanted to know.

"I don't rightly know, Cap'n," McQueen said. "But he found in some book that the cap'n can't force nobody to go to no religious service, 'n he contends as how this is a religious service, so he said they don't nobody have to go that don' want to."

"What about you?" Andrew asked. "What are you doing here?"

"I liked the boy, Cap'n, 'n I don' hold nothin' agin' you that I got to demonstrate for. I reckon that if nobody has to come, that mean that a body can come if he want to, 'n I want to."

250

"Thanks," Andrew said. He looked at Josiah and Kristin. "Well, then," he said, holding up his watch and looking at it, "if there are no objections, we shall get started right on time."

They all stood silent for several seconds, composing as it were a somber tableau. Andrew stared at his watch intently in order to start the ceremony right on the stroke of ten, while the others looked at the small, canvas-wrapped bundle that lay on the board. It was quiet except for the natural sounds: the wind whispering in the sails and the ropes creaking. At the helm, Gershom held the wheel. He would have been excused from the ceremony anyway, but Andrew noticed with some satisfaction that Gershom had at least removed his hat.

As the second hand reached the twelve mark, Andrew brought the watch down and raised the prayer book. It was *The Book of Common Prayer* for the Episcopal Church. It had been left aboard the *Cauldwell Morrison* by the last captain, and though Andrew wasn't Episcopalian, he found that the prayer book, with its prayers and sections clearly marked for every occasion, served his purposes well. And if he wasn't Episcopalian he wasn't anything else either, so this was as good as anything, he thought. He was aware of God. No one could see the immensity of the sea without being aware of God.

Andrew cleared his throat, and began to read: "Unto Almighty God, we commend the soul of our brother departed, and we commit his body to the deep; in sure and certain hope of the Resurrection unto eternal life, through our Lord Jesus Christ; at whose coming in glorious majesty to judge the world, the sea shall give up her dead; and the corruptible bodies of those who sleep in him shall be changed, and made like unto his glorious body; according to the mighty working whereby He is able to subdue all things unto himself, Amen."

"Amen," the others said.

251

Andrew nodded to McQueen, and McQueen lifted the end of the plank as easily as picking up a twig. Bright's body slid off the end of the plank and dropped into the water below. If it made a sound, it was lost in the splash of the bow wake and the constant whisper of the sea. His mortal remains, like the whole of his life, had exited this world in silence, or, worse, in protests that were muted by events that overwhelmed him.

"Ship's company dismissed," Andrew said. "McQueen, tell Truax I'd like to see him."

"Aye, Cap'n," McQueen said.

"You didn't eat breakfast this mornin', miss," Josiah said. "Would you like a cup of coffee now?"

"Yes," Kristin said. "Yes, thank you. I would like that very much."

"Thank you for coming to the service," Andrew said as Kristin started away with Josiah.

"I wouldn't have missed it," Kristin replied.

Their exchange was surprisingly gentle, considering the tumultuousness of their earlier meeting.

Truax came over to Andrew a moment later. "McQueen said you wanted to see me," he said.

"Aye. What type of demonstration were you making?"

"Demonstration?"

"You know what I'm talking about," Andrew said. "What you just did was close to mutiny, mister, and if you do something like it again, I'll have you confined to the orlop deck, so help me God!"

"Captain, you couldn't confine me for such a reason and we both know it," Truax said easily. "So why make threats?"

"You are wrong there, mister. As captain of this vessel, I can confine you for anything that I feel might constitute a danger to this ship. Anything that disturbs good order is dangerous to this ship, and what you just did was contrary to good order. Now I want to know what the demonstration was about."

252

"We were merely expressing our dissatisfaction over your refusing our request, tendered by me in good faith, that you return Mr. Bright's body to his family."

"I see," Andrew said. "And is there anything else you are dissatisfied with?"

"Now that you mention it, Captain, there is," Truax said.

"How surprising," Andrew said dryly. "And what would that be?"

"Your insane insistence that we continue on the quest for this record."

"My insane insistence? Are you calling me insane, Truax?"

"No, sir, not at all," Truax said, apologizing quickly. "Forgive me for the poor choice of words. I should have said your unreasonable insistence."

"And what would you have me do, Truax?"

"Me, sir? Or the men?" Truax said, smiling easily, confidently, over his control of the situation.

"Are you their spokesman?"

"On this issue, yes sir, I am," Truax said. "And it is their desire that you break passage, sign on a new mate and a second officer, and split us into three watches."

"And abandon the record?"

"Captain, you know that any reasonable chance for the record was lost two days ago."

"I know no such thing," Andrew said. "I stated that we would make this passage in eighty-nine days, and I intend to do so."

"Is that the message I should take to the crew, sir?"

"No," Andrew said.

"Then what message should I take, sir?"

"Take no message, Truax. I have no emissaries to the crew, nor will I recognize a crew emissary to me. I have always dealt directly with my men and shall continue to do so. You are dismissed, Truax."

"Aye, Captain," Truax said, easily. He looked up at

the sails. "You'd best tell Gershom to watch what he's doing, sir. We're spilling wind needlessly."

Andrew looked at the sails and saw that they were puffing slightly, rather than rounded full, as they should be. He looked back at Gershom and saw that the sailor had looped a rope through one of the wheel spokes and was enjoying a leisurely smoke. All helmsmen did it, and that in itself was no dereliction of duty. But it was up to the helmsman, even while relaxing in such a way, to ensure that the ship was in proper trim.

"Gershom, trim the sheets!" Andrew shouted.

"Aye, Cap'n," Gershom said easily, unlooping the rope and adjusting the wheel.

Andrew looked back at Truax. Even though Truax was not on watch, he had already gone aloft to adjust a stay. Whatever he was . . . and at this point Andrew wasn't sure what he was . . . Truax was a worker. And a sharp seaman. There weren't ten men in two hundred who would have noticed the loss of thrust in the sails, slight as it was. Andrew needed a new first mate, and he had the authority to issue officer's papers to anyone he felt was qualified. That obviously was Truax. But did he want Truax for his first officer? And perhaps, more to the point, would Truax accept the position if tendered?

Andrew didn't know the answer to either question, and it was not something he wished to dwell over right now. That, he decided, could wait for a while.

Chapter Twenty-five

Miles Chalmers examined the bottle carefully. The seal was intact. In fact, had it not been for the small mark so tiny as to be almost unnoticeable, he would not have known that this was the special bottle. He placed the bottle on the bar alongside another bottle of the same liquor, the second bottle opened and half empty, then stepped back to look at it. He smiled in appreciation of his plan.

After Miles assured himself that all was in readiness at the bar, he stepped into the bathroom and checked the linen closet. There he saw a small fruit jar, and in the fruit jar a slurry made up of charcoal and water. It was an uninviting-looking mixture to be sure, but one which would serve its purpose nicely.

Miles was alone in a small house that belonged to him, located on the very end of a small spit of land that protruded into the water. It had been built years before by Miles's father, Charles, and by design was remote and nearly inaccessible. Charles had used it for his many sexual liaisons . . . had in fact died there of dropsy while engaged in coitus with a sixteen-year-old girl. Because of its "soiled" reputation, neither Miles's mother nor any other Chalmers had ever visited it. Miles used it as his very own, private retreat. He did not use it to entertain women and was never visited in the house. In fact, there were very few who even knew of its existence.

One person did know, and Miles was waiting for him at this very moment. That person was Captain Raymond Woodward, and he knew of the house only because Miles had invited him out for a meeting and had given him instructions on how to find the place.

Miles had asked for the meeting because the situation was getting out of hand. It simply wasn't tidy anymore, and Miles was, above all, a tidy person. Everything would have been perfect had Captain Woodward just done the job he had been hired to do. But Woodward had gotten greedy. Twice. His first time to get greedy was when he kidnapped Kristin, instead of killing her quickly and cleanly as he was supposed to. That time he had held Miles up for the job of Chief of the Chalmers Security Police. Now acting in the capacity as chief, he was making more and more demands. Unreasonable demands . . . demands that Miles couldn't possibly acquiesce to.

Miles poured himself a drink as he thought of the situation, pouring the amber fluid from the open bottle and holding it up to watch the fireburst of color as it captured a sunbeam. He walked over to the window and sipped the liquid slowly as he watched the sea rolling in, wave following wave, one after another, stretching out across the flat, blue water, until the blue of the sea and the blue of the sky merged in an indistinct line, far to sea.

It was now April 30, nearly two weeks since Kristin's

disappearance. Aunt Constance was getting more and more depressed and had even missed the last three board meetings, allowing Miles to conduct them, sitting as the acting chairman. Of course, such meetings were useless, and Miles was powerless to do anything in that capacity. But it was giving him increased ammunition in his campaign to have her declared incompetent, and to that degree everything was going nicely.

Then Captain Woodward tightened his grip. Like the camel who just wanted his nose in the tent, Woodward had already thrust his head and shoulders in and was wanting more.

Miles was certain that a couple of warehouse robberies had been engineered by Woodward. The details of the operations were too precise, the plan too smooth for it to have been an outside job. Miles was even prepared to let them ride, figuring that they were part payment for Woodward's silence. But now Woodward had come up with a new demand. He would help Miles "get the old lady put away" in return for thirty percent ownership of the company.

"Thirty percent?" Miles had gasped. "Do you have any idea how much money that is?"

"A lot," Woodward said easily. "But look at it this way. If I had a vested interest in this company, I might be able to come up with a way to cut some of the losses. Why, I believe I could even stop those warehouse robberies."

"Yes," Miles said. "I believe you could at that."

"Besides, what are you kicking about?" Woodward asked. "If you go along with me, I'll help you get the old lady institutionalized, and you'll get control. That's what you want, isn't it?"

"Where will your thirty percent come from?" Miles asked.

"From you."

"Do you know how much stock that would leave me?" Miles protested.

"Sure. But according to the charter I couldn't vote my stock anyway, whereas you as the chairman of the board could. Then when the old lady dies, you'll automatically get her share."

"Don't count on it," Miles said. "Besides, she'll probably outlive me. She's as healthy as a horse."

"She'll live no longer than you want her to live," Woodward promised.

"No, thanks," Miles said. "In the first place, I've seen your work. It's sloppy. Kristin could still come back to haunt us. And in the second place, it would be too obvious if something happened to Aunt Constance now. She's going to live out her natural life span."

"Well, it's your company," Woodward said. "But I think you'd better act on this deal while you can."

That had been three days ago. Two days ago a fire of mysterious origin destroyed several thousand dollars worth of consigned cargo, and only yesterday the sea cocks of a newly arrived ship had been opened as the vessel was awaiting the unloading lighter. The seawater had spoiled the load. Last evening, Miles issued the invitation for Woodward to join him to "discuss" the situation.

Woodward assured him that his move was a timely one. "There's no telling what might have happened next," he said.

Now as Miles waited for Woodward, he crossed from the window to the front door and looked through it for the fifth time in as many minutes. This time he was shocked to see Woodward sitting calmly on the front porch swing.

"What the . . . ?" Miles asked. "How did you get here? I didn't hear a horse or a buggy."

Woodward smiled. "I've been here since before sunup," he said.

"What? I didn't see you. Where have you been? And why in the devil would you come so early?"

"You didn't see me because I didn't want you to see me," Woodward said. "I came early so I could nose around a bit and so I could keep an eye on you."

"An eye on me? What would you be watching me for?"

"Come on, Mr. Chalmers," Woodward said. "Don't insult my intelligence. We both know that you would be better off without me. Just as we both know that I have your arse in a sling, and you have to do what I say. Wouldn't you like to see me dead?"

"Well, I . . . I don't know. I certainly haven't thought of it," Miles said.

"That's bullshit, Mr. Chalmers, and you know it. You've thought plenty about it. You just haven't come up with a way to do it yet, that's all."

"All right, maybe I have thought of it," Miles admitted.

"There now," Woodward said, smiling broadly. "That's more like it. But just keep one thing in mind, Mr. Chalmers. I've made a lot of enemies in my life, and I've outlived them all."

"I'm sure you have."

"I have," Woodward said. "And do you want to know how I managed this?"

"I'm certain you are going to tell me."

Miles's irony was lost on Woodward, who tapped his temple with his forefinger. "I've got what it takes, up here," Woodward said. "That's why I came out here before sunup. I've examined every rock, hill, and tree. I've satisfied myself that there are no sharpshooters hidden out, waiting for their opportunity. I've looked through the house, and I've found no concealed weapons, and you don't seem to have one on your person, though I am going to search you."

"That isn't necessary," Miles said.

"I said I'm going to search you," Woodward said again, a bit more harshly. "Now put your arms out and lean against the front of the house."

259

"What? Look here, this is all very silly."

"Do as I said," Woodward ordered.

Miles, protesting, spread his feet and leaned on his hands against the house just as Woodward ordered. Woodward ran his hands up and down Miles's body, searching thoroughly for a concealed weapon.

"Well, now," Woodward said, smiling, as he concluded the search. "I guess all is in order. Unless you figure to take me on with your bare hands," he added, laughing at the joke.

"No," Miles said. "I have no such intention."

"I didn't think so."

"Shall we get down to business?" Miles asked, starting into the house.

"Not much business to it," Woodward said. "You know what I want. The only question is, are you going to give it to me?"

"It's not as simple as all that," Miles protested, pouring them both a drink from the open bottle, then handing one glass to Woodward. "Aunt Constance would wonder what was happening. It would cause questions."

"She won't need to know," Woodward said, holding the glass up to the light and looking at it very carefully.

"I'd like to see how we can keep it from her," Miles said. He held his glass close to his lips, but he didn't drink from it. When he caught Woodward looking at him, he looked away, refusing to meet his glance. "She's got to find out," he went on, "when she signs the authorization. Any stock transaction that large must have the approval of the board. And in this case, that means my aunt."

"We'll take care of that," Woodward said, eyeing Miles carefully. Neither man had tasted his drink yet.

"Aren't you going to drink?" Miles asked, holding his glass up.

"Certainly," Woodward said, "And you?"

Miles smiled nervously. "I . . . I've got to go to the bathroom," he said. "I'll drink mine as soon as I get back." He put his glass on the bar, cast a quick glance at Woodward, then went into the bathroom.

Inside the bathroom, Miles went straight to the linen closet. He removed the fruit jar full of the charcoal water, slurry solution, took a deep breath, then drank the sickening-looking stuff down. Two or three times as he was drinking it, he nearly gagged and would have vomited the stuff back up, but finally, he managed to get it all down. He put the empty jar back in the closet, stood there for a moment fighting the urge to throw up, then got it under control. He rinsed his mouth out, washed his lips, and checked his image in the mirror. There was some black in the cracks of his lips, but he decided it was noticeable only if someone were looking for it. He stepped back out of the bathroom and saw Woodward still at the bar, still holding the drink.

"Well, now, I feel like that drink after all," Miles said, picking up the glass from where he left it. He tossed it down quickly, then looked at Woodward. Woodward, smiling, drank his drink then.

"Miles, Miles, Miles," Woodward said, shaking his head knowingly. "Did you think I wouldn't see through that old trick?"

"What old trick?" Miles asked innocently.

"Simple," Woodward said. "You put poison in your glass. Then you find an excuse to leave the room for a moment to give me the opportunity to switch the glasses."

"You mean?" Miles started to ask.

"Don't worry," Woodward said. "I did switch glasses, but not like you wanted me to. You see, old buddy, I don't want you killed any more than I want myself killed. After all, you are the goose that lays the golden eggs, you know."

"What did you do?" Miles asked.

261

Woodward laughed. "I poured us both a fresh drink," he said. He pointed to the other bottle on the bar. "From the new bottle, with the unbroken seal."

Miles smiled broadly, and as he did so, the black of the slurry mixture he was unable to clean showed wickedly in his mouth.

"What the. . . ?" Woodward asked. Then along with the realization that he had been tricked came his first, telltale cramps. "What is it? What did you do?"

"You are so smart, Captain," Miles said, "that you outsmarted yourself."

Another cramp hit Woodward, this one so severe as to cause his knees to buckle. He tried to hold onto the bar, and when he grabbed it, he knocked over the two bottles and the glasses.

"I thought you would be playing detective," Miles said. "So I poisoned the whiskey. Oh, not the whiskey I poured us. That was perfectly good Scotch, and a rather expensive brand too, I might add. No, my dear fellow, I poisoned the other bottle. The bottle that you thought hadn't been opened."

"But the seal?" Woodward gasped.

"Can be bought if you have the right influence."

"You drank it," Woodward said. He was holding his stomach with both hands, and he dropped to his knees. "Why didn't it harm you?"

"You can't figure that one out, can you, Woodward?" Miles laughed. "I'll let you carry that little puzzle to your grave."

Miles walked over to a cupboard and opened it and took out a five-gallon can. He began leisurely sprinkling its contents on the floor.

"What . . . what . . . my God, that's gasoline!" Woodward said. "You're going to burn this place? Don't leave me here! Get me out of here! My God, man!"

"You'll be dead soon, it won't matter," Miles said as he spread the inflammable liquid around. Even as

262

he did so, Woodward fell to the floor, where he lay, jerking in silent spasms. Miles lit a match and dropped it, then jumped back in surprise when the gas flared up. He was not used to gasoline and had not realized how volatile it was. He let out a small cry of panic, then saw a window nearby and managed to leap through it. He hit the ground, rolled a bit, then got up and ran from the house. By the time he had reached a distance of no more than twenty yards, the house was a roaring inferno.

Miles turned to look at it, breathing hard from exertion and near panic; then as his breath returned and he realized he was safe, he began to smile. Finally, a strange type of euphoria began to overtake him. He started laughing. He was elated over what he had done. He had matched wits with Woodward and he had won! Now he was ready for anyone!

Miles's laughing brought on a spasm of coughing, and after the coughing, came the retching. He vomited up the hideous-looking mixture he had drunk in the bathroom, and the sight of it made him even sicker, so he vomited some more. But sick as he was, he knew that it was this mixture that had saved his life, for the charcoal had filtered the poison out of the drink.

Miles also noticed, for the first time, that he was burned and badly cut in several places, and was bleeding profusely. He had injured himself when he leaped through the window, and hadn't even realized it until this very moment.

"Are you all right, mister?" a voice called.

Miles was startled by the voice. The road leading into his house was private, and there should have been no one on it. He looked up the road to see who had yelled at him.

"No, I'm out here," the voice said. "I'm in the boat."

"I . . . I'm injured," Miles said, and even as he spoke, he felt himself passing out from loss of blood.

Chapter Twenty-six

MILES CHALMERS HERO IN FORMER POLICE OFFICER'S DEATH

Building Destroyed by Fire!

Mr. Chalmers Seriously Injured!

Miles Chalmers, President of Chalmers Shipping Company, was seriously injured yesterday, when his vacation cottage caught fire and was destroyed. Raymond Woodward, formerly Captain of Police, and an oft-decorated veteran of the Boston Force, was killed.

Raymond Woodward had within the month taken employment as Chief of the Chalmers Security Police. He and Mr. Chalmers were known to be good and fast friends, and they had adjourned to Mr. Chalmers's private retreat to discuss ways and means of combating the recent wave of robberies and arsons that have plagued Chalmers Shipping.

It is ironic that one of the problems they were discussing was the recent fire which destroyed much Chalmers equipment and cargo, when they were, themselves, in such grave danger from fire.

A witness, Mr. Elmer Hudson, told of seeing the building ablaze.

"Mr. Chalmers made a valiant effort to save Captain Woodward," Hudson said. "But the fire was too intense, and Mr. Chalmers had to jump through a window."

In jumping through the window, Mr. Chalmers suffered serious cuts, and a great loss of blood. Captain Woodward's body was burned beyond recognition.

Cause of the fire is not known.

"How is he today?" Constance asked Margaret.

"The doctor says he will be all right, if he is allowed to rest and take tonics to build up his blood," Margaret said.

"Oh, thank God," Constance replied, sitting down in a chair in the hallway, just outside Miles's bedroom door. "When I heard this morning that he was near death, I was sick at heart."

"Were you?" Margaret asked.

"Yes, of course I was," Constance said. She looked at the woman who had been her most bitter rival for forty years. "Margaret, whatever differences of opinion you and I have had in our past, I've never wanted injury to befall your son, as I'm sure you wanted no harm to come to Kristin."

Constance's message was delivered with such sincerity that Margaret was temporarily taken aback, and she looked at her sister-in-law for a long time. Finally,

265

she was unable to hold her tears in check, and she began crying.

"There, Margaret," Constance said, standing quickly and crossing to the woman. "There, there, now. Miles is going to be fine, I just know he is." She opened her arms to the woman, and Margaret came to her, resting her head on her shoulder, crying with the pent-up tears of someone who has carried the weight alone for years and suddenly found someone else to help share the load.

Constance put her arms around Margaret, patting her gently on the back, giving her what comfort she could. She knew the love a mother had for a son, and she shared Margaret's sense of relief that Miles wasn't killed in the fire. Despite their enmity, this was one thing they could be close on. Besides, if there had been one brief period of truce in their relationship, it had come twenty years ago when her own son was killed.

"So," Constance had said, standing in the bedroom of her son Jimmy and daughter-in-law Cynthia. "You have made me a grandmother."

Cynthia was lying in bed, and nestled next to her was a tiny rosebud of a baby.

"What have you named the child, Cynthia?" Constance asked.

"We've named it David Lee," Jimmy said jokingly.

Cynthia laughed. "Jimmy still hasn't accepted the fact that it isn't a boy," she said.

"Of course I have accepted it," Jimmy said. He came over to the bed and looked down at his wife and baby daughter. "How about it, Mother? Have you ever seen two more beautiful women in your life?"

"Never," Constance replied, laughing. "But you still haven't told me the child's name."

"It is Kristin," Jimmy said. "Kristin Lee."

Cynthia laughed again. "Notice how he got the name Lee in, after all?"

"That was Jimmy's father's name, and it is one the child will wear proudly, I'm certain," Constance said. She looked at the baby. "Hello, Kristin. I am your grandmother."

"I hope you are in a very grandmotherly disposition next week," Jimmy said.

"I shall always be in a grandmotherly disposition," Constance answered. "But why should next week be so special?"

"The cruise," Jimmy said.

"The cruise?"

"Mother, you know what a difficult and trying delivery Cynthia had. The doctor has recommended a restful cruise. We're taking my yacht to Bermuda."

"Jimmy, surely you don't intend to take this baby to sea right away!" Constance scolded.

"No, not at all," Jimmy said. "That's why I asked you if you were in a grandmotherly disposition. You will have to tend to the baby."

"But . . . what about the baby's feeding?"

"We've already taken care of that," Cynthia said. "Mrs. Emma Rittenhouse has offered to wet-nurse the child for us."

"You know Mrs. Rittenhouse, don't you, mother?"

"Yes, I know her," Constance said. "She's the wife of the grocer. She's always surrounded by children."

"Then, she should make an excellent wet nurse," Jimmy said, laughing. "Don't you think?"

"I imagine she would," Constance said, joining in the laughter. "Of course I will keep the child. You did have a difficult time, dear, and," she looked at the baby, "it's not many grandmothers who get to lavish so much attention on their grandbaby right after it is born. I will look forward to it with eager anticipation."

"Thank you, Mother Chalmers," Cynthia said. "You don't know how much we appreciate this."

Constance left the room, elated at the prospect of having Kristin all to herself for a short while. And she

267

had also discovered what to give the children as a present. She would make all the arrangements for the *Triton,* Jimmy's schooner, so that Jimmy could spend his time with Cynthia and the baby until it was time for them to leave.

One week later she rode with them to the docks, laughing and singing with them, almost wishing that she was going on their grand adventure with them. She held Kristin in her arms for the whole day, but just before Cynthia boarded the *Triton,* she turned and ran back to Constance to take the baby into her own arms. She looked into the child's face for a long, penetrating moment, then handed her back to Constance.

Cynthia's eyes were filled with tears and though it was only natural for a mother to cry at leaving her baby, even for the short time of three weeks, still there was a haunting quality in Cynthia's eyes that went right to Constance's soul. For one brief instant, she remembered standing here years ago, holding Jimmy in her arms, telling Lee good-bye. She had a flash of *déjà vu* and almost called Jimmy and Cynthia back to tell them not to go. She dismissed the idea as foolish, but for years afterward when Constance thought of that moment, she remembered the terribly haunting look in Cynthia's eyes. She saw those eyes in her sleep, or sometimes in a cloud, or a window, or a pool of water. But mostly, she saw them in Kristin's eyes, as Kristin grew up.

The *Triton* had a steam engine and paddle wheels in addition to her sails. At four-thirty in the afternoon of June 3, 1881, the *Triton,* while attempting to overtake the yacht *Fidelity* in a chance, friendly race, suffered a boiler explosion. Before the horrified eyes of the crew and passengers of the *Fidelity,* the *Triton* went down. Though the *Fidelity* stayed in the area for several hours searching for survivors, not one person was saved.

Constance was beside herself with grief when she

heard the news. Indeed, the whole city was distraught, for Jimmy and Cynthia Chalmers were one of the best-loved couples on the Boston social scene.

Margaret had expressed her sympathy over the mishap, and for a short time the war between the two women was called off.

And now if Constance had anything to say about it, the war would be called off again. Even though Miles hadn't been killed in his accident, he had been seriously injured, and that could be just as devastating to a loving mother. She extended a peace feeler to Margaret.

"Margaret, can there, at last, be peace between us?" she asked.

"I . . . I don't know," Margaret said, regaining her composure. She seemed to realize, as if for the first time, that she had been crying in Constance's arms. She backed away as if embarrassed by it and dabbed at her eyes and nose with her handkerchief. "There has been so much, Constance. So very, very much. I don't know if we can ever be friends."

"If we can't be friends, can we at least stop being enemies? At least until the safety of our children is decided. Your Miles and my Kristin."

Margaret looked at Constance and smiled a small, self-conscious smile. "We can try," she said.

Constance returned Margaret's smile with an even broader one. "If we would try not to be enemies as hard as we have tried to be enemies, then we're bound to make it. I have to tell you this, Margaret. In all these years, I have come to realize one thing for certain. You are a most determined woman."

"And you, equally so," Margaret replied.

Both women laughed, and Constance realized with a bit of surprise, that it was the first time they had laughed together in the more than forty years they had known each other.

Chapter Twenty-seven

SHIP'S LOG, Barkentine *Morning Star*, May 7, 1901, 21 days out of Boston, 30 degrees west longitude, 4 degrees north latitude.

Begins calm. Middle part same. 86 miles this day, noon to noon. Possibility of record passage beginning to be in doubt.

Sighted St. Paul's Rocks this A.M. Should cross equator by P.M.

Sounded bilges . . . found nine inches of water. Have had to man pumps every day for the last ten days. Fortunately, the leak did not worsen during the storm.

Offered first officer job to Julian Truax, but Truax

refused the job. Instead, he presented the author of this entry with a petition signed by all but Josiah Crabbs and George McQueen, requesting that passage be broken and vessel return for two new officers. At this point in the voyage, such a thing would be out of the question, even without the quest for a record. Truax seems to know this, and submitted the document more for agitation purposes than with the expectation of results.

Molasses making passage in good condition.

Miss Page is being cooperative and agreeable.

The *Morning Star* was a painted ship on a painted sea, rendered in colors of harsh white, glaring yellow, and brilliant gold. A vast, oppressive calm held over the equator. For twenty-four hours now, there had been a complete desertion of the trade winds. The sun that blazed overhead was pitiless in its intensity. The sailors were lethargic, and they ambled listlessly about the deck, as apathetically as if they were walking in their sleep. They stared up at the sky and then the sails, trying to remember the sound of the wind in the canvas and the ropes at strain. It was a sound that no one heard when the wind was right, but everyone missed when the winds had died. Its absence left a hollow spot in their very souls, and they ached for it, and tried to will it back.

The ship had all sails spread, but since there was no wind, the canvas hung lifeless from the sticks, moving only occasionally as if the ship were some living thing and the sails were its lungs, trying desperately to take a breath.

On deck, the men on the off-watch lay sprawled in the shade of the sails, engaged in the sailors' best way of passing time, sleeping. Below deck the temperature was well over one hundred degrees, and without a breeze it was impossible to spend any time there. Even Josiah had moved a portable stove onto the deck, where he and now Kristin prepared the meals.

The off-watch sailors slept through the heat and through the calm, and even through the constant thump, thump, thump of the manual bilge pump.

Sanders and Evers, two who were on watch, squatted in the small patch of shade thrown by the galley house. They were both working with rope ends, though in fact it was only to make it appear that they were working, for there were enough rope ends plaited now to serve four ships making the passage.

"I'll tell you one damn thing," Sanders said, working on the project as if it were the most necessary task on the ship. "If the cap'n don't do somethin' 'bout that damn leak, he's gonna work us to death on that damn pump." He pointed to the pump, where two men were working away, their backs streaming sweat under the sun.

"What does he care?" Evers answered. "You ain' seen him on it, have you?"

"The only thing the cap'n pumps on is Rose Page," Sanders said.

"What? You don't mean it. You mean the cap'n 'n Miss Page are . . ."

"Well, whatta you think?" Sanders asked derisively. "She's a whore 'n this here is his ship. If you was the cap'n 'n there was a whore on board, wouldn't you be takin' a little advantage of it?"

"You reckon she really be a whore, Sanders?" Evers asked, putting the OO sound in the word whore.

"Of course she is. Why else do you think that policeman would have brought her on this ship?"

"Well, maybe so," Evers said. "But I don't mind tellin' you. I ain't never seen no whore that looked like her before. 'N besides, she don't act like no whore. She acts real cultured, 'n she ain' come up to nary a one 'o us 'n propositioned us the way a whore does."

Sanders laughed. "Why, you poor ignoramus. You ain't never seen no whore at all what wasn't either down with the pox or so ugly it'll gag you jes' to look at her. But they's fancy whores too. The kind that lays with the rich men and cap'ns of ships. This here girl is one of them kind. Rose is a rich man's whore."

"You mean if I was rich, I could have her?" Evers asked.

"Just pay her price is all," Sanders replied.

Evers leaned forward and looked toward the foremast. There, peeling potatoes, Kristin was helping Josiah with the evening meal. "Look at that," he breathed. "What I wouldn't give for one minute alone with her."

"That time ain' likely to come," Sanders said. He pointed at the pump. "But like as not you'll be on that thing agin, soon enough."

"I'll be spellin' Hunt next," Evers said.

Truax came around then, and saw the two men sitting there, and he grinned at them. They returned his smile. The entire crew knew that Truax had been offered the job as first mate and had turned it down. In their eyes, that made him a hero of the first magnitude. There weren't many who would turn down such a cushy offer, just to stay with the men.

"You sounded the bilges?" Evers asked.

"When the watch commenced," Truax answered. He came over to stand in the shade for a moment. "We've pumped it down to just a little under three inches."

"Three inches? That ought to be enough to 'low us to have some rest," Evers said.

"Naw, it ain't," Sanders said. "Anythin' more 'n one inch, the cap'n's gonna get outta there. It'll slow the ship down, so's we can't make no record."

"Hey, Truax, whyn't we draw us up another paper?" Evers asked.

"What kind of paper?"

273

"One that says we don' want to pump on that damn pump 'till they's at least three inches of water in the bilges."

Truax laughed. "That'll do us little good, I'm afraid. He would treat that petition just the way he treated the other one. And our request to return Mr. Bright's body to his parents."

"Well then, what the hell good was it for us to do them other things?" Evers asked.

"No good at all," Truax answered. "And you want to know why?"

"Why?"

"Because this isn't a union ship."

"Hell, no, it ain't," Evers said. "That was what the sign said when we signed on. No union men."

"Well, then there's your answer," Truax said. "As long as there is no union to look out for our rights, we have no rights."

"I don't want no union," Evers said. "Unions keep a man locked ashore."

"Who told you such a thing?" Truax wanted to know.

"I've heard it," Evers said. "I've heard it lots of times."

"That's just the story captains tell to frighten you away from a union," Truax said. "In truth, there are more ships sailing with union crews now than without them."

"Is that a fact?"

"Aye, lads," Truax said. "As sure as I'm sitting here. And you can believe that if we were union now, we'd already have this ship turned around. There'd be no driving for a record . . ."

"I kinda wish we could get the record," Evers said. "I would like to have the extra money."

"Of course you would," Truax said. "We all would. But we all have sense enough to know when the record is no longer possible, too. And then, we could slack off

274

somewhat on the work load. There's no sense in killing us for no reason."

"What could we do about that if we was union?" Sanders asked.

"Why, we could strike," Truax said.

"Strike? You mean quit workin'?"

"Aye."

"But that'd be mutiny, wouldn't it? We could go to prison for that. Maybe even hang."

"Yes," Truax said. "If we weren't unionized. For a strike by a nonunion crew is mutiny. As a union though, we would have a right."

"Well, damn me, let's unionize!" Sanders said.

"We can't."

"What do you mean, we can't."

"We signed on to a nonunion ship," Truax explained. "We can't unionize during this passage. But when we get to San Francisco, we could. We could go down to the Union Hall, and sign up, one hundred percent."

"Huh! You'll never get one hundred percent of *this* crew," Sanders said.

"Why not?"

" 'Cause you ain' gonna get that old geezer of a cook that's sailed with the cap'n for so many years, 'n you ain' gonna get the nigger neither."

"I don't know," Truax said. "We've a long way to go yet. A lot can happen. This voyage could get so bad that the captain's own mother might join a union against him."

Over at the pump, Hunt raised up and examined the blisters on his hands, then called for Evers to come and spell him.

"If you ask me, it's damn near that way now," Evers said, groaning and standing to answer Hunt's summons.

Up on the quarterdeck, Andrew watched the girl peeling potatoes. Since the day they had buried Mr. Bright at sea, there had been a strange change in her personality and in their relationship. Andrew couldn't quite put his finger on it, but it seemed as if from that day forth a truce had developed between them. She no longer attempted to convince Andrew that he was making a mistake, and she accepted her fate for what it was. For that, Andrew was most thankful.

But there was another change. She no longer attempted to convince Andrew that there was something between them, as she once had. On the day they had last made love—the day Mr. Bright was buried—the girl had insisted that he must feel something for her. Now she no longer insisted. In fact, she made no reference to it at all. She was friendly but restrained. Andrew enjoyed the fact that she was being friendly with him and appreciated that every discussion or meeting between the two of them wasn't a confrontation of wills.

Andrew wasn't so sure about the other, though. He discovered to his surprise that he missed the girl's attentions and rather wished she would renew them. The subtle seductiveness of the girl's apparent nonchalance was even more maddening to his senses than her overt action had been. And yet he knew he wasn't in love with her. He couldn't be. She had all but admitted to him now that she was a whore. Besides, when thoughts of the girl filled his mind, he had only to shut his eyes to see the picture of her in bed with Mr. Bright.

Andrew forced thoughts of her out of his mind. He knew it would do him no good to dwell on her, for he couldn't change the way things were. Besides, he had other things to think of. Like what he was going to do with Truax.

Truax was beginning to be a cause of concern to him. Andrew had noticed Truax talking to the two men and though he couldn't hear them, something about their conversation bode trouble to him. He could tell it in the intimate way they whispered and in the furtive glances toward him.

Truax was going to mean real trouble soon, Andrew was certain of it. He shouldn't have offered him the job as first officer. Having the offer turned down was a slap in his face. And of course the rest of the crew had heard of it immediately, and that made Truax's position among them even more influential.

Andrew wished that he could appoint McQueen as his new first officer. McQueen could handle the job, and from the size of him Andrew believed he could handle the problems he would have with any of the crew who would resent working under a black man. But unfortunately McQueen didn't even have AB papers, and by law Andrew had to fill the vacancy from one of his ABs. That meant Truax, who had already said no. Moore, who was big enough and skilled enough but had as many muscles in his brain as in his arms, or Gershom, who was getting too old and too lazy for the job.

Josiah came back on the quarterdeck then, smoking a pipe and staring over the trail toward the shimmering horizon. Andrew looked at him and then up at the sails. As the last time he looked, the sails were hanging lifeless and the wheel stood motionless, even without a hand to steady it. Andrew was at the helm, because the slightest indication that a breeze was coming could be felt by the man at the helm first.

Josiah licked his finger and held it up in the air, turning it slowly all the way around.

"Do you feel a wind out there, old friend?" Andrew asked.

"Nary a whisper," Josiah answered. He thumped his pipe on the railing and looked into the bowl as if searching for a diamond in the embers. "Cap'n, we're nigh onto some trouble," he said softly.

"Truax?" Andrew asked.

"Aye. He's stirrin' up the men."

"Stirring up the men? You mean to mutiny?"

"No, sir, nothin' like that," Josiah said. "He's talkin' union talk to 'em."

"Union!" Andrew said, hitting his open left palm with his fist. "Of course, that's it! That's what all this is about!"

"He wants to sign on a full crew to the union when we get to port."

"And he's seeing to it that the crew will be in the mood for it," Andrew said. "This calm is made to order for him."

"Son of a bitch!" one of the men on the pump suddenly swore. He stood up holding the pump handle in his hand. "Cap'n, this son of a bitch just busted!"

Andrew left the helm and moved quickly to the pump. There, he saw in one glance that the damage was irreparable. A cast-iron flange had broken in two, and without it the handle wouldn't stay in place. And because of the location of the break, there was no way to jerry-rig a new flange.

"What'll we do now, Cap'n?" Evers asked.

"I'll tell you what I'm gonna do," Bradford said. Bradford was the man who had been working the pump with Evers, and was the one who had called out. "I'm gonna take myself a break."

"I'm afraid we won't be able to repair the pump, Captain," Truax said, looking at the pump.

"I know," Andrew said.

"And at the rate we're shipping water, we aren't going to be able to bail it out, that's for sure," Truax said. "I guess we'll be heading for port, won't we?"

"I don't know," Andrew said. He sighed disgustedly and walked over to the rail, then looked down at the water for a moment. Out of the corner of his eye he saw the girl approaching him, a look of concern on her face.

"Is it bad?" she asked.

"Bad enough," Andrew replied. He turned around and leaned against the rail, then looked into the faces of the crew. Nearly all had gathered around the pump then.

"What about the gasoline pump?" Josiah asked.

"It's been out since the first night," Andrew said.

"Maybe it can be fixed."

Andrew shrugged his shoulders. "This is the first such pump I have ever seen," he admitted. "I have no idea how one would even approach it."

"You might try to clean the fuel line," Kristin suggested.

"Clean the fuel line?" Andrew asked, surprised at the girl's comment. Surprised because it sounded like a logical thing to do, and he hadn't thought of it himself. "Yeah, that sounds like it might make sense. I'm not sure I can even find the fuel line, but it's worth a try."

"Show me where the gasoline pump is," Kristin said.

"Why? Do you know anything about it?"

"I've been around gasoline engines before," Kristin said. The father of one of her girl friends owned a gasoline buggy, and she had gone for rides with them in it. Most of the rides were punctuated by long stops on dirt roads while the man blew the dirt out of the fuel line. Kristin knew nothing else about gasoline engines, but she did know how to clean a fuel line.

"Come along," Andrew invited. "If you think you can do anything with it, you are certainly welcome to try."

Andrew led the girl below deck, and there, in the darkened, stifling hot hold permeated by the sickeningly sweet smell of molasses, he pointed out the small gasoline engine. It was lighted by a bar of sunlight that slanted in from the overhead hatch, so that it stood out boldly in the hold.

"This is the fuel line," Kristin said, pointing to a small rubber hose. She pulled it loose from both ends and tried to blow through it. It was stopped up.

"Just as I thought," she said. "I can't even blow through it."

"Let me try," Andrew said. He took the hose from

her and tried to blow. He had no better luck than she did.

"Well," Kristin said. "Whatever has that stopped up is your problem. Get that line cleared, and the pump will work."

Andrew held the line out and looked at it. "Maybe Josiah has something I can poke through it," he said. "Come on, let's get out of here. It's too hot and stuffy."

"You aren't going to give up, are you, Captain?" Kristin asked.

"Not if I can help it," he answered. "But why the concern? I thought you wanted to go into port."

"That was when we were still off the coast of the United States. I have no wish to put into a Brazilian port. Besides, I've come this far with you, I might as well see it through."

Andrew smiled at her. "And see it through you will, girl. Come topside; let's see if we can clear this line."

Kristin and Andrew climbed back up to the deck. The sailors were still standing around the damaged pump as if by looking at it they could fix it.

"Good news, lads," Andrew said, holding up the line. "We've discovered the problem with the gasoline engine pump. As soon as we clear this line we'll have that pump working, and the bilge'll be dried out in no time."

"You mean that pump'll do the work of two men?" one of the sailors asked.

"Two? Why, it'll do the work of all of you," Andrew said. "You'll think you're passengers on a cruise when this thing starts working."

"That sounds pretty good to me," Bradford said, and the others made noises of general agreement.

Everyone stood around watching as Andrew gingerly passed a long rod through the line. The rod came in contact with the obstruction, and Andrew worked it patiently until he managed to push it through and out the other side. It was a wad of paper.

"Must have been some of the packing material," Josiah said.

"Aye, I guess so," Andrew replied. "Well, gentlemen, in about one minute we'll see if we've repaired it."

Andrew went below deck to the small engine again, put the hose on, then jerked the crank over. After half a dozen jerks, the engine started. He smiled, went above again, and then looked over the rail toward the drainpipe. A stream of water half as thick as a man's fist was pouring out.

At that moment there was a sudden ripple of canvas, and everyone looked up in quick surprise to see the sails puffing out.

"The trades are back, gentlemen," Andrew said, smiling broadly. "And the pump is fixed. It could be that our luck is changing."

Chapter Twenty-eight

It had been four days since the return of the trade winds, and the *Morning Star,* moving at a brisk sprint, had taken them away from the equator and down into more temperate climes. Kristin had occupied most of her time during the past four days by reading the manual that came with the gasoline engine. She found it fascinating, and as none of the sailors, not even the captain or Julian Truax, seemed interested in anything mechanical, she decided that she would make herself expert in the complexities of the machine and take it on herself to keep it in proper working order. It would benefit everyone, and it would help her pass the time.

Boredom. That seemed to be Kristin's biggest problem now. Of course all hope of going back had long been abandoned, and now she wasn't all that sure she would want to go back if she had the opportunity. Oh, she wished there was some way she could ease her grandmother's suffering, since the poor woman was obviously grieving over her. But, she reasoned, it would make her homecoming all the sweeter when her grandmother discovered that Kristin had come back from the dead. Even such pleasant thoughts did little to relieve her boredom.

Kristin wondered about the others. They spent their lives at sea. Josiah, she discovered, had been ashore only a few months in the last forty years. What was there about the sea that could so capture a man's spirit and hold him its prisoner? She had observed the others, but they didn't seem to be affected by the long, empty hours.

The long, empty hours could have been filled had things worked out with Captain Roberts, but it was not to be. In her fantasies back in Boston, a dashing sea captain would take her away, and they would sail the sea in romantic bliss. But Captain Roberts clearly wasn't the man of her fantasies. At first she had been hurt and felt rejected. But she managed to put those feelings aside and finally accepted things as they were, with the same equanimity she accepted her confinement to this vessel. And with the sexual tensions relieved between them, she found conversation with Captain Roberts easier and the strain lessened. But the excitement was gone, and that she missed.

It was late, and Kristin had thought she was studying the gasoline engine manual. In fact, she suddenly realized that she had been on the same page for some time, not reading at all but merely reflecting upon things. She closed the book, then reached up to quench the lantern. She felt that a brief turn on the deck would make her sleep better, so she opened the door and stepped out into the passageway, walking quietly so as not to awaken Captain Roberts, who was sleeping in his cabin.

Despite everything that had happened between them, the anger and the anguish, the bitter and the bittersweet, and now the seemingly dormant aspect of their relationship, Kristin had to give Captain Roberts credit for the qualities that were to be admired. He worked twice as hard as any of his men, going aloft as often as any or working in the holds when necessary. And it seemed to her that it would be impossible for any man to sleep as infrequently as he did, so she was extra careful not to do anything that would awaken him on those rare occasions when he did get to bed.

When Kristin reached the deck, she caught her breath at the beauty of the scene. The night air was clear and sharp in the moonlight, and the sea stretched out from horizon to horizon in gently rolling magenta, given texture by the whitecaps that flickered like a candle flame when a wave spilled over.

The moon was a huge, hung lantern, and the movement of the clouds of canvas on the ship's masts caught the moonbeams and scattered them like bursts of silver through the night. Here, in the southern hemisphere, she could see the Southern Cross, and it was the most brilliant of all the constellations, winking and sparkling like diamonds cast carelessly upon black velvet.

Kristin walked to the ship's rail to better take in the beautiful sight, and she was treated to the appearance of hundreds of phosphorescent fish. She watched the green lights glowing from the sea.

"It's beautiful, isn't it, Kristin?" a voice asked.

"Yes, it is," Kristin said. "I wonder what makes . . ." Kristin stopped in midsentence and looked at the man who had spoken to her. It was Julian Truax, and he leaned against the rail maybe six feet away from her. His shirt sleeves were rolled up above his elbows, and he was looking down at the water. "What did you call me?" she asked.

"I called you Kristin," Truax said. He looked at her and smiled, and in the moonlight his teeth shone brightly. "That is your name, isn't it?"

"Yes," Kristin said weakly. "But I didn't think anybody believed me."

"I did," Truax said. "I believed you from the beginning."

"Are . . . are you with the men who kidnapped me and put me on this ship?" she asked, her voice laced with fear. "Has the time come for me to . . . to be killed?"

Truax looked at her with genuine surprise in his face. "Killed?" he asked. "My God, no, girl." He moved to her quickly, and in an effort to offer her comfort and nothing else he put his arms around her, pulling her to him. He could feel her trembling in his hands like a small bird. "Have you lived with that fear since you came aboard?" he asked.

"Yes," Kristin said, crying into his chest, her cries muffled by him.

"My God, girl, what a burden for you to carry! Believe me when I say that no one on this ship wishes you any harm. Not even the captain."

Until this moment, Kristin had no idea of the magnitude of the burden she had been carrying. Now, with at last someone who believed her and with the assurance that she wasn't going to be killed, she felt all her defenses being lowered. She relaxed nerves that had been drawn to a fine tautness for the last month, and she quit fighting the nameless terror that had held her in check, and she cried. She cried as if she had never cried before and had stored inside the tears of a lifetime.

"There, now, girl," Truax said, holding his arms around her, pulling her to him. "There now, let it all out. It's been bottled up inside you like a poison."

Finally, after several moments, Kristin regained her composure, and she pulled away gently, then turned to look at the sea once more. "How did you know about me?" she asked.

"I've seen your picture," Truax said. "And once I

led a protest march down to Chalmers Shipping. I saw you standing away, watching the demonstration."

"I remember that," Kristin said. "But . . . surely you weren't with them? They're anarchists."

"No, they are union men," Truax said. "Like I am."

"Then you *are* here to make trouble for Captain Roberts?"

Truax laughed. "And why should that bother you? He's certainly made his share of trouble for you."

"I . . . it doesn't bother me," Kristin said. "It doesn't bother me at all, except for my concern over the safety of the ship."

"You needn't concern yourself with the safety of the ship," Truax said. "I'm here to organize the men into a union and to secure their rights for them. I want to create something, Miss Chalmers, not destroy something."

"But unions destroy," Kristin said.

"No. Unions build. They build the dignity of man. It is my dream that one day all men will truly be equal, that one can look upon another without fear, or shame, and call that man 'brother.' "

As Truax talked of his dream, the fervor of his idea was transmitted by his voice. The sailor who had always been somewhat of an enigma to her now began to come into focus.

"Is that why you turned down Captain Roberts's offer to be first mate?" she asked. "So you would be equal with the others?"

"Yes," Truax said. "For if I had moved out of the forecastle, I would no longer be able to relate to the men on the same level. My mission is far beyond this voyage, Miss Chalmers. It is even beyond this crew. It is to see every sailor under the American flag united under the banner of human dignity. And that means unionized."

"I . . . I admire your ambition," Kristin said. "But I'm not certain that I agree with it."

286

Truax smiled. "I shouldn't expect you to. We are natural enemies, you and I, Miss Chalmers. For you are of the capitalist class and I am a worker."

"Do you feel enmity toward me now?" Kristin asked.

"This minute, you mean? No," Truax said.

"Then, doesn't that disprove your theory?"

"On the contrary. It proves it," Truax said. "You see, Miss Chalmers, a ship is a great laboratory for social experiments. Here, in the middle of the ocean, cut off from the rest of the world, we are like our own little country. It is as if no one exists but us. For all we know, no one *does* exist but us, for we are in total isolation. Therefore a social experiment that would take decades to prove ashore can be tested at sea in a matter of days. With the exception of the captain, we are a classless society. You, for all your wealth and power and influence ashore, are no more than the rest of us here. And since it is your wealth and power and influence that makes you my natural enemy, it is only natural that its removal would make you my friend."

"I see," Kristin said.

"I'm not at all certain that you do, but if you would be willing to discuss it at length, I would like to tell you more about it."

"Why?" Kristin asked. "Why would you want to go to all that trouble? I'm certainly not a candidate for your union."

"No, you aren't. But on the other hand, who better to espouse our cause than a member of the capitalistic class?"

"I shall enjoy holding discussions with you, Mr. Truax," Kristin said. "If only to relieve my boredom. But . . . I would ask one thing of you. A favor."

"Certainly."

"I would prefer not to have anyone know who I am."

"All right," Truax said. "Though it seems to me that you spent a good deal of time trying to convince everyone of your identity."

"It was important to me then. It is just as important to me now that I keep my identity secret."

"Very well."

"But I am curious," Kristin said.

"About what?"

"If you have known about me all this time, why have you remained silent? Why didn't you identify me when I wanted to be known?"

"I wasn't one hundred percent certain," Truax said. "And I must admit that I saw a possible advantage in keeping the situation as it was."

"What advantage could you have seen?"

"Why, this advantage, of course," Truax said easily. "The opportunity to talk to you, a representative of the oppressors, and tell you of our cause."

"I see," Kristin said. "You were going to use me."

"We are all being used, Miss. That's the point."

"I will listen to your side, Mr. Truax," Kristin said. "And, I must admit, I have found this evening's conversation an enjoyable interlude."

Truax started to walk away, but he stopped and returned to stand very near her. He looked down at her, and she thought she saw something in his eyes, a question perhaps. Or a challenge. Easily, and without fanfare, he put his arms around her and pulled her to him for a kiss.

It was a strange kiss. It wasn't demanding in its hunger and urgency as had been Captain Roberts's nor gentlemanly as had been Mr. Bright's. It was, like his eyes, challenging. As if telling her that he had the right to kiss her, no matter what her station in life. He was a man and she was a woman, and wealth, power, and influence could change none of that. Its very challenge made it stimulating and, even though devoid of the raw passion she had felt with Roberts, it was enough to leave Kristin's senses reeling and her mind spinning.

"Please," Kristin begged, turning her head away, gasping to recover her breath.

"Don't fear me, Kristin Chalmers," Truax said. "I will never come to you without an invitation. Because when that invitation is issued, I will know that you regard me as your equal."

"Don't put it that way," Kristin said. "If I never invite you, then you will think it is because I consider myself better than you. And I don't. Honestly, I don't."

"Then you will invite me," Truax said, matter-of-factly. He turned from her and walked away, disappearing into the darkness of the deck.

Kristin looked around, to make certain that no one had seen them, then squeezing her hands into fists of frustration, she turned back to the rail and looked once more toward the sea.

What was it about her? Kristin asked herself. What abnormality in her makeup would allow her to respond so easily to men? Captain Roberts had raped her . . . had forced himself upon her, and she had responded with an eagerness that was almost equal to aggression. And with poor Mr. Bright, she *had* been the aggressor, seducing him before he even understood what was happening. For a moment Kristin recalled the brutal scene in the warehouse and, with shame burning her cheeks, she remembered that even there she had felt nearly pleasant responses to the awkward caressing of her nipples.

Kristin watched the flashes of light from the fish in the water, then looked back at the stars. The Southern Cross was halfway up in the heavens before them, and she knew that the farther south they went, the higher it would go. When they were right under the Horn, the Southern Cross would be directly overhead. That was going to be about two weeks from now. What would happen in the next two weeks? What would happen in the next two months?

Kristin tried to think back two months, but she was unable to. Two months ago she didn't exist. The young girl who lived with her grandmother and watched the approaching ships through a telescope was a perfect stranger to the woman who was now standing on the starboard rail of a barkentine, trying desperately to control the racing passions that the last two months had unleashed.

Chapter Twenty-nine

SHIP'S LOG, Barkentine *Morning Star,* June 2, 1901, 47 days out of Boston, 60 degrees west longitude, 57 degrees south latitude.

Have had good northeast trades for 26 days. This, with smooth seas, has caused good sailing. Ran 367 miles this day, noon to noon. Fastest day since leaving Boston.

Twenty days now, since appointing Gershom first mate. He was compromise choice only. Moore couldn't handle it, Truax wouldn't accept it, and McQueen has no AB papers.

Miss Page has twice made repairs to the gasoline engine.

The Falkland Islands, which had been passed earlier in the day, were now barely distinguishable as lines of dark blue falling into the sea behind them. Andrew stood on the quarterdeck afterrail, looking back toward them. The *Morning Star* was still running before the wind, moving so fast that she was throwing a bow wake. But on the morrow, Andrew knew, all this would change. Then they would be under the Horn, where the thundering current of the extreme South Pacific, would crash into the raging swell of the lower Atlantic, raising waves as high as mountains and creating storms of a magnitude unparalleled anywhere else in the world.

Andrew thought of the task before them. He had doubled the Cape four times in his life. On one memorable occasion he had spent thirty-seven days trying to get through. Once he had gone through in one day, catching it when the Pacific swell had abated and the wind had come from the east, popping him through as cleanly as pulling a cork from a bottle.

It was here that the fate of the record passage would be determined. For there had been many a speed run in record time down the western coast of the Americas, only to watch the record fall while the ships stewed about, helplessly trapped at the southernmost tip of the inhabited world.

Andrew slapped his arms together to circulate his blood and hopefully warm his body. It was the dead of winter in these latitudes, and they were close enough to the South Pole to feel its influence. He held his hands up and blew on them, watching the fog of his breath as he did so.

"Eight bells, Cap'n; time for a watch change," Gershom said, coming on deck then.

Andrew looked up at the rigging. The stays, like the deck and railing of the ship, were coated with ice. The sheets themselves were frequently iced, but Andrew kept them clean by the simple expedient of lowering and raising them once or twice per watch. "I think the sails will stay clean until we heave to for the night," Andrew said.

"Are we going to heave to, sir?" Gershom wanted to know.

"Certainly. You weren't going to try and double the Cape at night, were you, Mr. Gershom?"

Gershom took a dip of snuff and looked out over the cold, rolling sea. "Well, now, Cap'n, iffen you had asked me to, why I reckon I woulda tried. Bein' as how you're shootin' for the record 'n all. But the plain truth 'o the matter is, I'da heap rather not."

"We'll make a run at it in the morning," Andrew said. He stretched and yawned. "I'd best rest while I can," he said. "There will be little enough sleep for me, after this night, until the Cape is southeast of us."

"Good night, sir," Gershom said.

Andrew took one more look at the sails and at the rigging before he left the deck. As he went through the hatch leading to the afterpassageway, he saw Duke lighting the running lamps, one mantled in red and the other in green. They threw squares of color against the deck, which was already beginning to collect hoarfrost.

"Good night, Cap'n," Duke said as Andrew passed by.

"Good night, Duke."

In her cabin, which shared the same passageway as Andrew's cabin, Kristin put the finishing touches to the dinner. Josiah had slaughtered one of the pigs, and after dressing it, rendering out the lard, and curing the meat, there had been a small chunk of ham left over. It was too small to cure or cook for the crew but too large a piece to throw away. It was just large enough to feed two people, so Kristin asked Josiah if she could prepare it especially for the captain and invite him to dinner in her cabin.

Josiah thought it was a very good idea, and he offered to help her cook it, even throwing in a bottle of wine. He was making an apple cobbler for the men, so he took two portions out and set them aside for her.

Kristin wasn't sure why she wanted to prepare a special dinner for the captain. There had certainly been no change in their relationship over the past few weeks that would indicate such a move would bear results. But, on the other hand, there had been no arguments in that time, either. And he had expressed his gratitude many times for her help with the gasoline engine. Anyway, the ham would just go to waste if someone didn't eat it, and who better than the captain?

Kristin had observed Captain Roberts very carefully over the last few weeks. She was convinced that he was starving himself as well as depriving himself of sleep. Never had she seen anyone who could stir her so. For the truth was, and now Kristin was ready to admit it to herself, she was in love with Andrew Roberts. And what's more she believed that Roberts was in love with her.

Roberts had never said anything . . . never even hinted with a word or a gesture. But sometimes she could feel him looking at her, and when she glanced around she would catch him in a look that betrayed his innermost thoughts. At such times, the captain would immediately clear his throat, or discover a mote in his eye, or check the set of the rigging—anything to divert attention from his soul-revealing gaze.

All right, if that's the way it is to be, Kristin decided, then she would do the captain's work for him. If it became necessary for her to take the first step, she would do so. Hence, this meal.

It was precisely for this reason that Kristin quit trying to convince Captain Roberts who she really was. For one thing, her continued insistence that she was Kristin Chalmers only served to anger him. But another, more personal reason was that Kristin wanted to see if Roberts could really fall in love with her. With the girl and not the name. Oh, it was being unfair to Andrew Roberts to believe that he could be moved by the thought of her money and position, she knew. But this way, there could never be the slightest question, or the least doubt. For if she could make him fall in love with Rose Page, a girl who had nothing but herself to offer, then she would know that the love was genuine.

When Kristin heard Andrew call good night to Duke, she lit the two tapers set in pewter holders on either side of the golden-brown ham. The dinner was set upon a sea chest, and she had borrowed a small chair from the chart room to give Andrew a place to sit. She would sit on the bed.

Kristin opened the door when she heard Andrew passing by.

"Andrew," she called. It was the first time she had called him Andrew since the first time they had made love.

"Good evening, Rose," Andrew said, poised by his door, ready to go in.

"Could you step into my cabin for a moment?"

"Certainly. Is anything wrong? Have you sprung a leak or something?"

Kristin stepped back to allow Andrew into her cabin. He saw the meal on the makeshift table.

"Well, now, what is all this?"

"I know you didn't eat tonight," Kristin said.

"No, as a matter of fact I didn't," Andrew said. He looked over the meal and sniffed the ham. "Uhmm, that smells good. But what is the occasion?"

"Oh, no particular occasion," Kristin said. "But I know we'll be doubling the Cape tomorrow, and Lord knows when you'll eat again. I just thought you should have a good meal, for a change."

"Well, Rose, I must say, that's very thoughtful of you," Andrew said. "And ham, too! Does Josiah know you did this?"

"Josiah helped," Kristin said. "Sit," she invited.

"That's not an invitation you will have to issue twice," Andrew said, taking the chart room chair. "Careful, girl. Treating me like this may make me decide to keep you aboard permanently."

"Make the offer," Kristin said.

Andrew, who was about to laugh at his joke, looked at Kristin with a surprised look on his face. "What did you say?" he asked.

"You said such treatment may make you want to keep me permanently. I told you to make the offer."

Andrew had picked up his knife and fork, but he put them down beside his plate. "I see," he finally said after a long pause. He sighed. "You'll do anything you have to do, won't you?" he asked coolly.

"What?" Kristin asked, surprised by his comment and his strange reaction.

"Just what is it the San Francisco police want you for?" Andrew asked. "What have you done that would make you go to all this trouble?"

"Andrew, I . . . I don't know what you are talking about," Kristin said.

Andrew got up from the table and walked over to the porthole to look out over the sea. It was closed, but since the room was not much warmer, the glass was not fogged over and he could see the white, flickering tops of the waves as they rolled endlessly by.

"It has been one deceit after another from the moment you've come aboard," he finally said. "I should have known." He turned to look at her. "It wouldn't surprise me, madam, to discover that you have been responsible for the breakdowns of the gasoline pump just so you could repair it and thereby get in my good graces."

"No," Kristin said quietly. "You have it wrong. You have it all wrong."

"I have been paid to deliver you to the San Francisco police, and I shall do so," Andrew said. "I would have thought that by now you would have discovered me to be a man of my word."

"I love you," Kristin said.

There was a moment's silence, and Andrew looked at Kristin with his face etched in shock.

"What did you say?"

"I said I love you."

"My God, woman, have you no shame at all? You would resort even to that to win me to your cause? Do not toy with my heart, madam, for that I shall not allow."

"But it is true," Kristin said. "Believe me, it is true!"

Andrew stood there looking at her, opening and closing his fists, with a nerve jerking in his temple, saying nothing.

"Andrew?"

Andrew raised his fist to his head, and then pinched the bridge of his nose between his thumb and forefinger.

"Andrew, say something."

"I wish you had never come into my life," Andrew said, turning toward the door and stepping quickly outside.

Kristin was still sitting on the bed, and she looked at the door in shock after Andrew left. Why had he done this to her? Why couldn't he accept her declaration of love for the truth it was? She fell across her bed and began crying into her pillow, muffling her sobs of sorrow and hurt and frustration, because she didn't want Andrew to hear her or have the satisfaction of knowing he had made her cry.

Later, when the crying was controlled and the tears were once more bottled up, she sat up again and saw the meal still sitting prettily on the table. Both candles had burned halfway down, and the wax had dripped, piling up on the pewter holders. The knife and fork by the plate that was to have been Andrews's lay crossways, just as he left them, and the plate was clean, mocking her with its emptiness.

Kristin let out a sobbing curse of anger, stood up, gathered the meal, plates, silverware, candles, and all into a bundle made by the tablecloth, crossed over to the porthole, opened it, and tossed the bundle overboard. When she turned back from the porthole, she wiped her hands together and felt a strange sort of satisfaction over her gesture.

Then she decided there was nothing left for her but bed, so she moved the sea chest away, turned down her covers, and began removing her clothes.

Kristin had been sleeping nude ever since they had arrived in the cold latitudes. It was a trick she had learned from Josiah when she complained once that she couldn't get warm at night.

"Do you take off all your clothes?" Josiah had asked, no more concerned about discussing such a delicate issue with a girl than he would have been discussing a cloud formation.

"Take off all my clothes?" Kristin had asked, half laughing, not knowing whether or not Josiah was serious. "No, I'm too cold, not too hot."

Josiah was rolling out dough for biscuits, and he continued to work, as he explained his theory of sleeping warm to Kristin.

"If you was hot, you'd want to keep your clothes on."

"That doesn't make sense," Kristin said.

"Sure it does. You see, if you take off all your clothes so that you are as nekkid as the day you was born, then climb in under the covers, why, the covers just sort of trap the body heat around you, and it builds up a cocoon, so's you're warm as toast, afore you know it. When you sleep in clothes, that body heat don't build up as quick."

"But what if . . . what if the ship went down," Kristin said. "Without clothes I'd freeze in the water."

"You'd freeze anyway, miss," Josiah said easily. "Besides, unless you figure you can swim two or three hunnert miles or more, then you just as well to freeze as drown."

Kristin had tried Josiah's theory that night, and to her surprise it worked. Now she slept nude every night, burrowed in a blanket, the blanket wrapped in a quilt, and the quilt covered with a comforter.

Just as Kristin finished undressing and wrapped herself in the blanket, she heard a very light knock at the door.

"Andrew?" she called. "Is that you?" Her heart leaped with hope.

"It's Julian Truax," a voice answered.

"Oh, Mr. Truax," Kristin said, unable to keep the disappointment out of her voice. "It's late, and I'm about to go to bed."

"I'm sorry if I've disturbed you," Truax said. "But I have that book we talked about. The one I thought you might want to read. I'll just leave it out here by the door."

"Yes, that will be fine," Kristin said. "Just . . . no, wait." In a sudden rush of bravado, Kristin decided to invite Truax in. Why not? He had been most attentive to her. He was certainly as much a gentleman as Andrew Roberts, perhaps even more so. And she had enjoyed the periodic discussions they had been having. He hadn't convinced her of his cause, but she was, at least, convinced that he was sincerely motivated and genuinely dedicated to the principle of dignity for man. She no longer believed him to be an anarchist . . . or worse, someone with a demented mind and misguided ideals.

Of course, if she invited him in dressed as she was now, wouldn't she be flirting with danger? What was it he said? *I will never come to you without an invitation. Because when that invitation is issued, I will know that you regard me as your equal.* Would he construe this as that invitation? Would she *mean* it as an invitation?

Well, why not? she asked herself. Why should she turn away his attentions if they were offered? What did she have to protect? Certainly not her virginity. Certainly not her relationship with Andrew, for there was no relationship with him. And as Truax had said, here on board this vessel, they made their own rules of behavior. They were in their own world. The social mores she had been bound to no longer existed, did they? Or if they did, they didn't exist in this world. Here everything had been reduced to the most elemental level. Eat, sleep, stay warm, stay alive. And if in addition to those basic elements, there was an opportunity to take the comfort and pleasure sex provided, then why not take it?

Kristin took a deep breath, girded her resolve about her like a suit of armor, and called out, "Come in."

The door opened and Truax stepped inside, holding the book in his hand. He saw Kristin standing there, holding the blanket wrapped around her, her legs uncovered from the knees down, and her feet bare.

"I'm sorry," he said. "I seem to have come at an awkward time."

"No, Mr. Truax," Kristin said in a voice that was small but resolute. "You have come at a most propitious time."

Truax put the book on the shelf and looked at Kristin with an expression of anticipation on his face. "You remember what I said on the deck?" he asked. "That night we spoke?"

"Yes," Kristin said.

"I won't force myself on you. If you want me to leave now, say so, and I shall go."

Kristin was quiet.

"Do you want me to stay?"

"I . . . I haven't asked you to leave," Kristin said.

"No, Kristin, girl. That isn't enough," Truax said. "You must ask me to stay."

Kristin looked at the floor, and two tears slid out of her eyes and down her cheeks. She began crying quietly.

"Ask me to stay, girl."

"Why, Julian?" Kristin finally asked. "Why must I ask you? Oh, God, am I such an awful person that I am to know nothing but rejection for the rest of my life?"

"Rejection? No, girl, no," Truax said, moving to her then and putting his arms around her. He pulled her to him and held her tightly. "Don't you understand what I'm saying? Despite all that I say, I . . . I would never consider myself good enough for you unless you told me so with your own voice. Unless you ask me. Only then will I know."

"Please stay," Kristin said. "Please stay . . . and make love to me."

"Yes, Kristin," Truax said, pulling her lips to his for a kiss. "I'll stay, and I'll make love to you."

A short time later, they were in Kristin's bed with their naked bodies pressed together. Kristin, who had planned this with Andrew, now accepted fully and eagerly this surrogate in the person of Julian Truax. Truax was a gentle and caring lover. He wasn't as virile as Andrew . . . he didn't bring the same animal strength into the bed. But he wasn't the overeager virgin that Mr. Bright was, either. He was somewhere in between, certainly skilled enough to arouse all the passions and hungers within Kristin and capable enough to orchestrate those passions and hungers to the point of rapturous release so that the keen edge of frustration which had gnawed away at Kristin for many days was removed, and she soared with the ecstasy of the moment, coming out on the other side, relieved and satisfied, and with the terrible hollowness filled.

And yet, even as Truax's shuddering moan of pleasure told Kristin that he, too, had been satisfied, she was aware of the vast difference between this and the times she and Andrew had made love. With Andrew, it had been one explosion of pleasure after another, going from peak to peak again and again and again, and yet, during all that, she had been aware of Andrew. She was not merely being with him, she was a part of him. This time she had nearly forgotten Truax, so lost was she in her own quest for fulfillment.

Later, with the pleasant warmth of Truax still with her and only their relaxed breathing to bind them together, Kristin closed her mind and her heart to any possible recriminations. She would not allow herself to feel guilt over what had taken place here tonight.

Chapter Thirty

The formal inquiry into the mental competence of Constance Ann Chalmers to continue in her capacity as Chairman of the Board of Chalmers Shipping Company was begun on the afternoon of Monday, June 4, 1901. It was a bright, sunny afternoon outside, and as the parties to the hearing arrived at probate court, they could hear the shouting and laughter of children playing in the park. Inside, however, the atmosphere was darker, since the courtroom was lighted only by a row of narrow, dusty windows located high on one wall. The sun that managed to get through the windows had to stab down through millions of floating dust motes so that what light did arrive was dimly diffused throughout the room, then absorbed by the heavy drapes and dark walls.

Those parties to the hearing were the sitting members of the board of directors, Tony Norton, counsel for

Miles Chalmers, and Anson Miller, retained by Constance Chalmers. Constance and Miller sat at one large, oak table, and across from them at another table some twenty feet away sat Miles and Tony Norton. The board members sat in the gallery with the spectators and the jury chairs were empty. The case was being heard by Judge George Waters and witnessed by members of the press and nearly one hundred and fifty spectators.

Anson Miller was seventy-three years old. He was head of one of the most prestigious law firms in the city, but he hadn't personally handled a case in nearly fifteen years. He had tried to talk Constance into using one of the young hotshot lawyers in his firm, but Constance had insisted upon having Anson there personally.

"I have to confess, Constance, that I have not kept myself properly informed on all the precedents. And Tony Norton is one very good lawyer," Anson warned again as they waited for the judge to enter.

"Anson, all you have to do is prove that I haven't lost my mind," Constance said. "That shouldn't be all that difficult, now should it?"

"We'll have one strike against us, Connie, when Judge Waters sees that you didn't have any better sense than to hire me," Anson joked.

"Then let the old coot rule as he will," Constance had replied. "You aren't only my lawyer, you are my friend. And you were Lee's friend, and John David's friend before that."

Anson reached over and patted Constance's hand affectionately.

"All rise!" the clerk called.

There was a scraping of chairs as Judge Waters came into the room, and everyone remained standing until the clerk called out the familiar opening phrases. A moment later, they were once more seated, waiting for the judge to start the proceedings.

Judge Waters settled into his seat behind the bench

and removed his glasses to clean them as he looked at the adversaries, the parties to the proceedings, the press, and the gallery of interested onlookers. It was a personal habit of his, totally unnecessary, for the glasses had been thoroughly cleaned while he was still waiting in chambers. Finally, after he finished wiping the spectacles, he slipped them back on and cleared his throat.

"Chalmers versus Chalmers. Is the plaintiff ready?"

Tony Norton stood and looked at Miles. Miles nodded his head slightly. "We are ready, Your Honor."

"Is the defendant ready?"

"The defendant is ready, Your Honor," Anson said. He didn't really stand; he just raised himself about one inch from his chair, then settled back as if having made a great concession to propriety.

"Very well, plaintiff, call your first witness," Judge Waters said.

"Your Honor, the plaintiff calls Dr. Frank Peters to the stand."

A rather small bald-headed man wearing pince-nez glasses and a Vandyke beard was sworn in. He was questioned by Tony Norton.

"State your name, please, sir."

"Frank C. Peters."

"What is your profession?"

"I am a doctor, specializing in psychiatry. That is a science which deals with the workings of the mind."

"Dr. Peters, have you observed the workings of Mrs. Constance Chalmers's mind?"

"I have."

"Where, and how, did you make such an observation?"

"I accompanied Mr. Miles Chalmers, yourself, and one of my colleagues, Dr. Thomas Goodwin, to Mrs. Chalmers's residence at Ocean House. I observed her there."

"And as a result of those observations, what conclusion did you draw?"

"I drew no conclusion at that moment, for a conclusion drawn from just one observation would have been completely unprofessional. I did determine a need for further investigation."

"Have you since drawn a conclusion?"

"I have."

"And what is that conclusion?"

"Mrs. Chalmers is suffering from disassociative realism. She has a total inability to accept death."

"I beg your pardon?" Judge Waters asked.

Dr. Peters cleared his throat, and looked up at the judge. "I said, Your Honor, that Mrs. Chalmers is unable to accept death."

"What do you mean by that statement?" Judge Waters asked.

"Simply this, Your Honor. She has closed her mind to reality. She believes John David Chalmers, her father-in-law, is still alive though he has been dead for well over thirty years. And more recently, she has refused to accept the possibility of the death of her granddaughter, Kristin, though an overwhelming amount of evidence points to death as the young girl's fate."

"Dr. Peters," Tony said, walking away from his witness and looking pointedly at Constance. "How have you come by such a decision?"

Peters removed his glasses and polished them industriously as he talked. "When I was able to observe Mrs. Chalmers the one time I did see her, she had locked herself in a room. The room was like a tomb of some sort. Always locked tightly shut and kept in the dark. The room was filled with artifacts from John David Chalmers's life. His books, slippers, toilet articles, even the newspaper he was reading at the time of his death, and ashes from his last cigar were still there."

"Why do you suppose the room was kept this way?" Norton asked.

"Those artifacts helped her sustain the illusion that John David Chalmers was still alive. It is my belief that Mrs. Chalmers would go into seclusion in this room and there talk with John David."

There was a small gasp of surprise from the gallery, but Judge Waters was able to quiet them with a wave of his hand. Judge Waters leaned over the bench. "Do you mean she was a medium?"

"No, Your Honor," Dr. Peters said. "Whatever you may believe about mediums, they, at least, recognize death, and when they supposedly talk to those who have died, they pass themselves off to be talking to people from the world of the nonliving. I believe Mrs. Chalmers thinks she is talking to a still-living John Chalmers."

"Are you certain of this?" Norton asked.

"Well, no," Dr. Peters admitted. "After all, psychiatry is a new field. It should in no way be construed as an exact science."

"Yet you would ask me to judge upon this person's mental competency," the judge said.

"Yes, Your Honor. Your decision must be a judgment, just as mine is."

"I need no instructions from you, thank you, Doctor."

"Your Honor," Norton put in quickly. "I'm certain Dr. Peters meant no instructions. He was merely trying to make available to you the benefit of *his* judgment in the field in which he is qualified."

"I will accept his judgment for what it is," Judge Waters said. "Have you further questions of this witness?"

"No, Your Honor."

"Questions by the defense?"

Anson Miller got up slowly and walked over to stand in front of the doctor.

"Were you able to question Mrs. Chalmers?"

307

"Well, not exactly."

"Is memory also an inexact science, Doctor? Surely you know whether you questioned her or not?"

"I didn't question her."

"And yet you are willing to make the observation that she is incompetent?"

Dr. Peters smiled. "No," he said. "That is a decision the judge must make. I can only make the judgment that she does not have a grasp of reality."

"Based on the one, brief observation you made."

"And the interviews with those who work with her and know her best."

"Thank you, Doctor. I have no more questions."

Dr. Peters was followed to the stand by Dr. Thomas Goodwin, whose testimony was substantially the same. After Dr. Goodwin, there was testimony from former housekeepers who swore they had heard Constance speaking with John David years after he had died, and one exceptionally damaging testimony from a young domestic who said that only three days ago she had observed Constance "having tea" with Kristin.

"She's lying, Anson," Constance said, leaning over to whisper in Anson's ear. The girl's testimony, however, was verified by two others, who swore they had been summoned by the girl to see what was going on.

"Do they have any reason to tell such a lie?" Anson asked Constance.

"None that I can think of," Constance said. "Except perhaps money. Perhaps Miles paid them to lie."

Perhaps all the testimony submitted thus far could have been passed off as the idiosyncrasies of an eccentric with little harm to her case. But then came the most damaging evidence of all. Several business associates, submitting documented reports, showed that in the last six months, and especially during the last four weeks, Chalmers Shipping Company had lost a tremendous amount of money due to ill-advised business ventures. There were statements showing that Chalmers

308

ships frequently padded the crew with "Widow's Men," fictitious crew members whose pay went to the widows and orphans of seamen. This practice alone was costing Chalmers Shipping several thousand dollars a year, and Constance knew about it but made no effort to stop it, despite the existence of a widow's pension. Documentation was also submitted showing that Constance habitually paid far more than the prevailing market price for goods and services she used, and a case in point was the recent acquisition of the *Morning Star,* now en route to San Francisco, for which she doubled the bid of the next highest company.

It was further pointed out that since the disappearance of Kristin Chalmers, Mrs. Chalmers had missed several board meetings. What business she did attend to was the expenditure of thousands of dollars in detectives fees plus a private security force with the primary duty of locating the missing girl.

"In fact, it was this very thing that caused the recent death of the honorable Captain Woodward," Norton said. "And nearly caused the death of Mr. Miles Chalmers himself."

"Objection, Your Honor," Anson called from his table. "I'd like an explanation of that statement."

"I would too, if you don't mind, Mr. Norton," the judge said.

"Your Honor, as we've pointed out in some of the documentation already submitted, Chalmers Shipping Company underwent a series of robberies and arsons in recent weeks. Mr. Chalmers tried to get the security police to act on these poblems. In fact, he believed it was for this reason that the force was established. But Captain Woodward informed Mr. Chalmers that his orders were quite specific. He and his entire private police force were to concentrate solely on locating Kristin Chalmers. Therefore, Mr. Chalmers suggested that they meet at his vacation house to discuss, in private, ways of dealing with the unreasonable request. It was while they were there that the unfortunate accident occurred that took Mr. Woodward's life and nearly took Mr. Chalmers's as well."

"Your statement made it appear as if Constance Chalmers's involvement in this was sinister," Anson said.

"Forgive me, Your Honor. That was not my intent."

"Do you withdraw your statement?"

"Yes, Your Honor."

"You may continue."

"Your Honor, I have no more witnesses to add to the parade of concerned citizens who have already appeared before you today to offer their expert testimony. I do have this resolution passed by the Board of Directors of Chalmers Shipping Company and signed by every member, stating that in their opinion Constance Chalmers is no longer competent to administer this company."

"That's not binding," Constance blurted out. *"I* control the board, *I* make the appointments, *I* render the decisions! I have not authorized release of such a resolution."

"Mrs. Chalmers, please," Judge Waters said. "You will have your opportunity to speak."

Anson put his hand on Constance's arm and made tiny shushing noises with his lips. Constance turned in her chair and looked scathingly at the members of the board. None of them would return her gaze.

"Now, Your Honor, I want it clearly understood that we find no fault with Constance Chalmers's intentions. She is a woman of good heart and has for many years been an inspiration to us all. But I feel that she is no longer up to the task before her, and too much rides on the fortunes of Chalmers Shipping. Directly and indirectly, there are thousands of people who depend on Chalmers Shipping Company for their livelihood. And financial disaster that befalls the shipping company affects all those lives. Look at her, Your Honor. Upon the tired, overworked shoulders of this poor, tragic woman rests the fate of thousands of hardworking citizens. For their sake, for the sake of the officers and family members who have vested stakes in the company, and for her own peace of mind and rest of soul, we ask not that she be stripped of her holdings but merely granted relief from the awesome burden she has been forced to carry for forty years."

Anson Miller stood up and shuffled over to the bench. During the hearing he had carried on the fight gallantly, questioning each witness extensively, examining the figures of the financial reports, challenging the contention that the reverses were brought on by incompetent management. But the forces aligned against him were overwhelming, and he knew it. There was only one recourse now, and that was to call Constance to the stand. That also meant that Tony wielded the tongue of cross-examination like a saber, slashing boldly here, hacking away there, until even those trained in courtroom procedure would be left stammering and gasping for breath. He had no idea how Constance would stand up under it, but he had no choice.

"Your Honor, I'd like to call Mrs. Chalmers to the stand, please."

Constance stood up, tall and straight, and walked directly to the stand without a sideward glance. She was sworn, then took the seat and waited patiently for the questions.

"Now, Mrs. Chalmers," Anson said. "The question here is very simple, regardless of all the extraneous material introduced by the plaintiff. Quite simply put it is this: Are you mentally competent to administer the affairs of Chalmers Shipping?"

"I am," Constance answered easily.

"Do you know the location of John David Chalmers?"

311

"I know the location of his mortal remains," Constance said. "He is buried in the Chalmers private cemetery on the grounds at Ocean House."

"Do you know the location of your husband, Lee?"

"I do not, sir. He was lost at sea."

"Do you know the location of your son, James?"

"I do not, sir. He was also lost at sea."

"Do you assume those two men to be deceased?"

"Yes, I do."

"Do you know the location of your granddaughter, Kristin?"

"I do not know," Constance said.

"Have you ever spoken to any of these dead or missing people, or served them tea, or in anyway seen them since they disappeared?"

"Of course not. The suggestion that I have is preposterous, and those who claim to have seen me doing so are lying.'

"Thank you. Mr. Norton, your witness."

"Mrs. Chalmers, is John David Chalmers dead?"

"Yes, of course he is."

"And Lee Chalmers?"

"I assume so."

"And James Chalmers?"

"I assume so."

"And Kristin?"

"No!" Constance said.

There was a mumble of surprise from the gallery.

"If she isn't dead, Mrs. Chalmers, then where is she?"

"I . . . I don't know," Constance said. "I fear she has been kidnapped."

"Have you received a ransom note?"

"No."

Norton ran his hand through his hair and turned his back to the witness, looking toward the spectators in the gallery, playing to them as an actor would to his audience. "Mrs. Chalmers, I'm afraid I don't understand," Norton said. "You say she has been kidnapped, but you haven't received a ransom note. Wouldn't you think that anyone who went to the trouble to kidnap the granddaughter of someone as wealthy as you would submit a ransom note so that their nefarious scheme would reap for them a profit?"

"I would think so, yes."

"But as yet there has been no ransom note."

"No."

"Mrs. Chalmers, were you shown a dress? A blood-stained dress that was positively identified as the one Kristin was wearing on the night she disappeared?"

"Yes."

"Has she contacted you since she disappeared?"

"No."

"Has anyone contacted you or told you that they know of her whereabouts?"

"No."

"Then it is obvious that she is dead, isn't it?"

"No," Constance said. "She isn't dead!"

"How do you know she isn't dead?"

"Because," Constance said, "if she were dead, I would know it."

"How would you know, Mrs. Chalmers?" Norton asked.

"God would tell me."

"Oh. *God* would tell you? Do you talk to God often, Mrs. Chalmers?"

"Yes."

Norton smiled broadly, then whirled around and pointed at her in triumph. "You talk with *God*, Mrs. Chalmers?"

"Yes," Constance said, smiling sweetly. "It's called prayer."

Those in the gallery who had no vested interest in the outcome of the trial laughed, and even the judge joined in the mirth. Norton coughed, then, with his face shining a brilliant red, excused the witness.

In summation, however, Norton recovered quickly.

313

He was brilliant. He wove the testimony of the two doctors and of all the witnesses into a tightly drawn web, supporting the contention of mental incompetence. He augmented their testimony with statements of fact from the business records and mentioned again the complete misuse of the private police force. And he tied it up neatly with the resolution passed by all the members of the board, stating that it was their considered opinion that Constance Chalmers was no longer capable of running a company as large as Chalmers. "I beg of you, Your Honor," he said in conclusion. "Find it in your heart to give this poor woman the rest she needs, the rest she so richly deserves, the rest she is unable to take for herself. I thank you, sir, for your indulgence."

Compared to Tony Norton's brilliant oratory, Anson Miller's summation was bumbling and ineffective. He tried to point out that the deteriorating financial condition of the company was at worst bad business and not necessarily indicative of mental incompetence. But the more he spoke, the worse he made it appear, until it began to look as if he were as guilty of incompetence as the plaintiff tried to make Constance Chalmers.

"Your Honor, if my client has shown any incompetence," Anson concluded, "it was in insisting upon retaining me as her personal counsel against my express advice. I ask now that you consider my ill-prepared attempt to defend her and weigh it against what you feel in your heart."

Anson returned to the table and sat down, then hung his head in sorrow and shame. He had been so badly outclassed by the young lawyer that he felt he had surely cost Constance her company. Constance reached over to pat his hand affectionately, reassuringly.

Judge Waters sat quietly at the bench for several moments. Finally, taking off his glasses and polishing them, he looked around the courtroom. He cleared his throat. "I shall retire to my chambers to consider this decision," he said. "It is a difficult one to make. I find

314

no fault with Mrs. Chalmers for clinging to the hope of life for her granddaughter, and I dare say that a close scrutiny of any major business in the United States today would reveal as many misadventures. But I do feel that I must weigh heavily the opinion of those who serve on the board with her and observe her day-to-day behavior. It is this opinion of her peers more than anything else that causes me distress in this case."

"Your Honor," a woman's voice spoke from the gallery.

There was another gasp of surprise as everyone turned to look toward the woman who spoke out.

"Mother, sit down!" Miles called. "We've concluded our case."

"Mrs. Chalmers, please," Tony said, starting toward her.

"Your Honor, may I say something?" Margaret asked. "Please let me speak!"

"Your Honor, I beg of you to excuse her," Tony said. "She's not used to jurisprudent behavior. I'll talk to her."

Tony walked over to Margaret, but she motioned him away impatiently. "Please, Your Honor, what I have to say is important to your decision."

"I see no harm in allowing the lady to speak," Judge Waters said.

Constance put her hand on Anson's and squeezed hard as she waited for Margaret to speak. She knew Margaret had waited forty years for this moment and was going to relish it. But what more could she say? What additional damage could she do?

"Your Honor, my name is Margaret Chalmers. I am the second largest stockholder of Chalmers Shipping, second only to Constance."

"Then you certainly have a vested interest in this case," the Judge said. "What do you have for the court?"

"I wish to withdraw my support for the board resolution," Margaret said.

"What? Mother, have you gone mad? What is this?" Miles shouted.

Tony returned quickly to silence Miles, but Miles wouldn't be silenced. He continued to yell and plead with his mother until Judge Waters, who had been pounding his gavel futilely, ordered the bailiff to silence him.

"Now, Mrs. Chalmers," Judge Waters said when Miles, angry and frustrated, sat down and buried his head in his arms. "You were saying?"

"For my son's entire life, I have driven him to this moment. But I did not want it like this. This is wrong," Margaret said. "Constance Chalmers is not only mentally competent, she is by far the best qualified person to run the company, and I want you to consider my opinion when you make your decision."

"Thank you, Mrs. Chalmers," Judge Waters said. "I think you have just made my decision relatively simple."

"Constance, did you hear that?" Anson asked. "We've just won this case!"

But Constance wasn't listening to Anson, because she had run to Margaret and the two women were embracing in tears while the gallery cheered.

Chapter Thirty-one

SHIP'S LOG, Barkentine *Morning Star,* June 7, 1901, under the Horn, 52 days out of Boston.

Begins with strong westerly breezes, sleet, and snow. Sea swells are very high.

Middle part winds come about. Sleet and snow abate. Seas continue to run heavy.

Five days under the Horn. Have three times transited as far west as 70 degrees, only to be blown back by strong westerly breezes.

Saw one ship today, heading east, running before the wind at good clip. Due to heavy seas was unable to speak. Do not know if he identified *Morn-*

ing Star or not. He was the *Swift Genoa* out of New York.

The leak has sealed itself again. It is odd that the leak occurs only during smooth seas and seals itself when the seas are heavy.

But it wasn't odd at all, Andrew knew. It wasn't odd if the leak was the result of sabotage, as Andrew believed now that it was. For on the last day the leak occurred, Andrew made a very tiny mark on the seacock valve. The mark was so small that only the one who made it would be able to see it. Then after the bilges were sounded and new water was found, Andrew checked the sea cock. It had been opened, there was no doubt about it. The mark had been moved. The result of that discovery left two questions in Andrew's mind. Who was doing it? And why? He believed he knew the answers to those questions. Of course, thus far it was only Andrew's belief that someone was doing it, though the belief was backed up by the evidence of the mark. That evidence, however, was too fragile for him to make an official entry in the ship's log; thus his suspicions were his own.

If Andrew had to make an accusation at this very moment, he would accuse the girl. She was a most enterprising person, of that he was certain. She had clearly shown herself to be imaginative enough to conceive the idea of opening the sea cock, and she had motive and opportunity, two things which had to be considered. Her motive was, clearly, to prevent this ship from reaching San Francisco. Her opportunity was her frequent visits to the gasoline engine. Even that added to Andrew's suspicions, for the girl obviously did not want the ship to founder. Therefore she taught herself the science of gasoline engines in order to ensure that the ship would not be placed in an excessive degree of danger. Substantiating that idea was the fact that when the ship encountered really difficult situations, such as a storm of great magnitude or seas as heavy as those encountered under the Horn, the leak stopped.

Andrew finished the cup of coffee Josiah had brought him a few moments ago and looked at the logbook, drumming his fingers on the table as he examined his thoughts. He told himself that the evidence was too fragile to enter in the logbook, but that was a lie. By all rights, his suspicions should be entered just so the record would cover him should anything happen. A logbook, after all, was not only a record of events but a record of a captain's thoughts and intuitions as well.

Why, then, did he not enter his suspicions about the girl's activity in the Ship's Log?

Andrew stood up and crossed over to the window to look at the slate-gray sea. He put his hands on either side of the window, leaning against it as he stared through the glass, feeling the intense cold of the outside even through the hull of the ship. He sighed, for he knew why he had not yet put her name in the book. Such an entry would cause only more trouble for the girl, and Andrew didn't want to cause her any more trouble. In fact, it bothered him that he was going to have to turn her over to the police when they did reach San Francisco.

There was much about the girl that Andrew admired. She was beautiful, of course, with a natural, wholesome beauty that Andrew had rarely encountered. Oh, he had seen other beautiful women, probably some who were even much more beautiful. But their beauty had been a studied beauty, classic lines augmented by the beautician's art. Rose Page had only the sun and the wind to arrange her hair, and the rain and the sea to apply its cosmetics to her face. And yet with no artificial aids to enhance her looks, her natural beauty blazed through like a beacon in the night.

Her beauty had drawn Andrew's attention first. But there were other things about the girl that he liked as well. Though she had attempted by persuasion and trickery to get him to turn back, or put into a port and let her off the ship, she had in other ways been a good sailor. She had not complained of the food, her cramped quarters, or any other aspect of the conditions at sea. She had voluntarily pitched in to help Josiah with his chores and always had a smile and a greeting for any of the crew. Andrew had never been in this close company with a woman for so long before this girl. He didn't really know what women were like. But he admitted, readily enough, that if Rose Page had been a man he would have liked him. For the qualities Rose Page possessed were the qualities Andrew most admired in any person.

Andrew also respected the girl's mind. She seemed to possess an inordinate amount of information about sailing. She used nautical terms easily and with understanding. She learned very quickly and was able to hold her own in any discussion, whether it be the abstract philosophies sprouted by Julian Truax or the aspects of shipping as a business. He had held several such conversations with her during the long hours at sea, slipping into the discussion so easily and quickly that before he realized it he was telling her his goals and plans for achieving those goals. Her contribution to the conversation had been mentally stimulating. She was more than a good listener, she was a good participant. And she had given him some intriguing ideas of her own. One idea she suggested was securing a mail contract from the U.S. government to carry the mail from the coast of California to Hawaii. The mail sometimes stayed piled up for weeks waiting for a courier, so the contracts could be had for the asking. And the mail would add significantly to the revenue of the trip without adding weight. Most captains avoided it because of the government paperwork involved, but the increased revenue was well worth the extra paperwork.

Yes, Andrew thought. Rose Page was a fascinating

woman. She was beautiful, she had the personal habits that he found likable in a person, and she was intelligent. All of these attributes paled, however, in the light of that which Andrew found most intriguing about her. Twice, since the girl had been on the ship, Andrew had had sex with her. The result of those two experiences had been nothing short of overwhelming. No woman in all of Andrew's experiences had ever moved him as this woman had. She had inflamed his senses and so filled his mind with thoughts of those two experiences that she threatened to dominate him. The day-to-day operation of the ship, the factors of command, even his personal goal to reclaim his ship were thoughts he had to force into his mind.

But therein was the rub of the entire relationship. Her ability to move him so and her sexual power over him were the result, he knew, of her life as a prostitute. She had the ability to make him feel that he was the most important person in the world when they were having sex. Andrew knew, however, that that was only an illusion. A brilliant illusion, created by a woman of remarkable sexual prowess. An illusion developed, no doubt, by the hundreds of men who had known her, who had seen her as he had, naked beneath them, crying with the joy of the moment, and giving much more than she was receiving.

Even as Andrew was thinking these thoughts, he felt a weakness in the pit of his stomach and a sweat in the palms of his hands, and he knew if he had the opportunity right now, this very moment, he would take her again.

He had been given that opportunity five days ago. She had prepared a dinner for him and invited him to her room, and there was no doubt in Andrew's mind where the dinner would have led. But then she told him she loved him.

Andrew had listened to those words in his mind a hundred times since then. No, a thousand times. And they hurt him as much each time he remembered as they did when she said them. He knew that the words were false, were only one more trick in her vast arsenal of weapons she could use against him. And she may have even known the power those words would have over him. Because he suspected that she knew the truth. The girl must know that he loved her.

"Cap'n Roberts, sir, the wind's right for another try," Gershom called from outside Andrew's door.

"Aye, I'm coming on deck, Mr. Gershom," Andrew answered. He buttoned his coat tightly about him and left the marginal comfort of his quarters to go on deck.

On deck the world appeared to be painted in various shades of gray and white. The deck was covered with snow and ice, and the ocean swells were gray, granite mountains, moving toward the ship. But with the wind behind, it was time to make another try at doubling the Horn.

The little barkentine plunged into the sea, and all the forward part of her went underwater. The sea poured in, threatening to wash everything overboard. In the scuppers, Duke and Bradford hauled on the foremast topsail stays and stood in water up to their waists.

"Truax," Andrew shouted. "Put a reef in your foresail."

"Aye, Captain," Truax replied, and he called for help from others as he sprang into action.

"Cap'n, the wind's coming ahead, sir!" Gershom shouted, and he pointed toward a large black cloud, rolling toward them from the southwest.

"Furl all sails," Andrew shouted. "Quickly, lads, or we'll be blown back to the Falkland Islands."

The gale grew worse, and carried with it more sleet and snow. The *Morning Star,* once more denied its transit, hove to and bobbed about like a cork.

By nightfall the storm finished, and the ship tossed on

the still heavy seas, but without wind and in the midst of a thick fog. The fog covered them like a blanket of cold, wet wool, and even finding one's way about on the decks was difficult.

"Girl, would you take the cap'n a sandwich?" Josiah asked. "He's scarce eat a bite now in the whole five days we been sittin' here in Satan's icebox."

"Yes," Kristin said. "I'll take it to him." She took the sandwich and a pot of coffee and, holding the coffee carefully and skillfully so the tossing of the deck would not cause any spillage, negotiated the distance between the galley and the captain's cabin without difficulty.

"Yes," Andrew called in answer to her knock.

"It's Rose, Captain Roberts."

The door opened, and Andrew smiled out at her. He stepped back and invited her inside.

"Josiah sent you something to eat," she said, showing him the sandwich and coffee.

"Good old Josiah," Andrew said. "A fellow never had a better mother."

"He thinks the sun rises and sets on you," Kristin said.

Andrew laughed. "I wish I could get it to rise down here. Tomorrow will be our sixth day."

"You'll make it through tomorrow, Captain. I know you will," Kristin said.

"Do you really think so?" Andrew asked.

"Yes," Kristin said. "And there will still be time for your record."

"The record," Andrew said. He laughed shortly, derisively. "I had nearly forgotten that."

"No, I don't believe that. Not you, Captain Roberts. You won't give up until the stroke of midnight on the eighty-ninth day."

Andrew laughed. "Perhaps you are right, after all," he said. He looked at Kristin seriously for a moment. "Rose, there's something I'd like to tell you."

323

"What?"

"It's about the other night," Andrew said. "The night you prepared the dinner for me."

"I . . . I made a fool of myself that night," Kristin said.

"No," Andrew put in quickly. "No you didn't, not at all!" He put his hand on hers. "Rose, listen to me. It was I who was the fool. You see, the truth is," he started, then he stopped, sighed, turned, and walked away from her. He stood with his back to her for a moment, then sighed and turned around looking at her. "Well, dammit, Rose girl, I love you."

"You what?" Kristin asked, not certain she heard correctly.

"I said . . . I love you."

A quick joy surged to Kristin's heart, only to be replaced by a sudden sorrow. No, not now, she thought. Not now. For although she loved him as much as she ever did and would have given anything to have heard those words five days ago, now, she knew, she didn't deserve them. For on the night she had felt betrayed, she had taken Julian Truax for her lover. Bitter tears stung her eyes, and she dropped her head quickly.

"Well?" Andrew said. "Well, isn't that what you wanted, girl?" He was surprised by her reaction. "Or was I right? Were you merely trying to use me?"

"No," Kristin said quickly. "I meant it when I said it."

"When you said it? How about now? Do you still love me?"

"Yes," Kristin said, very, very quietly.

Andrew smiled broadly. "Then will you marry me?"

"No," Kristin said just as quietly as before.

"What? What do you mean no? Goddammit, girl, I don't understand you!" Andrew bellowed. "Do you love me or not?"

"Yes, I love you," Kristin said. "Oh, Andrew, you'll never know how much I love you."

"Then why won't you marry me?"

"Because I . . . I . . ." Kristin broke down into tears, unable to tell him that she now felt stained. She no longer considered herself good enough for him.

"Listen, Rose darlin', I think I know what it is that's bothering you," Andrew said gently.

"You do?" Kristin asked in surprise.

"Aye, lass. You think it'll be troubling me to think of your former profession."

"My former profession?" Kristin asked, forgetting for the moment what he thought her to be.

"Aye, you know. You being a whore and all. I have to admit that it has taken some getting used to. But I'm willing to forget all that, Rose. And so help me, I'll never bring it up to you again."

"Oh, Andrew, you don't understand," Kristin cried. "You just don't understand at all."

"No," Andrew said. "No, Rose girl, I don't understand. I don't understand anything except that I love you, and you say you love me. And I want to marry you. That, I understand. Now, will you marry me or not?"

"Andrew, please," Kristin said. "Just give me a little time, would you?"

"Aye, lass. I'll give you some time. After all, that's what I have the most of at the moment."

Kristin smiled through her tears. "Thanks," she said.

"Get some rest, girl. We're going to try the Cape again tomorrow."

Kristin stepped outside and pulled Andrew's door to. She was just across the passageway from her own cabin, but she wasn't ready yet to go to bed. She had to talk to someone, to unburden herself of this terrible guilt she was now carrying.

But who could she talk to?

She considered Josiah. She had come to think a great deal of the old man. She respected his wisdom and appreciated his kindness. But she also knew his great affection for Andrew, and if she unburdened herself to

Josiah, she would just be placing the load on Josiah, for then he would have to protect her secret from Andrew, and it would be difficult for him.

That left only Julian Truax.

Well, why not? Kristin thought. After all, Julian Truax was the cause of her current dilemma. Until she had let him make love to her, she could have faced Andrew without shame, for Andrew already knew of Mr. Bright. Now she could not. Besides, Julian was a sensitive and intelligent man. Perhaps he would be able to help her.

Kristin knew that Julian was on deck, and she had a pretty good idea of where he was. Sailors who are cooped up together, so close for so many months, soon find a need for someplace to go to be alone. Like woodland animals claiming territorial rights, each sailor stakes out a few feet reserved only to him, and all others tend to respect his official proprietorship. Kristin learned of it as all new sailors did through observation and instinct. It was never verbalized because it was an unspoken law, and to put it into words would dilute its authority.

Truax had staked out for his place a small space of rail, just a few feet aft of the bowsprit on the starboard side of the ship. When Kristin found him, they were far enough removed from the others and so blanketed by the fog that there was, for the moment, the illusion that they were the only two people on the ship. In this desolate clime it was almost as if they were the only two people in the world.

"Julian," she called softly.

"Hello," Julian said, turning around and smiling at her call. "What are you doing on deck on such a cold night?"

"I want to talk to you about something," Kristin said.

"It sounds serious," Julian teased.

326

"It is," Kristin said. "Please, Julian, you are the only one I can turn to right now. You must help me."

"Of course I'll help you," Julian said. "If I can. What is it?"

Kristin moved up to the rail to stand beside him. She looked out into the fogbank as she spoke, knowing that the words would come easier for her if she didn't have to look him in the face. She told him everything that had happened to her. She told him of the rape and mistreatment when she had first been kidnapped, she told of the fear she felt after first coming aboard, and she told of falling in love with Andrew Roberts. Finally, she told him of Mr. Bright, and then of her experience with him. Because of those experiences, she said, she felt soiled and thought that she no longer deserved Andrew's love. When he mentioned it tonight, it broke her heart because it had come too late for her.

Julian was silent for a moment after Kristin finished her story. Finally, he spoke.

"If you had not been with Mr. Bright or with me, would you still have felt soiled?"

"No," Kristin said. "No, of course not."

"You must have a very low opinion of Mr. Bright and me."

"No, I don't," Kristin said quickly. "I liked Mr. Bright. And I like you, Julian. I like you very much. Why would you think my opinion of you would be so low?"

"Because," Truax said easily, "when the two rapists used your body, you did not feel as if they had soiled it. You considered yourself still pure for Captain Roberts. But with Mr. Bright and me, it is an entirely different story. We soiled you."

"No, I don't mean it that way and you know it."

"What way do you mean it then?" Truax asked.

"Well it's just that I . . . I wanted it with you," she said. "And with Mr. Bright." Her face flamed in the darkness. "And I enjoyed it."

"I see," Truax said. "So it is your mind you are policing and not your body, is that it?"

"I don't understand."

"Kristin, your body has known sex with four men besides Captain Roberts. Two of the men raped you against your will, and two of the men made love to you with your consent. The physical act of sex was the same. the only difference was your mental reaction to it. That which you found repulsive left you pure; that which you found pleasurable left you impure. But the purity and impurity is a state of your mind only, for technically all four events were the same. Now the question is . . . and this is the only question . . . do you love Captain Roberts?"

"Yes," Kristin said.

"Then that is a state of mind which should take precedence over all others. If you love him, tell him so. And if you are certain he loves you, then you have no problem."

"Should I tell him about the others?" Kristin asked.

"Why? Will it make it any easier for you to adjust yourself to it?"

"No," Kristin admitted.

"Then my suggestion is to tell him nothing. But . . ."

"But what?" Kristin asked.

"Be absolutely certain of his love for you, Kristin. You are a girl of exceptional worth, and I am not talking about your wealth. I am talking about you. It would be a sin to squander all that you are upon someone who does not give you his full measure."

"He has told me he loves me," Kristin said. "How else would one know?"

"How else indeed?" Truax replied. "That, my dear Kristin, is something no one but you can know."

Chapter Thirty-two

On the eighth of June the sun rose clear and continued so until twelve o'clock, at which time Andrew got an observation and fixed their position exactly. The winds were favorable and the sea somewhat abated. It seemed the perfect time to make another try for it.

"Do you want me at the helm, Cap'n?" Gershom asked.

"No, I'll take the helm. Keep your fingers crossed, Mr. Gershom. Maybe this will be our lucky day."

Everyone was on deck, ready to respond to any need the swiftly-changing conditions might create. Kristin and Josiah were going about, serving them a breakfast of biscuit and salt beef at their stations.

"Rose girl, if the sea gets too heavy, you go to your cabin and tie yourself to your bunk," Andrew ordered as she served him his breakfast.

"I'll be all right up here," Kristin replied.

"Please, girl, just do as I say. I wouldn't want you to be swept overboard."

"I'll be careful, Andrew. I promise you that," Kristin said.

With a following wind, the *Morning Star* proceeded westward, clipping through the waves at a pace that made everyone start to believe at long last the passage was going to be made, and an easy one at that. But ahead lay the last major obstacle. For ahead lay the confluence of the world's two greatest oceans, where the gigantic swells of the Pacific met by the powerful waves of the Atlantic create a maelstrom of whirlpools, eddies, currents, and seas, whose furious thunder can be heard for miles.

Kristin could hear the roar and see the ocean before them. It looked almost as if they were approaching a mountain range, and she wondered for a moment how the boat could ever be expected to sail uphill, and she marveled that any vessel ever made the passage.

"Excuse me, Miss Page, but you'd best get into harness if you intend to stay aboard," McQueen said. The big black sailor handed her a rope harness, then showed her how to put it on. It had snaps and clips that fastened to lifelines which had been rigged along the rails of the ship. It was designed so she could still move up and down the deck, but should she be swept overboard, she would still be connected to the ship, and if she was lucky could be pulled or pull herself back aboard.

"We're comin' into it, Cap'n!" one of the men yelled from the bow.

"Rose, hang on!" Andrew shouted.

The ship was tossed and slammed around at that instant more severely than at any time on the entire voyage. She was lifted up and thrown down, knocked along her port beams, then wallowed over and thrown backwards. She shuddered and slipped through the waves, sometimes giving the illusion of coming completely out of the water and other times going down by the bow, burying all the forward part of the vessel under the sea. If Kristin had not seen the need for the security lines before, she clearly saw the need now, for without them she and all the others would have been swept overboard.

"Captain, if we don't lay out there and furl the jib, we are going to lose the bowsprit," Truax suddenly shouted.

"Dammit!" Andrew swore, angry with himself. "Why the hell didn't I do it before we got into this sea? I can't ask anybody to do that. Truax, take the helm. I'm going to do it myself."

"You can't do it alone, Captain," Truax said.

"I can damn sure try," Andrew replied.

"Mr. Gershom," Truax called. "Would you take the helm, sir?"

"I'm still the captain of this vessel, Truax," Andrew said angrily. "I told you to take the helm."

"I'm going out on the bowsprit with you," Truax replied.

"Andy, don't be a fool," Josiah said. "You know damn well you can't furl that jib alone, and you also know Truax is the only one on this ship who can help."

Andrew glared at Josiah and at Truax, then with a resigned shrug of his shoulders said, "Come on, Truax. It's my mistake. I hope it's not your funeral."

Kristin moved forward with the two men, fearful for their safety, knowing, however, that what they were about to do had to be done. She breathed a quick prayer for their safety and realized at that moment that *she loved them both!*

Andrew's face was grimly set as he studied the bowsprit to ascertain just how best to accomplish this disagreeable task. Truax, she noticed, lay his hand once lightly on that section of the starboard rail he claimed as his own, almost as if telling it good-bye. Then with a wan smile he sprang to the starboard knighthead and crawled out onto the bowsprit.

Andrew went out on the other side, and both men, their feet in the footropes, held on by the spar as they worked their way out.

Truax had purposely chosen the leeward side, which was the more dangerous side, for the great sheet was flying with the wind and puffed out so that it was all he could do to keep from being thrown off the boom.

For some time the two men could do nothing but hold on. Finally they succeeded in furling the jib to a degree, at least enough to prevent it from tearing off the bowsprit.

"Thank you, Truax," Andrew shouted across the spar. "I must admit, sir, I would have been unable to do it without you."

"Glad I could help, Captain," Truax said, smiling back at him. At that moment, there passed through the two men a look of understanding. In the briefest glances, they told each other that they admired and respected one another as only adversaries of equal strength can. "Regardless of how our personal battle turns out," their eyes seemed to say, "you are a man I could like."

Suddenly two huge waves broke over the ship, and the vessel plunged into them. The men held on tightly, and the first wave brought them in freezing water up to their chins. The bow raised up out of the water so that both men hung suspended at a great height over the sea, dripping wet and freezing rapidly to the spar. Then the ship plunged back down again, and this time both men went completely under the water. Andrew was taking a breath just as they went under, and he got a mouthful of water, tasting the burn of the brine. He closed his eyes tightly and, when the ship lifted out of the water again, he was holding on for dear life, coughing desperately to get his breath. When he opened his eyes and looked across the jibboom, Julian Truax was gone.

Chapter Thirty-three

SHIP'S LOG, Barkentine *Morning Star* 132 degrees west longitude, 32 degrees north latitude. 79 days out of Boston, July 4, 1901.

Independence Day begins calm with freshening breezes by midmorning.

Forty nine days since leak occurred. Now know from two men who were witnesses to the fact that it was caused by Julian Truax, now deceased. Truax hoped to cause an increased work load and dissatisfaction among sailors so all would join union. Despite this, Truax goes down in this author's book as a good sailor although somewhat misguided.

The author of this log hereby confesses to the following misdeed and enters into the commission of same with full knowledge of its impropriety.

Tomorrow this vessel will make an unscheduled stop in the Southern California town of Los Angeles. There Miss Rose Page will be set ashore. This is being done to keep her from the hands of the law in San Francisco. If the San Francisco police department can be satisfied by the payment of a fine, then the fine will be paid. If they cannot be satisfied with a fine, then the captain of this vessel stands ready to accept the consequences of his action.

It now appears that the record is in sight though this unscheduled stop will surely mean the record will not be attained. The crew has performed ably, however, and they shall receive the same money they would have received had the record passage been accomplished. This will be paid from the salary due the captain and the hatch money. The $1,000 fee paid for the delivery of Miss Page will be surrendered to the San Francisco Police Department.

Andrew had been thinking of the entry in the log ever since he made it earlier in the day. He had told neither the girl nor any of the crew of his intentions. And as he was the one who kept the chart . . . Gershom was totally unequal to the task . . . no one else knew that the coast of California and the town of Los Angeles lay less than one hundred miles away from their present position.

Losing Julian Truax beneath the Horn had had a strange effect on the crew. They seemed to grow closer as a result. At first Andrew was willing to say that it was merely proof of the continued agitation of the sailor, and his death meant that there was no longer anyone to keep the sailors stirred up. But it was more than that. He may have been an agitator and perhaps an organizer for the dreaded union, but he was a sailor. He was, perhaps, the finest sailor Andrew had ever known. And it was typical of him to be engaged in the most dangerous job at the most dangerous time when he was killed.

The men all knew this as well. Among deepwater men there is no substitute for a man who always stands ready to do his duty and never shirks. When the rare person comes along who possesses that trait, he immediately earns the honor and the respect of all his crewmates. And if something happens to take him from their midst, they sometimes unconsciously pay homage to his memory by emulating his habits. Thus it was that there were none who shirked for the next thirty-six days, and with fair winds, smooth seas, and a hardworking crew, Andrew Roberts stood ready to snatch victory from the jaws of defeat.

But Andrew had not counted on the girl, and the closer he got to San Francisco, the less important the record seemed to be in his mind and the more important the prospect of surrendering the girl to whatever fate awaited her at that place. For that reason, Andrew had been gradually steering a course for Los Angeles, and tomorrow night they would be there.

Though the men had worked well on this day and they had run nearly three hundred miles, noon to noon, it was the nation's birthday, so Andrew ordered Josiah to slaughter the one remaining pig and roast it for a special celebration. Josiah had been cooking it for some three hours now, spitted whole and turning slowly over open coals so that the rich, succulent aroma permeated the ship and reached the nostrils of every man jack, whether he be at the helm, on the highest yard, or down in the orlop deck.

There was a spring to the step as the men walked, a

whistle on their lips as they worked, and a smile in their voices when they spoke. After weeks and weeks of moldy salt meat, biscuits with weevils, beans and rice, the prospect of fresh, spitted pork was a joyful one.

Kristin was as excited over the prospect as the men. Now, as she stood at the rail watching the others work and smelling the delightful aroma of the cooking pig, she tried to recall when she had looked forward to a party with more eagerness. She had, of course, attended hundreds of parties in her life, from her own and her friends' birthday parties as a little girl to the social extravaganzas she had attended as a debutante. But the most grand of those parties lacked the excitement of the one upcoming.

She wondered what it would be like; if by some feat of magic her friends could suddenly be transported to the deck of the *Morning Star* for the evening's dinner. How would they react? She laughed as she knew that all of them would react in absolute horror. But even as she laughed, she knew that she was once just like them. Seventy-nine days had changed her more than anyone could possibly believe.

"Ah, there you are, Rose girl," Josiah said, seeing her at the rail. She had taken the part of the rail once used by Truax. It had been an unconscious thing but one that was recognized, though not spoken of, by everyone else aboard including Andrew Roberts. "Would you make a rice pudding for the dinner?"

"A rice pudding? I'd be glad to, Josiah. I must confess, I don't know what to do. Will you tell me?"

"Sure, I'll tell you, lass. Though for the life of me, I don't know how any girl could grow to your age and not know any more about cookin'. You'd think you'd been raised in a fine house with cooks and servants to wait on you your whole life."

"I guess I just never paid much attention to it," Kristin said. "But I think I can do it if you tell me what to do."

"There ain't much to it, girl," Josiah said. "Come along, I'll get you started."

Late that afternoon, with the pig done and the rice pudding nearly so, the sailors amid much laughing and joking rigged up a sail canvas screen, then connected a hose to the gasoline bilge pump. Another hose went overboard to pick up the seawater, and the sailors thus created an effective shower. When Kristin first heard the sound of the pump and then a loud peal of laughter followed by an outburst of expletives, she stuck her head from the galley to see what was going on.

"Don't go forward, miss," she was warned by Hunt, who was standing guard for just such a purpose.

"Why not? What's going on up there?"

"The men are all takin' a bath, miss. For the dinner."

"A bath? My, this is an occasion, isn't it?" she said. For in truth, except for the captain's penchant for bathing and his generosity in allowing her the use of his tub, none of the sailors had taken a bath since leaving Boston. (She had no idea how long it had been for most of them before leaving Boston.) The sailors generally believed, and not without some reason, that their constant exposure to the rain and sea spray, kept them fairly clean. It was a rare occasion indeed when a sea shower was rigged.

One by one the sailors began showing up then, dressed in their shore clothes, with clean, red-striped or red-checkered shirts, and white duck trousers. Sometime later Captain Roberts appeared on deck, dressed in his captain's uniform, the one he wore for special occasions ashore.

"My, how handsome you all are," Kristin said as the sailors began gathering on deck, waiting for the dinner to be served.

"Cap'n," Gershom said, "can we give it to her now?"

Andrew smiled. "It was supposed to be a surprise for after the party."

"Yes, sir, but I figure she'd rather have it before the party."

"Aye, Cap'n. The rest of us figure that too," Bradford said.

"Very well, give it to her."

"Her? Are you talking about me?" Kristin asked.

"Well now, missy, you are the only *her* on this here vessel," Josiah said and his comment was greeted with more laughter.

"Give it to her, Cap'n," Gershom said.

"No, it's from you and the crew. You give it to her."

"Josiah?" Gershom said.

"Gershom, you're the one that made it. By rights, it should be you give it to her."

"Aye," the others said.

Gershom cleared his throat and one of the crew placed a package in his hand. "Well, miss," he said. "Well," he started again.

"For God's sake, Mr. Gershom, just tell her," someone urged.

Gershom thrust the package toward Kristin. "It was me that made it, miss, that's true enough. But the makings come from everyone's slop chest. Here."

"Well, what . . ." Kristin started, but as she was opening the package she saw what it was. It was a dress, handsewn by Gershom, who as a master sailmaker was as skilled as the finest seamstress. It was truly a beautiful piece of work, and since it was modeled after a picture one of the men had cut from a catalog . . . because he thought the girl pretty and meant to keep her likeness for company on the long voyage . . . it was very stylish. The material for the dress came from donated shirts, trousers, and other items, perfectly cut and matched as to color and weave. Kristin tried to say thank you, but when she opened her mouth to speak, the words wouldn't come. Tears slid down her face.

"She don't like it," Hunt said. "I told you that just

'cause you can make a sail ain't no sign you can make a lady's dress."

"Like it! I *love* it." Kristin said.

"But you're cryin'," Hunt said.

"Hunt, you dumb son of a bitch," Josiah said. "I ain't been ashore but one month ever ten years, but I know more about women than you do. They cry when they are happy. Now hush up 'n let her cry."

Kristin laughed and the laughter and the crying got all mixed up. The men looked on in embarrassed silence. Finally Josiah spoke again.

"If you want to get all dressed up for the party, why, I reckon we wouldn't mind the wait at all."

"I'll be right back," Kristin said. She looked at Andrew and he smiled.

"It's already drawn for you," he said, speaking of the bathtub in his cabin.

Andrew wasn't teasing. The bath had been drawn and sitting beside the soap was an ampule of bath oil and a vial of perfume. Kristin wondered where they had come from, but her curiosity wasn't half as great as her pleasure in discovering the unexpected treasure.

Kristin would have much preferred a long, leisurely bath, luxuriating in the soapy mixture and feeling the sensual delight of the oil and perfume. But she knew that the men were anxious for the party to start, so she bathed as quickly as possible, then returned to the deck.

The sun was setting in a fireburst of color, and the sea was smooth, and the breeze was gentle. On the deck a clean, white canvas had been spread, and a golden pig, with an apple thrust in its mouth, occupied the position of honor. To each side of the pig was a hoop of newly opened cheese, and there was wine, and, of course, her rice pudding.

"My God, miss," Josiah said. "I've never seen a more beautiful sight in my life."

At first Kristin thought Josiah was talking about the

dinner setting, but then she realized he was talking about her. She blushed though her skin had become so tanned from the sun that the blush wasn't as discernible as it once would have been.

"Nor have I," Andrew said, and the expression in his voice and on his face were just as reverential as those on the faces of the sailors.

At that moment, Kristin realized that a change had taken place. Whereas she had been thus far in the trip nearly one of the crew, she now suddenly was thrust back into the role of being a lady. It was a role that she knew she would occupy for the duration of the voyage. She felt a small pang of remorse for what she would be giving up, but even while feeling that remorse, she was glad to return to the role of being a woman again.

The meal was as magnificent as the aroma had promised, and afterward, when everything was eaten and everyone lay around in good spirits, one of the sailors pulled out a flute and began playing a lively tune, and a couple began to dance the hornpipe.

Andrew came over to sit beside Kristin. Since his declaration of love for her while still under the Horn, he had made no more overtures. Kristin had asked for a little time then, primarily to come to grips with those things that were bothering her. But Truax had been killed and, though it wasn't said, a moratorium was placed on everything. Andrew had said nothing more about his feelings for her but neither had he grown cool.

"Have you seen the hornpipe danced before?" Andrew asked.

"Not like this," Kristin said. She had seen it danced several times at parties in Boston. At one time it was considered very chic to get authentic entertainment, real Indians to do Indian dances, real sailors to do sailors' dances. But the difference between the rather stilted and almost embarrassing display at the parties and this natural venting of good feeling aboard ship was staggering.

"Now I understand," she said.

"Understand? Understand what?"

"I understand why a man could spend a lifetime at sea. There is so much joy in moments like this that everything else is worthwhile."

"Have you enjoyed your voyage?"

"More than I can ever tell you," Kristin said. "Though, there is sadness too when I think of Mr. Bright and Julian Truax."

"Aye. That too is part of the sailor's life," Andrew said. "And it's knowing that as you do that I'm still asking you to marry me. You wanted time to think of it, Rose, and now you've had more than a month. I'm asking now, and I've a reason for wanting an answer tonight."

Kristin looked at Andrew and at that moment she would have been the happiest girl in the world if she could just be Rose Page and forget the responsibilities inherent in the Chalmers name. As Rose Page, she would have only herself to answer for, and she could, and would, say yes, spending the rest of her life as his wife, sailing with him as captain's wives often did.

But she was Kristin Chalmers.

"Andrew . . . I'll not give you an answer this moment," she said. "But if you still want to marry me after we reach San Francisco, knowing what you will know then, I'll be glad to say yes."

"Then it is yes now, girl," Andrew said, smiling broadly. "For there is nothing in San Francisco that can change how I feel about you."

"Don't be so sure," Kristin said.

"Besides, you'll not be seeing San Francisco."

"I'll not be seeing San Francisco? What are you talking about?" Kristin asked.

Andrew smiled. "Mr. Gershom," he called.

"Aye, sir?"

"Muster all hands. I want to make an announcement."

"Aye, sir. All hands, stand to for the cap'n's announcement."

The flute stopped and the sailors gathered around, standing or sitting loosely by the remnants of the feast. The sun had completely set, and the ship sailed now under the deep blue of late twilight.

"Men, I promised you a bonus if we set the record."

"Aye, sir, that you did," one of the men said. "And we'll be settin' the record now, sure as a gun is iron."

"No," Andrew said. "We won't be."

"Cap'n, you mean we can't make it now?"

"No," Andrew said. "But it's not your fault. I steered a course that cost us a chance at the record. You're not to worry, though, for I can pay you the bonus out of my fees and hatch money."

"But why did you steer such a course?" Gershom asked.

"I think I know," Josiah said. He looked at the girl.

"Aye, Josiah, old friend, you are right. And you others, I hope will understand as well. As you know, I was supposed to turn Rose over to the San Francisco police. But I won't be doing that. Tomorrow, we'll land in Los Angeles and I'll put her ashore there."

"Andrew, no!" Kristin said. "You don't know what you are doing!"

"I know, Rose girl. I'm committing a crime. But I can't turn you over to them, can't you see that? I love you, girl. And I don't mind saying that aloud in front of all these witnesses. I love you and I'll not turn you over to the police."

"But the record! Your ship! You'll lose the chance to buy back your ship!"

"Then I'll save for it," Andrew said. "But there are some things more important than others."

342

"I didn't think anything was more important than your ship," Kristin said.

"You are, girl."

"The cap'n's right," McQueen said. "Cap'n, you don't owe me no bonus money. The way I see it, if we'd done our job proper, we'da had enough time to drop the lady off 'n still make San Francisco."

"McQueen's right," Hunt said. "You can have my bonus money too, Cap'n."

Within a short time, every sailor aboard had pledged to forgo his bonus money in order to see Kristin safely ashore in Los Angeles.

"You would all do that for me?" Kristin asked, moved by the demonstration.

"Aye, lass, we surely would," Josiah said.

Kristin smiled, and once again tears glistened in her eyes.

"Are you going to cry again, miss?" Hunt asked.

"No," Kristin said. "I'm going to do something even better." She smiled broadly, then put her arms around Josiah's neck and kissed him. The others whooped and cheered; then one by one she kissed every one of them.

"What about me?" Andrew asked.

"Yours comes later," Kristin said with a conspiratorial smile.

This time there were knowing, almost ribald laughs from the others, but strangely it did not bother Kristin. She felt as if she were one of them and she could afford the luxury of honesty.

She knew it would do no good to try and talk Andrew out of putting her ashore in Los Angeles, so she didn't even try. He would learn who she was in San Francisco, and when he came back for her, she would be ready.

Besides, she knew that there was no greater way for Andrew to show his love than to sacrifice his ship. She had no intention of denying him that privilege.

Chapter Thirty-four

BARKENTINE *MORNING STAR* SETS NEW RECORD!

SAILS FROM BOSTON TO SAN FRANCISCO IN 91 DAYS!

FASTEST EVER FOR SHIP OF ITS TONNAGE!

TO BE NAMESAKE FOR NEW RUM!

Arriving on the 17th instant, the Barkentine *Morning Star* under the able command of Captain Andrew Roberts established a new record for a ship of its tonnage in passing under the Horn from Boston to San Francisco in but 91 days!

Captain Roberts, when interviewed by this reporter, expressed some surprise over the record, believing that the mark to beat was 89 days. 89 days is indeed a record, established half a century ago by the clipper ship *Flying Cloud,* but the record of 91 days for a barkentine is no less inspirational when one considers that the *Morning Star* was exposing less than one-half the total canvas area and was carrying twice the weight.

Mr. Paul Yarber, president of Golden Gate Distillery, announced that a new rum bearing the name and likeness of the *Morning Star* would soon be introduced. "We expect sales to be brisk in honor of this magnificent achievement," Mr. Yarber said.

As many believe that a canal across the isthmus will be a reality, this may be a record that will last through all ages.

"Yes," Yarber said, leaning back in his chair, and staring across his large desk at Andrew. Through the window behind him the bay sparkled in the morning sun, and somewhere out there, among the forest of masts and trucks, lay the *Morning Star* though Andrew had no idea which one it was. "It is a real record," Yarber went on, answering the question posed by Andrew a moment earlier. "We had our researchers going through all the archives until we came up with it. It was quite necessary, you see, for we had already gone to the expense of manufacturing the bottles and releasing the publicity on our new rum. When you failed to arrive on the eighty-ninth day, we had to make a quick adjustment," Yarber laughed. "A shift in emphasis, so to speak."

"I am glad you were able to salvage something," Andrew said.

345

"You understand, of course, that we have actually salvaged only our product and not the record as per the terms of the contract," Yarber put in quickly. "The contract called for delivery within eighty-nine days for the prize to be paid. You did not deliver in eighty-nine days, thus there will be no prize."

"I understand," Andrew said. "But there will be hatch money?"

"Of course, my dear fellow. There will be hatch money and, if I may say so myself, there will be a rather sizable bonus indeed. It should amount to over one thousand dollars."

"Good," Andrew said, smiling. "That will make up to the crew the bonus money they lost."

Yarber leaned over the desk and picked up a letter. "I have something here that might interest you as well."

"What is that, sir?"

"I was interested in the tale you told me of the young girl you brought from Boston. The girl, Rose Page."

"You have information on her?" Andrew asked.

"You might say that. I have several influential friends on the police force, and I have discovered that the San Francisco Police Department has never heard of Rose Page."

"What? But of course they have," Andrew said. "I saw the extradition papers."

"I can tell you only what I know," Yarber said. "Rose Page is not wanted by the San Francisco police."

"Why, that's wonderful!" Andrew said, smiling broadly. "That means . . ." Suddenly the smile left Andrew's face as he realized what it did mean. The girl must have been telling the truth! "That means . . ."

"That she is my cousin, Captain," Miles Chalmers suddenly said, walking into the room.

"Mr. Chalmers! What are you doing here?" Andrew asked, jumping up in surprise at the entrance of Miles.

"I took the train from Boston when I discovered that my cousin might be on board your vessel. I must tell

346

you of ambivalent feelings on the matter. On the one hand, I hoped that it was true so that I could know that my cousin was still alive. But on the other hand, I felt betrayed that you could do such a thing to me."

"What do you mean, I could do such a thing to you?" Andrew asked. "I thought I was doing you a favor."

"You thought you were doing *me* a favor? By kidnapping my cousin?"

"I didn't know she was your cousin, Mr. Chalmers," Andrew said. "I thought she was a girl named Rose Page. She was passed off to me as being a young lady who was blackmailing you."

"My dear captain," Miles said icily. "In order to be blackmailed one has to commit some offense that is best kept secret. As I have committed no such offense, I am not subject to blackmail. Now would you kindly tell me where my cousin is?"

"My God," Andrew said, putting his hand to his head in total shock. "What a fool I have been! She tried to tell me, but I wouldn't believe her."

"Where is she, please, Captain Roberts?"

"She's at the Anchor Hotel in Los Angeles," Andrew said. "I instructed her to wait for me there. I intend to return for her as soon as the ship is off-loaded."

"It will not be necessary for you to return for her, Captain," Miles said. "I shall take a train this very evening. I cannot believe that you were so insensitive as to leave my cousin alone in a place like Los Angeles. If anything has happened to her, Captain, believe me, you will hear from me."

"She is all right," Andrew said.

"How do you *know* she is all right?" Miles asked in an angry voice.

"Believe me, that girl can take care of herself," Andrew said.

"That girl, as you call her, just so happens to be one of the wealthiest women in America. Do you have any idea what could befall her should someone discover that? She could be kidnapped again or murdered! All sorts of evil could be visited upon her and all because of your bungling, sir!"

"But no one knows who she is," Andrew insisted.

"She knows who she is, Captain. And I dare say those whom she tells will not be as stupid about it as you were. She is in great danger, I assure you."

"Then I'm going to her," Andrew said, starting toward the door.

"There is no need for you to trouble yourself," Miles said. "I will go to her."

"But you don't understand," Andrew said. "I must go to her. You see, I love her, and . . ."

Miles interrupted Andrew's sentence with a sudden, sharp, sarcastic peal of laughter. "Did you say you *love* her, Captain?"

"Aye, more than life itself."

"I see," Miles said. He stepped back and looked at Andrew, his eyes reflecting absolute contempt for the captain. "And you believe she returns your love, do you?"

"Yes, I do," Andrew said resolutely. "For she told me so."

"Because you have so much to offer her, I suppose. 'Marry me, Kristin and one day I shall have my own ship. Provided I don't lose it again through some stupid business venture,'" Miles mocked.

"No, it's not like that," Andrew said.

"Captain, has it ever occurred to you that Kristin was frightened out of her wits? I've no doubt that she told you she loved you. She is a bright and enterprising young girl. She would have made a pact with Satan himself if need be. But if you've one shred of human decency left in you, you will forget about her. Just sail away, Captain, and never see her or communicate with her again."

Andrew walked over to the window and looked out over the sparkling water. Was Chalmers right? Had the girl told him she loved him only because she was frightened?

No. That Andrew did not believe. The girl did love him, he was certain of that. And he loved her.

That was why he was going to take Miles Chalmers's advice and get out of her life now and forever. After all, what did he possibly have to offer a girl like Kristin Chalmers?

Slowly, Andrew turned from the window.

"You are quite correct, Mr. Chalmers. It would be best if I let you go to Los Angeles for her. I will apply for a cargo to China and leave without seeing her again."

Miles smiled broadly. "And I shall see to it that you get a China cargo, Captain. After all, I'm not inhuman. I know that you probably have a broken heart to mend, and the long voyage to China will have a great healing effect, I'm certain."

"Mr. Chalmers, it so happens that Golden Gate Distillery has a shipment for China at this very moment. Perhaps we can load it on the *Morning Star* as we unload our molasses."

"Yes, that would be . . ." Miles started, then stopped. "Captain, I know this is little recompense for your broken heart, but I have just hit upon the perfect solution. As a reward for finding Kristin, I shall make you a present of the *Morning Star*."

"You what?"

"I will give you title to the *Morning Star*," Miles said. "Of course, I don't have the title with me, but we can draw up a paper and have it notarized. Each of us can keep a copy and, when you return to Boston, you may apply for your title."

"But as a *reward?*" Andrew asked. "I scarcely see that I deserve a reward for what I did."

"Well, after all, you did deliver her safely to Los Angeles," Miles said. "Let's just say this is thanks from a grateful Chalmers family. Anyway, wouldn't you rather be on your own rather than come in contact with the Chalmers family again? Considering the way things. are?"

"Yes," Andrew said. "Yes, you have a point. I'll do it."

"Good, good," Miles said, rubbing his hands together. He looked at Yarber. "Mr. Yarber, do you suppose you could locate a notary for us?"

"Absolutely," Yarber said. "I'll have one here within the hour."

Miles looked at Andrew. "Then you, my friend, shall own your own ship within the hour. That should make you very happy."

"Aye," Andrew said sadly. "It should."

That evening Miles Chalmers slept soundly in the berth of the night train for Los Angeles. He had run into unexpected difficulty in trying to force the company away from his aunt. But he had not given up. Even now Tony Norton was compiling evidence to show that neither his aunt nor his mother were in their right minds. And once they were out of the way, the chairmanship of the board would fall to him.

Provided, of course, that Kristin was taken care of. And that little task he was going to do personally. He was going to Los Angeles to kill Kristin.

Kill Kristin, he thought, and as he thought the words, the wheels picked up the rhythm and sang the song back to him. *Kill Kristin, kill Kristin, kill Kristin, kill Kristin.*

Chapter Thirty-five

When Kristin came down for a late breakfast the next morning, she saw that the dining room was practically deserted. Only one table was occupied, and it was far in the corner. There a man sat alone so studiously perusing the menu that Kristin could tell nothing of his features.

But no matter. She didn't care whether her distant dining companion had agreeable or disagreeable features. She cared for nothing but the passage of the next couple of weeks, and the return of the *Morning Star*, and her dear, Captain Andrew Roberts.

Kristin picked up the menu and began studying it. They should have weevily biscuits and moldy salt meat, she said to herself. I would eat it then and be reminded of the *Morning Star*.

"Hello, Kristin. The family has been worried."

Kristin had been so engrossed in the menu and her

351

own thoughts that she hadn't seen the man across the room approach her. When she looked up, she was flabbergasted to see that it was Miles.

"Miles, my God! What are you doing here?" she asked.

"I've come to take you home, Kristin," Miles said. He pulled out the chair across from her table. "Your grandmother is in the hospital, so sick is she with worry over you."

"Oh," Kristin said, gasping and covering her mouth with her hand. "Oh, how thoughtless. I should have telegraphed Grandmother that I was safe."

"Yes, you should have," Miles said.

"I'll go to the telegraph office and do so at once."

"There is no need now," Miles said. "She knows you are safe. That is why I am here."

"But how did you find me?" Kristin asked.

"Captain Roberts told me where you were."

"Oh, then you've spoken to him? Where is he? Is he back in Los Angeles?"

"I'm afraid not, dear," Miles said.

"If you've spoken to him, then that means he knows," Kristin said. "He knows who I am, doesn't he?"

"He knows."

"Good. I'm glad he knows," Kristin said, sighing. "Now at last there can be honesty between us."

"I've taken a room here for the night," Miles said. "Tomorrow we shall leave for Boston. Your terrible ordeal has ended."

"Leave for Boston? No, not yet, Miles. I have to wait here for Andrew."

"You don't have to wait. I told you I have already spoken with him."

"But I do have to wait," Kristin insisted. "There's something you don't understand."

"No," Miles said gently. "I'm afraid there's something *you* don't understand."

352

"I . . . what? What is there that I don't understand?"

"You are going to tell me that you and Captain Roberts are in love, aren't you?"

Kristin blushed and looked at her plate on the table. "Yes," she said. "We are going to be married, Miles."

"Kristin, my dear Kristin," Miles said. He reached across the table and put his hand on hers. "You are only my second cousin, but in so many ways I regard you as my sister. Therefore, think of me as a brother now. As your big brother looking out only for your interest."

"What are you talking about?"

"Captain Roberts doesn't want to marry you, Kristin. He never did. Not from the beginning."

"Not from the beginning? Of course not. He thought I was a . . ." For some reason she couldn't bring herself to say the word *prostitute* in front of Miles. The word was far too intimate and, though she could say it and more to men of the crew of the *Morning Star,* to her cousin she could not.

"No, dear. Captain Roberts knew exactly who you were from the moment you set foot on his ship. It was all part of the plan, don't you see?"

"What plan?"

"The plan to get his ship back," Miles said. He sighed. "And much as I hate to admit it, the black-hearted scoundrel's scheme worked. He knew that we would place far more value on your safety than his ship. Therefore when he made the offer, we accepted."

"The offer?" Kristin asked in a weak voice. "What offer?"

Miles reached into his inside jacket pocket and pulled out his copy of the agreement he and Captain Roberts had signed. It was an agreement returning the *Morning Star* to the captain's ownership.

"You mean he . . . he traded me for his ship?" Kristin asked.

353

"I'm sorry," Miles said.

"Would the lady and gentleman care to order now?" the waiter asked, appearing at that moment.

Kristin stood up with tears stinging her eyes and ran from the dining room before the shocked eyes of the waiter.

"The lady has no wish to eat now," Miles said easily. "I should like eggs Benedict."

"Very good, sir," the waiter said, taking the menu and returning to the kitchen to give the order.

Andrew Roberts wasn't the only one with a broken heart. Though he was the one who was to marry Kristin, the entire crew had fallen in love with her in their own way. When he returned with the news that they were going to China and not back to Los Angeles, he had a near riot on his hands. Finally he was forced to tell them the truth, and they were now moping about, wearing their hurt as visibly as Andrew himself.

At about the time Miles's train was leaving San Francisco headed south for Los Angeles, Andrew was treating his crew to a fine dinner ashore. Normally this would have been a dinner for celebrating, and the wine would have flowed like water, and several of the crew would have been returned to the *Morning Star* in their cups. But tonight the mood was not at all gay.

"I'll say this for the young lady," one of the sailors said. "Be she rich or no, she was as good a sailor as I ever put to sea with."

"Aye, I'm agreein' with you on that point," another said. "And I ain' agreed with you since we put out from Boston."

"Cap'n, you reckon you'll ever see her again?" another asked.

"I don't think so," Andrew said sadly.

"Excuse me, gentlemen, but which of you is Captain Roberts?" a small, bespectacled man asked. He was holding a yellow envelope.

"I'm Captain Roberts," Andrew said. "What have you there?"

"I have a telegram, sir."

Andrew reached for it, but the man pulled it back ever so slightly.

"Give the cap'n his telegram, you little shit, else I'll have to stamp you up a mite," Pig Iron growled.

The man handed the telegram over quickly, looking at Pig Iron in fear.

"Here," Andrew said, handing him the tip he was hinting for in the first place.

"Oh, thank you, sir," the messenger replied. "Shall I wait for a possible return message?"

"That depends," Andrew said. "I don't know who it's from or if I'll want to talk to them."

"I'll wait, sir," the messenger offered.

"You do that," Andrew said. He pulled the message from the envelope, and began to read:

CAPTAIN ROBERTS
TWO PETTY CRIMINALS JESSE HELMS
AND WILLIAM PIERCE HAVE CONFESSED
TO CONSPIRACY IN THE KIDNAPPING
OF KRISTIN CHALMERS—STOP—THEY
HAVE INFORMED US THAT KRISTIN WAS
PLACED ON YOUR SHIP *MORNING STAR*—
STOP—HAVE REASON TO BELIEVE THAT
MILES CHALMERS WAS INVOLVED—STOP
—IF HE IS ALLOWED TO SEE KRISTIN IT
MIGHT MEAN DANGER FOR HER—STOP—
CONSTANCE AND MARGARET CHALMERS

"My God!" Andrew shouted, standing up so quickly that he knocked his chair over.

"Cap'n, what is it?" Josiah asked.

"It's Rose . . . I mean Kristin! She's in danger!" Andrew said. He showed the telegram to Josiah, and the others crowded around to read it too.

"Who is this Miles fella?" Josiah asked.

"He's her cousin."

"Well, why would her cousin want to hurt her?"

"Because he's an evil son of a bitch!" Andrew said. "You, messenger. Get a telegram down to Los Angeles for me right away."

"Yes, sir. Where does it go and what should it say?"

"Address it to Kristin Chalmers at the Anchor Hotel. Tell her that I'm coming for her. Tell her not to let Miles see her, that her life might be in danger."

"Yes, sir, I'll get that message out right away," the messenger said, taking the money from Andrew and starting out the door on the run.

"What are you going to do, Cap'n?" Josiah asked.

"I've got to get to Los Angeles right away!"

"Cap'n, we couldn't clear port tomorrow mornin' no matter how hard we tried," Gershom said.

"I don't have time for that. I'm going to take a train."

"Aye, a train. Come on, men," Josiah shouted. "Let's get down to the depot!"

It took three cabs to transport the entire crew to the railroad station, but moments later they were all there, running pell-mell to the ticket counter to shout at the clerk on the other side of the small wire cage.

"Hold your horses, hold your horses, I can't understand you if you all speak at once!" the clerk said. "Now who was first?"

"We was all first," one of the sailors shouted.

"Well, I obviously can't serve you all."

"You need serve only me," Andrews said.

"I'm sure the others might have something to say about that," the clerk said.

"He's the cap'n. Sell him a ticket to Los Angeles. It's an emergency," Josiah said.

"Well, why didn't you say so?" the clerk said. He took a small book of tickets and started to pull one out. "Your train leaves at six-thirty tomorrow morning."

"No," Andrew said. "That's not good enough. I have to go now . . . tonight."

"Oh, I'm sorry, sir, but that's quite impossible. The Night Eagle left . . . oh," the clerk pursed his lips and looked up at the big clock, "two hours and twenty-seven minutes ago. It will be in Los Angeles before your train even leaves in the morning."

"If that son of a bitch beats me to her, he'll kill her," Andrew said.

"Cap'n, ther's got to be somethin' you can do," Josiah said.

"I don't know what it would be," Andrew said.

"Maybe we could hire us a real fast ship that's all ready to go," Gershom suggested.

"No good," Andrew said. "The fastest ship wouldn't . . ." Andrew stopped in midsentence. "You've given me an idea! I can't hire a ship, but maybe I can hire a train!"

"A whole train?"

"I won't need a whole train," Andrew said. "Just an engine. Clerk!"

"Yes, sir?" the clerk said, returning to deal with them again but with distaste evident in his manner.

"I want to hire an engine."

It was nearly one hour later when Andrew climbed up the ladder to the cab of a waiting, steam-blowing engine.

"You the fella that hired this here engine?" the engineer asked.

"Aye," Andrew said. "I've got to get to Los Angeles before six-thirty in the morning."

"Impossible," the engineer said.

"Impossible? Why? Can't you go that fast?"

"I could if I had nothin' but clear track in front of me. But they's trains goin' both ways on these irons, mister, 'n they near 'bout all of 'em got priority over us."

"How soon can you get me there?"

"We can roll in there by a little after eight, I figure," the engineer said.

"Then, Mr. Engineer, let's roll," Andrew said.

Andrew watched the fireman as he shoveled the coal and the engineer as he twisted valves and moved switches. He had never been inside a locomotive before, and it was fascinating. Later, after they cleared the yard and were out into the countryside running at top speed, he discovered it was also somewhat frightening. He stood to one side and looked ahead, watching the slender points of switches as the train rushed toward them at sixty miles an hour. He heard the thunder of the bridges and saw the track shut in by rocky bluffs as the engine swept around sharp curves. He saw the telegraph poles light up in the night, picked up by the train's headlight, then whip by so fast as to be a blur.

And yet despite the excitement of the moment or the frightening sights and sounds of the run, all he could think of was Kristin and he prayed that he would be in time.

At that moment, a telegraph messenger walked across the lobby of Anchor Hotel in Los Angeles. He rang the bell at the desk.

"Yes?" the desk clerk asked.

"I have a telegram here for a Miss Kristin Chalmers."

"Kristin Chalmers? We have no one here by that name."

"Are you sure?"

"Of course I am sure," the clerk said. "At the moment, I have only one lady guest and her name is Rose Page. Do you think I don't keep up with the guests in my hotel?"

"What should I do with the telegram?"

"Why don't you leave it here?" the clerk suggested. "Perhaps she will check in tomorrow and I can give it to her."

The messenger handed the clerk the telegram, and

he put it in the "incoming guests" box. The messenger cleared his throat.

"You'll get your tip when I get mine," the clerk said.

"You won't forget?" the messenger asked, knowing he had just lost his tip but playing the game out anyway.

"I won't forget," the clerk promised.

And true to his word, the clerk didn't forget when he handed the telegram to Miles Chalmers the next morning as Chalmers was checking in.

"It is for Kristin Chalmers," he said. "Would you know her?"

"Yes, she is my cousin," Miles said. "I'll see to it that she gets it."

"I tipped the telegraph messenger two dollars," the clerk lied. "It arrived in the middle of the night."

Miles gave the clerk two dollars, thinking the price well worth seeing what message had been sent to Kristin. When he read it in the dining room while waiting for Rose Page to come down, he chuckled. So the captain was coming to rescue her, huh? Well, he would arrive too late. Miles would see to that. He would kill her as soon as he got her out of the hotel.

After Miles finished his breakfast, he went upstairs to Kristin's room and knocked lightly on the door.

"Who is it?" Kristin called.

"It's me, Kristin," Miles said. "May I come in?"

Kristin opened the door, then stepped back into the room. She had been crying, and her eyes were red, and she was holding a handkerchief to her nose.

"You look awful," he said.

"I'm sorry."

"Listen, I know how you must be feeling. Believe me, I don't feel so good for being the one to bring this news to you. But I've got an idea."

"What?"

"Let's go for a ride. I'll rent a carriage."

"I don't want to go anywhere," Kristin said.

359

"Of course you do," Miles insisted. "You don't want to be cooped up in here all day, do you?"

Kristin walked over to the window and looked outside. Birds were singing and the fronds of a nearby palm tree were rustling in the breeze. She set her shoulders resolutely. "No," she said. "You're right. I don't want to be here all day."

"Good, good," Miles said. "We'll have a fine time."

The engineer pulled the lever and the engine squeaked to a stop. "I'm not supposed to stop here on the main line like this," he said. "So you'd better hop down in a hurry. But I figured you'd save time if you'd get off here. The hotel you're wantin' is just over there. You can see the sign from here. You see that there anchor?"

"Aye," Andrew said. He hopped down from the engine, then turned to throw a wave and a grin to the two men who had brought him down here so quickly. "Good-bye, and thanks a lot."

"I hope you find your lady friend all right!" the engineer yelled, pulling the valve open again and forcing steam back into the piston. His words were drowned out, but Roberts caught the meaning and waved to him again, then started to the hotel.

Andrew was less than half a block away when he saw Miles and Kristin getting into a carriage.

"Kristin, wait!" he called.

Kristin turned around at the sound of Andrew's voice, but Miles flipped his whip against the team and the carriage darted off quickly.

"Wait!" Andrew called, starting after them on the run.

The carriage was too far ahead, and Andrew had no chance at all of catching them afoot. But as luck would have it, a cab came by at that moment. It already had a passenger, but Andrew jumped into it anyway.

"Hey, I have this cab hired," a fat, bewhiskered man shouted.

"Here," Andrew said, pulling out a ten-dollar bill. "Hire another one."

"Yes, sir!" the man beamed, taking the money eagerly.

"Mister, twenty dollars if you can catch that carriage," Andrew said, pointing to Miles now almost two blocks in front of him.

"You got it," the driver said, whipping the team ahead.

Both carriages raced through the city, eliciting yells of surprise and anger from the people they narrowly avoided. Finally Miles's carriage took a road leading out of town.

"We've got him now, mister," the cab driver shouted. "This road dead ends up here in about half a mile."

"Good, press him closely," Andrew said. "Don't give him the chance to get away."

Moments later, as the cab driver predicted, Miles's carriage came to a halt. He was trying to turn it around when the cab came right up behind them, trapping them there.

"It's too late, Miles, you can't get away now," Andrew said, standing in his carriage. "Why don't you just let Kristin go and give up?"

"What more do you want?" Miles asked. "I've traded you the ship for the girl's safety. Leave us alone, you fiend."

"What? What the hell are you talking about?"

"It's too late, Captain Roberts," Kristin said. "I saw the paper."

"What paper?"

"The paper where Miles traded you the ship in exchange for my freedom."

"In exchange for your freedom? Kristin, you were free. But you aren't now. Miles means to kill you. I

361

received a telegram from your grandmother, warning me about him. That's why I sent you the telegram."

"What telegram?"

"Well, I sent one last night," Andrew said. "Anyway, you have to believe me. Your life is in danger."

"It is but not from me!" Miles said.

"What the hell is going on here?" the cab driver asked, anxiously. "Mister, I ain't going to get involved in nothin' like this." He started to cluck to his team, but Andrew slugged him quickly, knocking him out cleanly. Kristin let out a small scream of fear.

"Do you see what I mean, Kristin?" Miles asked. "He is a violent man."

"Yes," Kristin said. "Miles, get me out of here. I'm afraid."

"Kristin, no, wait!" Andrew pleaded. "I can prove it to you."

"How?"

"Let's all go back together, and you can telegraph your grandmother."

"There's no need for that," Miles said.

"No," Kristin said. She looked resolutely at Andrew. "There was a time when I begged you to let me send a telegram and you wouldn't. Now, I'm going to let you send one, just to show you the difference between us."

"No," Miles said. "We don't have time for that foolishness."

"It will only take a short time," Kristin said. "And I have a point to prove."

"I said no," Miles said coldly.

Suddenly Kristin knew. She didn't know if it was the tone of his voice, the insistent resistance to the telegram, or the note of sincerity in Andrew. But she knew.

"It's . . . it's true, isn't it?" she asked.

Miles reached into his jacket pocket and pulled out a small pistol.

"Yes," he said. "It's true."

"But why, Miles?"

"Why? You have to ask me why? You and your grandmother have denied me everything that is rightly mine. I've had to live my entire life in your shadow, and you ask me why?"

"But we've denied you nothing."

"You've denied me everything!" Miles said. "Don't you see? *I* should be chairman of the board! *I* should inherit controlling interest of the stock! Instead, it's all going to you. It isn't fair. And now, on top of everything else, your grandmother has taken my mother from me."

"What do you mean? What happened to your mother?"

"She's double-crossed me," Miles said. "She's gone over to the enemy. Ah, but I'll take care of her. Yes, and your grandmother too! Once I finish with you, I'll go back to Boston and I'll have your grandmother and my mother declared insane." Miles giggled. "It's all perfect, don't you see? Two old women who have hated each other for years suddenly becoming such lovey-dovey close friends? That has to prove that they are insane, doesn't it? And with you out of the way . . . with you dead . . . why, that leaves only me. Only me," he said, and he laughed shrilly.

"How will you explain Kristin's murder?" Andrew asked. He was slowly, ever so slowly, reaching for the cab driver's whip.

"Simple, my dear captain. I shall kill both of you and declare it a murder, suicide. Everyone knows of your love for my cousin. When you found out who she was, you knew that such a love could never be. The emotional strain was too much for you so you killed her, then you shot yourself."

"Miles, you're crazy," Kristin said.

"I'm crazy? *I'm* crazy! No, dear, that's my game, remember? It's your grandmother who's crazy. Now get out of this carriage. Slowly, my dear, slowly. I think it would be nice if the two of you were found very close together. In each other's arms, so to speak." Miles stood up and motioned with his gun.

Andrew now had a solid grip on the driver's whip. He was watching as Kristin got out of the carriage, and just as she was on the ground and clear of the rig, he brought the whip down on Miles's team of horses.

"Kristin, get down!" he shouted.

The horses leaped forward and, when they did, the momentum jerked Miles off his feet, sending him tumbling to the ground. He let out a short yell, then was silent. Andrew jumped from the carriage and ran toward him, intending to wrestle the gun from him, but he saw at a glance that it wouldn't be necessary.

Miles Chalmers had landed head down beneath the carriage, and his neck was grotesquely twisted out of shape. His mouth was open with the silent scream still on his lips. His eyes were staring in surprise, but he saw nothing because Miles Chalmers was dead.

"Oh, Andrew," Kristin said, running to him, throwing herself in his arms.

"It's all over, darling," Andrew said, comforting her. "It's all over now."

Kristin let him hold her for a moment, then she pulled away and looked into his eyes, smiling at him with eyes full of promise. "No, my darling sea captain. It isn't all over. It's just beginning."

"Aye, lass," Andrew said, laughing happily and pulling her back to him again. "It is at that."

LOVE'S RAGING TIDE

by Patricia Matthews

This is the eighth novel in the phenomenal, best-selling series of historical romances by Patricia Matthews. Once again, she weaves a compelling, magical tale of love, intrigue, and suspense. Millions of readers have acclaimed her as their favorite story-teller. In fact, she is the very first woman writer in history to publish three national bestsellers in one year!

Patricia Matthews' first novel, *Love's Avenging Heart*, was published in early 1977, followed by *Love's Wildest Dream*, *Love, Forever More*, *Love's Daring Dream*, *Love's Pagan Heart*, and *Love's Magic Moment*. Now that you've finished reading *Ports of Passion*, we're sure you'll want to read *Love's Raging Tide*. The following is a brief excerpt from the first chapter.*

It was one of those late Spring days that only Mississippi can produce—a day so soft and balmy that the air felt like flower petals against the skin, a day full of awakening and promise—and the sight of it made Melissa Huntoon want to weep.

She stood on the spacious, pillared porch of her ancestral home, looking out over the broad acres that had belonged to her family for two generations, and her eyes burned with the effort to remain dry.

She swallowed past the hard lump in her throat and gripped the handle of the pink parasol that her granddaddy had brought her from Paris the year before he died.

The day should be gray, she thought; the clouds full of rain like unshed tears. Today, Great Oaks would ring to the auctioneer's hammer. The plantation itself—two thousand acres of Mississippi bottomland, some of the finest cotton land in the South—had already been taken over by the bank. Today, everything in the house would go to the highest bidder.

Melissa smoothed the full skirt of her dress with her hand. From a distance, she knew, she would appear well-dressed. Only close inspection would show the neat patches and darns that held the now-fragile cloth together. The dress, she thought, was like Great Oaks itself—impressive enough on general inspection, but badly flawed. In the case of Great Oaks, it was debts, endless debts, incurred against the property before and after her father's death. When the day was over, Melissa would be left with little more than the clothing she wore, and a few personal trinkets. It was not much to show for twenty-one years of life, not much with which to start a new life.

Bitterly, she watched the stream of horses, buggies, and carriages coming up the driveway. Like vultures, she thought; except that they couldn't even wait until their prey was dead!

Melissa knew very well that all of them weren't here to bid. Many of them were here simply to gloat on the downfall of the high and mighty Huntoons. Jean Paul, her father, would have greeted them with a round of buckshot; and she sorely wished that she might do the same.

However, she had no choice. Amalie, her personal maid, and the only one of the servants left beside Henry, had advised her to stay inside, out of sight until it was over; but Melissa could not bear the thought of hiding inside, as if she was afraid of these usurpers. She was the mistress of Great Oaks until the day was over, and until then she would appear before them as she and her family always had, proud, with her head held high. Let them stare, these nouveaux riches, these Johnny-come-latelies. Let them see what a Huntoon looked like. It might be their last chance to see real quality!

She heard soft footsteps behind her, and did not need to turn around to know that Amalie had come out on the veranda to join her. The knowledge lifted her spirits. Amalie had been with her as long as Melissa could remember. The older woman had been her nurse, her mother, her friend, and her confidante. And Amalie, at least, Melissa would be able to take with her when she left.

A shabby carriage drove by the veranda, and a woman's pinched, tight-mouthed face turned in her direction. The woman's eyes were bright with avid curiosity, and Melissa stared haughtily back as the carriage passed, going to the stable area where the horses of the prospective buyers were being tended.

Another of the sightseers, Melissa thought. In these Reconstruction times, there were not many in the South with the wherewithal to buy property and furnishings, even at auction prices, and obviously this woman was not one of the fortunate ones.

The traffic was increasing now, as more and more people arrived, and Melissa felt Amalie draw close to her side. "Are you all right, little one?"

Melissa nodded and reached for the older woman's hand. Not trusting herself to speak, she squeezed it fiercely.

Melissa's mother had died some years back, of a fever, and her father, wounded in the war, had come home to cough his life away. The war years had been difficult for Melissa, but not nearly so difficult as watching her beloved father, the man who had been so proud and strong, growing weaker every day, and seeing his face as he was slowly forced to relinquish his dream of once again seeing Great Oaks as it had been—a busy, thriving plantation.

Melissa, with the help of Henry and Amalie, had struggled to run the plantation on her own; but it was not to be. With the slaves freed, and the family fortune given freely to the Confederate cause, only the house and the land were left when the war was over. There had been no choice but to mortgage the property to the bank in town.

If the bank had remained in Southern hands, she probably would have been granted loan extensions, but the bank itself failed and was taken over, along with a stack of overdue mortgages, by a man named Simon Crouse—better known to the local populace as the Carpetbagger.

The Carpetbagger was a smallish man, who appeared taller because of the proportions of his body. He was, as some of the women were fond of remarking, "well set up," with small, neat hands and feet, and a large head with a thick growth of brown hair, which, if you didn't look too closely, gave him a noble air.

However, Melissa was one of those who *did* look closely. The war years had made her expert at judging human nature, and despite Crouse's façade of good manners and elegance, she had seen and taken note of the greedy flicker behind his dark eyes, and the unrestrained sensuality of his mouth, when he thought he wasn't under observation.

Always, from the first time they had met, Simon Crouse had made her uncomfortable. His dark eyes, moving cautiously over her body, made her feel violated, and she always felt a sort of dreadful *eagerness* in the man, a secretive greediness, that she was hard put to set into words, but which made her feel somehow threatened.

Melissa knew that many of the ladies around thought him attractive, even though he was a Yankee moneylender, a carpetbagger of the worst sort. If he kept on his way undeterred, he would soon have his greedy hands on most of Mississippi. She had to admit, in all fairness, that the fact he now owned Great Oaks had some bearing on the way she felt about him.

And speak of the Devil!

Coming toward her was a handsome carriage, drawn by a fine pair of matched horses, throwing up dust, and jouncing importantly up the great drive. She recognized the carriage as belonging to Simon Crouse.

But what drew Melissa's attention was the man on the large, black horse, riding alongside the carriage. The horse was magnificent, the trappings luxurious for these impoverished times, and the man himself was certainly imposing—young, well built, handsome, and expensively dressed. It was obvious that he was accompanying the carriage. What sinister connection could he possibly have with Simon Crouse?

The carriage moved around the curve in the driveway, and stopped at the bottom of the steps, in front of Melissa.

Melissa felt her heart begin to pound, and tried to compose herself. She must handle this confrontation with dignity. That was all she had left.

"Miss Huntoon!" Crouse had climbed down from the carriage, and stood awaiting her on the bottom step. He doffed his tall hat, and inclined his head.

He's like an actor, Melissa thought with distaste.

Crouse turned to the man on the black horse. "I would like to present my associate, Mr. Luke Devereaux. Mr. Devereaux, Miss Melissa Huntoon."

Luke Devereaux swept off his broad-brimmed hat. "It is my pleasure, ma'am," he said in a deep voice. His hair was rich brown in color, and his brown eyes had a slightly golden tint. His full mouth wore a slight smile.

Melissa returned his gaze coldly. "I am sorry that I cannot say the same, sir!" she said tartly. "The circumstances being what they are."

His smile remained in place. "I am in no way responsible for your circumstances, Miss Huntoon."

"Perhaps not," she directed a scathing glance at Crouse, "but you may be held responsible for the company you keep, and certainly Mister Crouse is responsible for my plight!"

"My dear Melissa, that is simply not true," Crouse said with a superior smile. "I have always deplored a lady involving herself in business matters. Not only is it demeaning, but the female mind simply has no grasp of the problems involved. Your plight is a prime example of that fact. The bank held the mortgage on this plantation, and the payments were sadly in arrears. My foreclosure is nothing more than sound business procedure."

"You may call it what you like, Mister Crouse, but that does not excuse this humiliating auction today!"

"That, Melissa, is not my doing. But you do have other creditors, my dear, and I suppose they believe they are entitled to due consideration."

"Daddy collected many fine art objects over the years,

paintings and the like. Many of them are priceless. Now, today, they will be sold off to people who have no idea of their true value!"

"Now there you are mistaken. I fully appreciate them," Crouse said with infuriating smugness. "And this is precisely why I am here today. There are several paintings that I fully intend to have for my very own."

"You?" Her voice was scornful. "What do you know of art, Mister Crouse?"

His smile grew strained, and Melissa knew that she had stung him. The thought gave her pleasure, but she was also a little intimidated by the suppressed fury in his eyes.

"I don't suppose that a young lady like yourself, isolated, as it were, in this charming backwater, has had a chance to learn much about the sophistications of the larger world," he said smoothly. "If you had, you would have learned not to judge people so quickly. The fact that I am a banker does not mean that I do not appreciate the artistic things of life. In truth, I already have an excellent and extensive collection of art, and I intend to add to it this day."

Melissa felt herself flush, and suddenly her bravado failed her, and depression took its place. "I don't suppose it really matters," she said dully. "After today, none of it will belong to the Huntoon family."

Crouse moved closer to her, turning his back on Luke Devereaux. Melissa stole a glance at the man on the horse, but he was apparently watching the parade of visitors as they came up the large, circular driveway.

As she looked back, Melissa saw that Crouse was now quite close to her. Too close! She could see the high color on his prominent cheekbones, and the hungry glitter of his dark eyes.

She wanted nothing so much as to draw back from him, but she did not wish him to think that she feared him.

"There *is* a way your lovely things can remain in your possession, Melissa."

She stared at him, as her heart leaped in sudden hope, then plummeted. She did not trust him. It had to be a trick of some kind. She whispered, "How?"

His voice was low. "Become my wife. Become Mrs. Simon Crouse."

Melissa felt as if her body had lost all heat. She could only stare at him in consternation, as he looked at her intently, his mouth slightly open, and his eyes bright with something that she could not put a name to.

Her mind was chaos. "Why?" she finally managed to whisper, although this was only one of the questions that tumbled pell-mell through her mind.

He smiled slightly. "I need a wife. I have spent years building up my fortune, and now I wish to enjoy it. I have chosen Great Oaks to be my permanent residence, and I would like you to share it with me."

He leaned even nearer, and his eyes burned into Melissa's with frightening force. "Be my wife, Melissa. I can make you happy. You will then not need to leave Great Oaks, nor the family possessions you hold so dear."

The stasis that had paralyzed Melissa broke, and she almost staggered backward, until she felt the stone of the steps behind her. The touch of it seemed to give her strength.

Again he moved toward her, and she swung her parasol around so that it formed a shield in front of her, the sharp point of it directed at Crouse's chest. His smile faded, and his mouth tightened.

"Mr. Crouse," Melissa said softly but clearly, "you presume too much! Whatever made you think. . . ?" She shook her head. "Simon Crouse, I would not marry you if I were starving and you had the last loaf of bread in the world! I look upon you as my enemy. I thought you knew that!"

Crouse's high color slowly faded, and his expression was blank with shock. Despite her own confusion, Melissa sensed that he really had no inkling of how she felt about him, impossible as it seemed.

"Take care, girl," he said, and his voice was as taut and sharp as the flick of a whip. "I am a dangerous man to cross. Perhaps you had better reconsider your words!"

Melissa, looking into those blank eyes, felt sudden fear. She shivered, as she thought of the water moccasin she had once stumbled upon, coiled by the side of a stream—Crouse's eyes now had that same deadly, mindless stare.

She conquered her fear. "I don't need to reconsider," she said, her voice as soft as his. "I spoke my mind. I hate you, Simon Crouse! You are everything that I find despicable in a man, and I could never, never become your wife. I would certainly much rather starve first!"

The corner of Crouse's mouth twitched, and he raised his hand as if to strike her, but paused as Luke Devereaux stepped between them.

"I think the auction is about to start." Devereaux's voice, speaking in a normal tone, seemed to break some kind of terrible spell, and Melissa found that she had been holding her breath.

Crouse turned away, and then, in a swift, lethal movement, wheeled back to face her.

"So be it," he said in an icy voice. "And what you said, about starving to death. That could very well happen, you know. In fact, I shall do everything in my power to see to it, and I have a great deal of power in Mississippi, far more than you know. Good day to you, Miss Huntoon."